Praise for *Chime*

"Part mystery, part fantasy, this beautifully-written page turner explores guilt, mercy, and love."

—Holly Black, *New York Times* bestselling author of *Tithe* and *Ironside*

★ "Extraordinary and moving."   —*BCCB*, starred review

"The language is rich . . . and the plot is tautly controlled."

—*The Chicago Tribune*

★ "A dark, chilling yet stunning world. . . . Exquisite to the final word."   —*Booklist*, starred review

★ "The magnificently dark romantic setting and lovely, lyrical language and imagery enhance a novel that is both lushly sensual and shivery."   —*SLJ*, starred review

★ "An entirely original concoction."

—*The Horn Book*, starred review

★ "Billingsley is one of the great prose stylists of the field, moving from one sparklingly unexpected image to the next and salting her story with quicksilver dialogue . . . Delicious."   —*Kirkus Reviews*, starred review

★ "Filled with . . . beautiful language, this is a darkly beguiling fantasy."   —*Publishers Weekly*, starred review

A rather curious request

I've confessed to everything and I'd like to be hanged.

Now, if you please.

I don't mean to be difficult, but I can't bear to tell my story. I can't relive those memories—the touch of the Dead Hand, the smell of eel, the gulp and swallow of the swamp.

How can you possibly think me innocent? Don't let my face fool you; it tells the worst lies. A girl can have the face of an angel but have a horrid sort of heart.

I know you believe you're giving me a chance—or, rather, it's the Chime Child giving me the chance. She's desperate, of course, not to hang an innocent girl again, but please believe me: Nothing in my story will absolve me of guilt. It will only prove what I've already told you, which is that I'm wicked. Can't the Chime Child take my word for it?

In any event, where does she expect me to begin? The story of a wicked girl has no true beginning. I'd have to begin with the day I was born.

If Eldric were to tell the story, he'd likely begin with himself, on the day he arrived in the Swampsea. That's where proper stories begin, don't they, when the handsome stranger arrives and everything goes wrong?

But this isn't a proper story, and I'm telling you, I ought to be hanged.

OTHER BOOKS YOU MAY ENJOY

chime

FRANNY BILLINGSLEY

speak

An Imprint of Penguin Group (USA) Inc.

SPEAK

Published by the Penguin Group

Penguin Group (USA) Inc., 345 Hudson Street, New York, New York 10014, U.S.A.

Penguin Group (Canada), 90 Eglinton Avenue East, Suite 700, Toronto, Ontario, Canada M4P 2Y3
(a division of Pearson Penguin Canada Inc.)

Penguin Books Ltd, 80 Strand, London WC2R 0RL, England

Penguin Ireland, 25 St Stephen's Green, Dublin 2, Ireland (a division of Penguin Books Ltd)

Penguin Group (Australia), 250 Camberwell Road, Camberwell, Victoria 3124, Australia
(a division of Pearson Australia Group Pty Ltd)

Penguin Books India Pvt Ltd, 11 Community Centre,
Panchsheel Park, New Delhi - 110 017, India

Penguin Group (NZ), 67 Apollo Drive, Rosedale, Auckland 0632, New Zealand
(a division of Pearson New Zealand Ltd.)

Penguin Books (South Africa) (Pty) Ltd, 24 Sturdee Avenue,
Rosebank, Johannesburg 2196, South Africa

Registered Offices: Penguin Books Ltd, 80 Strand, London WC2R 0RL, England

First published in the United States of America by Dial Books,
an imprint of Penguin Group (USA) Inc., 2011
Published by Speak, an imprint of Penguin Group (USA) Inc., 2012

5 7 9 10 8 6 4

THE LIBRARY OF CONGRESS HAS CATALOGED THE DIAL BOOKS EDITION AS FOLLOWS:
Billingsley, Franny, date.
Chime / by Franny Billingsley.
p.   cm.
Summary: In the early twentieth century in the Swampsea, seventeen-year-old Briony, who can see
spirits that haunt the marshes around their town, feels responsible for her twin sister's horrible injury
until a young man enters their lives and exposes secrets that even Briony does not know about.
ISBN: 978-0-8037-3552-1 (hardcover)
[1. Twins—Fiction. 2. Sisters—Fiction. 3. Supernatural—Fiction. 4. Guilt—Fiction.
5. Self-perception—Fiction. 6. Stepmothers—Fiction. 7. Secrets—Fiction.]
I. Title.
PZ7.B4985Ch 2011
[Fic—dc22
2010012140

Speak ISBN: 978-0-14-242092-8

Book design by Sarah Davis.
Typeset in Carre Noir.

Printed in the United States of America

• To Richard, for always •

Contents

The Trial

I've confessed to everything and I'd like to be hanged.

Now, if you please.

I don't mean to be difficult, but I can't bear to tell my story. I can't relive those memories—the touch of the Dead Hand, the smell of eel, the gulp and swallow of the swamp.

How can you possibly think me innocent? Don't let my face fool you; it tells the worst lies. A girl can have the face of an angel but have a horrid sort of heart.

I know you believe you're giving me a chance—or, rather, it's the Chime Child giving me the chance. She's desperate, of course, not to hang an innocent girl again, but please believe me: Nothing in my story will absolve me of guilt. It will only prove what I've already told you, which is that I'm wicked.

Can't the Chime Child take my word for it?

In any event, where does she expect me to begin? The story of a wicked girl has no true beginning. I'd have to begin with the day I was born.

If Eldric were to tell the story, he'd likely begin with himself, on the day he arrived in the Swampsea. That's where proper stories begin, don't they, when the handsome stranger arrives and everything goes wrong?

But this isn't a proper story, and I'm telling you, I ought to be hanged.

The Taste
of Burnt Matches

"I want to go home." My sister turned from the river and closed her eyes, as though she could wish away the river, and the barge on the river, and Eldric on the barge. But life doesn't work that way, more's the pity.

"We can't leave now," said Father. "It would hurt Eldric's feelings, don't you see?"

But Rose didn't see. She never saw, not about feelings. "I want to go home."

Villagers thronged the riverside, but they gave us plenty of room. I'd forgotten that, forgotten how they left a cushion of air around the clergyman and his porcelain daughters. We'd always be outsiders, even though Father's spent twenty years in the Swampsea, and Rose and I have spent seventeen. We've never been anywhere else.

"One hundred and eighty-three steps until home," said Rose.

The villagers never used to stare, though. If I were an ordinary girl, I might stare too. People like to stare at girls who've been ill, at girls whom they've hardly seen for three years, at girls whose stepmother has killed herself.

"Look!" said Father. "The barge is almost here."

But the villagers are wrong about Stepmother, and so is Father. She would never kill herself. I'm the one who knew her best, and I know this: Stepmother was hungry for life.

"One hundred and eighty-three steps until home." Rose was exactly right. I know; I've measured. The Parsonage sat exactly one hundred eighty-three steps behind us, its back to the river, its front to the village square.

"And," said Father, "just think how happy Eldric's father will be to see his son."

"That I will," said Mr. Clayborne, who was waiting with us in our cushion of air. He was more at home with the villagers than we were, even though he'd arrived from London only six months back. Perhaps it was because he was such a big, comfortable sort of man, while we Larkins are rarely comfortable, especially with ourselves.

"I don't like boys," said Rose.

Neither did I, but I knew enough not to say so.

"Rose!" said Father, but Mr. Clayborne was used to Rose.

"Eldric and I have never been apart this long," said Mr. Clayborne. "Almost six months."

Almost six months. Stepmother died two months and three days ago. I must never let myself grow used to Stepmother's death. I must never smooth out time the way Mr. Clayborne had. I'd never say she'd been dead *almost six months.*

I remembered the day she died with absolute clarity. I

remembered standing outside her sickroom door, wondering if I should enter. Why did I hesitate? I was afraid of awakening her, I suppose, which I'd call ironic if I were a poet, but I'm not, and anyway, I hate poetry. A poem doesn't come out and tell you what it has to say. It circles back on itself, eating its own tail and making you guess what it means.

Stop, Briony! Stepmother would tell you to stop. Stop dreaming about her, she'd say, and attend to Rose, who'd just gone into a fit of coughing. *Take care of Rose.* That's what Stepmother always said. I'd promised. I'd promised Stepmother I'd take care of Rose.

"Rose has such a cough, Father," I said. "Oughtn't she to be out of the wind?"

"Another few minutes won't hurt," said Father in his sermon voice, which is his favorite voice, the one he starches and irons every morning.

Have you become a doctor, Father? How do you know it won't hurt? Or did you hear it from God? You don't talk to anyone else.

The wind smacked at everything. It smacked the river into froth. It smacked the willow branches into whips. It smacked the villagers into streamers of hair and shawls and shirttails. The wind didn't smack us up, though, not the Larkin family. We were buttoned and braided and buckled and still.

But not all the buttons and buckles in the world can protect a Larkin from the swamp cough. When Rose started coughing last week, I actually talked to Father. I asked him whether she might have the swamp cough. Father said what he always says, which is nothing.

That's right, Father. Let Rose cough herself to death. Why

waste money on the doctor? There is, after all, no cure for the swamp cough.

The Shire horses came to a stop, steam puffing from their great pink nostrils. The barge had arrived. I looked for Mr. Clayborne's son among the passengers. I hoped he wouldn't be one of those grubby stone-throwing boys. But they all are, aren't they? I base my knowledge of boys on Tiddy Rex, nine years old, with the requisite grubby hands, but not altogether a bad sort.

At least I needn't talk to Eldric. I believe boys are not much for conversation. If Eldric bothered me, I'd mention Mucky Face. He's the resident river spirit and just loves boys. But to eat, Eldric dear. To eat.

"There he is!" said Mr. Clayborne. "See, on the left—tall, fairish hair?"

"What a good-looking boy!" said Father.

But I didn't see any version of Tiddy Rex, grubby hands or no.

"There!" Mr. Clayborne pointed. "Coming down the gangway. Surely you see him now? Light hair, well built."

"Oh," I said. I hadn't known he'd be so big. He was an enormous child. An enormous giant of a child, all six or seven feet of him.

"There's my bad boy," said Mr. Clayborne, waving Eldric over. He made it sound as though it were quite a good thing to be a bad boy.

Nor had I known he'd be so old. He was a university boy. I recognized the clothes from magazine pictures—the slim trousers, the checkerboard vest, the suggestion of a tie. I understood now why Mr. Clayborne wanted his bad boy to lodge at the Parsonage, with the clergyman and his daughters. I understood why he didn't want his bad boy to lodge with him at the Alehouse. Bad boys and alehouses are an explosive kind of mix.

"What do you think, Briony?" said Father. "Will the girls of the Swampsea be glad of a new and handsome face?"

I hate it when Father puts on a show, pretending we're the kind of family that chats and gossips and laughs. People always say one thing and mean something else beneath. I'm the worst of all, but at least I don't lie to myself about it.

Anyway, I have no idea what other girls feel, regular girls. I am not a regular girl.

I squeezed a peek at Eldric as he and Mr. Clayborne shook hands. Father was wrong, of course. Eldric wasn't handsome, not in a Greek statue kind of way, not like Cecil Trumpington, who wants to marry me. Well, Cecil actually wants to marry the idea of me. He wants a girl with ivory skin and corn-silk hair; he wants a girl with the face of an angel.

But not even Cecil has such gorgeous, slouchy clothes as Eldric. Everything about Eldric screamed of the things I'd never have, of London and theater and turn-on lamps and motorcars—

"I don't care to shake that boy's hand," said Rose.

And piped-in water—

Mr. Clayborne held Eldric at arm's length and smiled at him.

And piped-out lavatories—

Mr. Clayborne pulled Eldric back and kissed his cheek.

Kissing? Men kissing! We don't go in for that sort of thing in the Swampsea.

But we were country mice. Perhaps the history books will

report that, as the new century entered its second decade, men in London took to wearing mink coats, which led naturally to—

The constable stuck his great brass badge into our air cushion. The rest of the constable followed, which was a pity. The air cushion was filling up—now the Swamp Reeve, now Mayor Brody and his greyhounds, now Judge Trumpington and his wife.

Ah yes, the beautiful Mrs. Trumpington, and the beautiful Mrs. Trumpington's beautiful frock. Mrs. Trumpington, looking just like a May flower—although it was hardly April—a May flower in peach batiste with a lace underskirt and too much embroidery to mention, so I won't. Rose and I wore identical frocks, not to Mrs. Trumpington but to each other. We'd had them for ages and they made us look about twelve rather than seventeen. But Rose likes looking twelve: She also wore a pinafore and a pink hair ribbon. She wears them every day.

"I don't care to shake hands with that boy," said Rose. She has only one way of speaking, and it is loud.

Oh, Rose! Now Eldric would look at us and pity our shattered, fragile family and our shabby, childish clothes; and I'd be obliged to hate myself, and to hate him too, although I've had a lot of practice and it's not terribly burdensome. Hating, I mean.

I hate myself.

Eldric had certainly noticed us now, his eyes first on Rose, now swiveling to me, now back to Rose; assuring himself, as everyone did, that we were that interesting freak of nature, the identical twin. What did he think as he looked at our angel faces? What would he think if he knew what lay beneath the face of the angel named Briony?

"I don't care to shake hands with that boy."

Father gave up; I saw it in his shoulders. You can never win with Rose. He must have forgotten that while he was talking to God.

"Please allow me to introduce my daughter Rosy."

Rosy? Honestly, Father, there you go again, putting on your pretty mask, playing at the game of Perfect Family. We are not the sort of people who go in for pet names.

"How do you do?" Eldric smiled. He had golden lion's eyes and a great mane of tawny hair.

"I knew it," said Rose. "I knew it."

"Knew what?" said Father.

"I'm not rosy," she said, which is true. The two of us are alabaster girls, lovely to look at, or so we hear.

How could I bear it, Eldric living with us, this non-child, this boy-man? I'd have to keep on my Briony mask. I'd have to keep my lips greased and smiling. I'd have to keep my tongue sharp and amusing. Already, I was exhausted.

"And you?" said Eldric. After a heartbeat of silence, I glanced up. Eldric was looking at me, this golden London boy, looking at me with amber eyes. "What am I to call you?"

"You may call me Briony," I said, "which makes it awfully convenient because so does everyone else."

After a hiccough of silence, Eldric laughed. Then so did the others, except Rose. And me, of course. I don't have much laughter left. I've looked after Rose for years and years, and she drained me dry long ago. What's she feeding off now, I wonder. My soul juice?

I'd have to talk to Eldric, wouldn't I? Talk to this foreign boy-man animal. I knew nothing of boy-men and I didn't care to learn. And he wouldn't merely be living with us, but sleeping in Stepmother's sickroom, sleeping in the very bed on which she had died.

And eat with him?

Mealtimes had been so awkward after Stepmother died and Father started spending time at home again. Neither of us with anything to say, and Rose no great conversationalist herself. We hadn't had proper mealtimes while Stepmother was ill. Skipping meals is terrifically convenient: It gives one lots of time to brood and hate oneself.

Anyway, I hate cooking and I hate the kitchen and I hate Rose when she begins gulping air, which she was doing now as a way of limbering up for a fit of screaming. I'd warned Father, reminded him Rose doesn't like strangers, but Father never listens.

I used to be embarrassed when Rose screamed in public, but I was glad now. Once we got it over with, I could take the two of us home, peel off my mask, and let my face fall into its witchy folds.

But first there's the getting it over with. Rose's screams are like knitting needles. They jab right through your ear, into the soft squish beneath. She'd start any second. At least Rose doesn't hide what she feels. At least she's not silent, like Father.

There are several kinds of silence. There's the silence of being alone, which I like well enough. Then there's the silence of one's father. The silence when you have nothing to say and he has nothing to say. The silence between you after the investigation of your stepmother's death.

We've never spoken of the inquest, at which the coroner testified that Stepmother had died of arsenic poisoning. Of the inquest, at which Father testified that Stepmother might have taken her own life. Of the inquest, at which I testified that Stepmother would never have taken her life.

Not ever.

The air shattered; Rose's scream had begun. The others jumped, then looked about, wondering if they should pretend not to notice. But I was still thinking about silence.

Father's silence is not merely the absence of sound. It's a creature with a life of its own. It chokes you. It pinches you small as a grain of rice. It twists in your gut like a worm.

Silence clawed at my throat. It left a taste of burnt matches.

No, our family doesn't talk much.

A Crown
for the Steam Age

"I don't prefer to talk about it," said Rose from behind the cupboard door.

"She mislike all them new gentlemen, Rose do," said Pearl Whitby, except she was Pearl Miller now and I always forgot. She was Pearl Miller and she was married and she had an extremely ugly baby.

Pearl was right. She used to help out before Father remarried, and she knew that Rose didn't like strangers, especially not in the house. Eldric was bad enough, but Father had invited a third gentleman whom Rose had never even seen. I'd never have believed Father could do something so stupid, and I have a great deal of faith in Father's stupidity.

Didn't he remember that Rose hated surprises? That she'd especially hate a surprise guest, and a man, at that. She and I are not used to men.

"Happen Rose'd fancy a sweet?" said Pearl, flushed from

fighting the stove, which was possessed of a mercurial temperament.

I pressed my forehead into the kitchen window. "I know something that will be interesting to a certain girl named Rose."

I blew her name onto the window; breath-roses bloomed on the glass. "We're to have iced buns for tea."

There was only one reason I wanted to coax Rose from the cupboard: I could never leave off caring for Rose; which meant if she stayed in the cupboard, I had to stay in the Parsonage; which meant I couldn't call upon poor Tiddy Rex, who'd been stricken with the swamp cough; which meant I couldn't take note of Tiddy Rex's symptoms and compare them to Rose's; which actually wouldn't do me any good anyway, because if she did have the swamp cough, there was nothing I could do about it; but at least Stepmother couldn't say I wasn't doing anything, which she couldn't in any event because she's dead.

Except that maybe the symptoms wouldn't match up. Then, at least, I could stop fretting about Rose and the swamp cough and fret about something else.

The kitchen door groaned. It was arthritic and cranky from the flood, and it took advantage of every opportunity to complain. Red and yellow checks swam into the window glass, and I knew without turning that it was Eldric who'd entered. There was no mistaking that university waistcoat.

"I like iced buns," said Rose, her voice deadened by the cupboard—not that her real voice has ever been what you might call lively.

"A talking cupboard!" said Eldric. "I've always wanted to see a talking cupboard."

Rose would never come out of the cupboard now, not with Eldric in the kitchen. I was trapped in the Parsonage. I turned away from the reflected waistcoat to a flesh-and-blood Eldric, who quite filled up the doorway.

"I have a message for you." Eldric nodded at me. "Your father asks if you might step into the dining room."

"Who will care for the talking cupboard?" I said.

"I will," said Pearl. "You goes along, miss."

"You'll watch her like a hawk?" I said. "A hawk that can see through cupboard doors?"

Pearl laughed and said she would. Anyway, the dining room is only twenty feet away. I'd know if Rose needed me. Rose is not one to keep her feelings to herself.

But still I had to ask. "You're sure?"

"Us'll get along grand, me an' Rose."

"Thank you." But why should I thank Pearl? She was being paid. Anyone could stand a screaming girl if she was paid, but the sister of such a girl is never paid. I'd like to go farther than twenty feet. France would be nice, and I speak tolerable French. Or Greece, although I speak intolerable Greek, and only ancient. But if I couldn't manage to order a glass of wine, I'd order a wine-dark sea; and I like olives; and I believe I might like squid; and I would certainly like anyplace far away from Rose.

The dining room was absolutely littered with men: Father, Mr. Clayborne, Eldric, and the surprise guest, Mr. Drury, who was also Eldric's tutor. Men—their great boots clogging up the floor, their greedy lungs sucking up the air, their stubbly faces filling up the looking glass.

Men, I don't like them a bit. I'm not an ordinary girl, pining after romance and a husband. May the Horrors take me if ever I grow ordinary, like Pearl!

I know what Pearl had to do to get herself that baby with Artie Miller. I know, and I don't think much of it. Father would be astonished at what I know.

I leaned against the red damask wallpaper, which had once been so beautiful. But it was blistered and peeling now; like the kitchen door, it had never recovered from the flood.

Mr. Clayborne looked at Eldric; Eldric nodded. It was as though the Claybornes shared a silent language, which was utterly unlike the way we Larkins shared silence, which was not at all. We don't share anything.

I supposed that Mr. Clayborne's look meant, *Go talk to the clergyman's daughter*; and Eldric's nod meant, *Well, if you insist*, for he strode right over. What sort of excuse would he give for seeking me out? What sort of mask did Eldric wear?

"We didn't have a chance to become properly acquainted this morning," he said.

"My sister has a knack for making scenes in public."

Eldric nodded. "My father's mentioned Rose in his letters but speaks rather more frequently of you. He thinks you're quite the model daughter. He mentions you whenever he gets to wishing he had a model son."

Adults tend to view me as being mature beyond my years. I think it has partly to do with being a clergyman's daughter, partly to do with looking after Rose, and partly to do with being rather clever. But I can't take any credit; I'm stuck with all of it.

"A father tends to be disappointed," said Eldric, "when his son has achieved the great age of twenty-two and failed to graduate from university."

"You're to continue your studies here, with Mr. Drury?"

Eldric bent toward me, his whisper-breath warm in my ear. "It's *Mr. Dreary*, actually. Don't tell him, but I've given him a name that suits him better. Yes, Father insists I finish my studies."

I should love to finish my studies. I was to have gone to school in London after Father dismissed my own tutor, but in the end, I was obliged to stay in the Swampsea to care for Stepmother. Rose and Stepmother. And the worst of it is that I have only myself to blame.

"Am I to study with you?"

"Absolutely not!" said Eldric. "I can't have you showing me up in every subject."

Of course he couldn't. Girls weren't supposed to be cleverer than boys. It's quite a good thing I don't suffer from normal-people feelings, such as disappointment.

I felt rather than saw Eldric's gaze. "I didn't mean it, you know. Yes, you are to study with me, and outshine me in every subject." Eldric smiled, a long, curling lion's smile. "Every subject but one."

"What subject is that?"

"Boxing!" said Eldric.

Boxing? I should love to learn to box! Not only are girls supposed to be less clever, but content to sit by the fire and spin. Father believed this, of course, but Stepmother knew the truth. She knew that learning to run a household was a waste of a girl's time.

"This will come as a surprise to you, I know, but I have never studied boxing. I wish I'd thought to want boxing lessons. If I had, my stepmother would have seen to it, I assure you. She thought girls should study whatever they liked."

Stepmother encouraged me in everything I loved. I used to tramp about the swamp, and I wrote lots of stupid stories. She encouraged my writing, in particular, which was kind, for now I realize that my stories were simply awful. What a relief they burnt to cinders and no one will ever read them.

"I'm so sorry about your stepmother," said Eldric, which is something I've heard often these past two months and three days, but I still haven't gotten used to it. I understand it's not an apology, of course, but still, it sounds strange. I'm the one who should apologize. I don't exactly blame myself for Stepmother's death. I didn't feed her arsenic, and it was arsenic that killed her. But I did cause her to injure her spine. She might have died from that if the arsenic hadn't gotten to her first.

We fell silent. Eldric took to fidgeting with some fidgety-boy thing. I knew what he was thinking. In his position, I'm sure I'd be wanting to know all about Stepmother: It's so wonderfully interesting when a person kills herself. But she didn't, Eldric. She wouldn't!

The gentlemen had gotten on to talking about Mr. Clayborne's official business, which was to drain the water from the swamp. This was going to improve life in the Swampsea, at least according to Queen Anne. Less water meant more land. More land meant more crops, and more grazing for sheep and cattle. More land also meant no swamp and no swamp cough.

"Might we creep away?" said Eldric. "When Father starts talking of draining the swamp, he starts thinking he ought to put me to work, but that would be a disaster. I'd turn my shovel wrong way up, and set the water to running upside-down."

You'd think I'd despise this great shiftless lad. Here I was, caring constantly for Rose and complaining only to myself, which is not at all satisfactory; and there he was, doing nothing and boasting of it all the while. But I liked him. That is, I liked him as much as I liked anybody.

"I'll show you about the house," I said. "That will please Father."

It did, too. Father was delighted that his daughter was acting like a regular girl, playing hostess and chatting to a young man.

We set off down the corridor. The flood had been two years ago, but the cracked-plaster walls still smelled of dead water and mournful fish. The front parlor was rimmed round with windows, and in the light, I saw Eldric fidgeting with the most fascinating bits of curled wire.

"Are those paper clips?" I'd seen them in catalogs, but the pictures don't do them justice. They're beautiful, in an industrial sort of way.

Eldric poured a clinking waterfall into my palm. "Aren't they lovely! I can't keep my hands off them. But I give you fair warning: It was a box of paper clips that got me expelled."

"Expelled?"

"A box of a thousand paper clips," he said, his long fingers curling, coiling, twisting. "And a sack of colored glass."

"Expelled!" I might be a wicked girl who'd think nothing of eating a baby for breakfast, but I'd never allow myself to get expelled. It's far too public.

"Quite definitely expelled," said Eldric. "The dean left me in no doubt. But really, was it my fault? When the fellow down the hall bet me a thousand paper clips I couldn't chuck a certain stone far enough to reach a certain chapel?"

"You took the bet?"

"I ask you—for a thousand paper clips! Had I any choice?"

I acknowledged that he had not. "And the chapel?"

"Let's just say I have quite a good arm. Let's just say the stone reached the chapel with room to spare. Let's just say it reached the chapel with the kind of room that took it right through the stained glass."

Eldric laughed at himself, and I found myself laughing too. It had been ages since I'd heard my own laugh. It was rusty, but serviceable.

"Father will not find that an amusing anecdote."

"But you do," said Eldric, "which is far more important. When you're a bad boy, you find that people either laugh at you or with you. I prefer the *with*."

"You'll have some competition. Cecil Trumpington fancies himself the local bad boy."

"A rival?" said Eldric. "Shan't we have fun!"

I opened the door of Father's study, which is just a little less tidy than you'd expect. And he doesn't realize that his armchair smells of tobacco. *Do as I say, not as I do.*

At the end of the corridor lay the charred remains of the library.

"A flood and a fire!" Eldric looked at the blackened floor, at the boarded-up windows, at the great black cavern that had once contained bookshelves. It still whiffed of smoke. "You've had more than your share of misfortune."

I nodded, but it actually had nothing to do with misfortune and everything to do with me. Six months ago, the library shelves held all my stories. Then I set the fire and cremated them all.

And I have the scar to prove it.

But I don't mind, really. I don't read much anymore.

"Father would want me to point out the church, which lies just to the other side of the library." The church and the library shared the wall, conjoined like Siamese twins. "But you probably don't care about the church, being a bad boy, that is."

"Don't tell your father," said Eldric.

"I probably have an obligation to point out all the local hazards. When they say *safe as houses,* they weren't thinking of ours." I led Eldric through the foyer and flung open the front door. "You'll notice the porch has fallen right off."

"Good Lord!" Eldric's eyes were very bright. It was because of the whites of his eyes—yes, that was it. They were whiter than anyone else's.

I explained we lost the porch to the flood. "Father hasn't gotten around to rebuilding it, although he's quite a good carpenter. He says if Jesus was a carpenter, it's good enough for a clergyman. But I don't remember that Jesus let his house fall down."

Beyond the ghost of the porch lay Hangman's Square, its cobblestones strewn with the lengths of steel that were growing into the railroad line between London and our village of Swanton, which meant that Swanton was living beautifully up to its reputation as the end of the line.

Eldric stared at me with those bright eyes. What a contrast we must have made: my eyes, blacker than black; his eyes, whiter than white, plus an interesting little scar that dipped into his eyebrow.

Eldric stood very still, yet hummed with energy, just as London did. The London I'd never see, strung with electric wires and brilliant with switch-on lamps. I've always wondered whether they string lamps into the lavatories, or do even Londoners think there are certain things best left in the dark?

I'm aware that I'm mixing my metaphors horribly. How can I compare Eldric to a lion in one description and to electricity in another? But I don't care. It's my story and I get to make the rules.

Back into the parlor, where the mirror over the mantel shelf caught Eldric's face. Not mine. I'm not tall enough, and anyway, I've outgrown my reflection.

Eldric turned away from the mirror, holding out his hand. In the cup of his palm lay his fidget of paper clips. But the fidget had blossomed into a crown. An allover-filigree crown, with a twisty spire marking the front.

I stared at it for some moments. "It's for you," said Eldric. "If you want it."

"I'm seventeen," I said. "I haven't played at princess for years."

"Does that matter?" Eldric set it on my head. It was almost weightless, a true crown for the steam age.

In a proper story, antagonistic sparks would fly between Eldric and me, sparks that would sweeten the inevitable kiss on page 324. But life doesn't work that way. I didn't hate Eldric, which, for me, is about as good as things get.

I mustn't get back to thinking of myself as princess, or wolfgirl. All the silly things I used to imagine. Stepmother was right. It doesn't matter that you look like a princess on the outside. You're a witch on the inside and nothing will change that. It's best not to look at yourself at all.

"I'll show you where you're to sleep." I pushed through the swinging door into what had been the sewing room. Stepmother slept here when she was ill. Stepmother died here, with no one about to mark her passing. Why didn't I check on her, sit with her? I knew she was dying. But that's what witches do, isn't it? They leave people to die alone.

It was hard to imagine Eldric in this room. How would that mixed-metaphor lion- and London-boy fill Stepmother's empty spaces?

What did mixed-metaphor boys possess? Football things? Trophies? Sweaty jerseys?

Eldric turned on his high-tension muscles to the window, which overlooked the swamp. "Do you go out there and tramp about?"

I used to visit the swamp every day. I used to imagine myself into a wolfgirl and prowl and lope and sniff and howl. "Not for a long time." I knew exactly how long: three years come September.

"What's it like?"

"Wet." I remembered that September day with terrible clarity. It was the day Stepmother told me I'm a witch. I'm still astonished she had to tell me. How could I not have known? Or at least guessed? I had, after all, left a trail of destruction behind me, wide as a football field.

"It's very beautiful."

Beautiful? The swamp stretched as far as the eye could see, a gray shimmer, bronzed with reeds and cattails. I used to think it beautiful, but I have no particular feeling for it anymore. I suppose the old wolfgirl Briony would have disliked the idea of draining the swamp, but why should I care? I could never visit the swamp again.

"Pearl did what she could to make the room comfortable, but please tell us if you need anything."

Strange to think of Eldric hanging his university jacket and trousers in the sewing cupboard, which had once been filled with needles and spools of thread and embroidery frames. That was back in the days when Father thought his daughters had to be educated in the domestic arts—a hideous phrase, which is of course why Father chose it. He hired Pearl's mother to help domesticate us, but along came Stepmother and set us free.

"I'll ask Pearl to attend to the fire."

Stepmother had never cared for fires. They made her too warm, she said. I had to wrap up when I came into the sewing room to care for her. The sewing room was a sad place then, and I always think a clean-swept grate is desolate.

The light from the window caught at Eldric's wide lion cheekbones, and at a rougher sweep down his cheeks. Whiskers? Did this boy-man shave? Of course he did, foolish, ignorant Briony. He was twenty-two. He'd be shaving away in this room, in the very room where Stepmother died.

I was suddenly aware of him, of the overwhelming Eldricness of him, of his busy London blood pumping just inches away. Of his paper-clip energy and switch-on eyes.

"Miss Briony!" It was Pearl calling—screaming! "She runned out. Miss Rose runned into the swamp!"

I slammed through the swinging door. I'd done the very thing Stepmother had warned me about. Or rather, I hadn't done it.

I hadn't been caring for Rose.

I hate myself.

You must take care of Rose. Stepmother had said that again and again. *Take care of Rose.* And I had promised.

I'd learned how to do it. I'd learned I had to hate myself.

I crashed into the kitchen. The cupboard door was ajar.

When you hate yourself, you don't neglect your responsibilities. When you hate yourself, you never forget what you did.

I'd even forgotten about Rose's cough. How little it took, two bright eyes and a couple of paper clips. What if it's the swamp cough and she dies, Briony? How will those bright eyes look then?

Let's review the rules, Briony: What, above all, mustn't you forget?

You mustn't forget to hate yourself.

· 4 ·

Such a Pretty
Little Rosy!

One hundred eighty-three steps to the river.

I hurtled down the riverbank.

One hundred eighty-three . . .

Other footsteps now, joining mine—no, pouncing over mine, catching me up.

"You can't come with." I threw the words over my shoulder.

But Eldric was already at my side. "Your father made a plan," he said. "You and I are to search the swamp, while he and my father search the fields."

One hundred eighty-three steps.

"And he gave me a Bible Ball."

"Then mind your feet," I said, "else the bog will have you for supper." The Horrors couldn't touch him, not if he carried a Bible Ball.

"Your father says you know the swamp better than anyone." Eldric ran beside me on quiet lion paws.

But it had been three years. I'd changed; perhaps the swamp had changed. "Mind your feet."

One hundred eighty-three steps are quickly taken. We turned onto the towpath, ran beside the river.

"I have Bible Balls for you and Rose," said Eldric.

The bridge rose ahead. How many steps? Rose would know. Already I was winded. I'd lost the old Briony, that long-ago wolfgirl who could lope endlessly through the swamp.

I spattered over the pebbles at the foot of the bridge, trying to keep up with myself. My breath grew hot and sharp.

"You can't help Rose if you overtax your strength." Eldric took my arm, reined me into a trot.

"I know you've been ill," he said. "Ill for almost a year. I can't even imagine. Please don't overtire yourself and make me have to rescue you."

I might have smiled, but the problem with bridges is that they go up before they go down, and I hadn't the strength. It's true, I'd been ill for a long while. I had a queer sort of illness that made me feel as though I were a music box in want of winding, moving and thinking more slowly with every passing day. Thinking—that was the worst. I'm used to being clever, not dull.

We tipped over the rise of the bridge. Downhill now, into the swamp.

The swamp hadn't changed. Lucky me, to see it again, before Mr. Clayborne drained the water. It was just as I remembered, a foreverness of mud and water, water and mud, and to the west, a blackness of trees.

"Rose left no tracks," said Eldric.

She hadn't, she couldn't. The swamp is too oozy and flowy

26

and drifty to hold an imprint. In April, the swamp smells of winter, but the snow has melted; the season of mud has begun. Beyond the stretches of mud and water lay the end of the world, where the air turned blue.

But slow-poke Rose could never run to the end of the world, not in a quarter hour. Unlike me, she's never been quick. I pointed to the blackness of trees.

"She's in the forest?" said Eldric.

"The Slough." But if she wasn't . . . Stop, Briony. Make a plan.

"There are three bits to the swamp. We're on the Flats now, which is all reeds and shallows. Rose will have come to no harm here."

Unless one of the Horrors—

Stop!

"In another quarter mile, we'll enter the Quicks. That's the bit that likes to gobble you up. If she didn't come to grief there, she'll be in the Slough. Tread only where I tread through the Quicks. It's only two miles, but every step is treacherous. When we reach the Slough, go on ahead." No need to say I couldn't keep up.

"You'll need your Bible Ball," said Eldric.

I snatched a crumple of paper from his palm. Strange that a thing so small keeps a person safe in the swamp—unless that person is Briony Larkin, who isn't actually a person, which is the reason she needs no Bible Ball. The Horrors can't hurt her: She's a horror herself.

"You keep Rose's," I said. "You'll find her first."

The wind sang through the reeds. "Mistress!" said a voice, and another—"Mistress!" And now a chorus of melancholy voices, calling my name. Or, rather, the name by which the Old Ones called me back in the days when I was wolfgirl, back in the days when I'd used to roam the swamp.

"Where hast tha' been, mistress?"

"Such a vasty time to bide away!"

"Aye, a vasty time."

"Listen to the wind," said Eldric. "It's lovely, the way it blows through the reeds."

I nodded. Eldric saw only the reeds, heard only the wind. He hadn't the second sight.

The second sight.

I tried to disbelieve Stepmother when she told me I'm a witch. I knew she was right, yet I tried to make a case for myself, pecking at the proof Stepmother offered—pecking at it, turning it over, saying it didn't exist. Then pecking at another bit, and another, until Stepmother took pity on me. If I wasn't a witch, she asked, how else was it that I had the second sight?

"Talk to us, mistress! Make us our sweet story!"

Stepmother had leaned toward me then, taken my hand between the two of hers. Her hands were always cool. "I wouldn't tell you if I weren't obliged to," she said. "I only want your happiness."

It was true. Stepmother wanted nothing but the best for us. She wanted us to follow our dreams, helping in every way she could. She made sure I always had paper and ink and pens; she made sure I had time and privacy in which to write. And even Rose—well, Stepmother never minded the scraps of paper Rose left scattered about the Parsonage; she never minded helping Rose cut them into bits, paste them into collages.

"Mistress!"

The voices of the Reed Spirits faded.

"Make us our sweet story!"

Did the Reed Spirits know what had happened to the stories I'd written for them? Did they know those stories had burnt?

The mud-and-water of the Flats gave way to the water-and-mud of the Quicks. Jellied trickles turned to tricky jellies; the land quivered.

"Mistress!"

What a queer feeling; I'd never ignored the Reed Spirits before. It wasn't simply that I mightn't speak to them in front of Eldric. It was that I mustn't ever speak to them, not ever. Stepmother was very clear. She'd told me again and again: Briony plus the swamp plus the Old Ones is an explosive combination.

I had to break my promise now, but Stepmother would understand: I had to rescue Rose.

I gave all my attention to the Quicks, to the fleshy plants and splatty bogs that lick their lips as you pass by.

"Careful," I said. "The Quicks are always hungry."

We crept round glints of scummy water and slimy reeds. My feet wanted to run, but my head told me not to be foolish. I couldn't help Rose from the bottom of a bog. Patience! The Quicks were only two miles across—not even two miles! But a mile lasts forever in the Quicks.

"What's that smell?" said Eldric.

"We're almost to the snickleways. They have a fearsome smell."

"Snickleways?" said Eldric.

"Waterways—you'll see in a moment; they snickle all

through the Slough. They won't gobble you up, though—unless you can't swim. You may run—now!"

He ran terrifically fast, which was depressing. I used to run fast myself. Stop now, Briony: That sounds like jealousy, and you know what happens when you get jealous.

Your witchy jealousy breeds firestorms, gales, floods—disasters of Biblical magnitude. Wouldn't Father be proud!

I ducked through tangles of scrub, prickles of black fir. The snickleways were the color of tea, crossing the Slough, then doubling back to double-cross each other.

"Rose!" I called.

"Rose!" called Eldric, deep in the Slough.

I slipped through twisted branches, plunged into the first snickleway, slogged through the muck. "Rose!" I emerged caked with mud to the chest.

"Rose!" called Eldric.

I brushed past ferns. I pulled against foot-sucking mud.

The water caught at bits of my reflection. Now a dark eye, now a slim nose, now a fall of bright hair. A face belonging to a shattered girl. A girl, scattered through the Slough.

"Rose!" I called.

Scream, Rose! You're so good at screaming. Go on, jab your screams into my ear-squish.

I never lost my internal compass, although every landmark had multiple copies of itself. The snickleways looked all the same, scum and duckweed and tea-water and reflection shards. The mud looked the same, every teaspoon, and so did the trees and logs and ferns and stumps.

"Rose!"

I crashed in and out of snickleways, dislodged smells of

sulfur and rotten eggs. The wolfgirl Briony never used to crash. She slipped silently through the Slough; she could run forever. But it's three years later now, and I know all the wolves are dead. Isn't education a wonderful thing?

Another snickleway, more egg-and-sulfur vapors, which prickled tears into my eyes. But they were false witch tears, not real people tears. Witches can't cry.

"Rose!"

More tea-dark water. The sulfur sting grew sharper; my tongue arched and spat. My hands and legs shook; I stumbled over scraps of my face. I pushed myself from the muck, I listened, I stumbled, I pushed myself from the muck, I listened, I—

Rose's trademark scream, distant, but unmistakable.

"Rose!"

"Fires are dangerous!" Rose's voice.

A crashing now, Eldric and I running, converging upon Rose.

We ran at each other, Eldric and I. We ran through trees furred with moss.

"Fires are dangerous!"

But there were other voices. "Rosy, dear!"

"Take my hand, Rosy!"

The voices of girls!

"So pretty as you be, Rosy!"

Eldric and I, plunging into black spruce.

"Fires are dangerous!"

A green dimness now. Needles of sunlight, glancing off Rose's hair. "Fires are dangerous!" She stood screaming, her eyes squeezed shut.

"Us got us some visitors!" said a girl's voice.

The girl was— Look up, Briony; you have to look up. Higher—into the treetops!

Three figures, dashing and darting through the trees.

"Such a pretty Rosy!"

They sat astride black branches—no broomsticks for these Swampsea witches!

"Doesn't you be wishing to come along with us?"

I crunched my fingers round the Bible Ball. "Get away from her!"

The black capes, the gnarled branches, swirled around Rose. "You be making such a pretty little witch, Rosy!"

Rose clapped her hands to her ears.

What if I proclaimed my own witchiness? Would they leave Rose in peace—honor among thieves, and all that? But I couldn't, not with Eldric listening. I shook my Bible-Ball fist at them.

"Ooh, doesn't I be scareful!" said one of the witches, although the branch she rode bucked, like a startled horse. Wisps of carrot-colored hair floated from her hood.

"I be trembling in my drawers," said another.

"Such a woeful lie!" said the third. "You doesn't wear no drawers!"

"No drawers for us witches!" How they screamed and laughed.

I darted forward, pecking the Bible Ball at them.

"Look at them eyes she got!" said the redhead. "Like to coals, they be."

The witches rose on their branches, screeching with laughter. "It be fine not wearing no drawers." The redhead again. "Look Rosy, such a treat it be!"

Rose didn't look.

Pine needles swirled about our feet, stirred by an unnatural wind. I smelled the tart-treacley scent of magic. The wind corkscrewed up to a miniature whirlwind, a tornado of pine needles, spiraling up and under the witches. Now, at last, the capes decided to follow the laws of nature, billowing up and out, leaving us with a spectacular view of three naked backsides.

My hands jumped like startled birds. I ought to have looked away, but the sight was horribly fascinating. Fascinatingly horrible. Eldric grabbed my bird hands, and together we stared up at the three gnarled branches circling the glade, up at the twin-moon backsides.

The witches laughed. This was no old-hag cackling but peals of girlish laughter. Eldric and I stared. The witches circled and descended upon Rose. More laughter as they pulled away, one of them dangling Rose's hair ribbon from her finger.

"Now girls, for t'others!" The witches dove upon us. Eldric and I ducked—they'd smash into us—but the branches reared back, then hovered an Eldric's arm's-length away. There came a rearrangement of legs and capes. They laughed and laughed as we stood, looking up into their inner girl-parts.

Eldric crunched my bird hands. I jerked my chin to my chest. I felt my face boil with my own hot blood, which in an alabaster girl is a terrible thing to see—shades of crimson coming but never going.

I felt rather than saw the witches circling, then rising, now above the trees, now out of sight. But their shrills and shrieks of amusement blew to us on that unnatural wind.

That unnatural wind—think about that, Briony. Think about anything rather than what you're thinking about, which you mustn't name, because then you'll think about it.

The unnatural wind is a perfect memory to stuff into your mind. It will make you remember you hurt Rose. It will make you remember the swings, the froth of petticoats, Rose's screams—those knitting-needle screams, which even when Rose was only seven, sounded just as they do today.

You must remember so you can hate yourself. It's been ten years, but you mustn't let yourself forget what you owe Rose.

It was Easter Day and Rose and I wore our white, frothy frocks. It was a day of froth: the froth of spring blossoms, the froth of lace on Stepmother's hat, the froth of petticoats as Rose and I pumped ourselves higher and higher on the swings.

Stepmother wasn't Stepmother yet; it would be years before she and Father married. We knew her well, though, Rose and I. Perhaps she meant to help the poor Reverend Larkin with his motherless daughters. That would be like her. Father was forever fretting that he didn't know how to raise girls properly. Poor man, his wife dying in childbirth.

I remember so clearly how Stepmother's pretty fingers flew like hummingbirds. How she played a game of catching at our legs, pretending to pull us down. How she pulled at Briony's legs, Rose's legs. Briony's legs, Rose's legs.

Rose's legs. Rose's— Rose's— Rose's—

When you're jealous, your spit turns to acid. When you're jealous, you eat yourself from the inside out.

When you're jealous, and when you're seven-year-old Briony Larkin, and when you're a witch, you raise a wind. A wind that makes Rose whimper and complain; a wind that makes Rose scream that she didn't prefer to swing; a wind that makes Rose lose her grip on the ropes; a wind that makes her fall, so that she smashes her head on a rock.

It would make a better story if I could describe how her skull made a sharp crack, if I could describe how her blood pooled on the rock, how it matted the grass and dried in her yellow hair. But I have learned that life is both less exciting and more horrid than stories.

No crack, no blood, just Rose crumpled on the ground. Just Rose screaming.

Rose, screaming. Rose screaming in the memory-time of the swings; Rose screaming in the now-time of the Slough.

Eldric crunched at my hand.

"That hurts!"

"Sorry!" Eldric let go at once.

"Go ahead, plug your ears," I said, not looking, never looking at him, never looking at him again. My face must be in the crimson-streak stage, which lasts forever. "It's not rude, not if it's when Rose is screaming." Pine needles drifted round our feet.

"But I don't want to miss anything!"

What would that be like, not wanting to miss anything? How wearisome to be forever grabbing at bits of life. Look at Eldric now, stepping over to Rose, bending over her, asking perhaps if she'd been hurt. I sat at the foot of an alder, leaned against its trunk, just waiting. Light-needles glinted off the pale gold of Rose's hair. I felt a little distant from myself, as though I sat in the audience of a production of my own life.

There would be no surprises in this production. I'd be caring for Rose in every scene. In the next scene, for example, the curtain would open upon me hanging about Tiddy Rex's sickbed, comparing his cough to Rose's. I mustn't neglect to play that scene, even though it had just occurred to me that a person with the swamp cough might be unable to scream so very enthusiastically. But I couldn't take any chances. It's my fault Rose is the way she is.

It's my fault that Rose screams. That she screamed this morning, that she was screaming now. She screamed like a river, the longest river you could imagine, and from time to time, words bobbed to the surface, like sticks. I could make out the words, although I doubted Eldric could. Rose screamed for her hair ribbon. It was her favorite ribbon and it matched her frock. And although she didn't say this, I knew that without the ribbon, she'd refuse to wear the frock.

Rose is finicky about colors.

Finish the story, Briony. You know the rules. You have to tell yourself the other horridly unexciting events. That you jumped from your own swing, rather hoping you might hurt yourself, just a little, so that Stepmother would fuss over you too. That Stepmother spent such a time crouched beside Rose, touching Rose's head. That the hummingbirds had flown from Stepmother's fingers.

That Stepmother rose and looked down upon you. That you looked up at her, at the crisp V of her jaw, at the thin openings of her nostrils. That she waited such a while to speak.

"Oh, Briony!"

That was all she said at first, and then:

"We mustn't ever tell your father."

Help to Get Them Witches

"Flying branches?" said Mr. Clayborne, who'd only been in the Swampsea six months and had never seen a witch.

"It be a snag," said the Swamp Reeve, who'd taken the chair nearest the fire. The Brownie used to curl up under that chair, back in the old days, before Stepmother and I forbade him the house. "Us calls it a snag."

The firelight played over the bit of frayed carpet where the Brownie used to lie. I used to look at him and marvel that no one else could see him. But now I had to remember that it was better he was gone. That he and I were dangerous together, the Old One and the witch.

"A snag rode by a witch," said the constable.

"Us needs must talk to Miss Rose." The Reeve wore his neck-skin too tight. You could see his Adam's apple bounce around, which made my backbone cringe. "She be the lass them witches thinked to thief away."

I shifted in my seat but couldn't get comfortable. The old swamp craving had returned. I hadn't felt it for years. It had come upon me the first few months after I stopped visiting the swamp, after Stepmother realized the Old Ones ignited my wickedness, made it run out of control.

"I want Briony to read to me." Rose sat beneath the parlor table, bits of paper scattered around her. Rose is attracted to paper of all sorts, sweets wrappers, shopping receipts, Valentine's Day cards, instructions for games we never played, the last page of any book—this, in particular, is annoying.

When Father is irritated, he speaks more precisely than usual. "Please come out from under the table, Rose." He curled his sentences as carefully as a schoolgirl curls her hair. "You are a grown-up girl now."

"I don't prefer to." Rose shuffled the papers about. I knew she was testing the colors, deciding which combinations would look best in her collage. "I want Briony to read to me."

But Rose was not a grown-up girl. She would never be a grown-up girl. She knew perfectly well that my stories were nothing but cinders, and she was not unintelligent, so what was she thinking? Did she suppose I could paste the ashes of my stories together, the way she pastes her bits of paper into a collage?

Rose has great faith in my abilities.

"Happen I might approach Miss Rose?" said the constable.

"Scissors are dangerous," said Rose.

"Danger?" said Eldric from across the room, where he and Mr. Dreary were stuffing Clayborne books into Larkin shelves.

"I need someone to cut my papers," said Rose. "Stepmother used to cut for me, but she's dead."

"I'm just the man for a dangerous job," said Eldric.

"Happen I might talk to Miss Rose direct-like?" said the constable. "Tell her us needs her help to get them witches."

"Certainly you may," said Father.

Certainly, Father? Do you have any idea what's going to happen once the constable sticks his face beneath the table? That face of his, with those saggy eyelids turned inside out and the red bits showing?

"I don't prefer to speak to the constable." Rose's breath snagged on her words and set off a spasm of coughing.

"Hand to your mouth, Rose," I said.

"He's only going to ask you a few questions," said Father. "If you act like a grown-up girl and answer them properly, you'll never see those witches again."

The constable approached the table. Forge ahead, O mighty enforcer of the law. May you be stout of heart and eardrum.

When Rose takes to screaming, she starts loud, continues loud, and ends loud. Rose has a very good ear and always screams on the same note. I'd tested her before I burnt the library, and our piano along with it.

Rose screams on the note of B flat.

We don't need a piano anymore now that we have a human tuning fork. In any event, Rose and I never played very well, despite Father's insistence that we practice an hour a day. We'd never be like Mother, who'd played the piano beautifully, or so Father said. I sometimes wondered if Father really remembered her. Seventeen years is a long time.

It was wonderfully restful to stand back and do nothing. I heard Father call in the reinforcements, who are named

Pearl. I watched Pearl escort Rose from the room. I heard Rose scream all the way upstairs.

The pitch of B flat has uncommon carrying power.

Strange how her screams eased the swamp craving, just a bit. It's like rubbing your elbow after you bump it, I suppose.

The mighty enforcer of the law returned to his seat. Eldric had taken Rose's place beneath the table, fidgeting with bits of paper and working the scissors. There's little to compare between Eldric and Stepmother, except they were the only people I'd ever seen join Rose under the table. How patient Stepmother had been, her hummingbird fingers cutting the papers into bits at Rose's direction, and those bits into smaller bits, and those smaller, and smaller still.

There fell what a novel would call an "awkward silence," save for the sound of Eldric chopping at the air with the scissors. I fixed my gaze on the bookshelves. Before the flood, they'd been filled with a rainbow of fairy tale books and dog-eared Latin histories and all the novels of Jane Austen and Charles Dickens and the Brontë sisters (except that sniveling Anne). Now they were empty, begging hands. The flood had turned the books into bloated corpses that had to be shoveled up and hauled away in barrows.

I used to like books and reading, but I destroyed our books in a couple of fits of witchy jealousy. Had I meant to drown our books? Had I meant to burn our books? Honestly, you'd think a witch would know what she'd meant to do. I was, after all, a great girl of seventeen when I set the library fire. But I'm not a proper witch: If I'd had a proper witchy education, I'd certainly not have burnt my hand. A proper witch would avoid that unimaginable pain, that horrible healing, that horrible itching. Sometimes my scar itches unbearably. I have to bite at it so I don't scream.

The constable dragged up his eye folds. His sausage eyes slid about until they landed on me, which was a greasy sort of feeling. "Us been told you seen them witches, Miss Briony."

I nodded.

"Did you see 'em close-like?" said the Reeve.

I'd seen them close-like, all right, but what should I say? If I'd had a proper witchy education, I'd know the rules. Does one betray a fellow witch?

The Reeve took my silence for fear. "Us knows them witches be right scareful to think on, Miss Briony. But them memories you got, they be the very things to get 'em hanged."

"Briony scared?" said Eldric. "I've never seen anyone less scared in my life. She has nerves of iron."

It's true: I don't get scared; I keep my head in emergencies. People think me a sort of Florence Nightingale, but I have no heroic qualities. I simply don't feel very much.

"You got memories too, Mister Eldric," said the constable. "Didn't there be nothing peculiar about them witches?"

Peculiar? No, nothing peculiar, just the normal run of witchy backsides and witchy girl-parts.

"Him an' me," said the Reeve, "us be sniffing round for evidence, see? The Chime Child, she do her job proper. She don't take to hanging when there don't be no evidence."

"A child?" said Mr. Clayborne.

"It's only a title," said Father. "She's rather old, really."

"One of the witches had red hair," said Eldric, now lying on his stomach and crinkling the pages of the *London Loudmouth*. That's what Father calls the London newspaper.

Oh, well. There went my attempt to save my fellow witches, although I can't say why I tried. None showed any sisterly affection.

Was Eldric thinking of those witchy girl-parts too? Had he ever seen those bits of a girl before? Most girls would blush to think such thoughts, but when you've been as wicked as I, you don't have any blushes to spare.

What do twenty-two-year-old shaving boy-men get to see?

"That be evidence o' the most excellent sort." The Reeve's Adam's apple strained against his neck skin, which is a thing that should be illegal. "Thank you kindly, Mister Eldric."

Pearl pushed through the door with a tray. We've had lovely teas since Pearl came to us. There's always soft white bread, like clouds, and butter, and two kinds of jam. The sweet today was lemon cream and butter biscuits.

I adore lemon cream!

Pearl glanced upstairs, where Rose continued to cough and drill through the floor on the pitch of B flat.

"Sorry, Mr. Reverend, sir," said Pearl, "but I doesn't got no tricks to quiet Miss Rose."

I did, though. I had a few Rose-calming tricks, which often as not succeeded one time out of ten. So why was I sitting here, dreaming about lemon cream? My job was to care for Rose, for nothing and no one but Rose.

I stood, made for the door.

"You mustn't fret about it, Pearl," said Father. "Rose is difficult to calm."

Is she, Father? Is she! How would you know? You've hardly seen us these three years past.

"And Briony," said Father, "where are you going?"

What do you think, Father! Who do you think has been caring for a screaming Rose while you've been chatting to God?

But there was no point saying anything. There never is.

"Nowhere."

"I've always wanted to go *Nowhere*," said Eldric.

"You mustn't leave," said Father. "These gentlemen will have questions to put to you still."

Stepmother always said we didn't have to mind Father. "He's a good man," she'd say, "but he doesn't know much about girls, does he?" We let him think we were minding him, though. It was easier that way.

She was terrifically skilled, Stepmother was: She was skilled in the art of not-minding-but-pretending. But I, witchy, tricky Briony Larkin, didn't know what to do.

Eldric squiggled out from beneath the table. "What if I went *Nowhere* and gave this to Rose?" Of a sudden, he was kneeling before me, a paper rose blooming in his hands. He'd fidgeted the rose right out of the *London Loudmouth*. The paper was coarse, but the rose was a miracle of ingenuity and engineering. You could look into its whorled petals forever, into petals within petals within petals.

"Rose will go mad for it," I said.

"Yes, go on," said Father. "Do give it to Rose."

"Just follow the screams," I said. Eldric smiled at me over his shoulder.

Another awkward silence fell, but Mr. Clayborne did what people in novels always do: He broke the silence by clearing his throat.

"What is this Chime Child of which you spoke earlier?"

"Who," said the Reeve. "The Chime Child, she be a *who*."

"But a special sort of *who*," said Father.

"She be special, right enough," said the Reeve. "The Chime Child, she don't be no Old One, no Old One proper, but she don't be no proper person, neither."

Mr. Clayborne only looked from Father to the Reeve and back again.

"She has a foot in both worlds," said Father. "One foot in the world of the Old Ones, the other in the human world. It would be a miscarriage of justice to try a witch without someone present who understands the Old Ones."

"You doesn't need to fret none, Mr. Clayborne." The constable worked his sloppy lips. "There don't be no miscarriage: Us does it right an' us does it proper. Any witch us seizes, she get a trial with the Chime Child an' all t'other trimmings."

"Then us hangs her," said the Reeve.

"Why do you need a trial?" said Mr. Clayborne. "Can't you tell that you've caught a witch if she flinches from a Bible Ball?"

But not every witch reacts to a Bible Ball. They don't affect me, for instance, which is convenient. Just imagine: the clergyman's daughter, unable to touch the Bible?

Awkward.

"Not every Old One is susceptible to a Bible Ball," said Father, "and in any event, even an Old One is entitled to a trial."

We all fell silent, and as though choreographed, so did Rose. Eldric must have succeeded with his fidget.

It was so quiet, you could hear every little clink and tap as Pearl passed the tea things. You could hear the chimney wheeze.

Two dollops of lemon cream for the constable; two dollops of lemon cream for the Reeve.

You could hear a chunk of coal crack and spit; you could hear footsteps coming down the stairs.

Two dollops of lemon cream for Mr. Clayborne; two dollops of lemon cream for Mr. Dreary.

You could hear the swish of the door pushing past the doorjamb. You could hear Eldric's lion feet and Rose's tiptoe feet. Rose held the paper rose just as Eldric had, in the bowl of her hands. There was an unfamiliar softness to her face, as though she might smile.

Two dollops of lemon cream for Rose; two dollops of lemon cream for Eldric.

"I want Briony to read to me," said Rose.

Three dollops of lemon cream for Briony!

"I want Briony to read to me," said Rose, spreading her skirts on the carpet, just as Stepmother had always done, except that Rose's were white and Stepmother's were always the colors of the sea. It was surprising how entirely at home Stepmother had looked, sitting beneath the table, following Rose's instructions. But it was not at all surprising how not-at-home I had felt, watching Stepmother with Rose, watching Stepmother's infinite patience as she cut the papers to slices, to slivers, to splinters.

It was jealousy, of course. Jealousy makes you feel small as a splinter. Jealousy makes you feel empty, makes you want to reach for the Brownie. But the Brownie's bit of carpet was empty, save for biscuit crumbs and a bit of coal-sputter.

Eldric took his tea on the floor. He did look comfortable, leaning against the wall, and when he smiled, he reminded me of Stepmother. She often smiled when she worked with Rose. She had a great flash of a smile; it echoed her pearls and foaming lace.

But Mr. Dreary chose the chair next to me. He was too starchy for the floor. He was unlike Eldric in every way, including the depressing whiff of tinned soup—of which, I neglected to mention, Eldric does not smell.

"Here be the properest thing to do," said the constable. "If Miss Briony an' Mister Eldric will be so kind as to take the Reeve an' me, us'll examine where them witches was."

Not I! Hadn't I sworn yesterday I'd never leave Rose alone, not even twenty feet's worth of alone?

"I'd be glad of a walk," said Mr. Dreary, stretching his puffy little legs. He was from America and had a most peculiar way of speaking.

"A walk!" Eldric jumped to his feet, the very picture of a wild boy, pouncing and bouncing with his long, curling lion's smile. "A walk is so . . . so healthy!" He was ready for another swampy adventure filled with danger and naked backsides.

"I want Briony to read to me."

"But Rose," I said, although I knew it would do no good, "don't you remember the library fire?"

Rose did.

"What happened to our books?"

"Your stories, do you mean?" said Rose, ever precise.

"Yes, my stories." Rose was right. Ever since the flood last year, the library held only the stories I'd written. I hardly remember that time, though. That's when I'd fallen so ill, when I was winding down.

46

"I like the stories where I'm a hero," said Rose.

"What happened to my stories?" I said.

"They burnt," said Rose.

"Am I then able to read them to you?"

"Stories?" said Eldric.

"No," said Rose. "I liked the stories where I'm a hero." She gave her little pre-cough sound.

"Hand to your mouth, Rose," I said.

"What stories?" said Eldric.

"Foolish stories about me and Rose." And the Old Ones. I'd always been writing the stories of the Old Ones. "I'm too old for them now. I'm glad they burnt."

I was, too. Sometimes I wonder if I called up the library fire simply in order to destroy them.

"I wish my book had burnt in the fire," said Rose, which is what she'd taken to saying whenever the subject of the library fire arose.

"A book you wrote?" said Eldric.

Rose shook her head.

"Who did, then?"

"It's a secret." Rose was full of secrets.

Mr. Clayborne's voice rose, and so did Mr. Dreary's peculiar accent. Mr. Dreary didn't want to carry a Bible Ball into the swamp. He didn't believe in the Old Ones.

"I must insist," said Mr. Clayborne. "How can it hurt? It's no more than a bit of paper scribbled with a Bible verse."

"I'd feel foolish," said Mr. Dreary.

"It don't matter if you feels a fool or if you doesn't," said the Reeve. "Them Old Ones, they be real as real, an' don't it be better to feel foolish than to feel dead?"

"The Old Ones are dangerous," said Eldric, his eyes sparkling whiter than white. "There's the Dead Hand, who will rip your hand off. There are the Wykes, who will lure you into the bogs. There's the Dark Muse, who will suck away your spirit."

"I'm glad to see," said Mr. Clayborne, "that my son is capable of acquiring and retaining at least some information."

"If there's enough blood and wickedness," said Eldric. "I stopped in at the Alehouse this afternoon, which is better than any library. I am absolutely stuffed with information. Do you know there exists a person who's only half of an Old One? Something like that, anyway."

"The Chime Child was born at the Mirk and Midnight Hour," said Rose, who was dotty about birthdays.

"The Mirk and Midnight Hour," said Eldric. "Lovely. I wish I'd been born then."

"I prefer that you not be born then," said Rose.

"I shall accede to your wishes," said Eldric.

"Mightn't it be better if you postponed your trip into the swamp?" said Father. "It will be dark soon." Father would think of that, wouldn't he? Didn't he ever get sick of living with himself, of being so—so prudent?

"But I don't want to miss the Boggy Mun," said Eldric. "Not the king of the swamp! See how much I know, Father. Isn't that every bit as good as memorizing the kings and queens of England?"

"I hears you, Mr. Reverend, sir," said the constable. "But evidence, it be right fragile. It might to be blown away, an' that were a woeful thing."

"Our English monarchs are so unimaginative," said Eldric. "They execute people in such tediously conventional ways."

I had to bite back my laugh before I could speak. "I'm sorry, but I cannot accompany the constable."

"Why ever not?" said Father.

What could I say now? I couldn't tell him I'd promised Stepmother never again to enter the swamp. I couldn't tell him that Briony and the swamp, together, are deadly.

How did Stepmother manage to ignore Father so neatly, with him never realizing for a second?

It was then that the plates of the earth shifted beneath me. Gravity reversed itself and ran uphill. I tasted lightning. I was falling, falling up into witchiness.

A skull sat on Mr. Dreary's shoulder. It stared at me as though we were acquainted, which we were. We'd met once, but I couldn't think where.

The eyes of the skull were black holes held into place by bone. They were no more than holes, but they recognized me. The skull worked its jaw back and forth.

When a person has already seen Death—seen it once, at least—you'd think she'd remember whose shoulder it had been sitting on. But this particular person did not. She only knew that that person had died.

She knew that Mr. Dreary was soon to die.

How could I have forgotten who it was? I rarely forget the little things, much less the big ones. Perhaps I'd seen Death during the last months of Stepmother's life, when I was ill and foggy. I remember little from that time.

Death must have perched on Stepmother's shoulder when she was fading out of life, but I hadn't seen it then, of course. No, not Briony, the girl who let her stepmother die alone.

Death had no lips, but it was smiling.

49

No one else could see it, not Eldric, not Father, not Mr. Dreary himself. Just me, Briony, third-class witch. I'd promised Stepmother not to leave Rose. I'd promised her never again to venture into the swamp.

But what if I might prevent Mr. Dreary's death?

Dead finger-bones chittered. It was waving? Yes, a friendly little finger twinkle, waving good-bye. Death vanished all at once, and I fell back into human-ness, with Father folding my fingers around a Bible Ball. "It's all decided, then. Pearl will care for Rose while you help the constable and the Swamp Reeve."

This just shows you how much Father knows about me, which is exactly nothing. Giving me a Bible Ball to protect me from the Horrors is like throwing a life preserver to a fish.

I oughtn't to go into the swamp, but Mr. Dreary was to die. Would Stepmother approve of my following him into the swamp to make sure he was safe? How could I know? What if I just wanted to return to the swamp because the hinges of my jaws still ached with craving?

Could it be that I truly wanted to save Mr. Dreary?

I doubted it, but I'd go. I hadn't the knack of only pretending to do as Father wished. Did I want to save Mr. Dreary?

I'll never know. We witches don't go in for self-knowledge.

· 6 ·

Please
Let Him Live!

I drifted across the Flats. Drifting—that's the proper way to navigate the swamp. Not chasing after Rose, not pounding past the Reed Spirits, with no chance to stop for the singing of the reeds. I drifted beside Eldric, listening to his low whistle. How could I have forgotten that the swamp has no beginning? How could I have forgotten that the swamp simply seeps into existence? That it bleeds and weeps into existence?

The itch was gone—the itch of my scar, the itch of the swamp craving. How lovely to seep and bleed and weep into the swamp. It would take more than three years for me to forget. If I could love anything, I'd love the swamp.

Is this what a nun feels when she runs wild? Perhaps running wild needn't mean dressing in satin and taking to cigarettes. It might mean running into the wild, into the real, into the ooze and muck and the clean, muddy smell of life.

Eldric's whistling slid into words. "Your father says you know the swamp like the back of your hand."

"I am not at all interested in the back of my hand."

"But you're interested in the swamp," said Eldric. "So why have you stayed away for so long?"

"Who told you that!"

"You did," said Eldric.

Had I? Eldric and I drifted through the swamp. We wept across the Flats, we bled around the remains of ancient trees. Mr. Dreary had fallen behind us; he didn't know how to drift. He splatted along on his dreary legs.

"I see you love the swamp," said Eldric.

I didn't love anything. But I couldn't say that, and I couldn't explain why I'd abandoned the swamp.

There were so many things I couldn't say. That Stepmother had proven to me that the swamp and I, together, were dangerous. That I'd promised her never again to set foot in the swamp.

When I was hollowed out with craving, I'd remind myself that the swamp and I were a combustible combination. When I bit at my own teeth, I'd remind myself that my swampy combustions hurt people.

"There's always Rose to look after," I said. "She wants a lot of minding."

But I wasn't minding Rose, not right now. I was in the swamp, for the second time in two days, leaving Rose in the Parsonage. But it was all right, wasn't it? Pearl had promised never to take her eyes from Rose, not even for a moment (although I'd told her she could blink). It was all right, wasn't it, because I was doing it for the best? I was doing it to save

Mr. Dreary—wasn't I? A witch is wicked enough to fool her own self.

Best check on him—yes, there he was, in the finest of dreary fettles. Don't fool yourself, keep checking.

"But you've always had Rose to look after," said Eldric.

"Don't forget we all fell ill," I said. "First Father, then I, then Stepmother. Rose too, just a bit, toward the end of Stepmother's life. We each of us had to mind the other."

All, that is, save Father. He didn't mind anyone, and I mind that. He'd been quite ill for the first year or so after he married Stepmother. But then he got better and went off, or maybe he went off and got better. I don't know and I don't care. All I know is that he came home only to sleep. We rarely saw him.

"She didn't kill herself, you know."

I hadn't known I was going to say this, but it was too late to take it back. "My stepmother wasn't the type to kill herself."

"She was murdered?" said Eldric.

I tried to answer without answering, as this was not a popular hypothesis. "She wouldn't have killed herself."

"No?" said Eldric.

I looked up at him, his cheeks not exactly rosy, but pinkish gold. "You don't believe me?"

He paused. "I don't not believe you."

I should never have said anything. Of course he didn't believe me. I wouldn't myself. Why didn't I think about it all the time? Why didn't I turn into Mr. Sherlock Holmes and bring her murderer to justice?

We fell into silence. Eldric fell back to whistling; his

53

whistling slid into singing. "Gin a body meet a body, comin' thro' the rye." Beyond the Flats lay the fields. I had used to love lying in them in the fall, the rye waving above my head, bronzed and feathered.

"Gin a body kiss a body, need a body cry?"

Eldric and I bled and wept round twists of black branches. It was most peculiar to hear Eldric sing. I felt he was singing just for me. I'd not felt that since Father stopped singing to us, at bedtime. I suppose we'd grown too old for that, Rose and I, but still, I'd missed it for a long time.

Now I had to struggle to keep up with Eldric. He wasn't short of breath; he was fresh as the proverbial daisy. Unfair! This is my swamp and I'm wolfgirl, tireless and fierce. Unfair! I wished I could uproot him and pluck his petals, one by one.

He loves me.

He loves me not.

He loves me.

But I already know how it will end.

He loves me not.

"Let's slow down," said Eldric. "No need to rush, not today."

"You think I'm not fit," I said.

"It's Mr. Dreary who's not fit," he said. "It's you who've not been well."

"But I'm not a fragile, faint-y sort of girl," I said. "Once, I could run forever." I can't even remember when I learned to run forever. It seemed that I'd always been wolfgirl. Father had never minded my going into the swamp until I turned ten. Then he began to have doubts. He told me I ought to be more ladylike. He never quite forbade me, though, and thank goodness Stepmother came along to say I might visit the swamp as much as I liked—until, of course, she told me I mightn't.

> *Gin a body meet a body,*
> *Comin' thro' the rye,*
> *Gin a body kiss a body,*
> *Need a body cry?*

He had a nice voice, not beautiful but pleasant. He sang as naturally as he spoke.

> *Ilka lassie has her laddie,*
> *Nane, they say, hae I,*
> *Yet a' the lads they smile at me,*
> *When comin' thro' the rye.*

He returned to his subterranean whistle. Drift, weep, bleed through the black labyrinth of trees, through the ancient forest. Drift, bleed—

Blast!

Blast Mr. Dreary, calling for us to wait up. His Dreariness was slow and puffy. His little legs weren't drift-worthy, only drear-worthy.

"Hold tight to your Bible Ball," I said. "We're about to enter the Quicks. They'll gobble you up if you're not careful."

"Unless," said Mr. Dreary in his tinned-soup way, "I happen to come across a Horror who's immune to the Bible." How could a tinned-soup voice sound mocking? Mr. Dreary didn't believe in the Horrors.

"How does a Horror come to be immune?" said Eldric.

"Natural selection," said Mr. Dreary, very proud no doubt to have heard of Mr. Darwin.

"Not enough time," I said. "The Bible only came to the Swampsea during the last century. Natural selection doesn't work that quickly."

"How do you also come to know so much?" said Eldric.

"Father engaged a brilliant tutor for me. Henry Fitzgerald was his name, but we called him Fitz. He didn't mind. Sometimes we called him the Genius. He didn't mind that, either. He was interested in everything—in Mr. Darwin, in Dr. Freud, in those machines that photograph people's bones."

"My feet are wet," said Mr. Dreary.

"You lack the proper gear," I said. We teetered along a trickle of land that wound between water and mud. "Here in the swamp, even the swans wear rubber boots."

"Not for long," said Mr. Dreary. "Give Clayborne a couple of years, he'll drain the swamp dry."

Oh, dreary me!

"But the swamp's so beautiful," said Eldric. "I don't care for the idea of draining it."

"It's progress," said Mr. Dreary. "You can't stand in the way of progress."

"I can so," said Eldric.

"But Miss Briony understands," said Mr. Dreary. "She knows what progress will mean to the Swampsea. Cattle, crops, education, commerce, medicine."

Miss Briony understood no such thing, but just then, a brace of pheasant had the good sense to blast out of the reeds at our feet. Mr. Dreary jumped. Eldric and I pretended not to laugh.

We skirted the hungry bog-holes, which were simply dying to drink down any unwary traveler. Well, actually, it's the traveler who'd be doing the dying. But the swans had nothing to fear and were feeding at the bog-holes, poking about with their yellow bills. The water shone yellow, reflecting the yellow sky and the white swans and the bronzed reeds and the yellow bills. The ground quaked beneath our feet, breathing in air, breathing out mist.

"Tell me about the Horrors," said Eldric.

"Later," I said. "We ought to catch up with the constable and the Reeve. The swamp is unfriendly at night."

I called, but they'd drawn too far ahead.

"I can throw my voice as far as I threw that stone," said Eldric. "You remember, the stained-glass-smashing one?"

He threw his voice, all right, and with the proper shattering effect. The constable and Reeve turned about and waited.

"Don't worry," I said as we sped up. "You'll experience the Horrors soon enough."

London seems an exciting place, far more exciting than the Swampsea. But it occurred to me that the Swampsea might seem equally exciting to Eldric. He wouldn't have seen any of the Old Ones: So many had died in the great cities—in London, and Manchester, and Liverpool. No one knew it was the machines and metal making them sick, killing them.

Only the vampires can survive. They're remarkably tough, which is lucky for them, as they don't embrace country living.

By the time we reached the constable and Reeve, the sunset had turned to dust. We'd only two lanterns among the four of us. The water was gray, the reeds were black. With every step, we squeezed at the lungs of the swamp. It breathed out mist and poison.

Mr. Dreary coughed and rubbed his eyes. "Smells like the Hot Place."

I said nothing, not having had personal experience.

Now that dusk had fallen, came the Horrors. Voices wailed about us, voices of the dying and the damned. Twigs snapped beneath invisible feet; an invisible something smacked its lips.

Mr. Dreary whirled round, and round again.

"Don't run!" I grabbed his sleeve.

"It don't be naught but the Horrors," said the Reeve. "They delights in making folks scareful, but you got yourself a Bible Ball."

"Don't run!" I tightened my hold on Mr. Dreary's sleeve, turned to the others. "Don't let him run!" A chorus of screams cut through my words. Hold tight, Briony. This is why you're here, to save Mr. Dreary.

"Look at the lights!" Mr. Dreary's voice scratched like an old nail. "A village, we'll be safe there!"

"No!" The Reeve, the constable, and I spoke over one another, trying to explain. "They're false lights; they're the Wykes; they're luring you into danger!"

Mr. Dreary was not fit, but he was strong enough, in a horizontal sort of way. He tore his sleeve from my grip, fled deeper into the Quicks.

I flew after him, hitching up my skirts. "Stop!" Mr. Dreary puffed, and wheezed, and slipped. I lurched at his coattail, but up he bounced, hurtling toward the cluster of lights. They shone softly, in fair imitation of a village whose inhabitants understood the value of a good fire and a stout door.

"Don't run!" Eldric bolted after us. A fringe of light caught Mr. Dreary's coattails. Mr. Dreary screamed. Eldric spun forward, but all he illuminated was the dark heart of the swamp.

"The two o' you follows him that way," shouted the constable. "The Reeve an' me, us'll come at him from t'other."

What a fool I was! I should never have come to the swamp. I should have kept my promise to Stepmother. I should have remembered that in the swamp, my wicked energy adds up to disaster and death.

"Don't look at the lights," I told Eldric. "The Wykes will trick you just as they did Mr. Dreary. They'll trick you right into the Quicks."

"Hell!" said Eldric.

"It may come to that."

We couldn't run, not in the dark, not in the Quicks, where speed equals death. I picked along bits of mud, walked tightrope between bog-holes. Eldric followed, holding the lantern high. Starlight swam on the darkness. "We're looking for grassy bits that will support us," I said. "They rise from the Quicks, like islands."

I drew a deep breath. "Mr. Drury!"

"Don't move, Mr. Drury!" shouted Eldric. "We can save you if you stay put."

Please, let Mr. Dreary live. Please let him live!

But witchy magic doesn't listen to please and pretty please, and anyway, I didn't really care. I only pretended to care because not caring makes me a monster.

The star-dimpled water shone before us. We leapt onto a tussock, which quivered beneath us. Stars floated in the pools, lanterns floated in the pools. Not just one lantern, not just our lantern. Scores of lanterns, hundreds of lanterns, flickering about us.

"The Wykes again," I said. "You can't help seeing the reflection of their lights, but don't look at them straight on."

"Mr. Drury!" called Eldric.

Black water stretched as far as we could see, black water, grassy tussocks. Maybe we could save him. Maybe. I coiled myself tight as a spring. We jumped to the next tussock. Eldric landed beside me, almost tumbling me into the ooze. He grabbed my elbow.

We leapt from tussock to tussock. We squished the lungs of the bog. It breathed its poisoned breath. We coughed and rubbed our eyes.

Smells like the Hot Place.

"But aren't we forgetting something?" said Eldric. "He has his Bible Ball."

"It will protect him from most of the Horrors," I said. "But it won't protect him from his own foolishness, from allowing the Wykes to lure him to the most treacherous part of the swamp. No Bible Ball can prevent him from slipping and drowning."

But it was your own foolishness, wasn't it, Briony? This is just what Stepmother had been talking about. You, in the swamp, with your witchy jealousies and rages boiling always beneath. You don't think you mean harm, but harm you do. You'll kill Mr. Dreary just as you killed Stepmother—or you would have, if the arsenic hadn't gotten her first.

You have to remember it, remember that you were the one who called the tidal wave. Remember! Surely you remember your witchy rage, how it set the river to boiling?

I know you remember standing beside the river, looking up at the Parsonage. Looking at the back garden, at the apple tree, where the swings had once hung. Looking at Stepmother, bending over the vegetable beds. You remember the boiling river, you remember Mucky Face rising—rising from the river—rising ten feet, fifteen feet, curling over himself.

Curling himself into a wave.

You'd called Mucky Face and he came. He came rearing like a snake, rising to the height of the Parsonage. He was a curl of iron, hard and black, save for his whirlpool eyes, his foaming mouth.

He smashed himself upon the Parsonage, he smashed Stepmother and the vegetable garden. Mucky Face flooded the Parsonage, but nowhere else. Mucky Face injured Stepmother, but no one else.

But it was enough. Mucky Face drowned our books, Mucky Face injured Stepmother's spine.

"Look!" Eldric raised the lantern.

It shone on a Dreary-shaped space, a black space where no stars shone.

"Don't move, Mr. Drury!"

Stepmother would have died from her injuries had the arsenic not found her first. Even then, I didn't understand. I had to ask Stepmother—ask her as she lay in bed—ask her if she was sure about the dangers of my wandering into the swamp. It didn't make sense: I had, after all, been standing across the river from the swamp when Mucky Face appeared.

Stepmother instructed me to look out the window into the garden. She asked me how wide the river was. I said about thirty feet. She asked me where Mucky Face lived. I said he lived in the river. She asked me whether Mucky Face would be able to hear me calling him from the swamp side of the river. I said he would. She asked me whether Mucky Face would be able to hear me calling from the non-swamp side of the river. I said he would.

Perhaps he'd have come sooner had I been in the swamp itself. Sooner and stronger. I don't know, and anyway, he was quite strong enough.

"Don't look at the lights!"

"Hold on to your Bible Ball!"

The swamp slurped and swallowed. The stars rubbed out the Dreary-shaped space. Eldric shifted behind me; the tussock gasped and gurgled.

The swamp plus Briony . . . Briony plus the swamp . . .

Next time, Briony, keep your promise to Stepmother. Don't pretend you're interested in doing good. How long can a clever girl trick her own self? It's been three years since you learned you're a witch. Perhaps you didn't kill Stepmother, not technically, but that doesn't mean St. Peter's going to wave you through the pearly gates.

Slurp and swallow, slurp and swallow. Mr. Dreary had vanished. Too late to pull him out. The false lights had vanished. Everything had vanished except Eldric and me. Everything had vanished except the two of us, the lantern, the stars, and the swamp, which breathed slowly through its jellied lungs.

7

Girl What Can Hear Ghosts

Rose and I stood in our usual place, facing Father and the headstone. We usually stand beside the grave, but there'd be no grave for this funeral. You need a body for a grave, and Mr. Dreary's body had been taken by the swamp.

Taken by the swamp. No, Briony, please try to remember! Not *taken*. The Wykes lured Mr. Dreary into the most treacherous part of the Quicks, where he fell and drowned. Where anyone would have drowned, unless he could walk on water, which I venture to say Mr. Dreary could not.

But I could not forget how the swamp slurped and swallowed. Those were not the sounds of falling.

Father had prepared a sermon on the meaning of Mr. Dreary's life. That's what stories do, they try to create meaning from nothing. But there's no meaning to Mr. Dreary's life. He lived, he smelled of tinned soup, he died.

When we were small, Rose and I used to play a game

called connect the dots. I loved it. I loved drawing a line from dot number 1 to dot number 2 and so on. Most of all, I loved the moment when the chaotic sprinkle of dots resolved itself into a picture.

That's what stories do. They connect the random dots of life into a picture. But it's all an illusion. Just try to connect the dots of life. You'll end up with a lunatic scribble.

But Father has to try. It's his job.

He looked up; the crowd fell silent. Fall silent; fall into the Quicks. Slurp and swallow. Stop, Briony! Please try to remember: Mr. Dreary had a Bible Ball.

Rose and I faced Father; the congregation gathered behind. I was used to playing clergyman's daughter, dressed in funeral black, down to my ribbons and lace mitts. Rose was identically dressed, but she wasn't playing. Rose can never learn how to play.

"Black isn't a color," said Rose.

I shook my head. "Hush, Rose!"

The daughter of a clergyman will attend hundreds of funerals. She may attend as many as two or three a week when the swamp cough is on the prowl. I'd stood beside dozens of graves since Stepmother died, but hers was the one I remembered. I remembered the dark oblong; I remembered its corners, clean and sharp, like the angles of a hospital bed.

"I match up with pink," said Rose. "I don't match up with black."

I put my finger to my lips. "Father's speaking."

But Rose doesn't like to be hushed. "Black isn't a color. I want my pink ribbon."

The crowd rustled behind us. They'd be staring, of course,

at the reverend's peculiar daughter. I don't mind the disapproving ones so much. It's the tolerant ones I can't stand, the ones who smile at Rose, who speak to her ever so slowly and gently. They don't realize how very intelligent Rose really is. They're just terrifically pleased with themselves. *Look at me!* they all but shout. *See how broad-minded I am! How wonderfully progressive, how fantastically twentieth century!*

"I match up with pink."

"Come along, Rose." I turned round; she followed me into the graveyard. I used to stop by Mother's grave, but I haven't recently, not for several years. I used to stop to talk to her and tidy up a bit. I used to trim the ivy on her headstone. But now ivy and lichen have run riot over the gravestone carvings, which are not the usual cherubim but sunflowers and daisies—Mother's favorite flowers. They're exquisitely carved. I'd say you could almost smell them, except sunflowers and daisies haven't much of a smell. I wish I might have known Mother. I wonder whether I'd have taken such a very wicked path if she hadn't died when we were born. She knows I'm a witch, I suppose. I imagine her looking down on me and shaking her head and sighing.

I can't face her.

Stepmother ought to rest here too, in the Larkin plot, but no: The Reverend Larkin didn't fancy giving his second wife a proper burial.

I led Rose to the far end of the graveyard, to a tenement of tiny gravestones. They sprouted round our feet like pale mushrooms. So many children had died of the swamp cough this winter. The gravestones were uneasy newcomers, perched at the edge of their seats.

The earth tilted beneath my feet. I sat so I wouldn't fall. The second sight was coming upon me. Not the ordinary sort of second sight, the sort that links me to the Old Ones. It's the other sort, the sort that links me to the spirit world.

The sort that, only three days ago, linked me to the skull of Death.

The world shook herself like a dog. She tried to fling me off, but I clung to the nearest gravestone. This sort of second sight is never roses and moonbeams, but death and blood and the smell of fear.

From the grave beneath came a little voice. "'Twere the Boggy Mun what sended the cough what taked me."

It was a child's voice, thin as skimmed milk. The world swung off its axis and ran uphill.

"The Boggy Mun," said a second child from the next-door grave. "The Boggy Mun, he be that angry his waters been took away."

The earth tried to scratch me off, like a flea. "Taked me, an' the baby too," said a third. "Them last minutes, they was bad, with old Death hisself a-leaning on my chest."

"An' now us be asking you for help, girl what can hear ghosts."

Don't ask me! Thunder fizzed at my fingertips. *Girl what can hear ghosts.* I can't help—I won't help! But the words stuck to my mind like flypaper. *Us be asking you for help.*

"Them London men, they oughtn't to have took the Boggy Mun's water."

"Tell 'em the Boggy Mun sended the swamp cough, he be that angry."

Us be asking you for help.

"An' now my baby sister, she be took with the cough."

The ghosts thought I could appease the Boggy Mun, who would then snatch away the swamp cough. Poor ghosts—well no, they're not really ghosts. They're Unquiet Spirits who can't rest until something in the living world has been set to rights: their murder avenged, their sins confessed.

Their baby sisters cured.

The children's voices grew thinner.

The Boggy Mun had ruled the swamp since before our human time began. He was lord of the swamp, of the water and the mud, and all swampy states in between. He could be kind, he could be savage. He could kill with the swamp cough, and why not, when his water was stolen away?

And still thinner.

"They oughtn't to have took no water."

"Tell the grown folks to fetch it back."

Until Mr. Clayborne called a halt to the draining of the swamp, the Boggy Mun would strike with the swamp cough, and strike and strike again.

Strike and strike again—oh, you idiot Briony: Ask the ghost-children, quick! "My sister—does she have the swamp cough?"

"Them London men oughtn't to have took—"

"Don't go—does she have the swamp cough? Please tell me!"

Please tell me *no!*

"Them London men—"

The children's voices skimmed themselves into extinction. Gravity turned itself right side out. The world bounced up to chase her ball, which was sick making, although it would soon be over. But I'd wish myself sick again if I could do it over. I'd asked the question too late.

"I don't have the swamp cough." Rose came into focus. She smiled her anxious-monkey smile, which is the only smile she knows how to make.

"Of course you don't," I said, just as Rose hunched herself into her chest for a comfortable paroxysm of coughing. What exquisite timing. If she weren't Rose, you might think she was indulging herself in a paradox. In a paroxysm of paradoxysm.

But she is Rose.

"It's time for the funeral-baked meats," said Rose, squeezing her words past the last crumbs of coughing.

"Right you are, Rose." We were alone in the graveyard. Even Eldric, the newcomer, knew that every good mourner makes merry in the Alehouse with roast pork, and pies, and funeral biscuits, and sherry and ale. Especially the sherry and ale. A funeral is a thirsty piece of business.

I was dizzy and seasick. "Give me a minute."

"People can't give minutes," said Rose.

Rose, literal Rose. "It's just one of those things people say. We talked about that, remember, when Father tried to catch the barkeep's eye?"

"Quick!" said Rose, all in a rush. "Cover your ears!"

I clapped my hands to my ears, pretending I couldn't hear the church bells chime twelve o'clock. Rose has a peculiar relationship to the notion of time: She won't let me listen to the clock strike twelve. I can't say why—I've told her often enough that I like the hour of noon—but there's no understanding Rose.

"It's time for the funeral-baked meats."

"Off we go, then." *Us be asking you for help, girl what can hear ghosts.*

"I want you to read to me," said Rose. "I want a story where I'm a hero."

Oh, Rose! I launched into my litany of the library fire and the books burning, and then she said what she always said:

"I wish my book had burnt in the fire."

That blasted book again! Just tell me about it, Rosy dear. I'll see that it burns. But Rose never tells her secrets. That would be breaking the rules.

Us be asking you for help. Don't think about that, Briony! Rose never breaks the rules.

But reminders of the ghost-children were everywhere. In the cemetery, the ground puckered with death. Outside the cemetery, the gravestones pointing every way but up, like bad teeth.

Stepmother lay beneath one of those careless gravestones, in the unconsecrated ground set aside for murderers and witches and suicides. How could Father have been married to Stepmother and not known she'd never kill herself?

The cemetery lay on Gallows Hill, the highest bit of the village. In the distance, the swamp stretched out in a crinkle of gray crepe. Below sat Hangman's Square, anchored on the south end with the Siamese church-and-Parsonage twins. The other sides of the square offered everything one might need in life: the Alehouse, the jail, and the gallows. Sometimes, when a person visits the Alehouse, he goes right on to visit the others.

The present occupant of the gallows was Sam Collins, of the upriver Collinses, each of whom was born with an extra finger, the better to steal from you, my dear.

The ghost-children wanted me to tell the villagers how to stop the swamp cough. Let's pretend I do. Here's how it would go.

It would turn into a *House That Jack Built*.

This is the girl called Briony.
This is the girl called Briony; who lived
in a swamp that was being drained.
This is the girl called Briony; who lived
in a swamp that was being drained;
which angered the Boggy Mun.
This is the girl called Briony; who lived in a swamp that
was being drained; which angered the Boggy Mun;
who sent the swamp cough.
This is the girl called Briony; who lived in a swamp that
was being drained; which angered the Boggy Mun;
who sent the swamp cough; which Briony found out
about through the ghost-children.
This is the girl called Briony; who lived in a swamp that
was being drained; which angered the Boggy Mun;
who sent the swamp cough; which Briony found out
about through the ghost-children; whom Briony was
able to hear because she has the second sight.
This is the girl called Briony; who lived in a swamp that
was being drained; which angered the Boggy Mun;
who sent the swamp cough; which Briony found out
about through the ghost-children; whom Briony was
able to hear because she has the second sight; which
Briony has because she's a witch.

This is the girl called Briony; who lived in a swamp that
was being drained; which angered the Boggy Mun;
who sent the swamp cough; which Briony found out
about through the ghost-children; whom Briony
was able to hear because she has the second sight;
which Briony has because she's a witch; which the
Swampfolk found out when she had to explain how
she knew.

This is the girl called Briony; who lived in a swamp that
was being drained; which angered the Boggy Mun;
who sent the swamp cough; which Briony found out
about through the ghost-children; whom Briony
was able to hear because she has the second sight;
which Briony has because she's a witch; which the
Swampfolk found out when she had to explain how
she knew; which meant she was hanged by the neck
until dead.

That *was the girl called Briony.*

I'm not really the sacrificing type.

"It's time for the funeral-baked meats," said Rose.

We descended Gallows Hill, each in our own way. I'm no longer a wolfgirl, but still, I'm fast and Rose is slow. She's slow and clumsy and afraid of heights and speed and danger.

An' now us be asking you for help, girl what can hear ghosts.

This is the girl called Briony; who wanted to hurry to
the Alehouse; which would distract her from the
memory of the ghost-children; which kept coming
back to her until she wanted to scream; which she

felt like doing anyway, because Rose doesn't know how to hurry; which goes to show that Briony's always waiting for Rose, and if Briony ends up on the gallows, it will be for murder.

This is the girl called Briony.

8

When in Rome

"I don't like that man." Rose spoke loud enough for Mad Tom to hear.

"Where be my wits?" shouted Mad Tom, who, aside from being irritatingly mad, stood between us and the funeral-baked meats. "They be lost, O my stars an' strumpets. Lost forever an' aye."

"I don't like that man."

He rattled his umbrella. "It be you lovelies what taked my wits. I seen you when you done it. I spied you with my little eye."

He's harmless, poor thing. That's what everyone said. It was true, but who cares? Lots of people are harmless, but that doesn't mean I have to like them.

"Two hundred twenty-six steps until the Alehouse," said Rose. "But we have to pass that man."

"And pass him we shall," I said, for Tiddy Rex was sure to be in the Alehouse, and I needed to listen to his cough. Just let it be different from Rose's. Please let it be different!

"I want the funeral biscuits," said Rose.

"Come along, then."

"Doesn't I spy two black-eyed lovelies!" Mad Tom flapped his umbrella at us as we passed. "Has you such a thing as a pair o' wits about you?"

"I want the funeral biscuits," said Rose. But we'd already pushed through the Alehouse door, into the smells of tobacco and lantern oil and the ghosts of fried sausages. A hand snuck into the crook of my arm.

"I was afraid you weren't coming."

I looked up, into Eldric's switch-on eyes.

"You came just in time," he said. "I was about to auction off your seats. They're going for a fortune."

There weren't many fortunes to be made in the Swampsea, but neither were there many chairs. Mourners crammed windowsills, leaned against walls, talking, laughing, drinking, as all good mourners do. But there, at a table occupied by Mr. Clayborne and Father, were two seats, tipped onto their front legs to show they were taken.

How would a regular girl feel if an Eldric boy-man saved her a seat? Eldric, from exotic, faraway London.

Would a regular girl be happy? I don't know much about certain feelings, like happiness. I have thoughts, of course, but thoughts stay in one's head. Thoughts don't feel.

"Introduce me to the new fellow, won't you?" said Cecil Trumpington.

Cecil was Judge Trumpington's son, but he didn't mind sharing the next-but-one table with the ratcatcher and a fellow from the willow yard. Cecil was democratic when it came to drinking.

Cecil and Eldric shook hands. Two lovely boys, face-to-face: Cecil, all dark ringlets; Eldric, all tawny mane. Cecil a bit the taller; Eldric a bit the broader. Cecil, all pale and dead-poet-ish; Eldric all electric and alive.

Cecil leaned over me; he smelled of money. "It's been such a long time since I've seen milady!"

Milady. Such an old-fashioned word makes him feel clever. "Only five days," I said.

"You count the days too!"

How would a regular girl feel if a Cecil boy-man stood looking at her with his pale fish-eyes, pressing a hand to his chest? Cecil, whose house has stained-glass windows and curved stairs, and a porch fixed securely to the front.

Would a regular girl want to smack him?

"I'm hungry for funeral biscuits," said Rose.

"Funeral biscuits?" said Eldric. "Shall I hunt them down? Are they dangerous?"

"You're mad!" said Cecil, but he rose to accompany Eldric. Two boy-men, stalking the wild funeral biscuit.

I let my mind go wandering. I pretended I was a regular person. I breathed in greasy air and sour ale, just like a regular person. I listened in on the conversation behind me, just like a regular person.

Eavesdropping is such a regular-person activity.

"Hark to my words," said the constable. "The witch is like to be that Nelly Daws. She got that wicked red hair."

Nelly Daws, from the Coracles, the smallest-but-one village in the Swampsea. She had red hair and dancing feet.

"Nelly Daws," said Davy Wallace, a fisherman known principally for having caught a hundred-pound sturgeon with his one hand. "I always knowed her for a witch." But you can't trust what Davy knows: He's not a knowing sort of person. He's the sort to accept a wager to spend the night in the swamp without a Bible Ball. He's the sort to meet up with the Dead Hand and come home minus one of his own.

Could Nelly have been that red-haired witch, screaming with laughter and swooping through the trees? It was hard to imagine.

"She got them sharp witch eyes," said the Swamp Reeve. "I marked it well last time I seen her."

Now I wished I weren't eavesdropping. I didn't want to hear about catching witches, and hanging witches. But you can't just stop eavesdropping. Too bad a person can't close her ears.

"Us mustn't go by eyes," said the Chime Child. "Too many people what doesn't be witches been hanged as witches." I pictured her, wind-roughened face, thinning hair. She was utterly unremarkable in appearance. You'd never guess she had a foot in the world of the Old Ones. You'd never guess she had the second sight.

"Witchcraft be a sin," said the Chime Child, "but hanging an innocent, that be a sin too."

"The Chime Child," said the constable, "she be in the right o' it. There can't be no hanging o' Nelly, not 'til us matches up the evidence."

"An' I doesn't like hanging nobody," said the Hangman, "without I be sure as sure. I doesn't like hanging no girl what be said to be a witch, an' she don't turn to dust."

The Hangman was a great ox of a fellow. I pictured him

watching the hanged girl, waiting for her to turn to dust. The Hangman need only wait a quarter hour, and if the body continues to swing, he can be sure she wasn't an Old One.

He can be sure that Judge Trumpington and the Chime Child made a mistake.

It works the other way too. Imagine Briony struck dead by a runaway horse. Imagine Father looking on, fretting about the cost of coffins these days, when of a sudden, his daughter's body turns to dust. He'd made a mistake too. He'd never really known her at all.

"I got you some evidence," said the coastguard chief. "I seen Nelly one midnight, dancing widdershins 'neath a horned moon."

"Did you see her close-like?" said the Chime Child, as though she knew the answer would be *no,* which it was. "I be getting on in years. My mind, it don't be clear like 'twere. I be scareful to judge *yes* when the truth, it be *no.* A person can't just be thinking it be Nelly Daws dancing. He needs must know it be Nelly Daws."

Now came Eldric and Cecil, laden with pies and pork and biscuits and ale and sherry, and now Rose had something to say, which put a blessed end to my eavesdropping. When Rose speaks, you can't hear anything else.

"I knew it!"

"Knew what?" said Father.

"I knew the food would be brown. I don't like brown."

It was true, everything was brown: the pie, the sherry, the gravy, the biscuits, the caraway seeds on the biscuits.

Brown or not, it looked delicious. I reached for my fork.

I'd grown used to eating with my right hand. I was rarely tempted to use my left. It would be harder if I still wanted to write, but all that's behind me.

It's just as well I switched hands: Witches are thought to be left-handed. Perhaps it's true. Rose is no witch and she uses her right hand. We are mirror twins, she and I. What's left for me is right for her; and if I wanted to feel sorry for myself, I might say nothing's right for me.

But Rose was using neither hand. "I need Briony to cut for me."

Cut for her? After all these years of teaching her to cut her meat? Of telling her knives weren't dangerous if properly used? On the day I break down and slap Rose, I'll probably use my dependable left hand.

"But you cut your meat ever so well on your own."

Rose raised her clenched fist. "My hand prefers to be occupied."

"What do you have, Rose?"

"It's mine," said Rose.

"Of course it's yours, but I'd like to see it." One never knew what hideous things Rose might pick up.

Lamplight glinted off the pewter tankards as they went up and down, although where Cecil was concerned, there was a lot of *up* and not so much *down*. Rose uncurled her fingers. On her palm lay a crumple of paper.

"He dropped it," she said. "He didn't prefer to have it."

"It's a Bible Ball," said Cecil, stating the obvious, which was his specialty.

Father sat up very straight. "Who dropped it, Rose?"

"Mr. Drury didn't prefer to have it, so it wasn't stealing."

"The fool!" said Mr. Clayborne. I'd never heard him raise his voice before. "And after all my warnings!"

Yes, Mr. Dreary had been a fool, letting the Quicks have him for tea. He didn't believe in the Bible Ball, he'd left it behind. Slurp and swallow. I'd been right. The swamp reached out and gobbled him up.

"His Bible Ball?" Eldric leaned forward, the very image of a boy who didn't want to miss anything. Least of all Mr. Dreary; no, Eldric didn't miss him. Why was it that Eldric could get away with a thing like that—not being sorry when a person was supposed to be sorry?

Cecil put on a solemn face for about five seconds, which happens to correspond with his attention span. "When in Rome," he said, shrugging wisely.

"We're not in Rome," said Rose.

"What Cecil means," said Father, "is that people who travel to foreign places ought to follow the rules and customs of that place."

"But we're not in Rome," said Rose.

"Quite true," said Eldric. "We're far from Rome."

"In the Swampsea," said Cecil, showing off his geography. I still can't understand how Cecil and my old tutor, Fitz, got along so well, when we often called Fitz "the Genius" and avoided calling Cecil anything at all, so as not to be rude.

"We're in the Swampsea?" said Eldric. "Surely not! I'm certain I took the express train to the Dragon Constellation."

Cecil put on his best dead-poet face. He's far too highbrow for silliness.

But Rose laughed. She does sometimes understand when

something's meant to be silly. I never can predict when. But the laughing set off a fit of coughing. What was I doing, filling my belly and licking my burns? I needed Tiddy Rex and his cough.

"Don't tell me you haven't heard of the Dragon Constellation!" said Eldric. "It's very far, indeed, from London, and I for one intend to follow all its customs. If a native from the Dragon Constellation tells me to carry a Bible Ball, then it's a Bible Ball I shall carry."

I spotted Tiddy Rex warding the Alehouse against the Old Ones. The barkeep often asked him to perform the odd job, now that he'd achieved the great age of nine.

"Then you must learn our customs," I said, waving at Tiddy Rex. "Here's a boy who'll teach you everything."

Tiddy Rex came bouncing over. "Doesn't you look beautiful, Miss Briony!"

"Thank you, Tiddy Rex!" I said. "And here I'd been thinking this frock makes me look slightly dead." Black is not a happy color for me, but then, funeral clothes do not specialize in happiness.

"Not a bit o' it, Miss Briony," said Tiddy Rex. "You doesn't look a bit dead!"

Tiddy Rex is the one person who can make me smile. He's a very decent specimen of nine-year-old boyhood.

"You've heard of Mister Eldric, I daresay," I said. "But I'll tell you something about him you must never tell anyone else. Promise?"

"Promise!"

"Mister Eldric doesn't come from our planet at all. He comes from a faraway place out in the sky called Earth."

When Tiddy Rex smiled, each of his several million freckles lit up.

"But now that he's here, in the Dragon Constellation, he has to learn our ways, so he can protect himself against the Old Ones. You were warding the Alehouse, just now. Explain it to Mister Eldric, will you?"

"Us mixes wine an' bread, Mister Eldric, an' puts it round by the door an' the windows so them Old Ones doesn't come creeping in."

Tiddy Rex paused, then added, "Wine an' bread be church things, you knows, Mister Eldric, an' them Old Ones, they doesn't care for church."

Wine and bread. This has always seemed rather ghoulish to me, as though one were smearing the threshold with Puree of Christ.

"Thank you, Tiddy Rex. Such things are undoubtedly puzzling to a person from Earth."

"You're a fine lad." Cecil made a great show of opening his fingers to reveal a coin. "Such a deal of money. I wonder how many toffees that will buy you?"

"Sixpence a bag," said Tiddy Rex. "But licorice be the thing for me, begging your pardon, Mister Cecil."

"I like licorice," said Rose.

"Tiddy Rex," I said, "how do you like pork?"

"I likes it fine, Miss Briony."

"Please help me with this," I said. "They've given me such a lot—the whole pig, minus the squeak."

Tiddy Rex laughed and snickled in between me and Eldric, and once we got to eating, the idea of happiness returned to me. Not the feeling, the idea. Would a regular girl be happy simply eating a hot meal with a great deal of chew to it? Maybe happiness is a simple thing. Maybe it's as simple as the salty taste of pork, and the vast deal of chewing in it, and how, even when the chew is gone, you can still scrape at the bone with your bottom teeth and suck at the marrow.

"Robert's birthday is June twenty-seventh," said Rose, apropos of absolutely nothing.

Robert is the fireman Rose most admires.

"When's your birthday?"

She meant Eldric, which I found interesting. She's never asked about Cecil's birthday.

"It's a very special birthday," said Eldric. "It's the only birthday you can make into a sentence. Can you guess what it is?"

I thought about it. "Yes, oh August One," I said, which set Eldric to laughing and Tiddy Rex asking me to explain.

"I was joking," I said. "My real guess is that it's March fourth, as in, *March forth!*"

"You be ever so clever, Miss Briony," said Tiddy Rex.

It's lovely to be clever and have little boys remark on it and have big boys smile curling lion's smiles.

Hurrah for the smell of gravy, all blood and butter and yum!

Hurrah for the smell of pork, all sizzle and dark and chomp!

Hurrah for a snickly boy, all round and grubby and snug!

"Briony hasn't any birthday," said Rose.

"I feel certain she does," said Cecil, whose birthday I happen to know is April Fools' Day.

"No birthday?" said Eldric.

"It's one of our strange customs, here in the Dragon

Constellation," I said. "I'll tell you about it later." But I had nothing to tell. Rose has such very peculiar theories on the passing of time. I mustn't listen to the chiming of midday or midnight, I have no birthday. When I ask why, she says it's a secret.

"The Chime Child," said Rose, "was born at the Mirk and Midnight Hour."

"Hush!" I said. "She might hear. It's rude to talk about a person behind her back."

There came a sudden rush to the bar. The music was about to begin. Quick, Tiddy Rex—cough!

Tiddy Rex didn't cough.

"I like the fiddle." Rose turned her chair to face the musicians.

"I like it too." Father stood up, holding his old fiddle.

A murmur arose from the people standing about. "You astonish me, Larkin!" said Dr. Rannigan. "I thought you'd given up the fiddle for good."

Dr. Rannigan couldn't possibly be as astonished as I: I'd seen Father lock away his fiddle. He locked it up, literally, in the silver cupboard. He didn't throw away the key—he's not showy enough for that—but he did the next best thing: He dropped it into his pocket and vanished from the Parsonage. He did come back every evening—one does have to keep up appearances—but he came home only to sleep, and then, never with Stepmother.

"Good lad!" cried Mr. Sly. "Us been missing them fingers o' yours."

"I'll be rusty," said Father.

How ill he'd been then, falling into ever-longer stretches

of confusion, his eyes unnaturally bright, as though he were burning up from the inside. And after Stepmother had nursed him with utter devotion, what does he do but lock away his fiddle and absent himself from our lives. He did make a full recovery, though, which is too bad.

But I mustn't think about it, for it makes me angry, and anger and I do not get along.

"Will you sing with us, Briony?" said Father. "Just as we did in the old days?"

How dare he ask! He, Father, who'd been well for three whole years but not brought out the fiddle until today. How dare he!

"I like Briony singing," said Rose.

"I should like to hear you," said Eldric.

I shook my head. I wouldn't sing, not with Father. He'd broken off our ritual of singing every evening, and never a word of explanation. He sang wonderful songs, or so I'd thought. I must have been fond of him then.

Anyway, I can't sing anymore.

Father had grown rusty, but only a little. I don't like to admire Father, but it's true that the old tunes sounded complete with the fiddle added back in. The fiddle stitched all the other sounds together—the whistle, the accordion, and the drum, which Davy Wallace played remarkably well despite his missing hand.

Eldric's fidgety fingers reached for the salt and pepper shakers. Pepper bowed to Salt; Salt bowed to Pepper; and away they went, gliding through the cutlery and plates and splashes of gravy.

Eldric leaned toward me. He smelled of pine and thunder

and soap. London soap must be the cleanest soap in all the world. "I always forget," he said. "It's Pepper who's the man, isn't it?"

"It certainly is," I said. "At least here in the Dragon Constellation." Eldric was not unlike Tiddy Rex. He could make me smile too.

Father played the opening bars of "True Thomas." I couldn't imagine Father was actually going to sing. Then he'd have to open those scratches he pretended were his lips.

But Father looked my way. "Do you still know every verse?" No, of course he wasn't going to sing, not Father.

I declined to answer. He wasn't going to flatter me into singing with him. He couldn't disappear for three years, then go all smiles and rainbows and expect the same back. I particularly remember the day Father disappeared. It was the day Stepmother told me I'm a witch.

It was, in the end, Mrs. Whitby, Pearl's mother, who sang. Salt and Pepper changed their steps to match the slow melancholy of "True Thomas." Most people can't fidget and listen at the same time, but Eldric was dead opposite to most people. He could listen only if he fidgeted; and he was fidgeting and following the story of True Thomas, who was stolen away to Fairyland, where he stayed for seven years, unable to tell a lie. That last bit sounds ghastly. If I couldn't lie, I'd be dead.

Once the song was done, Eldric launched Salt and Pepper into a polka. "Does that happen here? People being stolen into Fairyland?"

"We're not glamorous enough for Fairyland," I said. "That's

for ballad-y places, like Scotland. In the Swampsea, you'll merely get your hand ripped off, like Davy Wallace, or your wits snatched away."

"That's the Old One for me," said Cecil.

"How do you mean?" said Eldric.

Listening to Cecil's explanation was rather less enlightening than anything Mad Tom might have said, but we finally understood that if any of the Old Ones was to attack Cecil, it would be the Dark Muse. She feeds only on the energy of truly artistic men, draining away their wits, and we were given to understand that Cecil was just such an artist. He wrote poetry, you see.

And indeed he did, as for example, in my birthday poem where he rhymed "seventeen" with "Halloween." I actually do have a birthday; it's November first.

"What about Briony?" said Eldric. "Which of the Old Ones would attack her?"

"The Fairies," said Cecil. "They love golden hair and beauty and wit."

"They also like good housekeepers," I said, "so there's an end to that."

"Which Old One would take Eldric?" said Cecil.

I was allowed to look at Eldric now, stare at him if I liked. "I don't know him well enough." I flatter myself that I am quick to see what sort of mask a person wears, but I hadn't yet with Eldric.

When Tiddy Rex returned to our table, he laughed and laughed to see Salt and Pepper dancing. He'd traded Cecil's sixpence for licorice, and he gave quite a lot to Rose.

Cough, Tiddy Rex! Cough!

He really was a very nice little boy. Too bad he'd have to grow up.

Wait! I didn't really mean that, not the way it sounded. I wanted him to live to grow up. I didn't want him to die of the swamp cough. Not Tiddy Rex, the boy with the star-powered freckles.

But you'd think he'd live forever at the rate of not-coughing in which he was currently engaged, which was one hundred percent. That's the way of the swamp cough, though. You can live with it for months, comfortably enough, and only at the very end do you get dreadfully ill.

They oughtn't to have took the Boggy Mun's water.

The Boggy Mun's water.

The Boggy Mun.

I couldn't speak to the villagers about the swamp cough without ending up swinging beside Sam Collins. But what if I called on the Boggy Mun? What if I spoke to him? He's killed people; we'll probably get along. What if I promised to give him something he wanted in exchange for taking back the swamp cough?

The Boggy Mun couldn't have what he really wanted. I was the only person who could stop the draining, because I was the only person who knew the connection between the draining and the swamp cough. But I'd never stop it, because I value my neck. So why not take back the swamp cough like a good little Boggy Mun and take the next best thing, which is blood and salt.

There are certain things the Old Ones can't abide, such as Puree of Christ. There are certain things the Old Ones go mad for, such as blood and salt. That then is what I'd offer the Boggy Mun, salt from the kitchen and blood from the witch.

It was a good scheme. I could save Rose from the swamp cough—if she had it—without risking my neck. I'm not like that fellow who thought it a far, far better thing to trade his life for that of another. I'm nothing like him: I'd never volunteer to lay my head in the lap of Madame la Guillotine. No, that fellow was a hero and I'm not a hero at all.

·9·
A Good Little Boggy Mun

The sky was the color of porridge. The wind slapped at the ancient trees. It slapped at me too, but I slapped back and pushed ahead. I mustn't miss my opportunity. The Boggy Mun shows himself just as the evening mist rises, and he keeps strict business hours.

A V of geese flew above, strung beak to tail as though on a wire. The Flats turned into the Quicks and gobbled up my feet.

In my pocket, I carried a paring knife. Pearl keeps the kitchen knives bright and sharp. If you believe in justice and a connect-the-dots world, you'd think I'd trip and die on my own knife. But I'd wrapped it in multiple sheets of the *London Loudmouth* and carried it point down.

I arrived at the Boggy Mun's bog-hole just as the mist was rising. A melted-butter sunset pooled on the horizon. The mist was thickening over the dark splat of the bog-hole. It grew thicker, now still thicker. I set a twist of newspaper on an island of moss. Against it, I set the knife.

A burble of water—that meant the Boggy Mun was stirring. A wailing of wind—that meant the Boggy Mun was rising.

I opened the twist of newspaper, sprinkled salt onto the moss. Next came the knife. Which hand to use, left or right? My left hand is nimbler, but my scar constricts my range of motion. I took the knife with my right hand.

Slicing yourself is harder than you'd think. Your skin doesn't slice, not like bread or cheese. Your flesh pushes back. It's resilient, like the skin of a mushroom.

I pushed at the knife. My mushroom skin pushed back.

I thought of what I did to Rose. I thought of what I did to Stepmother. I pushed through my mushroom skin. Self-hatred is powerful: Out came the blood, drizzling into the salt.

"Boggy Mun, I, Briony Larkin, come to beg of you a boon."

Should I tell him I'm a witch, or would he already know? If he knew I was one of the Old Ones, might he be more likely to grant my request? A trade discount, so to speak?

The water lip-lapped; the wind wailed.

"You have sent the swamp cough to us, to the people of the Swampsea. Our loved ones are dying and dead. If you will take back the swamp cough, I promise to visit this spot every evening and give to you our salt, and give to you my very own blood."

The wind wailed.

"Every evening," I said. "I promise faithfully."

"An' church days?" said a dry little voice.

A witch can feel surprise, but it takes her only a minute to swallow it down.

"Church days too."

The water lip-lapped.

"The blood don't satisfy," said the Boggy Mun.

"But it's my own blood!" I said, because that's how the Old Ones like it best—the personal touch. "And still warm."

"I got me a few years' experience wi' the human fo'ak," said the Boggy Mun. "Aye, a few years. I learned more on you fo'ak than you learned on your own particular selves."

The mist pressed against me, as though the air had thickened. As though it were mist thickened with beard, the Boggy Mun's beard.

I sat back on my heels, but the beard-mist pressed at me.

"She be a lovely lass," said the Boggy Mun. "Oh my, yes. A lovely lass."

He was speaking to me, I realized. He could see me.

"Happen this lovely lass got herself a sweetheart?"

I shook my head. "You can see me but I can't see you."

"I fixed it up that way," said the Boggy Mun. "I thinks it be a grand system. What do the lass think?"

"Grand," I said.

"I sees thee, right enough," said the Boggy Mun. "An' what I sees tell me tha' doesn't be all mortal, though it be a puzzlement what sort o' the Old Blood tha' has."

"I'm a witch."

"There be a deal o' mortal in thee. I hasn't been learning on mortals all these years that I doesn't know there be someone tha' needs must save. Tha' be certain tha' doesn't got no sweetheart?"

"No sweetheart."

"But there be someone particular tha's o' the mind to save. There always be someone particular."

"My sister," I said. "My twin sister." I thought of Rose, back in the Parsonage, in Pearl's care. Pearl, sworn to keep her eyes on Rose, except for blinking. "We are identical, she and I."

"What be the name of this sister?"

"Rose Larkin."

The moment I said those words, I knew I'd made a mistake. The sky leaned on my shoulders, all ashes and smoke.

"It want but a moment for a body to be striked wi' the swamp cough." The Boggy Mun paused. "There, now it be done. Tha' sister, she be striked wi' the swamp cough. If'n tha' be o' the mind to save her, tha' best stop these mortal fo'ak from taking the water from my home. Water what be mine."

The Boggy Mun was gone. I rose, the ground trembled beneath me. I was a fool. I'd thought to make a bargain with the Boggy Mun, but he'd given Rose the swamp cough.

I'd pretended to heed Stepmother's warnings about the swamp, but I broke my promise, and look what had happened! Mr. Dreary, dead. Rose, struck with the swamp cough.

My thoughts drifted like cold ashes. I didn't want to hang. I was responsible for Rose. I promised Stepmother to care for Rose. But I didn't want to hang.

It's strange how a person can have a distinct distaste for herself, but still she clutches on to life.

I hate myself.

It doesn't matter, Briony. You have to remember how you hurt Rose, because now you've hurt Rose again.

Tell yourself the story. Remind yourself how you hurt Rose. Remind yourself of the swings, the froth of petticoats, Rose's screams.

You must remind yourself. You must hate yourself.

Remind yourself what Stepmother said to you, not once, but many times. Remember how she'd look at you, how she'd say, "Never tell your father."

Remember how those words would make your heart lurch and cut off your breath.

"I'll protect you," Stepmother would say. "I'll lie if I have to." She'd tell me that if Father knew what I did to Rose, he'd turn me over to the constable. "He's a righteous man, your father," she'd say. "He'd not exempt his own daughter from the law."

Overhead, the plovers called out. *Full moon! Full moon!* The Quicks were a scribble of charcoal.

Remind yourself what you did to Rose; remind yourself what Stepmother did for you. She hid your wickedness. She tried to stop it too. She knew you ought not to enter the swamp. You thought at first it was nonsense. You argued with her. You pointed out that you weren't in the swamp when you called Mucky Face, but she reminded you that you were standing at the very edge of the river. That it didn't matter that you were on the Parsonage side, because even in the swamp, you couldn't possibly have gotten any closer to Mucky Face.

You pointed out that the swings weren't in the swamp, but Stepmother reminded you that they too hung as close to the swamp as could be.

By the time I reached the Flats, the moon had risen. *Full moon! Full moon!* I was mid-stride when I saw her, saw the Chime Child, drifting across the Flats. I stood flat and still, a paper doll cut from moonlight. She mustn't see me. I edged into the shadows. If the Chime Child saw me, she'd want to know my business in the swamp, a thing I was disinclined to divulge.

I didn't want to hang. Not hanging involves keeping my mouth shut, a thing at which I excel. I didn't want Rose to die, but Rose living means Briony dying. I didn't want to hang.

I prayed that she not turn, I prayed she not see me.

Why was I so determined to hold on to life? I've so often wished I could stop breathing and let go.

The Chime Child drifted back toward the village. I'd prayed that she'd do so, but actually, I don't believe in prayer. I believe in good luck. I don't mean to be ungrateful, but if someone's out there answering prayers, mine's not at the top of the list.

Back in my wolfgirl days, I'd often met the Chime Child in the swamp. I'd almost forgotten. She and I were the only people who regularly visited it. But who cares, anyway? This particular witch has other things to think about, such as whether she's willing to reveal she's a witch in order to save her sister.

I'd wait until I reached the river. Then I'd decide.

Moonlight floated on the water like spilt cream. The bridge stretched before me. I'd cross the bridge, then I'd decide. Remember, Briony, remember how Rose screamed. You must always remember.

The bridge yawned its reflection onto the river. My feet took me onto the planks. My feet pushed me toward the decision. My feet were turning the far bank into the near bank; they were turning *then* into *now*. What was the point of anything?

Of course I'd do it. I had to save Rose. I'd known that all along, of course. I'd just been pretending.

I'd tell someone tomorrow. I'd let myself have until tomorrow.

Father is not a fire-and-brimstone sort of clergyman, but he does sometimes talk about Hell. I think Hell's a myth, but don't tell Father I said so. I think strands of Hell are woven into our everyday world.

Take this example.

As I pushed open the gate to the Parsonage garden, the smell of mint and apple sprang up at my feet. I recognized it at once.

"I told you to go away." I would not look at him, no, not at the Brownie, creeping around my skirts on his horrid stick legs.

"That you did, mistress," said the Brownie. "But now, with the stepmother dead and gone—"

"Don't you speak of her!" I said.

I'd banished the Brownie after the library fire. I didn't argue with Stepmother this time, not when she said that the Brownie and I were a dangerous combination—even the mint-and-apple Brownie—and that the Brownie must go. Not when she said the library wasn't near the swamp, which meant my witchy anger must have ridden upon the Brownie's power to call up the fire: He was the only Old One anywhere near. He was always very near, in fact. He tended to follow me about.

The Brownie crept alongside me on his double-jointed legs.

"Go away!"

95

Silence.

"Go away!"

Silence.

I slammed the Parsonage door behind me, but that was only for show. Doors mean nothing to a Brownie. He squirmed inside in his own oily way. The Brownie was back, the Brownie who'd helped me call up the fire. There's a bit of Hell for you.

Another strand of Hell:

I return from my visit to the Boggy Mun, knowing that Rose has the swamp cough. The Parsonage appears empty. Pearl has left for the evening. I walk about; there is a slant of light beneath the parlor door. Shall I knock?

Go ahead, Briony, knock. That's what a regular person would do, and really, it's not so very difficult. But I was lying to myself.

I always lie.

Father sits beside Rose. Eldric sits beside Dr. Rannigan. I'd almost forgotten Eldric lives here, that he's slept here for ten whole nights.

"How are you, Rose?" I say.

There comes a long pause, and Father answers for me. He tells me that Rose has the swamp cough. He tells me that the cough's not terribly bad—it never is at first—and that scientists in London are working on a cure, and that surely before Rose falls very ill, the scientists will have found a remedy.

Father always lies.

Dr. Rannigan knows Father is lying. He says there's nothing to do when the cough gets bad, save for injections of strychnine to stimulate her heart. And morphine, of course, morphine at the end, to ease her passing.

Ease her passing. The words rang in my head like the bells of some lunatic cathedral. *Morphine to ease her passing.*

"Rose," I said, "I've a mind to call at the firehouse tomorrow. Would you like to join me?"

Father glanced at Dr. Rannigan. Dr. Rannigan nodded and said a bit of fresh air wouldn't hurt, and went on to tell us how to wrap her up and how long she might stay out, but I was too busy regretting my offer to listen. Rose is besotted with the firehouse and the firemen, and a besotted Rose is a tedious thing indeed.

Morphine to ease her passing.

Father looked from me to Rose and back to me again. For the first time since Stepmother died he noticed our clothes. He muttered something beneath his breath that sounded remarkably like "Good God!" He said we couldn't go about dressed like twin versions of the Little Match Girl; and that we certainly couldn't testify at Nelly Daws's trial like that; and that Pearl would know how to fix us up.

We were to have new clothes.

We were to have new clothes because I tried to bargain with the Boggy Mun and he outwitted me. I should feel guilty, but I don't. Father shouldn't feel guilty, but he does. We were to have new clothes because I made Rose sick.

This, to me, is Hell.

On and on ring the lunatic bells.

Storybook events come in threes. So, it seems, does Hell. Here's the third strand of Hell woven into that night.

I lay in bed, listening to Rose cough. It was a wet, skin-scraping cough, very different from her earlier cough. Rose had never had the swamp cough. I was a fool.

I was a fool, yet I was clever.

It was the clever Briony who'd called up Death. She called it up so she might go into the swamp, so she might save Mr. Dreary, who wouldn't have died had she not called it up. It's rather unbearably circular.

But there are more unbearable circles.

It was the clever Briony who dreamed up a plan to save Rose. She dreamed up the plan so she might go into the swamp, so she might save Rose, who wouldn't have contracted the swamp cough had she not gone into the swamp.

The clever Briony knows that when she enters the swamp, people die. The clever Briony intended that Rose contract the swamp cough. She has always been jealous of Rose.

This to her is the third strand of Hell.

10

Lo: the Gloriousness

That night, the swamp craving returned.

What a strange word, *craving*. What is it, really? It's hard to describe, despite the fact that it keeps you up all night. It's trickier than pain. It's an itch stuck below your skin. You lie awake on your side of the do-not-cross line, listening to your sister heave and cough. You scratch at itch-ants that tunnel through your bones. You never can reach them.

It makes me sympathetic to Fitz the Genius's craving, which was for arsenic. It sounds a peculiar thing to crave, but apparently more people than one might expect are addicted to the stuff. That's what Father said after he dismissed Fitz, even though that meant I had no tutor. Even though he was still a genius. I couldn't see that the arsenic affected him a bit.

Father sacked the Genius, I banished the Brownie, and then I was alone.

Night faded into blue ink. I was bored, I didn't want to be

hanged. I was bored. I buttoned myself into collar and cuffs. I tied myself into ribbons and shoes. Dawn clung to me like cobwebs.

I find it impossible to be bored when I help Rose get ready for the day. That's because I'm too busy loathing her. Loathing and boredom don't mix.

"Five hundred sixty-four steps to the fire station," said Rose.

"Before you take any of those steps, you must put on your shoes."

"Five hundred sixty-four steps to the fire station."

Honestly, if I don't save her life, I'm going to kill her!

Despite her cough, Rose was in unusually good spirits. That was irritating. If I'm to trade my life for Rose's, I'd appreciate her exhibiting a touch of melancholy. Also acceptable would be despair.

"You talked last night while you were asleep," said Rose.

"Your shoes, Rose!"

"How can you talk when you're asleep?"

I could blame myself for her good spirits, if I wanted to, which I didn't. Rose's fascination with the fire station began when I set the library fire. I'm still astonished that it was Rose herself who alerted the fire station. She told me all about it—how the alarm bell went off, and the firemen went rushing about, harnessing the horses and checking the ladders, and how it was the handsome Robert himself who lifted her onto the fire wagon and stood right behind her so she wouldn't fall, and off they went, the hose-carts rattling behind.

"I prefer that you not talk," said Rose.

I myself preferred not to talk, but I'd have to talk to say so. "Robert wears shoes."

"I don't like my shoes," said Rose.

"I'm wearing my shoes and you don't see me complain."

"You only hear a person complain," said Rose. "Not see."

How has Rose lived for seventeen years and no one has ever killed her, not once?

"Perhaps you ought to put your shoes on in the wardrobe." Rose was irritatingly agreeable. She crawled into the wardrobe and shut the door. Rose has a theory that time goes more slowly in the wardrobe, which may be true, given the amount of time she spends in there.

"Five hundred sixty-four steps to the fire station."

"How many steps to the breakfast table?"

"I don't want breakfast," said Rose. "I want to go to the fire station."

We ended up compromising. We'd have toast, only toast, which as Rose said, is quick to eat. But Eldric was waiting for us in the dining room, wearing one of Pearl's ruffled aprons. "You look very beautiful," I said. "Is this a special occasion?"

"I suppose you could say so," he said. "I'm in charge of breakfast this morning."

"Boys don't wear aprons," said Rose.

"This boy does," said Eldric. "He does when he's cooking eggs."

"But Pearl cooks our eggs," said Rose. "Anyway, I prefer toast today and so does Briony."

I looked at Eldric, into his eyes. My fingers knotted themselves together. Eldric looked at me all the while he spoke.

"Pearl's baby died." He swallowed, cleared his throat. And

then, because he already knew Rose well enough to know she might not understand, he said, "She's very sad and wants to stay at home."

My fingers hurt. I looked down. They were twisted all about one another.

I didn't know what to say, but Rose filled the silence.

"I like poached eggs," said Rose, "but Briony thinks they're disgusting. She likes fried eggs. I think scrambled eggs are disgusting because they're all one color."

"No scrambled eggs." Eldric curtsied with his apron and vanished into the kitchen.

"I know what you're going to say," said Rose. "That we should eat the eggs because it's Eldric making them."

I nodded.

What did one say when a baby died? I should think of something before Eldric joined us, practice something regularly girlish. But it turned out he wasn't to eat with us. Perhaps he'd lost his appetite. Perhaps he thought it heartless that I could eat my fried eggs. Unfair that Rose could eat her poached eggs and no one would think anything at all.

"Now for your cloak." Wearing a cloak is on Rose's list of the thousand things she hates most. The problem is that each of the thousand is ranked number one.

"But Dr. Rannigan says you must, and anyway, it hardly weighs a thing, it's so full of holes." I swung mine round my shoulders. Rose hates any bit of clothing that constricts, but I say, Chin up and bear it. Life is just one great constriction.

"*Ventilated*," I said, "that's the word. Our cloaks are terrifically ventilated."

The Brownie waited for us beside the door, then followed

us like a double-jointed cricket. By all Brownie rules, he ought to have stayed in the Parsonage. He made a poor Brownie. He worked no mischief in the house; he helped with none of the chores. He was reserved and affectionate, devoted to me, or so it seemed.

"Go away!"

He didn't go away.

The sky was white and went on forever, and so did the wind, right through our ventilated cloaks.

Mr. Clayborne's men were at work, clanging about with the lengths of steel that were to grow into the London-Swanton railroad line. Too bad it hadn't been built while my Genius Fitz was still here. He was forever going off to Paris, and Vienna, and other places with delicious pastries, and complaining about how long it took just to get out of the Swampsea. I might be happy about the train myself had I any opportunity to take it. But I'm stuck.

In front of the jail stood a gangle of boys throwing stones at Nelly's cell. At her window, actually, which was shut and barred, but it was the principle of the thing that counted. It's not that I dislike every boy in the world, but this particular pack was uncommonly hateful, all snips and snails and puppy dogs' tails.

They'd throw stones at me too, once I was in jail. But at least I was a witch and deserved it. I wasn't so sure about Nelly. You'd think I'd recognize a fellow witch, but no: I'd find out with everybody else. If Nelly was a witch, she'd turn to dust once she was hanged. If not, we'd know we made a mistake.

Petey Todd, leader of the snips and snails, must have spotted us, for a moment later, the boys' voices rose in a singsong chant.

When Daftie Rosy passed away,
What do you think they done?
Sold her off as fishing bait:
A copper for a ton!

Daftie Rosy. I couldn't let that stand. I approached Petey. He was only thirteen, but big as a man.

"Fe-fi-fo-fum." I poked my finger at Petey's chest. "I smell the stink of a big boy's bum!"

I was in a fighting mood. *Daftie Rosy* set me off, of course, but there was also Pearl's ugly baby. The baby had died and I wanted to fight.

"Hey!" said Petey, then his invention dried up.

Dearie me! What to say?

You don't have to be big to do a lot of damage with your elbow. I jabbed mine into the front bit, where Petey's ribs gave way to some softer stuff. Down he went. I stamped on his stomach, which resulted in a most satisfactory sound.

I flung myself upon him, grabbed his ears.

"Help!" he bellowed. "She be like to pull 'em clean away!"

"They're wonderfully handy," I said. "Big as soup plates." Up went his ear-handles, down went his skull. Crash! Onto the cobbles.

You can win a fight if you don't care about getting hurt. I have a good head, and I used it. Crack went my skull against his.

Petey howled.

"See the lovely stars, Petey?"

I saw them myself, red blobs splatting against my eyeballs.

"She's kilt me!" screamed Petey.

104

Not just yet, Petey, but give me a minute: You'll wish you had been kilt.

Crash!

"Dear, oh dear!" I said. "A splat of brains just dribbled out your ear."

I lifted his head for the third crash. "Pity your mother didn't cook you longer."

Blast! An arm scooped me round the middle, lifting me up. Lifting me off Petey.

Whoever it was would be sorry. When I rammed my elbow this time, it connected with muscle and bone, which is far more satisfactory than blubber. A person feels she's really doing something.

"Steady, miss." It was Robert's voice. It was Robert's arm that had picked me up and was setting me down.

"I fetched him," said Rose. "I didn't prefer you to fight."

"She were in a pother, Miss Rose were, an' so, miss, I taked the liberty."

Now that's true poetic irony. I rush into battle to defend the fair name of Rose Larkin, and what does she do but fetch Robert to stop me.

"I don't match up today," said Rose. "I wish Robert could have seen how my ribbon matches my petticoat, but the witches took my ribbon."

Robert blushed.

I turned away from the Brownie, but he followed along, his absurd knees clicking every which way. I mustn't talk to him again. If I kept on, it would be easy to slide back to my old ways, stepping into the world of the Old Ones, letting my powers run wild.

Ten paces away, a bubble of villagers surrounded Petey. "Did I kill him?" I said.

"No, miss," said Robert.

"Pity."

"I knew Robert would stop the fight," said Rose. She smiled at Robert, an actual smile. Her teeth were matching strings of pearls. "I knew it."

Had I ever seen Rose smile before, a real smile?

The villager-bubble burst, revealing Cecil and Eldric, drag-pulling Petey toward me.

"You're all over blood," said Eldric.

"The boy shall have a proper beating," said Cecil.

"But I beat him already," I said, "and don't tell me I didn't do it properly. I'm touchy about these things."

Eldric looked me up and down with his lightning eyes. "I'd never say you beat him improperly."

"But the blood—" began Cecil.

Could Cecil never shut up?

"It's Petey's blood," I said. "I can tell by the stink."

"I sent Robert a birthday card," said Rose.

"That you did, miss, an' 'twere a pleasure to receive."

"But the sheer cheek of this fellow fighting you!" said Cecil.

"It's the other way round," I said. "I fought him. He was rude to Rose."

"Robert sent me a birthday card too," said Rose, "but he couldn't send one to Briony because she hasn't any birthday."

"I don't care about who fought whom," said Cecil.

"Your father would care," I said. "A judge would care who started it."

Cecil's eyes scuttled about like pale beetles. To Petey, to me, and back to Petey. Eldric stood before Petey, speaking to him in a lovely plum-jammy sort of voice and tick-tocking his finger in front of Petey's eyes.

"Damn it all, Briony," said Cecil very softly in my ear. "This Eldric fellow is keeping you to himself." But I imagined I knew what Cecil really cared about. He cared that it was Eldric, not he, who looked so easy and expert. That it was Eldric who looked our way and said perhaps Dr. Rannigan should see the boy.

"I thought we had an understanding," said Cecil, still very soft.

We did?

"Cecil, would you please escort Petey to Dr. Rannigan?"

Cecil paused, but there was no way he could politely protest.

Poor Cecil. It's hard to be a devil of a fellow in these modern times. No stagecoaches to hold up. No princesses to rescue. Just Petey Todd to escort, while the easy, expert fellow walks the pretty girl home.

But perhaps the pretty girl should go straight to the jail. Perhaps it would be easier to turn herself over to the constable now rather than waiting until teatime.

"Robert will walk me home," said Rose. "I asked him, and he said yes. He will walk me three hundred sixty-three steps until home."

"Yes, miss," said Robert. He gave her his arm and she actually took it. Extraordinary.

"All of our books burnt," said Rose.

"Yes, miss," said Robert. "I be right sorry for that."

"But my book didn't burn," said Rose.

"No, miss?" said Robert, and off they went: step one. Only three hundred sixty-two more to go.

So there we were, Eldric and I, alone in the square, except for Mad Tom, and Mr. Clayborne's men laying the London–Swanton line, and a few dozen snips and snails running about, puppy dogs' tails between their legs.

"You're a grisly sight," said Eldric. "Best mop up before you go home. May I?"

He took my shoulders, faced me toward the sun. I leaned against the village well.

"I know a bit about head wounds," he said, "having given and received so many myself." I thought of the scar that dipped into his eyebrow, naked and pink as a baby mouse.

"Spit!" He held out his handkerchief.

I spat.

The handkerchief dabbed at my forehead. "Ouch! You'll have a fine-looking bruise tomorrow."

"Then you'll be able to distinguish me from Rose."

The handkerchief paused. "I could tell you apart from the beginning. You're quite different to each other, you know."

Perhaps he could tell, in the obvious ways. The odd one was Rose; the other odd one was Briony.

The handkerchief went to work again.

"So," said Eldric.

It wasn't quite a question. It was more of an invitation to tell him whatever I chose. I could talk about Petey, I could not talk about Petey. I could talk about Pearl's baby or not talk about Pearl's baby. Eldric gave me a choice, and it was this that made me want to tell him everything.

I'd never met anyone I'd wanted to tell. I wouldn't, of course, but the thought was comforting.

Comforting in a suicidal sort of way.

"If Petey were a color," I said, "he'd be puce."

"Yes, of course!" said Eldric. "What if he were an animal?"

"Rat."

"Historical personage?"

"Robespierre."

"Robespierre and the reign of terror," said Eldric. "Fancy that—I remember Robespierre. Some of the bloodier bits of my lessons must have stuck. Is Petey engaged in a reign of terror?"

"The word *reign* is a bit resplendent for Petey," I said. "He's just a two-bit bully. He and his lads were throwing stones at Nelly Daws just now."

In a few hours, they'd be throwing stones at me too.

"If you were an historical personage," said Eldric, "you'd be Robin Hood."

"You must have missed the Robin Hood lesson. He's not historically real. You're wrong about me, in any event. I'm no hero."

"I must respectfully disagree," said Eldric, which was nice, but ignorant.

"What animal would I be?"

Eldric thought for a bit. "A wolf. It has to be a wolf."

"I like that," I said. "Cecil would have made me into a talking mouse with a ruffled bonnet."

"Anything but that," said Eldric. "You're quick and elegant, loyal and fierce."

Loyal? I wouldn't correct him.

"If you were a sport, you'd be boxing."

Ooh, boxing!

"I'll teach you if you like."

Some invisible string jerked at a squishy bit behind my ribs. "I should like that."

Except, first I'd be in jail, and then hanged.

But hanging didn't seem quite real just then. Perhaps it was because Eldric was taking care of me, which was something that had ceased to be real long ago. I only just remembered it, that hot-bread comfort of being cared for.

When I was ill, before Stepmother came, Father used to spread crisp, white sheets over the library sofa and tuck me up in a special goose-down comforter. I loved running my thumb over its shiny, satiny edging. He'd sit on the end of the sofa and count my fingers and toes, which were always all there. Then he'd pretend to snatch away my nose and tell me I had adorable apricot ears. There was always hot chocolate, and sometimes the smell of lemon and sugar.

"We'll take it slowly," said Eldric. "We'll ease you into being a bad boy. First boxing. Next, stone hurling, which leads naturally to the breaking of windows. You'll start with an ordinary window, work your way up to stained glass."

"What next?" I said. "Set your father's drainage project on its head? Set the water to running backward?"

"There!" said Eldric. "I knew you had proper bad-boy instincts."

There are certain advantages to having a conversation. One is that a person like Eldric might make you laugh, and you might begin to remember how pleasant that is. Another is that you tell yourself things you didn't know you knew.

Set the water to running backward. That's easy. You don't even have to be a witch. You just open the sluice gates at flow tide, and all the sea comes rushing back into the swamp.

I had to have this conversation in order to understand how to save my neck from the noose.

"Spit!"

I spat.

I mostly hate talking to people, but talking to Eldric revealed a dazzling possibility. I could sabotage the draining project, and lo, the gloriousness that would ensue: The water would stay in the swamp; which meant the Boggy Mun would be appeased; which meant he'd lift the swamp cough from Rose; which meant that everything would be fine, except for the small matters of concealing my witchiness, and controlling my powers, and keeping Rose safe from me. But once you've imagined your head in the noose, these inconveniences are as nothing.

How light I felt. I was ready to play! "We could have a club," I said. "A bad-boy club."

Eldric embraced this idea with proper bad-boy spirit. "It must be a secret, of course. We'd need a secret handshake."

"And a secret language," I said. "We'll speak in Latin, so no one will understand."

Except Father, and who talks to him anyway?

"Here's the problem with Latin," said Eldric. "It's so very secret, I can't understand a word. Being expelled takes a toll on one's Latin."

"Oh, not that sort of Latin, not the ordinary sort," I said. "It's the difficult sort of Latin no one speaks anymore. But I'm sure you know it already. It comes from rarely attending to one's lessons. Here, tell me what this means. *Fraternitus.*"

"Fraternity?" said Eldric.

"Very good," I said. "And what does fraternity mean?"

"Brotherhood?" said Eldric.

"See, you do know the difficult Latin. What does this mean? *Bad-Boyificus.*"

"Bad boy," said Eldric. "You're right. I did learn the difficult Latin back in my perhaps not-so-misspent youth."

"And *Fraternitus Bad-Boyificus?*"

"Bad-Boys Fraternity," said Eldric. "No, I mean *club.* Bad-Boys Club! We'll need an initiation, of course."

"Lovely!" I said, which is not, perhaps, initiation-appropriate vocabulary, but I meant it sincerely. An initiation! The very word conjured visions of dark rooms and candles and initiators wearing Spanish Inquisition–style headgear.

"Here's the most interesting thing about an initiation," said Eldric. "You never know when it's to be. So you must watch for it, listen for it, and trust it, even if you're called at the dead of night. Your fellow fraternitus will never let you come to harm."

"Frater," I said. "It's fellow frater."

"Done!" Eldric stepped back. "At least you don't need stitches, which I fear poor Petey will need."

Poor Petey. I'd like to say I could almost feel a tender spot for poor Petey, but the truth is I'd rather feel at the tender spot on his head and give it a poke.

"It's a fine day in the Dragon Constellation for us frater," said Eldric. I agreed and didn't even correct his Latin. Who needs plurals anyway?

It had in fact grown sunny, warm enough that the greengrocer set a cart of vegetables outside his shop, and Davy Wallace sat on a stoop, grading pheasant feathers, which he did astonishingly quickly with his one hand. If one were an optimistic person, one might say that it was really quite warm.

The day had turned itself inside out. How fragile life is; it can turn on so little. Pearl's baby dies, but then there comes a spat-on handkerchief, the creation of a brotherhood, and the end of the swamp cough.

Was I really so happy not to die? Was this feeling simply relief? Or was it that Eldric was taking care of me? Stepmother cared for me during those long, foggy months of my illness. I don't know how she did it, with that injury to her spine. I didn't deserve care at all. But every time I awoke, there she was, with a bowl of soup, or an herbal plaster, or my writing materials—I couldn't bear to tell her I was too tired to write: She was so very delighted to be giving me the opportunity.

There is much, I suppose, that I don't recall of my illness. I had grown so very dull-witted. But should I ever again sink into illness, I'm sure I'll remember Eldric.

I'll remember he cared for me. I'll remember that some-one at last had taken the time to touch my face.

11

The Chiming Hour

"Mistress! Just a word, mistress!"

Not the Brownie, I absolutely would not talk to the Brownie. I slammed the garden gate behind me.

"Have a care, mistress. You almost caught my nose!"

Then you shouldn't have such a long one.

"Won't you write the stories again, mistress? I ask not for myself alone, but for all of the Old Ones."

I wouldn't give him the satisfaction of asking. I absolutely would not ask why he'd linked his power to mine in order to call Mucky Face.

Why he'd had me injure Stepmother's spine.

Tonight, I'd keep the world safe from Briony Larkin. No talking to the Brownie. No going into the swamp, not really. I'd only to cut across a corner of the Flats and from there, strike out through the fields of wheat and rye.

Worry buzzed round me like a gnat. There was no one in the Parsonage to keep an eye on Rose. Pearl was still at home, mourning her baby, but even if she'd returned, I couldn't have asked her to stay past midnight. The whole of the village was asleep. But Rose was asleep too, and Rose sleeps very soundly. That is one way in which we are not at all identical. Rose tells me I talk in my sleep, that sometimes I scream. I'd worry about blabbing my secret, except it's only Rose. I must make it a point never to sleep with anyone else.

The lantern had already grown heavy, but I held it high. Its yellow light bounced ahead, off the Flats, broke across the fields of rye. It was midnight, the chiming hour, the favorite time of many of the Old Ones—the Dead Hand, the Dark Muse, the Devil.

The Dark Muse is the most wicked of the three; at least I think so. She doesn't steal the man himself, as the Devil does. She steals his soul and his wits. That counts for a lot, if you ask me. I'd rather be in Hell with my soul and wits, than in the outside world without them.

But the Dark Muse is one of the few things I need not worry about. She only preys on men.

I'd meant to creep up on the pumping station, but instead, it crept up on me. The night was cloudy, no moon shone. My arm sagged under the weight of the lantern, leaving my toes most beautifully illuminated.

Suddenly, there it was, a rise of red brick, striped with new mortar.

A fingernail of fear scraped down my back. Someone might spot me, mightn't they? None of the Swampfolk was likely to be abroad at the chiming hour, but what about Mr. Clayborne's men?

Mr. Clayborne might have posted a guard. The station was the heart of the draining operation. If it was destroyed, the draining must stop, and rebuilding would take a deal of time.

I crept round the pumping station—no guard here, no guard at all: Mr. Clayborne trusted the Swampfolk.

I stepped back, forcing the lantern light off my toes, onto the station. It put me in mind of Petey Todd, show-offy and muscular. He was going to be just like the pumping station when he was grown, puffing out his chest and punching his chimney into the sky.

If Petey were a building, he'd be a pumping station.

Petey Todd: disgustimus!

The doors were sneery and unlocked. The polished hardware said, clear as anything, "Wipe your feet!"

I did, but only because I mustn't leave any traces. Machines hulked in the shadows. The lantern glanced off bits of polished brass and glossy paint. I shone it about, found the switch.

Let there be light!

I flicked the switch.

Behold: There was light!

Illuminating gas is extraordinarily clean and white, as though it were piped straight from the stars. The machines sprang from the shadows, fierce as Roman legionnaires in red and gold.

I brought out my weapons: three candles and a book of matches. How small they looked next to the machines, like David's slingshot next to Goliath. But we know what happened to Goliath.

I pulled at the windows; they closed smoothly—no stick or squeak or scowl. Mr. Clayborne kept his house in good order. I drew a match across the striker's gritty lip. The flame shone yellow in the piped-in starlight. I lit the candles, one, two, three. There: I was done, save for shutting the door behind me when I left.

An open flame, plus a sealed room, plus illuminating gas—these things added up to an explosive situation. I prowled round the outside of the pumping station, pushing and pulling at doors and windows. All shut tight.

If I was lucky, the explosion would spark a fire.

"Mistress!"

My hands jumped. They're always the first to be afraid.

My thoughts followed more slowly. *Mistress.* My thoughts turned the word upside down, then right side up again. *Mistress.* I had not been caught—not by anything human.

"I needs must speak to thee, mistress."

The voice splashed and slapped.

Not human.

I turned toward the estuary, where a wave stood on its tail, like a fish. You think it must fall, but no: It can stand as long as it needs. This I knew from the last time I'd seen it, which was also the first time.

"Two years I been waiting," said Mucky Face. "I been waiting, but tha' didn't never leave tha' dwelling. I been waiting to tell thee it broke my heart."

"What do you mean?" I turned away from the pumping station. Best draw away: The station might explode.

"I misliked to strike tha' stepmother like I done." Mucky Face followed me along the estuary, beating the water with his tail. "The call, though, it come too strong."

"But I was the one who called you." My thoughts lagged

behind the meaning of his words. "I told you to strike Step-mother."

"No, mistress!" said Mucky Face. "'Twere an Old One what called me. 'Twere an Old One o' the wicked, solitary kind. Its power were monstrous an' catched me at ebb tide." He paused. "That power, it kilt the minnows what be my friends."

I shook my head. It was I who'd called him. I'd been angry, of course, and later, Stepmother and I worked out why: I'd been jealous.

Jealousy is never a nice thing to look back upon, but even in the nastiness, I remember the thrill of calling Mucky Face. I didn't have a word for it then, but I do now: power. Such thrilling power we witches have—over the wind, over the tidal wave, over so many of the Old Ones.

I wish I knew what I'd been thinking. I'm nearly sure I meant only to frighten Stepmother, remind her I'm a witch, make her pay attention to me, not Rose. If I were a praying person, I'd pray it was just power run amok, helped along by the Brownie. Brownies are mad for practical jokes. I'd pray that I'd only meant Mucky Face to stand on his tail, to stretch his boiling strength over the Parsonage, over the garden. That I'd never imagined he'd smash himself upon Stepmother.

I remember it, all of it. I remember the gray water surging from the river, smashing itself to spray, washing over a blue dress. I remember my throat filling with acid, wanting to run to Stepmother, not wanting to run to Stepmother.

I had to save Stepmother. I couldn't endure life without her. I couldn't endure life with the guilt of having killed her. I'd barely left the house in a year, since Stepmother had told me I was a witch. Dr. Rannigan. I had to fetch Dr. Rannigan.

I had so many memories. My words couldn't begin to do them justice. "I called you to crush my stepmother."

"No, mistress," said Mucky Face. "'Twere an Old One what called me, an Old One what were born o' water. Tha' doesn't be born o' water, mistress. I needs must speak direct. Tha' doesn't be near strong enough to call me. Tha' doesn't be near strong enough to draw me five miles upriver to tha' dwelling."

I wished I could believe him, but I am an Old One, I have that power. I called him and he came.

"Forgive me, mistress."

"Don't say that anymore!"

I remember running, running from Stepmother's body to the Alehouse, where I found Dr. Rannigan. My memory now speeding into a jumble of people and voices, into the flooding of the Parsonage. My memory lingering on Stepmother, whom Dr. Rannigan and the Hangman lifted ever so carefully onto a stretcher—

"What do you want of me?" I said.

"I been wanting to come back into the story," said Mucky Face.

The story, the story, always the story! "All the stories are burnt."

"Can tha' not scribe 'em again?" said Mucky Face.

"It's too late for that."

"But tha' needs must scribe 'em, mistress! Scribing, it don't never die, but a story what be on a person's tongue—well, there don't be no person what lives forever an' aye. Scribe o' my power that it don't be forgot. Scribe o' how I surges into the fringes o' the sea. Scribe o' how I dive—"

It was then that the pumping station blew up. Mucky Face tipped backward, exploding into foam. I tipped forward, exploding into a run.

You can run and run. You can run and grow fitter and faster. You can run so much and so fast, you turn back into wolfgirl, running endlessly, effortlessly, through the swamp.

I knew I'd called Mucky Face. I knew Mucky Face had injured Stepmother. But I was running, running like wolfgirl, outrunning my memories.

You can outrun your memories, but sometime, you will have to stop. And when you do, there will always be Stepmother, waiting to be remembered.

12

Wolf and Lion

Look at me, Briony, walking and talking with a boy-man. Tonight is the first meeting of the Fraternitus Bad-Boyificus. Eldric and I walk along the towpath. The sun sits on the river like a great orange yolk. Eldric and I admire it.

It feels as though it's been months since Eldric arrived, but it's been only five weeks. If you want to stretch out your life, here's my advice: Look about for new experiences, lots of them. It slows down time. Here are the experiences I recommend: Sit down to breakfast with a person, actually sit and eat and talk. Plan the details of a secret club while your father reads the paper, and even if your father realizes what you're doing, it's all right, because you've kept the important thing secret.

No one knows about the fraternitus.

Pardon me: Fraternitus. It's the sort of word that simply begs for a Capital beginning.

The Shire horses have marked the path with their great dinner-plate hooves. We put our feet inside their footprints, we laugh.

Briony feminina regularitatis est.

She is a feminina regularitatis who deserves a holiday, just for this one evening. Listen to what she did. Hark unto the extreme cleverness of Briony Larkin.

This is Briony Larkin.

This is Briony Larkin; who burnt down the pumping station.

This is Briony Larkin; who burnt down the pumping station; which made the Boggy Mun happy.

This is Briony Larkin; who burnt down the pumping station; which made the Boggy Mun happy; which prompted him to cure the villagers of the swamp cough.

This is Briony Larkin; who burnt down the pumping station; which made the Boggy Mun happy; which prompted him to cure the villagers of the swamp cough; which cured Rose Larkin.

This is Briony Larkin; who burnt down the pumping station; which made the Boggy Mun happy; which prompted him to cure the villagers of the swamp cough; which cured Rose Larkin; which meant that Briony Larkin deserved a holiday, and she wasn't even obliged to sneak out at night and worry about being caught, nor was she obliged to worry about Rose waking and bolting into the swamp in a panic, because Father and Mr. Clayborne are looking after Rose, will wonders never cease?

This is Briony Larkin.

I deserved a holiday, and I deserved to dispense with the laces and trusses expected of a clergyman's daughter. I wore my oldest frock, which looked remarkably like a potato sack, and I wore very little beneath. I should never have imagined how lovely that feels. It's most freeing, and it gives you the delicious sense you're on your way to moral degeneracy. I shall soon be painting my lips and drinking gin.

The first meeting of the Fraternitus Bad-Boyificus was also to be my first fighting lesson. I made a fist and showed it to Eldric.

"Fistibus Briony." I shook my fist. "Eldric terrorificorum est?"

"Terrific? I'm terrific!"

"Not terrific!" I said. "Quite the opposite. Listen carefully: terrorificorum."

"Hmm," said Eldric.

"Grant me patience, O Jupiter Magnificum!"

"Not terrified!" shouted Eldric at last. "Never terrified of Briony's fistibus!"

We laughed and laughed. I was aware that I didn't hate myself, which left me in a philosophical dilemma. Should I hate myself for not hating myself?

Briony destere Briony.

It doesn't quite have the same ring.

I initiated conversation, like this:

"Do you think you'll return to London?"

I found myself truly interested in what the answer was to be.

"Not for some time," said Eldric. "Father intends to find another tutor willing to spend at least a year in the Swampsea. I feel it my obligation as a bad boy, and a founding member of the Fraternitus, to complain whenever he speaks of staying on. So please don't mention how very glad I am to stay."

"Mumibus wordium," I said, although I knew that Mr. Clayborne knew Eldric was fond of the Swampsea, and that among the three of us—Mr. Clayborne, Eldric, and me—each of us knew the others knew. There's an example of the Clayborne family language. It's a silent language, but dead opposite to Father's. And I, Briony Larkin, was beginning to pick it up. I learn languages quickly. Have I perhaps mentioned that?

"Speaking of tutors," said Eldric, "I wonder that your father let you go without lessons since that Genius Fitz of yours left. I hope I'm not being a nosy parkerium."

"You can't blame Father," I said. "Or, rather, you can blame him, and I certainly invite you to do so, but it will have to be for something else. Father intended to send me to school. It was all arranged, and my trunks were packed, but Stepmother fell ill and I stayed to care for her."

"Surely there were other suitable people who might have done so?"

"It's difficult to explain."

It was impossible to explain. *Stepmother fell ill.*

But that wasn't quite true. Stepmother also fell. *Stepmother fell.* Mucky Face smashed her, and she fell. Which made her fall ill.

I made Stepmother fall and she fell ill. I made Rose fall, and she fell ill.

I hadn't known what I was doing at the time, but I

remember both incidents entirely. My life changed in the few minutes it took for Stepmother to tell me about them. I couldn't leave her then, of course, not the Stepmother I'd injured. I couldn't leave her ill, and alone, to care for Rose, whom I'd also injured.

I may be wicked, but I'm not bad.

Eldric turned toward me on soft lion's feet. Some witchy antenna picked up waves of indignation: Eldric was ready to pounce. "So you sacrificed—"

"Not *sacrifice!*" I hate that word. Father used it in his one-sided arguments with Stepmother. *Is it fair that Briony sacrifice her life for you and Rose?*

Father lost control of his voice when he and Stepmother argued. It was no longer the crisp, laundered voice of the clergyman, or even the curling ribbons of his irritated voice. Instead, he shouted. The Reverend Larkin actually shouted.

But in this particular argument, Eldric was the quiet one and I was the one with a throat-full of shouting. Shouting is angry, and Briony plus anger is dangerous. Briony plus anger results in something like Mucky Face.

I ought not to shout. I ought to forget that I'd been longing to go to school after Father dismissed Fitz. That I'd have seized the chance to go anywhere, but especially to London, and school!

Eldric and I had stopped walking now. We had stumbled into an argument.

"You don't understand," I said. "Father and Stepmother told me to go, but I refused. I unpacked my trunks."

I'd sat that day at Stepmother's side in the sewing room. She couldn't manage the stairs, not with the injury to her

125

spine. Her beautiful black hair streamed over the pillow. She smiled her generous smile—how could she bear to smile after what I'd done? She'd be in pain for the rest of her life.

Fitz was not always kind about her; he said her teeth were too big. But he was jealous, I think. We'd been the best of companions, he and I, but when Stepmother came into our family, she became my best friend and Fitz second best.

"I know things are done differently here in the Dragon Constellation," said Eldric. "And I know that when in the Dragon Constellation, it's wise to do as the Dragon Constellationers do. But I can't help bringing up a tradition from my native Earth. Parents there are expected to give their children opportunities. Not every parent, of course, but parents like your father, and mine. We expect them to open doors for their children so they can march forth into the world."

March fourth. Eldric's birthday.

March forth!

"But I told you, Father gave me opportunities."

"And your stepmother?"

"I told you that too. I was the one who wanted to stay— who decided to stay!"

Stepmother had taken my hand in her own cool one. She was always cool, and that day, the sewing room was positively chilly. She disliked fires, even on the coldest nights. "You do see what happened," she said. "Don't you, darling?"

I did see, much as I wished I didn't. She laid out the events, like puzzle pieces. She never told me what happened. She left me to draw my own conclusion.

Puzzle piece number one: Stepmother had been sitting

126

under the parlor table with Rose, helping her with those infernal collages.

Puzzle piece number two: I'd stood in the parlor door, watching, and I said something about not understanding how Stepmother could bear the tedium.

Puzzle piece number three: I stood gazing across the river, to the swamp. Stepmother came into the garden, Mucky Face rose from the water.

I did see what I might have been thinking. I knew exactly what I'd been thinking. I was jealous that Stepmother had spent such a deal of time with Rose. My jealousy had called up Mucky Face.

"If your stepmother really wanted you to march forth," said Eldric, "she shouldn't have accepted your—well, I won't say sacrifice."

"Except that you just did," I said. "And in any event, you don't understand."

But my argument was slipping away from me. I knew I was right, but I couldn't explain why. We turned toward the bridge. Our feet whispered over the silvered wood. The lion-boy was quiet; the wolfgirl was quiet. I've been training the wolfgirl, running her up and down the stairs, when no one's about to see. It's marvelously exhausting.

In May, the mud has melted into slush. The peat moss is emerald and the sundew plants show their bright, yellow faces. You might think they resemble happy schoolchildren, until you learn of their flesh-eating habits. We cut across a corner of the Flats, oozed across scrub and moss, trod on bright, carnivorous smiles.

I'd forgotten how wolfgirl could change direction mid-stride, how within the space of a heartbeat, she could turn from the Flats toward the estuary. Eldric did the same, wolf and lion, shifting quick as wind.

"You're fast," said Eldric.

"I'm catching up with myself," I said, which made Eldric laugh.

At least we wouldn't be going into the heart of the swamp, which meant I was unlikely to hurt anyone. The fighting lesson was to take place in a meadow called the Scars, not because we were interested in acquiring any, but because it was dryish and largish and free of crops. At the far end of the Scars rose the pumping station, or at least what was left of it.

"Funny about the pumping station," said Eldric.

"Funny," I said.

The pumping station was already being rebuilt. As soon as it was all brash and red-brickibus, Rose would fall ill. I had another plan, though. We could stow away on the London–Swanton line, once it was up and running. It was behind schedule, which was troubling. Rose had to leave the Swampsea while she continued well. No matter how far we traveled, Rose would die of the swamp cough if the Boggy Mun infected her again before she left.

It turns out there are two ways to make a fist. If you make one sort of fist, you punch your opponent. If you make the other sort, you break your thumb.

Eldric curled my fingers into place, set my thumb upon them, just so. How casually he did it, as though he touched girls every day. Perhaps he did. Had he ever really touched a girl, touched her in the Pearl and Artie way?

Such a nosy parkerium, Briony!

"Soften your knees, sink into your heels. You want to keep yourself low."

"I have an advantage there." I softened, I sank.

Eldric punched, slowly, just to show me, keeping his arms close to his sides, turning his fist to make the punch, turning it back when he snatched it away. "It's the snatching away that gives it power," he said. "Also, by pivoting from the hip. Never punch from the elbow."

"Of course not," I said. "Only a stupidibus would fight like that."

Guess what? I can punch as well as make people laugh.

Soft knees, weight low, sink into heels. Hips pivot—wham! My fist flew forward.

"Nicely done!" said Eldric, although it had glanced off of his palm like a pebble.

"Why aren't you begging for mercy?"

"I make a point never to do so," said Eldric. "It puts one at a disadvantage."

He laughed and I laughed, but the clergyman's dutiful daughter didn't laugh. That girl was gone; wolfgirl had returned. Wolfgirl, who was leaf dance and moon claw and tooth gleam. When Jupiter sizzled the air with lightning bolts, she caught them on the fly.

"Nice throw, Jupiter!"

"Nice catch, wolfgirl!"

Her mouth was a cavern of stars.

Eldric adjusted my hands. "You want to draw your right hand in a bit."

The witch nodded. Eldric assumed she was right-handed. But the witch was left-handed, and she had the second sight, which meant she saw the Strangers wriggling from beneath the great stones that dotted the Scars. She saw the Strangers weaving and wobbling toward her on their tiny string legs. But Eldric hadn't the second sight; he was blind to the Strangers, so she pretended blindness too. She showed him her new fist-making skills; he gave her fist his undivided attention.

One doesn't laugh at the Strangers, despite their spaghetti arms and legs, despite their outsized heads that loll about on spaghetti necks. The Strangers are proud and powerful. The Strangers control the harvest.

"Excellent fistibus," said Eldric, but he wasn't done with my hand. He inspected my left palm, the pucker of scars.

"There's no fortune to be read in that palm," I said, but of course he wanted to know about it; of course he'd been dying to ask since we first met. "Do you want the version of the story in which I'm a hero, or do you want the true version?"

"Both," said Eldric.

"Greedy!" I said.

"I was quite ill," I said, which I mentioned not because it's true, although it is, but because it makes people feel sorry for me. Even a witch wants sympathy. "My memory of the event is rather foggy." This is also true. "But I know I was writing one of those stories Rose is forever mentioning, and I suppose I smelled the fire—in any event, I found myself at the library door."

Here's where my account of the fire diverges from the truth. I had, indeed, been writing, but the Horrors alone know what possessed me to stumble into the library. What made me call up the fire?

I don't think I'll ever know. Not even Stepmother could

venture any theories. And burning my hand—well, I'd been ill, and perhaps I hadn't been strong enough to control the fire.

"You must remember," I said, "that this is the heroic version."

"I have it well in mind," said Eldric.

"I attempted to rescue my stories, not for my own sake, but for Rose's. The stories soothe her, and there are so very many she loved. I knew it would take me years to write them all again, and even then, they'd never be the same."

"I believe that," said Eldric. "Heroic version or not." He curled my fingers into a fist.

"As for burning my hand in the attempt," I said, "I think I must blame my illness."

It's unsettling to straddle two worlds, one foot in the human world, speaking to Eldric of scars and fires, the other foot in the world of the Old Ones, where the Strangers look at me all slanty and sideways beneath their toadstool bonnets, their tongues flapping from their lolly-bobbing heads.

It seems odd that a day given over to bad boys and boxing should turn into a day of memories. But so it was. My memories were dull and gray, like a photograph. The books were black, the fire gray. A cloud of white lace rushed into the library. I didn't recognize her at first, not Stepmother, because it wasn't possible that she be there. She couldn't rise from her sickbed. Her bracelets were the color of cinders, although they jangled in the key of gold.

Flames leapt into the room. They sharpened their teeth on the floor. And then I couldn't see, there was only sound—a jangle of gold, a woman's voice, a girl's screams. The girl had burnt her hand.

How much pain, though, must Stepmother have endured to rush to the fire? To try to save me? I never asked, of course.

"My turn." I've always wanted to know about the scar that dips into Eldric's eyebrow. Eldric treated me to an account of the Great Pudding Caper, which made me laugh so hard I had to stop fighting to catch my breath.

"Mistress!"

Now the Strangers spoke. "Make us our story, mistress!"

They spoke one at a time, their voices identical, one picking up precisely where the last left off. If you were to close your eyes, you'd think it a single voice.

Punch, kick, block. I must get rid of my skirts if I am truly to kick.

"Make us our story, mistress! Our story, it need must be telled. The story o' the dark earth, o' the roots, the roots what us tends all the spring long that you fo'ak might have victuals an' beer."

Kick, punch, block, punch. All those stories, the stories of the Old Ones, they burnt in the fire.

"Scribe it to us, mistress. Scribe o' the clay. Clay, it be right comely, but you fo'ak doesn't see it. You doesn't see the crystals what it got, you doesn't see 'em sliding and gliding."

The Strangers are the ones to know such things. The Strangers rule the underground, not the Devil. They ripen the corn and paint colors on the flowers and gild the autumn leaves.

"Make us stories o' the underground. Make us the story o' the Unquiet Spirit what tosses in her winding sheet. She be lying with them cold worms an' don't nobody hear her shrilling."

132

Punch, block, kick.

"The Unquiet Spirit, she be shrilling out a name. Tha' knows it fine, that name. It be tha' own particular name. It be *Briony Larkin.*"

Stepmother screamed my name the day of the fire. Stepmother, who ran to the library despite her injury. I have a theory about how she might have managed to pull off such a feat. It comes in the form of an equation: Love + Fear = Herculean Strength. It's how mothers come to fling runaway motorcars from their children. It's how . . . well, actually, I oughtn't to speculate, never having experienced the Love portion of the equation. But I did read about the mother and the motorcar in the *London Loudmouth.*

"Make us our story, mistress. Make us our story."

Eldric caught at my fist, examined it, made sure I hadn't slipped into thumb-breaking mode. "Your fists are beautiful," he said.

Beautiful! He said my fists are beautiful! How I wished I could tell him about the Strangers.

"Thank you," I said. His hand was warm around my fist. "Yours are adorable."

He squeezed my fist in mock protest. He smiled his curling smile. How I wished I could tell him everything.

Secrets press inside a person. They press the way water presses at a dam. The secrets and the water, they both want to get out.

Beautiful! That's what a friend would say. A friend would touch a person's hand. But Briony, you mustn't think about having friends and touching hands. If all goes as planned, you and Rose will leave the Swampsea. You'll leave the

133

Swampsea on one of Mr. Clayborne's trains, but nothing will really change. You'll live alone, except for Rose, you'll live in the dark with the dust and the crumbs, and when you hear a noise, you'll scuttle into the cracks of the wainscoting.

Friendship will get you nowhere. You have to keep your secrets. You mustn't speak of the Strangers, now lob-bobbling away from you. Now vanishing beneath the rocks. You mustn't believe that the pretty boy from London will keep your secrets. Do you want to exchange the pressure of all those secrets for a rope about your neck?

Guess what it is that turns plants to coal.

Pressure.

Guess what it is that turns limestone to marble.

Pressure.

Guess what it is that turns Briony's heart to stone.

Pressure.

Pressure is uncomfortable, but so are the gallows. Keep your secrets, wolfgirl. Dance your fists with Eldric's, snatch lightning from the gods. Howl at the moon, at the blood-red moon. Let your mouth be a cavern of stars.

13

The Trial

Pearl returned to us the day before Nelly's trial. We welcomed her, and we shook her hand, and some coins passed from Father's hand to hers, and we went our various ways, all except Edric, whom I overheard offering to help with supper.

Pearl said it was very kind of Mister Eldric but she didn't need no help, and anyways, she knew her place, she was sure, which was more than she could say for Mister Eldric; and Eldric said never mind about that, he thought she might like some company just now; and Pearl burst into tears and cried and cried, with Eldric saying things too low for Briony to hear; and Briony realized she should admit she was turning overhearing into eavesdropping, in which case she might as well sit down and enjoy it, which she did; and she heard Pearl's sobs turn to laughter from time to time, as when Eldric tried to peel an onion with the butter knife or said he didn't mind gathering herbs from the garden if Pearl could tell him where to find the mint sauce.

How does Eldric manage this so easily? When I told Pearl

how sorry I was about her baby, she merely said, "Thank you, miss," and turned back to the sink. Perhaps she could tell I was sorry about her baby, but only in my head. That's just a thought, not a feeling.

The next morning, Eldric also helped out in the kitchen, or pretended to help but really spent most of his time making up disrespectful rhymes about Judge Trumpington and the Chime Child. He even made Father and Mr. Clayborne laugh, although Father couldn't help but comment that *Judge Trumpington* does not rhyme with *wages of sin*, and never will.

We were on our way to the courthouse, more than an hour later, when I realized that the whole morning was a trick of Eldric's to set us all at ease. Rose and I, in particular, were nervous.

How does he manage it?

The courthouse was tucked behind the jail, overlooking a sullen little street, clotted year-round with mud. Father and I paused on the courthouse steps to have an exchange of words. They were actual words with actual meanings attached to them. It was not a pleasant experience.

"But you've been called as witness," said Father. He kept his voice low, as we were in public. No one must suspect that the Larkins have their little family disagreements.

Father and I, together with Rose, Eldric, and Tiddy Rex, made an inward-facing circle, like cows, only more intelligent. The Brownie stuck his long nose between Eldric and Tiddy Rex.

Go away! But I didn't bother saying it anymore.

"Eldric is nice," said Rose. "Do you think he's nice?"

"Very nice," I said.

"He gave me a pink ribbon," said Rose.

"So he did."

"He gave it to me because the witches took my first pink ribbon." Rose was talking now to Eldric. "When I told Briony you gave me the ribbon, she said, 'Oh, that Eldric!' She meant you're nice."

"When you've been summoned as a witness," said Father, "you are obliged to enter the courtroom."

How had Stepmother managed to shrug off Father's notions of propriety? She always said he needn't know what we girls were doing. That it wasn't lying, that it kept him from worrying and kept us free to do what we wanted to do.

"But I can't testify if I'm ill." My words had actual meanings, but none of them penetrated Father's mind. It appeared to be hermetically sealed. "I always get ill in the courtroom."

"Always?" said Father. "You've only been there once."

"I saw Briony be ill," said Rose. "I didn't prefer her to, but she did."

"It's the way the courtroom smells," I said. "It smells of eels."

Father sighed. "Please spare me these arguments of yours."

"Whose arguments should I use?"

Father's clergyman mask slipped. His scratch-lips actually ripped themselves apart. But he couldn't have been more surprised than I was. The shock of hearing myself uncoiled like a spring. One might be wicked, but one wasn't pert. Not to one's father.

My own mask stayed just where it ought. I've had lots of practice.

"Listen here," said Father. "I'll not tolerate this sort of rudeness."

"What sort of rudeness will you tolerate?" My Briony mask hadn't slipped. That was exactly the sort of thing she'd say, only more so.

When did the pictures start sliding through my mind? Perhaps I'd been seeing them all along; perhaps that's why I had a headache. I saw pictures of Stepmother—Stepmother, as she was at the beginning, wrapped in pearls and lace. Stepmother, as she was toward the end, her hair spread across the pillow. Stepmother, as she was at the end, her skin like waxed paper.

They were not quite memories. Perhaps they were dreams, or merely reflections of memories—memories caught on broken glass.

I had a headache; I sat on the steps, let my head droop over my knees. Father spoke behind my back. "The inquest of her stepmother's death took place here not four months ago. Briony was terribly upset."

I haven't gone deaf, Father. I can hear you. But do you really think I'm upset because of something that happened here months ago? Have you been reading Dr. Freud? Don't tell me you believe in psychology!

"But of course I wouldn't wear a pink ribbon with this new frock," said Rose. "I'm wearing a blue ribbon."

"You have quite an eye for color," said Eldric. "The ribbon exactly matches your sash."

"Why, so it does," said Rose, which was exactly what Father said when she pointed out her matching ribbon and sash, but Father said it with an exclamation mark.

"How pretty you be, Miss Rose," said Tiddy Rex.

Rose and I wore new frocks for the first time in years and years. Father had asked Pearl to see that we had something suitable to wear to the trial. She and her mother started our frocks, and when Pearl's baby died, Mrs. Trumpington had her seamstress finish them, which was very kind. They were made from the same midnight blue merino, but mine was far more grown-up than Rose's: It was cut very trim (no childish flounces for this girl, thank you!), with alabaster buttons down the side of the neck and along one shoulder.

Tiddy Rex sat beside me on the step; he slipped his hand into mine. "I'll bide with you, miss. Happen you got one o' them migraines?"

Oh, Tiddy Rex! If I were fond of children, I'd kiss that red-radish cheek of his. "Just a headache, Tiddy Rex." One has to believe in psychology to have migraines.

"Look at that woman," said Rose. "She is wearing a most beautiful blue, which I prefer she wear because I have an eye for color."

"Thank you," said a voice, belonging, I supposed, to the blue-wearing woman. "Blue and green are my favorite colors."

Everyone but me turned toward the voice, fragmenting our clever-cow circle, and there followed a general twitter during which names were offered and accepted, and greeting cards too, and hands extended and taken, and a pair of blue leather shoes tip-tapping into my range of vision. They were lovely shoes, all creamy leather and satin ribbons.

Huge, though.

When I learned that the owner of the shoes was named Leanne, I made a bet with myself. I bet that despite her enormous feet, Leanne would be very beautiful. I glanced up.

I won.

She was everything I am not: tall, full-figured, sloe-eyed, dark. You could easily picture her in a sultan's palace, strands of rubies plaited into her hair. Her frock was of peacock blue silk—silk, for an afternoon in the courtroom? But on her it looked wonderfully right—right out of the harem.

"How kind you all are." She spoke in a dark-river sort of voice, as though her throat were filled with dusk. She was staying in a village not twenty miles off, but her dusky voice made it sound like an island of spicy winds and bursting pineapples. Just the place to be marooned.

She despised witches, she said. It was witches that had driven her uncle Harry mad. It was in honor of his memory that she made it a point to attend the trial of every witch she possibly could, in his honor that she celebrated every conviction and hanging. She could only do so, of course, during the summer months, when she visited her cousins. Otherwise, she lived with her family in London, which was mercifully free of witches.

Presently, Eldric sat beside me on the step. "Here's a possible solution: You and Tiddy Rex and I will stand at the very back of the courtroom, and if you feel ill, we'll leave."

"Fine." The taste of ashes rose in my throat. Just fine! Let me be ill in front of everyone and die of humiliation.

Tiddy Rex kept hold of my hand as we entered. I remembered the depressing courtroom smell of cardboard and eel and moths—and please don't tell me moths don't have a smell. I assure you they do.

The court had been called to silence. Eldric leaned in to

whisper, "Who's the person sitting beside Judge Trumping-ton?"

"She's the Chime Child," I said.

"The Chime Child?" said Eldric. "Your father said she wasn't a child, but I hadn't quite imagined—"

"She's very old," I said. "She says she's getting too old."

"The Chime Child, she got to be grown," said Tiddy Rex. "She got herself a job too scareful for brats."

"Too scareful?" Eldric looked at me for explanation, but the glass-pictures were coming to me again, slicing me full of memories. Stepmother, lying back on her pillow, saliva creeping out the sides of her mouth.

"You tell him, Tiddy Rex."

"A Chime Child be a person what see the Old Ones an' spirits an' the like."

Saliva dripping down Stepmother's chin.

But this was a dream memory, not a true memory. This was how I imagined Stepmother must have died. It was foolish, no doubt, to have inquired into the symptoms of arsenic poisoning: Once I stuffed the information into my memory, I couldn't stop imagining each stage of Stepmother's death.

"At the trial o' a witch, or any Old One, there got to be someone from the spirit world, because—well, it's like they knows more about witches an' such-like than us regular folks."

"She looks remarkably corporeal," said Eldric. "Not at all like a spirit."

"She don't be no spirit," said Tiddy Rex. "Leastways, she don't be no proper spirit—do she, Miss Briony?"

I would simply ignore my dream memory of Stepmother

leaning over the basin, ignore the bloody . . . Quick someone, say something!

Eldric could be counted on to oblige. "How, then, does she come to be an improper spirit?"

"She don't be improper!" Tiddy Rex's voice went into a squeak. "You got it wrong, Mister Eldric."

"He's teasing, Tiddy Rex. She has a foot in the spirit world only because she was born at midnight. So she was born on neither one day nor the other."

"Or on both days?" said Eldric.

I nodded. "And she belongs neither to the human world nor the spirit world, or as you suggest, to both. She has the second sight."

The constable had been called to the stand. He spent a long while delivering his testimony, but it could be summed up in a few words. Nelly had red hair: One of the witches had red hair; Nelly was one of the witches. Nelly denied it, but a fellow can't trust nothing what might be said by a witch.

Rose was called next. Eldric and I exchanged a glance. Each of us understood that he'd leave me to my eels and accompany Rose to the witness box. A glance. Hadn't I once wondered at the way Eldric and his father understood each other so well without saying a word? I was growing fluent in their language. I believe I must have spoken it when I was small. It tugged at little strings that were not quite memory—nostalgia, perhaps? That longing for something you cannot describe.

Rose was all anxious-monkey smiles and indirection. She had a great deal to say about the fire department and the letters she'd written the firemen, and she spoke about the dangers of fire, and somehow got on to confiding that she didn't like the same-colored food all on one plate. But about her experience with the witches, she'd only say that they'd taken her ribbon.

"Which is not very clever," she said, "because a pink ribbon does not match up at all well with red hair."

"You speaks on color, Miss Rose." The Chime Child spoke in the accent of the Swampsea, with its round vowels and pinched-off consonants. "What does you think on the color o' yon Nelly's hair?"

All heads swung toward the prisoner's box. Nelly held her chin high, looking neither left nor right. It brought to mind her feet, dancing round the Maypole. It must have been four years ago or more, but I hadn't forgotten her dancing feet.

"Do her hair match the hair o' the witch you was speaking on?" said the Chime Child. You'd never guess from her plain, gravelly voice that she lived in a world of midnight births and the second sight. "The witch what thinked to thief you away?"

"The witch's hair and Nelly's hair don't match at all." Rose was very firm on this, but she started to waffle when she went on to say that despite that, neither of them should wear pink, and before she'd finished, you could tell that Judge Trumpington and the Chime Child had lost whatever confidence in her opinion they might have had. Their opinion was doubtless confirmed when Rose shrieked that I must cover my ears (it was almost noon), and they summoned the next witness, who was Eldric.

The air was saturated with yawns when he took the stand. His long fingers fidgeted about for want of a paper clip or a saltshaker or a scrap of the *London Loudmouth*. I found myself wondering what he'd think when Rose and I stole away to London. Who'd tell him we were missing?

Eldric seemed quite a different person in the witness box. I'd never seen him so—so efficient, for want of a better word. There were no humorous asides, no hint of the bad boy. His account of the truth, the whole truth, and nothing but the truth was precise and complete in every detail, except for the bit about the naked backsides. That, he left out.

I noticed particularly.

I had, so far, withstood the courtroom and the eel-sick. But after Eldric had finished, the reflection-slices returned. I saw Stepmother and the white pillow and the black hair and blood and spit. I saw myself too, saw my own bird hands holding a spoon. My hands were feeding Stepmother. My hands were feeding her soup.

And then the sick-sandy smell of eel saturated the court-room. I tore my hand from Tiddy Rex's, I pushed through the courtroom door. But the smell followed me down the courthouse steps, round the side alley, where only the dogs could see me heave my breakfast onto the cobbles.

14

Nineteen Chimes

The village children were playing on the railroad tracks, which reminded me that the maiden run of the London–Swanton line had been delayed for want of a permit. But I wouldn't think about it. I wouldn't let myself slide into that Möbius strip of worry, where I remind myself that once Mr. Clayborne's men have finished rebuilding the pumping station, the Boggy Mun will re-infect Rose with the swamp cough. That it will then be too late to run away to London because Rose will only bring the swamp cough along with her.

See how I'm not thinking about it?

Eldric was playing with the children. He rose from a clot of boys tossing horseshoes and waved me over.

I waved back. *I'm coming!*

This was the fourth Friday afternoon we were to meet at the Alehouse. Friday is an exciting day. It's payday, and market day, and bad-luck day, and Pearl-looking-after-Rose day, so you never know what's going to happen.

Eldric said that my education had been sadly neglected. How, he asked, could a girl grow up in Swanton never knowing that the close of market meant the beginning of Two-Pint Friday? That customers and merchants alike simply slid a few feet north, into the Alehouse, where two beers could be had for the price of one, and the fish and chips were always hot and steaming.

I settled my hat (the ribbon is a very pale pink), I smoothed my gloves (pink monogram on white). Father must have suffered quite a shock when he finally noticed that Rose and I went about in a state of acute ventilation, for he'd ordered up more new clothes. I know it's only that Father doesn't want to appear mingy, but I confess, I like new clothes. I adore new clothes.

Perhaps I'm shallow. Yes, I'm shallow, I don't mind admitting it. Perhaps I should admit that there's no end to the depths of my shallowness.

Off I went, into the bustle of Friday market, which on this particular Friday was all squashed with oilcloth tents: A storm was blowing in from the north.

Tiddy Rex detached himself from the horseshoe-tossing boys and trotted toward me. He passed a group of girls skipping rope, grubby pinafores flapping, voices rising thin and high.

> *Tie the baby to the track.*
> *Look! The one oh one!*
> *The train goes click, the train goes clack,*
> *Look, the baby's done,*
> *For,*

Five,

Six,

Seven . . .

Tiddy Rex touched my hand. "Mister Eldric, he brung that rhyme all the way from London."

All about us, life carried on in its disordered way. A donkey passing, carrying spices and flies. Mad Tom, poking his umbrella into rubbish bins and rabbit holes, looking for his lost wits. Petey Todd, pinching an apple from the greengrocer's bin.

Petey has a spacious view of what belongs to him.

"Mister Eldric!" called one of the skip-rope girls. "I maked ninety-four, I did."

"Ninety-four!" Eldric pounced to her side. "You should get a blue ribbon or a gold medal! But I haven't either."

He paused, as though considering. "Could you make do with a blue-ribbon bit of fish?"

How the girls laughed!

"Or a fish fried like a medal?"

"I found milady at last!" said Cecil's voice from behind. He turned me about by my shoulders and looked me up and down—at my skirt (four pleats, checkered in two tones of white), at my shirtwaist (dusted with glinting beads), at the netting (placed strategically across the chest).

"Staring is rude." I suddenly wished the netting hadn't so many holes.

"You don't mind when *he* stares at you." Cecil jerked his head toward Eldric.

"He doesn't stare," I said. "He looks."

147

"I'm desperate to talk to you," said Cecil. "We've never even mentioned it."

"It?" I said.

"You know," said Cecil. *"It."*

But I didn't know.

"What are you playing at, Briony?" Cecil stared with his flat, fishy eyes. "I don't deserve this kind of treatment."

I stared back. I'm not jolly enough to play at anything.

"You want to pretend it didn't happen?" said Cecil. "That's what you always wanted; I see it all now. You putting me off after she died. First, *Oh, but there's the inquest!* And then, *Oh, but there's the burial!* And then, *Oh, but we're in mourning!* I never thought you'd betray me."

Tiddy Rex squeezed my hand. "What be the betrayment you done, Miss Briony?"

"I've no idea," I said, although I hated to admit it. Even if Cecil doesn't know what he's talking about, I usually do.

"That's the worst of all," said Cecil. "If you're going to betray me, at least be honest about it."

"Let's talk about this another time, shall we?" I said.

"Oh, but there's the inquest!" said Cecil, in a squeaky female voice. *"Oh, but we're in mourning."*

"Is that the way I sound, Tiddy Rex?"

Tiddy Rex shook his head. "No, miss."

I never thought I'd be glad to see Petey Todd. A person like Petey can only have so much fun stealing apples and must perforce increase his enjoyment by clipping Tiddy Rex on the shoulder and circling round to see the tears in Tiddy Rex's eyes.

"Cry, baby, cry!" said Petey.

Yer mam is going to die.
Hitch yer sister to the plough,
She don't matter anyhow . . .

"Never mind." I put my arm around Tiddy Rex's shoulder. "Petey can't help himself. Poor thing. You know what they say about him?"

"They doesn't say nothing!" said Petey.

"They say he's soft in the head. They say he eats worms for breakfast."

"Doesn't!"

"Did you know, he can't learn his letters?"

"I got me my letters," said Petey.

"You do?" I made a clown face of amazement, big eyes, dropped jaw. "Can you make the first letter of your name?"

"Sure can! I can make a *P*."

"You can make a pee?" Another clown face of amazement. "How lovely! But don't do it in front of the young ladies."

"It don't be like that!" Petey stumbled into an explanation of his code of honor as it appertained to girls. But I turned away. I was done with Cecil, I was done with Petey.

But there are always more people one has to deal with, and on this particular unlucky Friday, it was Leanne. She'd sprung, seemingly, from nowhere, although she was rather robust to be an apparition. The skip-rope girls surrounded her, reaching for her green lace overskirt, which floated over some silvery, satiny stuff. The effect was very pretty and watery, although water doesn't wear huge ropes of pearls.

"I'm glad you like it," said Leanne. "But no hands, please."

Eldric must have seen her since the trial; of course he had.

149

Just look at the way he came prowling over, crunching his tie into genial disorder.

"What a pleasant surprise." He shook Leanne's hand. "Come and play!"

"Your frock, miss, it be ever so fine," said one of the skip-rope girls.

"Them flowers in your hat," said another. "They doesn't be real, does they?"

The flowers weren't real, but what lay beneath the netting at Leanne's breast was. It was real. She was, in short, like a gland.

Swollen.

Leanne feminina regularitatis est.

But she didn't breakfast with Eldric every morning, as I did. She didn't laugh with him as they expanded their bad-boy Latin vocabulary. She didn't have boxing lessons with him, and surely, he never admired her fist. Did he?

The sky turned to ashes. It snapped and growled.

"To the Alehouse!" Eldric promised fish and chips all round, and a blue-ribbon fish for the ninety-four-times rail-jumping girl.

The children stuck to him. They clung to his arms, they snatched at his jacket.

I hate children.

Cecil took my arm. "I made a botch of it before. Let me try again, talking to you, that is."

"Talk away," I said, following the group to the Alehouse. It was a kind of test. Can Cecil Trumpington walk and talk at the same time?

"You're not as kind as you could be."

How true, lamentably true. I'm sorry, Father. I do not love my neighbor as myself.

The bloated sky opened up. Rain fell in ark-loads. Cecil and I ran for the Alehouse. The children were already seated at the bar, in fits of laughter because Eldric had ordered a plate of gold-medal fish and chips.

"I don't see what's so funny," said Eldric.

I'd have liked a plate of gold-medal fish and chips myself, but the rules were clear. Fisher-brats at the bar, gentry at the tables.

Leanne, Cecil, and I gazed at one another. The three of us, together, were thin as gruel. We needed Eldric as thickening agent.

The longer I looked at Leanne, the more I saw her as a bundle of clichés. Raven's-wing hair, laughing eyes. Ruby lips, shell-like ears. You could probably mix them up and it would make no difference.

Ruby ears and shell-like lips?

Heaving cheeks and scarlet bosom?

I was rather surprised to find Cecil gazing not at the scarlet bosom but at my face. He'd spoken to me. He was waiting for my response.

Leanne helped me out, gazing at me with her curling eyes. "That frock does suit you wonderfully. Pity, it's the sort of thing I can't wear. It wouldn't suit me at all."

What did Leanne mean beneath her talcum-powder words? Was this one of those compliments that turns around to bite?

Then a marvelous piece of conversational good fortune came our way: The Hangman rose and walked past us. He was an enormous fellow. Heads turned, following him. Conversations faltered, leaving dribbles of silence, until he pushed out the door.

Don't think about it, Briony; don't spoil the day! Nelly's hanging has nothing to do with you. It doesn't matter that she's a witch and is going to hang. Or that she's not a witch and is going to hang. Just count yourself lucky you've avoided her fate so far. Just fall into the conversation about witches and hangings and ooh, isn't it exciting!

Leanne was quite the witch hunter. Her entire family had been plagued by witches. Not only had witches driven her uncle mad, they'd brought her cousin out in boils; he had the scars to prove it. Not to mention her sister-in-law—

Leanne delivered herself of this information with a terrible sort of gusto. Her cheeks shone, her eyes were rosy. News of Nelly's trial had brought her to Swanton initially, and now she'd returned to see Nelly hanged.

Don't let her guess what I am! Let's hope she's like the others, who look only at the surface. Let's hope she'd never think that a girl with black-velvet eyes and cut-glass cheekbones could be a witch.

"Please excuse me." Leanne turned to the window. She didn't want to miss a single thrilling moment. I understood now why she'd chosen a table by the window, despite the chill. I understood why every table next to a window was taken. A hanging is a good bit of fun, but not in the rain. Best get yourself a pint and watch from inside.

Two pints, rather. Don't forget, it's Two-Pint Friday.

I rose. "I'll help Eldric with the food." But he was already on his way back, loaded with hot pies and pickled eggs and bees-wine and ale. "And lemon tart for after."

I pretended to be busy. I pretended I might need something at the bar. Let's see, what was it? Oh, yes: I needed not to watch Nelly hang.

The spectators roared. I jumped. If we were in Spain, they'd have shouted *Olé!* That's right, think about Spain, not Swanton.

You've a lot not to think about, Briony. You mustn't think about the delay of the London–Swanton line. You mustn't think about what's happening in the square, not about the crash of the trapdoor, the jerk of the noose, the twitching of—

Don't think about it!

But you can't ignore a hanging when you're surrounded by the beating of fists and the stomping of feet and the cries of general good humor that accompany an execution.

The first chime. The Alehouse fell silent. The second chime, the third. A chime for every year of Nelly's life.

The fifth chime—the seventh—twelfth—

Would Rose mind my hearing twelve chimes of a person's life?

The eighteenth—the nineteenth—

Silence now. Nelly's life had been counted out to its end.

Leanne swung back to her food. "Pity," she said.

Pity?

"Father will be cross," said Cecil. "He so dislikes making a mistake."

A mistake. Nelly hadn't turned to dust. She'd been no more than a girl with red hair.

"Here's an idea," said Eldric. "Let's play that game where you ask the questions—you know the one, Briony."

I could slap him—punch him! Didn't he care that they'd hanged the wrong girl? "Most every game asks questions."

My fingers arranged themselves into a terrifically non-stupidibus sort of fist.

"Questions such as, 'Which Old One would you be?'" said Eldric. "Or, 'Which Old One would attack you?'"

"Old Ones!" said Leanne, with a double-barreled sort of exclamation mark, perhaps to fill the world with all the exclamation marks Rose never used. Conservation of matter, and all that.

"The metaphor game." I'd punch him on that squarish corner of his boy-man jaw.

"What invention would Leanne be?" I said, thinking of the rack and the skull crusher.

"The very thing!" said Eldric. "To which I have just the answer. If Leanne were an invention, she'd be a motorcar."

"I adore motorcars!" said the fine horsewoman, raising her tinkling eyes and laughing her twinkling laugh.

"But not the careful, boxy sort of motorcar," said Eldric. "The lower, longer sort. Black, I think. Calf-leather interior."

"What a lovely game!" said Leanne, clapping her sultry hands. "Let me think of an invention for Eldric."

The electric light, of course. But Leanne had her own idea.

"The telephone, I think."

Because he talks too much?

"You're ever so good at bringing far-flung people together."

She was right. I hated her.

"What would I be?" said Cecil.

The X-ray, of course. Cecil likes to look through girls' clothes.

The barkeep lit the lanterns. They flared blue with a stink

of the Hot Place, then paled when Father walked in. He tends to have that effect.

Father headed straight for our table. What would Father be if he were an invention?

"Will you sing with us, Briony?"

I had to look up.

Father can't be an invention. He's only old, nothing new.

"Please do!" said Cecil. "You have a lovely voice. I haven't heard you in ages."

"Another time, perhaps," I said. But there'd be no other time. When Father stopped singing, so did I. I stopped so thoroughly I can't sing anymore.

"Please?" said Father. "Please, Briony Vieny?"

Briony Vieny? He hadn't called me that in ages. *Rosy Posy. Briony Vieny.* Give it up, Father. There's no Briony Vieny anymore, or Rosy Posy. We grew out of those girls while you were away. They died.

"Will you choose a song?" said Father.

How does love die? In the first year, Father touches Stepmother's hair and sings *Black is the color of my true love's hair.* In the fourth year, he buries her and says, as usual, nothing.

"'Black Is the Color.'" I turned away before Father's face began to disappear, before his eyes went pale, his lips white.

Sorry, Father. You were the one who asked.

I grasped the fork with my right hand, just as all non-witchy girls must do. I stabbed into the pie. Steam burst from the crust, smelling of cinnamon and wine.

I set down my fork. One reason to cook with cinnamon and wine is to disguise the taste of eel. But you can't fool me.

"Shall I get you something else?" said Eldric.

155

I shook my head. The very thought of eel brought up the taste of sick. I sipped at the bees-wine. It buzzed about my mouth but didn't buzz away the taste. Why hadn't he brought fish and chips as he had the three Fridays past? Did he think Leanne a touch above Two-Pint Friday fare?

Quiet again in the Alehouse as the Hangman slid back through the door. Rain dripped from his hat brim, flicked off his jacket as he hung it up. Everyone looked at him; he looked at no one. He took his old seat, he looked at no one.

"What a nasty job," said Leanne, proponent of ridding the earth of witches. She smiled, exposing her heart-shaped teeth. "I wonder that he can bear to eat."

Cecil said he wondered too, but I didn't. Let's say you do something wicked, such as smash your sister's wits. Does that mean you shall have no more cakes and ale?

No. Your heart must go on ticking, and your mouth must go on eating, and your brain must go on sleeping; and if you enjoy the occasional pint, what of it? You may as well enjoy the pint. If someone makes a joke, you may as well laugh.

Your heart ticks on, that's all there is to it. Life goes on, that's all there is to it.

Black is the color of my true love's hair.
Her lips are like some rosy fair.

"I like girls with golden hair," said Cecil to no one in particular, and he snatched at a bit of my hair.

He was tipsy. "Leave me be, Cecil." How could Fitz have stood his company, Fitz, my tutor genius.

But look at Eldric. Was he also tipsy? Look at him, slipping off his chair, onto his knees. Look at him, kneeling at Leanne's feet. Look at him, strumming an imaginary guitar.

The sweetest face and the gentlest hands.
I love the ground whereon she stands.

I stood up. What was I doing here? I hated other people my age. How stupid they were. I should hate to be a regular girl with a sugar-plum voice. I should hate to have swan-like lashes, and a thick, sooty neck. I sound as though I'm joking, I know, but I should truly hate to be like Leanne, so charming and ordinary and stuffed with clichéd feelings. I'm glad I'm the ice maiden. Who wants to be crying over every stray dog?

Not I. Scratch my surface and what do you see? More surface.

I excused myself. I said I mustn't neglect Rose, which Eldric would have known was a lie, if he'd been attending properly, which he wasn't. He knew perfectly well that Pearl looked after Rose on Fridays—on quite a lot of other days, as well.

The square ran with water. Light spilt outside the window, dripped off Mad Tom's umbrella.

"You be going out in this weather, miss?" said Tiddy Rex.

"What other weather could I go out in?"

The Alehouse door slammed behind me. Mad Tom crouched beneath broken umbrella fingers. Hangman's Square was a witch's brew of mud and sewage and drowned rats. I stepped into the square, where everything was oozing and bubbling and churning. The wind wound itself through the gallows. It danced with Nelly Daws. Nelly danced with the wind, danced on her poor, dead, dancing feet.

Nelly was no witch. She was a nineteen-year-old girl who, once, had danced round a Maypole. Judge Trumpington had been wrong; the Chime Child had been wrong. Couldn't they have listened to Rose about the different colors of red hair, Nelly's and the witch's?

Don't think about it, Briony. There's no point. Remember: You're the girl with nothing below the surface. Scratch it and what do you find?

More surface.

· 15 ·

Communion

I'd left Eldric behind in the Alehouse. I'd left Nelly behind in the square. But I couldn't leave Rose behind, I could never leave Rose. I stood outside the bedroom we shared. I listened to her cough.

Rose had been feeling poorly, Pearl had said. Rose had gone early to bed.

I was glad to hear it. I needn't tell Rose at once. I needn't tell her she'd been right, that Nelly had been no witch, that the witch's hair didn't match Nelly's, that the judge and the Chime Child ought to have heeded Rose. But the judge and the Chime Child had dwelt mostly on the fact that Nelly could not account for her whereabouts on the night of the flying snags.

Rose coughed as I trudged up the stairs. Rose coughed as I set my hand on the doorknob. Rose coughed. She had a wet, skin-scraping cough. She had the swamp cough.

I let my hand drop. There was nothing for me in that room. If I went in, I'd just lay myself in our bed, in the hollow I'd left of myself.

Life and stories are alike in one way: They are full of hollows. The king and queen have no children: They have a child hollow. The girl has a wicked stepmother: She has a mother hollow.

In a story, a baby comes along to fill the child hollow. But in life, the hollows continue empty. One sister continues lonely and unloved; the other coughs behind the door. I sat in the hall. I waited. Father returned from the Alehouse. I waited. He sat before the fire in the parlor. I waited.

Sometimes, of course, the sister's the wicked one, not the stepmother.

I'd lived in a hollow all the past year. A Fitz hollow, a Brownie hollow, a Stepmother hollow. When you live in a hollow, your life is small. It's all paper snips, and dust, and cold wax drippings, and the scab on leftover gravy.

I waited. Father went to bed. No more waiting. Time to go, little witch. Your sister has the swamp cough.

Wind had replaced the rain. It slammed sticks and scum and willow peels against the far bank, it slammed me across the bridge. The fishermen have a name for the northeast wind. Don't tell Father I know it. They call her the Bitch.

The Bitch thwacked the Flats with the side of her hand. She thwacked the breath from my lungs.

The Bitch could easily push a seven-year-old girl from a swing. Was it the Bitch I'd called that day? Was it the Bitch who'd smacked Rose to the ground?

Probably.

If Briony Larkin, age seven, wanted to call up a wind, she'd have called up the most powerful wind she could. She might not have been quite aware of what she was doing, but I know enough about that younger Briony to know that when she did a thing, she did it thoroughly.

So did the Bitch. She had the water on the run. Gone were the stagnant pools, the creeping trickles. She turned the ooze to slither, which whipped along on its belly, smacking its lips.

The Bitch kept me on the run too. She pushed at me, she tugged at me. She made me long to turn back. She made me yearn to lie in the warm hollow of myself and hate myself in comfort, but I had to keep on.

Try to care about someone other than yourself, Briony. Think about Rose, lying at home, coughing her lungs into bits. Remember Rose, as the Bitch snickers round you, whistling beneath her breath. As you slog through burble and splat, as you sloggle through slurple and smack.

I had no other choice. I'd once thought I could turn myself in and save Rose. But I knew better now. Remember what the constable said at the trial? *A fellow can't trust nothing what might be said by a witch.*

What would have happened if I had turned myself in as I'd planned? If, after having trounced Petey, I revealed everything to the constable. I'd have been hanged and the draining would have continued.

The pumping station rose just ahead, even more red brickibus and stuck-upimus than before. None of the Old Ones was out. Not tonight, not with the Bitch on the prowl. They were staying snug in the jellyfish earth.

I clawed through the Bitch, leaned against the pumping station wall.

I'll huff and I'll puff and I'll blow your house down!

screamed the Bitch. She pelted me with leftover rain and sea salt and grit and twigs and venom.

She didn't have a chance. The bricks might be stuck up, but they were stuck up tight. I edged along the wall, toward the door. Just a few yards more and I'd round the corner into that lovely little nook, where the Bitch couldn't reach.

Round I went. The lantern flew from my grasp. "Nabbed!" said a great voice. There came a crash of darkness, a crunch of collar. I couldn't breathe. I swatted at a jacket, at a sleeve.

"Well, I'll be," said the voice. "A girl!"

Light again, pressing into my Bitch-squinted eyes.

"Miss Briony!"

The hand let go. I tumbled onto brick. Air leapt into my lungs like silver fish.

Robert? I tried to speak, but my voice was folded flat.

"Sorry you taked such a tumble, miss." Yes, it was Robert, Rose's firefighter. He drew me to my feet. "But I never been so—what I means to say, well, it be you, miss? You what be the—?"

Robert paused, swallowed, and into the silence came Eldric's voice.

"It's all right, Robert. You may leave Miss Briony to me."

Robert's light bobbed about, shone on Eldric. Why was I surprised that he looked so utterly like himself, a greatcoat, a tease of a tie?

"Begging your pardon," said Robert, "but it be your pa what setted me to watch this place come the darklings. He told me to seize the culprit an' fetch him to his own particular self."

"Culprit?" said Eldric. "You don't mean to say you suspect Miss Briony!"

Robert looked at me for a good while. "I can't say how sorry I be, miss," he said at last. "Sorry to treat you so rough-like."

"It was your job, Robert." I wheezed through my accordion throat. "You had to do your job."

Robert left, still apologizing and protesting. Eldric and I were alone, in the quiet. I looked at Eldric. Could I come up with a plausible excuse? I'd never get lost in the swamp; Eldric knows that. Eldric looked at me. Each of us was waiting for the other.

"I'll start," said Eldric. "I saw your lantern through the window, and being the nosy parkerius that I am, decided to come along."

I refrained from correcting his Latin. "Did you know your father had posted a guard?"

"Yes," said Eldric.

"Did you suspect me?"

Eldric paused. "I didn't not suspect you."

"Now you know," I said.

"Now I know."

A little silence. Good thing Eldric started. He saw me leave—he'd have known any story I might have invented to be a lie.

"Shall I ask why you did it?"

I slid down the wall, sat.

"Good idea," said Eldric. "Let's make ourselves comfortable and wait for the wind to die down."

I slumped against the wall.

"Why did you do it?" said Eldric.

"I can't tell you."

"Perhaps I can find out this way." He brought the lantern to my face. "Don't they say the eyes are the windows to the soul?"

I closed my eyes.

"But now, the only thing I can discern is the vivid blueness of your lips."

He heaped his greatcoat around me. I protested, as one must do; I even opened my eyes for extra politeness. But he insisted he was warm in his slouchy tweeds. He defied me to find a trace of blue in his lips.

This is what I want. I want people to take care of me. I want them to force comfort upon me. I want the soft-pillow feeling that I associate with memories of being ill when I was younger, soft pillows and fresh linens and satin-edged blankets and hot chocolate. It's not so much the comfort itself as knowing there's someone who wants to take care of you.

"What are you thinking?" said Eldric.

"I'm thinking of what will happen when you tell your father, and he tells my father." I'd been thinking of exactly that, but in an inside out sort of way. I'd receive the very opposite, the opposite of satin edges and hot chocolate.

"And finally the constable will show up to fetch me."

"And you'll spend your life in jail?"

I closed my eyes again. Eldric thought I was joking.

"Father's a righteous man," I said.

"You're mad!" said Eldric. "Of course he's not going to call the law on you."

"Not if your father does it first," I said.

"Do you really believe your father would turn you in, or mine?"

I did believe it. Stepmother had believed it too. That's why she promised again and again never to tell Father. She knew what would happen were he ever to find out.

I thought of the constable, of his droopy eyes and sloppy lips. Would he have to touch me to arrest me?

"I won't tell anyone," said Eldric. "My father, your father, no one."

"But that's not fair!"

"How is that?" said Eldric.

"I destroyed a very expensive pumping station, and haven't paid anyone back, and besides, it wouldn't be fair to Robert. He's supposed to tell your father."

"Let me take care of my father," said Eldric. "I'll lie if I have to. And if you need to pay me back, here's what you can do. I've been wanting to have a garden party, at the Parsonage, but I'm a visitor and don't like asking your father."

"You want me to ask Father?" I said. "That hardly makes up for an expensive pumping station."

It was wonderfully comforting that Eldric would lie for me. He would? Really, he would?

"There's such a thing as being irritatingly ethical," said Eldric. "That's you, right now."

That's a pleasant change. Witches are rarely accused of being irritatingly ethical.

"Now," said Eldric, "for a talk about the Fraternicus."

"Fraternitus," I said.

"I was just testing you," said Eldric. "You passed. Now, tell me the meaning of *Fraternitus*."

"Fraternity." Where was this going?

"And what's a fraternity?"

"A brotherhood."

"In a brotherhood," said Eldric, "each of the members trusts the others."

Oh-ho! "You're not going to talk me into telling you why I did it."

"It appears not," said Eldric. "But I have something I want to say. I feel it with every fiber of my bad-boy being. When I put my unscholarly mind to work on why you'd destroy the pumping station, I can think of only one thing: You're in some sort of trouble."

"Maybe I'm one of those people who likes to watch things burn."

"You're being irritatingly ethical again," said Eldric. "But without the ethical bit."

"I'll show you how ethical I am." I reached for the satchel and drew out a bottle.

"It's from the church?" Eldric spoke softly, as though he were praying.

"From the church."

"Communion wine?"

"Communion wine." I knew that Mr. Clayborne was no fool, that he wasn't the man to let the illuminating gas cause a second accident. He'd have turned it off, or contained it somehow. So I'd stuffed my satchel with the kinds of treats that appeal to fires—paper and rags and paraffin and alcohol.

"Brilliant!" said Eldric.

How lovely to no longer have the option of destroying the pumping station. What a relief! It wouldn't be a relief the next day when I awoke to hear Rose coughing. But I might as well enjoy it for now.

I drew off the cork. "How does one drink it?"

"Right from the bottle."

"A swig?" I said. "I've never had a swig."

I drank. The smell shivered against the roof of my mouth. I wiped my mouth with Eldric's coat sleeve, just like a bad boy. "I've swigged." I handed the bottle to Eldric. "Or is it swug?"

"Swug," said Eldric. "It is in bad-boy circles, at least." He swug. "It tastes much better outside church."

"It's the picnic principle," I said. "Things taste better outdoors. And if it's a forbidden thing, so much the better."

"I'm sorry I called you irritatingly ethical," said Eldric. "I was clearly mistaken. Now back to my idea, from which you are clearly trying to distract me. I'm not saying that Fraternitus members mayn't have secrets from each other. Sometimes that's inevitable. But don't you think we can trust the other and ask for help?"

There was no point in saying what I really thought. I nodded and swug again.

"Perhaps our initiation will bind us in mutual trust and aid."

"I've been waiting and waiting," I said, "but no initiation."

"Keep waiting," said Eldric. "Now that I've mentioned it, I shall have to delay it for months. The initiation must never come when you expect."

We were most companionable, passing the bottle between us. I made myself forget about the next day. We leaned against the wall, very gradually sliding toward each other. I leaned my head on his shoulder; he rested his head on the top of mine; and the astonishing thing is that it wasn't at all awkward.

I wouldn't worry about tomorrow. I'd let today be enough.

167

We laughed a lot and I grew warmer still, lovely and warm. I do realize that some of that warmth was due to the wine, but there was much more to it than that. There are two distinct aspects to Communion wine: one aspect is the wine itself, the other is the idea of communion. Wine is certainly warming, but communion is a great deal more so.

The Party's Always
Over at Midnight

"I don't like all one color," said Rose, "but I like our frocks."

I knew she did. She'd been saying so all day. She liked the way they matched up with themselves, which is to say they were white, white, white.

But that's what young ladies wear to garden parties. White.

Rose was to attend the party. Dr. Rannigan said she might.

"Robert will like the way I match." Rose turned so I might do her buttons.

I pressed my lips together so I wouldn't say what I'd said so often in the past few days. That Robert might choose not to come; that he might feel awkward; that he wouldn't have any friends at the party.

But Rose had heard me often enough. "I'm his friend. He would come because I'm his friend."

"You're all buttoned, Rose."

Once, I would have called her Rosy.

Or Rosy Posy.

Funny how I kept thinking of our pet names since that rainy Two-Pint Friday at the Alehouse, when Father called me Briony Vieny.

"I look pretty," said Rose.

She did, too. The dress was drifty and Grecian in shape, with a high bodice that flowed into a great shoulder bow. Mine was identical. The party had proved to be a lot of work, and in the end, Pearl abandoned her plan to design two dresses. We'd look like twin Grecian oracles, rather pale from staying in our cave. Also minus the prophetic powers, which was a pity. If I could look into the future, I'd know how I saved Rose from the swamp cough. I hadn't had a single idea, so far. Two weeks and no ideas.

"Do you suppose Robert's here yet?"

"Why don't you go see," I said, which left me to do my own buttons, but that was better than going mad. "Don't forget, Dr. Rannigan says you must wrap up well, and that you mustn't stay at the party past ten o'clock."

It also left me with some brain-room to think about how to save Rose. One needs an entire absence of Rose to be able to think about her. If she died, I could think about saving her all the time.

There's a riddle in there. I'll suggest it to the Sphinx.

Rose came dancing over the moment I descended the stairs. "Leanne is here, and because of my eye for color, I said her frock is Persian green, and she said, 'Right you are!'"

Her cheeks were actually faintly pink. Rose smiled her pearl-strand smile, her real-girl smile.

"I asked her how old she was," said Rose, "and she said she was very old indeed. Father said it was rude to ask, but Eldric said Leanne was joking and I mustn't believe her. He said she's just his age, which is twenty-two."

Rose led me through the kitchen, which was a most peculiar feeling. Usually it's I leading Rose.

"Eldric has decorated the garden in blue and white. He said it was inspired by the Orient, but Leanne said it was *À la Japonaise*."

We stood at the kitchen door. "May I open it now?" Eldric had forbidden any of us even to peek at the garden. He'd been most secretive about his arrangements for the party, and had taken to skipping meals in order to work on the final details.

"I see you put on your shawl," I said. "Very good."

But Eldric had taken dinner with us yesterday—I suppose he couldn't very well not show up, as Father had invited Mr. Clayborne. Mr. Clayborne said it looked as though Eldric was working hard; and Eldric gave him a gray little smile and said he was; and then Mr. Clayborne had to go and say he wished he could once, just once, see Eldric work hard at something useful, such as university, or a profession.

"I prefer that you open the door," said Rose.

Blast Mr. Clayborne! Why did he have to go and refer to his blighted hopes, with Eldric looking as though he'd worked himself to death? He was still six or seven feet of boy-man, but he no longer hummed with energy. I don't know how a great boy like Eldric can look translucent, but he did. He was burning out, all wick and no wax.

"I prefer that you open the door," said Rose.

The door? I came back to the world. Sorry Rose, yes, the door.

This is the difference between Eldric and me. Had it been my job to transform the garden, I would have removed the clothesline. Clotheslines always make me think of undergarments, and although I've never been to Japan, I don't imagine a memory-whiff of undergarments is at all *À la Japonaise*.

But Eldric had added clotheslines, strung them all about to encircle the garden. From them hung sheets, lined up hem to hem, and tethered to the ground with stakes. He'd created a three-sided walled garden. The fourth side opened to the river.

I hadn't known Eldric could paint. The sheets were white, the paint was blue, and together, they blossomed into a blue-and-white landscape: cranes and spray-foam seas and snowy mountains and cherry blossoms.

The western sky was bright. Eldric's shadow slouched against the garden wall, quite dwarfing him. I bounded toward him, bursting to tell him he was a genius—as much a genius in his own Eldric way as Fitz was in his own Fitz way—but then slithering up the wall came a second shadow, all bouncing ears and shell-like hair.

I un-bounded at once, which was both embarrassing and un-oracular. Where was my Delphi cave? I needed to hide.

The garden was filling with *Oohs* and *Aahs*, which were accompanied by guests and the rustle of evening wraps and little tendrils of scent. Pearl appeared bearing a great roast beef, and the energy of the crowd surged toward the banquet table. Corks popped and glasses clinked and Father, who'd been put in charge of the roast beef, said "Ouch!" as he cut himself.

I wandered to the river. Paper lanterns dotted the apple tree, where the swings had once hung. It was a crabbed little thing. It's hard to imagine Rose and I were ever small enough to swing from it.

Footsteps came up behind me, with quite a bit of pounce. Eldric?

"Champagne, milady?"

What a dreadful thing, to have confused Cecil with Eldric.

But Cecil was pouncy all over. He seized my hand and said, "I've had a rather interesting thought."

Imagine, a thought!

The sun was orange and setting fast. Its reflection oozed up and down the river in thick marmalade ripples.

"Don't you want to know what it is?"

"Don't you think," I said, "that Eldric ought to have built one of those curly little bridges over the river?"

"I beg your pardon?" said Cecil.

"It would have fit in so well with the Japanese theme. My theory is that the rivers in Japan are only an excuse."

"Come sit down and talk sensibly for once." Cecil tugged at my hand. "The food is lovely and you might quite like my idea."

"An excuse, you see, to build those cunning little bridges. Eldric would have painted it blue, of course."

"Damn it all, Briony! It's always *Eldric this* and *Eldric that* with you. I don't wish to speak of Eldric. I wish to speak of us."

He scooped up my arm, swung me round.

"Let go, Cecil," I said. "I've a strange dislike of being forced."

"But Briony," he said, "I'm so full of good spirits. I could walk to London, I think!"

Why didn't he?

After a moment, I realized we'd turned into an audience for the production of *Garden Party*, by Eldric Clayborne. The stage was illuminated with candles and paper lanterns and glowing cigars and little fires just starting up in a half-dozen braziers.

To the left unfolded the drama of Father and the Carving Knife.

Sorry. Stage right is what I meant to say.

Upstage center unfolded the drama of Mrs. Trumpington's heel and a bit of soggy earth.

On stage left unfolded the drama of Rose and the absent Robert. She stood between Eldric and Leanne, and although I couldn't hear her words, I knew she was inquiring after him, and I imagined Eldric was probably saying that no, he didn't think the invitation could have gone astray.

How tiny Rose was between the two of them. I saw exactly how I'd look should I ever stand next to Leanne, which I shall endeavor not to.

Rose looked like an underdone sugar cookie.

Downstage center unfolded the drama of the Brownie and Mad Tom, both making straight for Briony Larkin. "Black-eyed girl!" called Mad Tom. The Brownie was silent.

"I'll get rid of the fellow!" Cecil knotted his fists and sprang forward. It was all I could do to catch at his coat.

"It's only Mad Tom!" I said.

There was a tacit understanding among the villagers that he might wander in and out of parties and weddings and other private events. But *tacit* implies the ability to make inferences, which is why Cecil didn't know.

"It be you what taked my wits," said Mad Tom. "I knows it by the blackness o' your eye."

And it had been Mad Tom who'd carved the sunflowers and daisies on Mother's tombstone. Well, not exactly Mad Tom, but the person Mad Tom used to be before he went mad.

"I needs 'em, black-eyed girl. I needs 'em sore, I does."

"I haven't got them. But if you take yourself there"—I pointed to the banquet table—"you shall have bread and roast beef."

And a bit of the Reverend Larkin's blood.

"I'll get us a table, shall I?" said Cecil. "In one of those warm nooks. I know milady is often cold."

I liked the word *warm*, but I disliked the word *nook*, as it meant sharing a small space with Cecil. And there was still his idea to endure.

He took up too much space in the nook. Not his body, although it was large enough, but his energy. I'd seen him like this upon several occasions, but I'd never been trapped with him.

"You're out and about so much more these days," said Cecil. "Why don't you join us on Blackberry Night?"

This was his great idea? "You're mad!"

Good girls didn't romp about on Blackberry Night. Father has strong opinions about it. His biggest, fattest sermon of the year is all about Blackberry Night, which is also Michaelmas, when is also when the Archangel hurled the Devil from Heaven. Naturally, this annoyed the Devil considerably, and he goes about on that night, spoiling the blackberries.

"I'll protect you," said Cecil, laying his hand over mine.

175

I whipped my hand away. "Cecil!"

On Blackberry Night, the lads and lasses run barefoot through the swamp, pretending to try to catch the Devil; but it would appear the Devil catches them instead, for they consume quantities of beer and wine, and they shed their clothes, and there are always a number of surprise weddings come Advent.

How does Father feel about Blackberry Night?

He's against it.

"I'm so in love with you," said Cecil.

I looked into his fallen-angel eyes. How convenient if I could fall madly for him. I could marry into stained glass and a lawn made of money.

"All the more reason I should decline your kind invitation." What did regular girls see in him that I didn't?

"I won't touch you," he said. "I'll protect you."

Some girls choose to marry into stained glass without the madly-fallen bit. But I, at least, would need quite a lot of stained glass.

"I can protect myself."

"You don't know Blackberry Night," he said. "You'll find, I think, that your father has kept you rather ignorant of the world outside the Parsonage."

There wasn't enough stained glass in the world that would convince me to marry Cecil Trumpington: aspiring highwayman and prig.

"I know more than you give me credit for," I said.

This was the wrong thing to say. It was provocative. It made Cecil lean in still farther and say, "Do you," with a most unpleasant inflection on the *do*.

Cecil teased me to reveal my worldly knowledge, and I found amusing ways to sidestep his questions, and on we went with this for quite a while until it occurred to me that this is what is called flirting.

It's a tedious exercise.

It takes no more than a single brain cell to flirt, making it perfect for Cecil and leaving me another few billion to admire the paper napkins, which Eldric had folded into pagodas. To smile at the long-toed dragon feet Eldric had crafted for the braziers. Their claws were painted gold. And to glance from time to time at Eldric and Leanne. Mostly they were wandering about drinking champagne, but I once caught her hiding from Mad Tom behind Eldric. What? The superb horsewoman afraid of poor Mad Tom? She did look ridiculous.

I was jealous, wasn't I? I wanted to be Eldric's only friend. But that's not the way the world works, Briony. You have only one friend, but regular people have dozens.

Yes, I was jealous. I was practicing one of the seven deadly sins (although it doesn't actually take much practice). I probably had all seven.

Anger?

Absolutely. I was especially gifted there. So have a care, Briony! You don't want to blow them all to cinders.

Gluttony?

Just look at my shining plate.

Pride?

Absolutely. I hated myself, but I also loved myself in a hateful way. I loved being clever, I loved being special, I loved being a witch.

Lust?

Don't think about that! But my eyes wandered to Eldric and Leanne. Had they done what Pearl and Artie had done? Stop, Briony! Bad things happen when you're jealous.

Cecil leaned in too close. I felt his hot breath on my cheek. Why didn't I care whether he'd engaged in the Pearl-and-Artie activity? "You've gone all dreamy," he said.

I leaned away. He'd gone all lusty.

"I can't take my eyes off Leanne," I said. Look at someone else, Cecil. "Don't you think her beautiful?" Don't lust after me, Cecil. I'm not a regular girl.

"Too bold for my taste." Cecil took possession of my hand again, tugged me toward him. "I prefer the white goddess style."

The white goddess rose, the Brownie rose. "What did I say about forcing me about? Are you tipsy?"

"Not tipsy!" said Cecil. "No, not that, and I promise I won't— Look here, I'll fetch you a sweet!"

He leapt up, bounded for the sweets table. It looked very much as though he was drunk. But he bounded steadily enough (for a bounder, that is), and he returned with three dishes of trifle, Eldric, and Leanne.

They'd been playing at Metaphor, which had set them to laughing immoderately and sploshing champagne every-where except inside of themselves. Just as well, perhaps, as I suspected they already had plenty inside. Eldric pulled out a chair for Leanne, but she preferred to stand, and so, of course, did he.

"Leanne is a Klimt, of course," said Eldric.

"Is she?" I'd never heard of a Klimt, but I was in no danger of exposing my ignorance, for Eldric staggered into an explanation of what was Klimt-ish about her.

It seemed that Klimt was a painter in Vienna, and it also seemed that Eldric had visited Vienna. He'd told Leanne but not me. Eldric knew just how Klimt would paint Leanne, which was all in gold, with flowers growing from her hair, and he'd arrange her clothes, just so—

Leanne interrupted. "She's a little young for Klimt, don't you think?"

"Oh sorry, sorry, so sorry!" said Eldric.

Eldric was tipsy. Cecil was something else.

I was young, I was dressed in white, I was an underdone sugar cookie next to Leanne's shot-silk taffeta, glinting blue and green, except that there were fewer glints than there might have been, which was because there wasn't as much taffeta as there might have been, which was because Leanne wore her skirts right up to her ankles, quite exposing her enormous feet.

"But I found myself stuck on the sculpture," said Eldric, and for a moment I pictured him impaled on a monument, until I realized that he was still playing at Metaphor. "What sculpture would Leanne be, do you think? You're so clever, Briony, you'll know at once."

An old one, missing its head.

"Unlike you, I haven't traveled," I said, and dug into my trifle, which I'd ordinarily have enjoyed, as it was simply bursting with cream and custard and rum. But I wore white and I'd never been to Vienna, so what was the point of anything?

"I know what Briony would be," said Cecil. "She'd be a Dresden figurine."

"One of those dancing ladies?" I said. "They're not sculptures, and anyway, I'd end up breaking myself."

"I absolutely must step away from the fire," said Leanne,

shaking her laughing hair and looking at Eldric with her curling eyes. As the two of them moved back, Mr. Clayborne joined us to wish Leanne a very happy birthday.

"It's your birthday?" I said.

"Tomorrow, actually," said Leanne.

"We're going to raise a glass at midnight," said Eldric.

This was a birthday party. I was glad her birthday was tomorrow, which was the first day of August. I didn't want her to have been born in July. July was a jolly sort of month, not all hot and puffed up on itself.

Oh, August One! I remembered making Eldric laugh that day in the Alehouse, when I was guessing at his birthday. And here we were: Leanne was an August One. Wouldn't Eldric remember how we'd laughed?

I paid little attention to the conversation, although I did hear Mr. Clayborne say that Eldric looked perfectly dreadful, which I'm glad to say he did.

"Briony!"

I jumped, but it was only Rose, tugging at my sleeve, announcing that the Mirk and Midnight Hour was upon us.

I pressed my hands to my ears. What had I been thinking—or not thinking! I'd let Rose's ten o'clock bedtime slide by, but Rose had kept an eye on the clock. She'd warned me of the midnight chimes.

My hands on my ears hardly muffled the chimes, which are wonderfully penetrating. So was Eldric's voice, calling for attention. "Let us raise our glasses to Leanne on this, her twenty-third birthday!"

"Why, Eldric!" cried Cecil. "I never thought you'd take up with an older woman!"

That's about as clever as Cecil gets, but everyone laughed. It was the champagne, no doubt. Cecil positively glowed. I do have to admit he has lovely skin.

Rose pulled my hands from my ears.

Eldric acknowledged Cecil with a flat Cheshire Cat smile, then tugged it into a real smile as he saluted Leanne with his glass. "To Leanne, the best companion a man could ever have."

The guests broke into a chaos of laughter and teasing. Eldric blushed. Leanne didn't. Perhaps she runs on petrol, not blood.

Eldric had been thinking of Leanne that night, the night of our communion, the night of the Bitch. He hadn't been communing with me at all. He'd been communing with thoughts of Leanne.

"The party's over." Rose's voice was choked with tears. "And Robert didn't come."

"The party's not over," I said, which was idiotic, as I oughtn't to encourage Rose to stay up.

"Yes, it is," said Rose. "It's always over at the Mirk and Midnight Hour."

"Let's go, then." I couldn't bear to look at Eldric with Leanne anymore. I was jealous. And why not?

There are no preconditions for jealousy. You don't have to be right, you don't have to be reasonable. Take Othello. He was neither right nor reasonable, and Desdemona ended up dead. I wouldn't mind Leanne ending up dead. I wouldn't mind exploding her into fireworks of peacock and pearl.

Who cares about pearls, anyway? They're overrated, in my opinion. What is a pearl but a bit of sand and oyster spit?

Rose and I went inside. I didn't say good-bye. This is the advantage of having a sister like Rose. You never have to say good-bye.

Up we went, up the crumple of stairs to our room, with Rose crying the whole time and worst of all, the Brownie following. He wasn't begging yet, but he soon would be, begging for his story.

"Read me a story," said Rose.

"But Rose—"

"Please, mistress!" When the Brownie looked up, one saw mostly the sharp tip of his long nose. "Make me my sweet story!"

"There are no stories!" I spoke to Rose, of course, only to Rose. The Brownie needn't think I was speaking to him.

I said what I always said about the books having burnt, and Rose said what she always said about wishing her book had burnt, and I didn't ask what I always don't ask, which is what on earth is her book? Then I laid myself down where I belonged, on my side of the do-not-cross line. I belonged in the imprint of my own self, which as always, was right next to Rose.

· 17 ·

Mooncrumbs

I awoke at once. Darkness leaned on me, panting in my ear. I looked over the do-not-cross line into the moonlit window. Eldric's face floated in the glass. I clutched the neck of my nightdress before sliding out of bed. There was too much Briony, too little nightdress.

I pulled at the casement, released his face from the glass. He reached through the window, his beautiful hand, his five beautiful fingers outspread. If I were a poet, I'd write about hands, nothing but hands. I touched the whorled petals of my fingertips to his; our hands made the roof of a house.

But, wait: Eldric had been ill only five days ago, the night of the garden party. How could he be so entirely recovered?

"The time has come," he whispered. "Time for wolfgirl to come into the night."

Into the night! An electrical thrill ran between my shoulder blades. "But my nightdress?"

"Into the night!"

I gave him my hand. My whorled fingertips bloomed. Into the night!

The roof was slippery with moonlight. A skitter of roofs ran below, the view spattered with dormers, chimneys, corbels, oriels. Our descent was planned in ingenious bad-boy fashion. Ropes ran over the roofs, dipped over edges to roofs below, where other ropes waited.

Eldric showed me his bad-boy technique. You lay your middle on the rope and squizzle yourself along the rope and over the edge. It is generally thought a good idea to hold tight.

Down he went. I did the same. You might read about such an adventure in a book, but it's different in the moonlight, different to experience it in three dimensions—the rope pressing into your middle, feeling thicker than it looked; the slates too, larger than you'd imagined, smelling of dampness and stored-up weather. Your nightdress bunching up beneath as you slip over the edge, and the passing thought that at least you're wearing undergarments of an unventilated variety. Your feet finding a knot in the rope, which you don't need, but getting another little thrill when you realize that the lion boy-man attended to every detail with you in mind.

Eldric would never plan an initiation for Leanne. He never could. Even if Leanne didn't mind sacrificing her blue-green skirts to the rooftops, she'd never be able to haul herself up and down ropes. She had too much heft up top.

I was fast, I was strong. I almost laughed to see Eldric strolling about on the roof below, as though he weren't tensed to leap should I fall. But I had my own bad-boy muscles. He'd learn to trust them as I did.

We scribbled down the last ropes, tumbled into the garden, which was heavy with the scent of azaleas. Eldric must be feeling very much recovered indeed, to have arranged not only for a full moon, but one of unusual brightness. She was dazzling, glinting off the Flats and the Quicks.

I looked at Eldric. The moon hung in his eyes.

"Into the Slough, wolfgirl!"

Into the Slough!

Impossible that Eldric could love Leanne. Not a girl who thrilled to the hanging of a witch. Not a girl who in the land of metaphor game was a motorcar.

"Bible Ball first." Eldric snatched a gossamer bag from some fold of air.

From what I understand, motorcars are all hot air and rude noises, vented from certain unmentionable regions.

Eldric tied the bag round my wrist with pale taffeta ribbons. Within lay a Bible Ball. Even a Bible Ball was dressed up tonight!

Wolfgirl and lion-boy loped past tangles of blueberry bushes. The moon followed us into the Slough. We snickled through ferns and scrub and moon shavings and root tangles and logs frilled with overlapping mushrooms.

We leapt into snickleways, waded through velvet ooze. We dripped out the far side, trailing smells of sulfur and rotten eggs.

We laughed at the sulfur. We laughed at the rotten eggs. We laughed at the drifts of moon-peel. We laughed.

"Behold the task that lies before you." Eldric took my shoulders and turned me toward a log. "Follow the trail of breadcrumbs until you have found the great treasure of the swamp."

Breadcrumbs?

Shimmering drops ran the length of the log, leading your eye farther into the Slough. Creamy toadstools grew from crevices in the trunk, and in between the crevices were the glittering, glancing mooncrumbs.

"Not breadcrumbs," I said. "Mooncrumbs."

Clever Eldric! You had to look very close to see that the mooncrumbs were nothing but dribbles of lime. They glowed fluorescent in the moonlight.

"Quite right," said Eldric. "That was a test. Your journey is now begun, and remember: Do not return until you have claimed the treasure. Many have sought it; none has returned."

I followed the mooncrumbs to the end of the log. There they dribbled onto the ground and farther into the Slough.

I followed the mooncrumbs, always the mooncrumbs. They made an enormous, luminous treasure map, looping me along paths, circling back upon themselves, beckoning me across snickleways.

Clever, clever Eldric!

I plunged into a snickleway, into a skim of moonlight, into the dark and ooze.

I disappeared. My feet, my knees, my waist. I sank to my chest. Laughter now, Eldric laughing as I plashed about.

"I shall have my revenge!" I shouted.

Oof, ooze to the chest, hard to push, hard to push, but the Amazon of the Swampsea can push through anything, can scramble out the other side, shake herself, lope on. A crash-splash came behind me; Eldric had leapt into the snickleway. I loped ahead, leaping logs frilled with mushroom pantalettes; sploging through ooze and splat; following the mooncrumbs until they ran into nothingness at a cobweb of roots cupping a bundle of oilcloth.

I waited until Eldric caught up with me. I felt like a kettle on the boil, hiss and steam. This—yes, this must be the feeling of happiness. I must hold on to this feeling.

I opened the oilcloth. Inside lay a small, square box. I opened the box. I sat back on my heels.

I didn't know what to say. A skylark sang. It was almost dawn.

In the box lay a wolfgirl made of wire and pearls. Gray pearls. Tiny wires, tiny pearls, twisted round and round into the very shape of a wolf, into the very shape of a girl, into the very shape of Briony.

I didn't know what to say. I clutched the wolfgirl Briony.

"Off we go." Eldric reached for my hand. His eyes were white and gold. "One of the tricks to being a bad boy is not to get caught. My father will be rising soon."

I flew to my feet, mucky to the shoulder, he mucky to the chest, his curls flecked with mud, my own hair hanging over my shoulder in muddy rats' tails.

He wouldn't have made a treasure for Leanne, would he? And anyway, what Eldric-fidget could possibly represent that tangle of clichés?

Birdsong rose all about as lion-boy and wolfgirl walked home. They were hardly tired. "You seemed ill last week," I said. "Especially on the night of the garden party. But here you are, quite—"

Quite what? Quite well? Such a feeble word for an electric boy.

"Quite!" said Eldric. "And in tip-top bad-boy fettle. I attribute my recovery to the restful week I spent with Father, reviewing the letters of application from all my would-be tutors, poor fellows. I resent feeling unwell, you know, as I can no longer say I never fall ill."

We left the Slough for the Quicks. We passed a slurp of green water where an egret stood laughing like a madman.

"It was quite nice, really, spending a week with Father. I hardly wanted to sneak out at all."

By the time we reached the Flats, a silver eyelid winked from the eastern horizon. It winked the Quicks into emerald splotches and pale shimmers.

We reached the back garden. The gray slate roof skittered up and up to my bedroom window. "It's going to be harder going up," I said.

"Mmm," said Eldric. I felt rather than saw that his attention had shifted. "Do you remember what I said just now?"

I followed the direction of his gaze.

"That it was quite nice spending a week with Father."

The garden door was ajar. Father and Mr. Clayborne sat on the stoop, waiting.

"I've changed my mind," said Eldric.

18

Sticks and Stones

We sat in teams of two. Eldric and I at one side of the dining room table, smelling of plant squish and rotten eggs. Father and Mr. Clayborne at the other side, smelling of strong tea and leftover sleep.

It brought to mind the day Eldric arrived. I remembered standing in the dining room with all those men gobbling up the air and clogging up the mirror. But the numbers had changed, the alliances shifted. The teams were equal now.

Mr. Clayborne cleared his throat. "Eldric!" But instead of looking at Eldric, he looked at Father. Father looked at Mr. Clayborne, who cleared his throat again. "I always thought you good-hearted, despite your eternal pranks and mucking about."

"I like mucking about." Eldric turned a couple of toothpicks into swords, which leapt into mortal combat.

"But I never thought you could do anything so wicked."

"Wicked," said Father.

Wicked? I was the wicked one.

"Mucking about isn't wicked." Eldric wore his lazy lion's smile. He didn't mind what he was called. He was a sticks-and-stones sort of person.

"Imagine my surprise," said Father, "when I came to look in on the girls and what do I find?"

His voice hadn't undergone its morning ironing. "Or, rather, what I don't find. I don't find Briony."

"You check on us at night?" How horridly reminiscent of Dracula, a Dracula clergyman, who has just a little trouble with crosses.

"From time to time." Father drew his palms down his cheeks. "It takes me back to the days when we'd sing together at night." He stretched out his eye-wrinkles.

"But I was awake then," I said.

"Yes," said Father, his eye-wrinkle insides all soft and raw. "You were awake then."

"En guard!" Eldric's toothpick-swords leapt to ready position. "Parry—thrust!" The toothpick-sword leapt at my finger.

"Don't touch my daughter!" Father's scratch-lips ripped apart. His teeth were too big.

A horrid, heavy silence followed, a Dracu-clerge silence, while Father reset his lips into their proper scratches.

"So that's what you think." Eldric rolled the toothpicks between his thumb and forefinger.

"What else are we to think?" said Father's wrinkled voice. "The two of you, missing all night."

"Have a little trust!" Eldric's voice rose. "I may lounge about and laugh, but to think you'd believe I'd behave— that is to say, your daughter and I—and I, a guest in your house!"

Snap! Bits of toothpick-sword fell to the table.

Understanding came like a kick to the stomach. They thought Eldric and I were together—together the way boys are with girls.

"Returning at dawn," said Mr. Clayborne. "Together."

"For God's sake!" shouted Eldric. My shoulder-wings jumped. Now they were all shouting, Eldric, Father, Mr. Clayborne.

I plugged my ears. I hate shouting. It makes my ribs go tight.

It was stupid to think I could be a bad boy. Of course I couldn't. There's no point in trying anything new.

You try your first step. What then? You have to walk everywhere.

You have your first conversation with the Boggy Mun. What then? Your sister gets the swamp cough.

You try your first initiation. What then? You have to—

Eldric tapped my arm. I unplugged my ears.

"We appear to have misjudged the situation." Father's eye-wrinkles had slipped back into place. "Mr. Clayborne and I are sorry."

I waited for the *but* part. There was bound to be a *but*.

"It seems I am a bad influence on you," said Eldric. "This comes as quite a surprise, as I have found you wonderfully impervious to influence."

They were to forbid me to see Eldric, weren't they? I needed a safe place to put my gaze. It was easiest to look at the bits of toothpick-sword.

"It's really more that you're a bad influence on Eldric." Mr. Clayborne smiled to show he wasn't serious. "Eldric's

new tutor, Mr. Thorpe, is to arrive next week. You and Eldric were to have lessons together, as you know—"

"I'm not to share Eldric's tutor?"

"I told them you help me learn, but they didn't listen,"
said Eldric.

"I miss Fitz," I said. My brilliant Fitz. "When shall I ever
have lessons?"

"Fitz was hardly suited to be a tutor," said Father.

"Just because of the arsenic?" I said. "It never interfered
with our lessons."

"One doesn't leave one's daughter alone with such a man,"
said Father.

"Why ever not?"

But of course he wouldn't tell me. Which means, of
course, he couldn't think of a single reason why.

The early light came in at the window and glanced off the
stubble on Father's jaw. Father hadn't ironed his voice, and he
hadn't shaved, either. But Father always shaved. Where was
the father who left me alone?

"It's not that you're a bad influence on Eldric," said Mr.
Clayborne. "Of course not. But I've come to see that he's
steadier, more level-headed, with young women who are
rather older than you."

Not Leanne!

Not that rather older young lady!

Yes, Leanne. "She is a clever young lady," said Mr. Clayborne, "and has been wanting to continue her studies, but
her circumstances have been rather straitened of late."

Leanne to study with Eldric? To sit across from him, every
day? She'd take pains, I supposed, to resemble a painting by

this mysterious Klimt—all in gold, flowers in her hair, in a state of tasteful undress.

The rather older young lady, who was very old, indeed. Or so she'd told Rose, oh how terrifically funny, ha-ha, top marks! I let myself imagine she was telling the truth. If she were very old indeed, she'd have to be an Old One, and Eldric would discover her true nature and cast her off in her petticoat . . . No, best keep her in her clothes. I was an Old One, but I'd never be very old indeed. Unfair that we witches live only a mortal lifespan, that we're deprived of the infinity of experience that makes the Boggy Mun so tricky.

The Boggy Mun and his tricks . . . How had I not seen it before? I had a perfectly trick-free bargain to offer the Boggy Mun. A bargain he'd be glad to accept: He'd cure Rose and get what he wanted.

Up you get then, Briony. Put an end to this affecting scene. Paste on your angelic face, tell one of your pretty lies. It's not Father's business where you're going. It's just between you and the Boggy Mun.

19

Make Love Story!

The Quicks sputtered, the sponge squished beneath my feet. I was a bit squishy myself. I'd had no time to bathe: I wanted to catch the Boggy Mun during his morning hours. I had to reach the bog-hole before the mist burnt off.

Eldric and Leanne? Leanne and Eldric! Leanne, sitting in my seat, laughing with Eldric.

Shut up, Briony!

Eldric and Leanne, sharing an inkwell. Eldric turning his pen into a boat, sailing it over his blotter—

Shut up, Briony!

The Quicks breathed slowly, their poisoned breath smelling of sulfur and infection and overripe flesh. They smacked and swallowed, smacked and swallowed.

Soon the Boggy Mun would open up shop. I wore no cloak and had no pockets. I carried my knife and salt in a basket. Little Red Riding Hood, skipping off into the woods. And whom will she meet?

Why, her own self, of course: the wolf. My hand flew to

the gray-pearl wolfgirl hanging about my neck. If I didn't know I couldn't love, I might have thought I loved her.

I sprinkled the salt. I sliced through my mushroom skin. I drizzled my blood onto the salt.

The Boggy Mun came just on time.

He came in the mist, in the midst of his long beard. He came in a tangle of mist and midst. The ancient face peered from the tangle, the crepe-paper skin, the crumpled eyelids.

"I came before," I said.

"Aye."

"You did not grant my request."

"I did not."

"Twice, I have spilt blood and salt."

"Aye," said the Boggy Mun.

"I come today not to beg but to bargain."

The crumpled eyelids lifted, hung, waited.

"I know how to keep the water in the swamp."

The eyelids waited.

"But I shall have need of your help."

The water ran, the wind wailed, the eyes waited.

"I can act on All Hallows' Eve, but not before." I'd let the ghost-children speak for themselves, tell the villagers of the Boggy Mun and the draining and the swamp cough. But I'd have to wait for Halloween, for it is only on that night that ordinary mortals can see and hear the dead.

"I can do something that will make the men turn off the machines. If they do that, the water will stay in the swamp. But you must do your part. You must cure Rose of the swamp cough."

The mist hung motionless.

"If Rose has died, or is near death, I shall have no reason to act."

"Cured, no," said the Boggy Mun. "If'n she be cured, I got me a notion tha'd flight wi' her to them dry lands beyond my reach."

He had a reasonable point.

"This be my bargain. Tha' sister, she don't continue no worse, she don't continue no better. Tha's got no need to fret on her 'twixt now an' All Hallows' Eve."

Halloween. The night the dead rise and walk the earth.

"Tiddy Rex too," I said.

"Tha' sister an' the lad shall survive All Hallows' Day," said the old-parchment voice. "An' if'n matters comes about as tha' says, the cough shall be lifted from tha' sister, an' from all t'other fo'ak what be striked."

The wind wailed, the water ran, the Boggy Mun was gone.

It seems unfair that I can feel worry but not relief.

There, there, Briony: You're asking for too much. After all, the Boggy Mun was surprisingly agreeable. You got what you wanted, didn't you?

Mostly.

Then please shut up.

It was the ghost-children, of course, who should tell the villagers about the draining and the swamp cough. What an idiot to ever have thought of telling the villagers myself. *A fellow can't trust nothing what might be said by a witch.* But they'd believe the ghost-children.

And even if they believed me, they'd know me for a witch and hang me. This way, I'd have a chance to escape. I'd call the ghost-children from their graves. I'd escort the ghost-children to the villagers, urge the ghost-children to tell the villagers their tale. Then I'd disappear. I'd lose myself in the swamp. Best start now, start finding places to hide and crannies in which to store provisions.

I pressed into the shady margins of the Slough.

"Pretty girl!" said a chorus of small, chiming voices. "Pretty girl, make story."

I hadn't thought about the Bleeding Hearts for three years. I'd forgotten how prettily their voices chimed together. On the other hand, they talked far too much and had the most appalling grammar.

"Pretty girl, make love story."

"People don't make stories," I said. "People *write* stories. They *make* tables."

"Make tables!" Their pink blooming faces turned up toward me like thousands of glorious hearts. "Make tables!"

A person could never talk to the Bleeding Hearts.

"Pretty girl, make story at table."

"Use your articles!" I said. "Make *a* story—I mean, write *a* story at *the* table. Or, write *the* story at *a* table. Or—"

"Love story! Love story!"

"Not unless you use your articles."

"Articles! Articles!"

They gave me a headache.

"Pretty girl love!

"Pretty girl love!"

Enough! "Pretty girl love what?" I said.

Stop, Briony! You mustn't start speaking as they do. "What is the object of your sentence?"

"Object! Object!

"Love is object!

"Love is object of desire."

Shut up! You're making me think of Eldric and Leanne turning their pens into boats and swimming them across an ink-blotter sea. There'd be a pirate ship, of course, and a deserted island— Why didn't I just kill myself?

"Pretty girl love pretty boy."

Boy? "I don't love any boy."

"Pretty girl laugh with pretty boy."

Eldric and Cecil were both pretty boys, but you couldn't laugh with Cecil.

"Pretty girl laugh with pretty boy."

At last they'd put an object to the sentence.

"Pretty boy! Pretty boy!

"Laugh!

"Play!

Light nibbled at the edges of my vision. Blue flames skittered over the muck, yellow flames dove into the earth. The Wykes were out early today, glinting, flirting, teasing, luring.

"Love story!

"Pretty girl love!"

The Bleeding Hearts were idiots.

Laughing and playing with Eldric was fun, but it wasn't love. But the Bleeding Hearts were spirits of love and romance. They had no room in their tiny minds for a person who didn't love anyone.

"Love story!"

I turned away. There's no point in saying good-bye to the Bleeding Hearts. It's not in their vocabulary. "Make story, pretty girl." Off I went, but their chiming voices carried a long way. "Make love story!"

Forget them, Briony. Think about the early hours of All Hallows' Day. Think about how the villagers will scrabble after you, all arsey-varsy, armed with anything to hand: pitchforks, horsewhips, toothpicks. You can elude them if you get a good head start. It's the scent hounds you want to worry about. You'll have to make a few circumspect inquiries about how to muddle your tracks and muddle your scent and muddle the hounds. You'll muddle them further by taking to the snickleways. Pity you haven't a boat.

On I went, through spinachy water, into a gray incandescence and the smell of rot. The incandescence insinuated itself beneath my hand as a dog might insinuate its head. I sprang back, but the tattered flesh did not. It quivered.

The Dead Hand slithered and oozed. It tapped finger to thumb as though biting the air. But tapping is crisp; this was all flab and squish.

"No!" I said.

The bloated fingers slimed over my hand, oozed round my wrist.

"You can't!" I said.

The Dead Hand oozed tighter.

"I'm one of you," I said. "I'm a witch!"

The Hand pulled. Tightened and pulled.

What should I do, what should I do?

It wasn't painful, not yet, but the thought of the pain to come was itself a kind of pain.

I sat back on my knees, pulled away. The Dead Hand pulled toward. The bog-hole spat and chuckled.

The Dead Hand did not absorb my warmth; I absorbed its chill. The Wykes sparked up, yellow, blue, glinting, laughing—everything was laughing, the bog, the wind, the Wykes. But not the Dead Hand. It didn't laugh.

The slop splashed at my knees. The wind snickered.

The Dead Hand was silent. It pulled. I pulled back. The earth trembled.

The Dead Hand was silent. It pulled.

Articles, articles! Use your articles!

The Dead Hand pulled and squeezed, pulled and squeezed.

I'd brought no articles, no Bible Ball.

"I'm a witch!"

The Hand didn't care.

But I'm a witch, a witch!

Crack! My wrist went *crack!* It was the sound as much as the pain that made the sick come spraying from my mouth.

The Hand didn't care. It pulled.

Pull and *stretch*. It wasn't just bones that held my wrist together. There were other things for which I had no name. Things that could be pulled, things that could stretch. Why had I never known them, given them names?

My wrist was small. How could it fit so much pain? *Stretch!* The *crack* had been fast, the *stretch* was slow. How could one wrist occupy the universe of my mind?

Crack, and *stretch*, and now *snap!* I had nothing in my stomach to lose.

Someone shouting now. "Bloody hell!"

The pretty boy.

The pretty boy pulled. He was London soap and pine.

200

The pretty boy cracked and stretched and snapped. He was tawny flesh and lion's paw. His paw dug for my hand.

"Hold on!"

But it was the Hand holding on. It was the Hand squeezing.

"Hold on!"

Hold on to the pretty boy? I could hold on to him only with my thoughts. *Pretty boy laugh! Pretty boy play.*

The Hand squeezed. *Love is object of desire.* Those chiming words, hold on to them, hold on.

The Hand squeezed. *Pretty girl love pretty boy.* Hold on to those words, hold on.

But the Hand squeezed. It squeezed out my thoughts. It squeezed out my brain-light. I was disappearing. I saw my brain-light go drip-drip-dripping out my mind.

Out it went, drip-drip-drip, until I was snuffed out.

· 20 ·

Happily Ever After

Dark and light, dark and light. That was the world. The world was like lace. Lace is dark and light. Stepmother wore lace. Leanne wore lace.

Leanne and Eldric, dark and light.

When we think of lace, we think of white, but without the dark, the in-between bits, there'd be nothing to look at.

Dark and light, dark and light.

Bones are hollow. Bones are webbed with lace.

Anesthesia, Dr. Rannigan!

Bones can hurt—how they can hurt!

Take a hand, crush it slo-o-o-o-w-ly, splinter the bones, crumble the lace, squish away the negative space.

Anesthesia!

"Drink it down." Eldric's voice pressed a spoon to my lips. "There you go, every last drop!" Liquid trickled down my throat.

All those airy hollows, gone.

I swallowed. Swallowing tore my hand.

Anesthesia!

Dark and light, the world was dark and light.

Dark and light, mint and apple.

Go away!

But my voice was lost, and anyway, the Brownie never listened.

Mint and apple. Dark and light.

The smallest eye-twitch tore my hand-lace.

"Every last drop!" Eldric's voice was honey.

The honey voice sang.

> *I know where I'm going,*
> *And I know who's going with me.*
> *I know whom I love,*
> *But the dear knows whom I'll marry.*

Once I had been in the roar-time of my life. Now I was in the hush-time. The people who sat with me were in the hush-time. They made hush-time sounds: a mouse-squeak as they sit in the chair, a crumble of rockers on wood. Father singing, lullaby-soft.

> *O I fear ye are poisoned, Lord Randal, my son!*
> *O I fear ye are poisoned, my bonny young man!*
> *O yes! I am poisoned; Mother, make my bed soon . . .*

Stop: That's not a hush-time song!

> *I got eels boiled in eel broth; Mother make my bed soon,*
> *For I'm weary wi' hunting and fain would lie doon.*

That's a roar-time song. Stop!

Father didn't stop.

Eldric sat on the end of my bed. His end went down; my end went up. *O I fear ye are poisoned.* I had to erase that song.

"'I Know Where I'm Going,'" I said.

"Briony?" Eldric's end of the bed went up. He stood at the pillow end. My eyelids felt his gaze.

"Did you say something?" His voice was thick as porridge.

"'I Know Where I'm Going.'"

"Shall I sing it?" he said.

I flapped my good hand. Yes!

My end of the bed went up.

Eldric cleared his throat. He sat so long, now silent, now clearing his throat, that I slipped back into darkness.

"I have here a ladies' hatpin," said Eldric. "I know you are wondering what this superb specimen of masculinity would want with a hatpin. But what you don't know is that Tiddy Rex and I are building a castle, and of course, every castle needs a catapult, and what every catapult must have is something to pult. Even as I speak, this hatpin is being transformed into an enormous medieval stone."

Eldric's voice was hush-time, but a catapult is not a hush-time pursuit, and neither was the smell. It was a roar-time smell: wood smoke, mixed with a warm, brownish spice, mixed with a whiff of the fruited soaps sold at the Christmas fair.

"It takes a dozen men to heave this stone into the catapult—or women, of course, if they are boxing champions, like you."

When a person is ill, a whiff of roar-time is better than any tonic. I opened my eyes. Sun slanted in the window. It lay curled in the palm of my left hand, my wicked hand.

Where was my virtuous hand? My virtuous arm was

heavy, too heavy to raise itself. I couldn't see the end of it.

I lay in the sewing room. I didn't like that. This is where Stepmother had lain. The smell of sickness had infected the room. I memory-smelled it, a bloated oozy smell, toad-scum, stagnant water. It crimpled the underside of my tongue.

I memory-smelled eels. Eels in eel broth. That was a sick-making smell. Where was my mint-and-apple Brownie?

It was good to open my eyes. It let light into my brain. I was in the sewing room, but the toad-scum smell was gone. It was now just wood smoke and brown spice and fruited soap.

Eldric had brought new smells with him. He'd brought new sounds with him. The sound of his hollow whistle: *If a body meet a body, comin' thro' the rye.*

Stepmother had never cared to light a fire, but there was a fire in the grate.

I heard him look at me: The chair went *crumble–crumble*—stop!

My heart ticked off the seconds until Eldric bent over me; then his face filled my mind.

"There you are!" he said. "I've been waiting for you."

He'd become gaunt, hollow as his own whistle, save for the under-eye bits, which were scribbly and pale.

"You look tired." I'd grown a stranger to my own voice. It made the faintest of chimes, like the ticking of a fingernail on glass.

"That's what I'm supposed to say to you." His smile pouched out the under-eye bits.

I had all sorts of deep, meaningful questions to put to him, things to tell him, but I couldn't think what they were.

"I'm also supposed to tell you that talking might overtire you."

"This is Briony, remember? Since when did talking ever tire her!"

Eldric sounded more like himself when he laughed.

"I'll be listening," I said, "even if I close my eyes. Talk to me. Tell me what you've been doing while I've been ill."

"I've been right here."

I closed my eyes. "Tell me about the harvest festival."

"I didn't go," said Eldric. "I've been right here."

That was interesting.

"Tell me about the hayride." I'd had visions of Eldric and Leanne on the hayride. Drinking from the same thermos; sharing a blanket; and when their fellow hay-riders left, lingering, perhaps, in the hay—

"I'll go next year," he said.

"What about Mr. Thorpe?"

"Boring," said Eldric.

My lips were too tired to smile. "But lessons?"

"I couldn't have lessons when you were so ill. When we thought you might die!"

No lessons with Leanne!

"Any excuse to avoid lessons," I said.

But Eldric didn't answer. All he could do was clear his throat.

It may have been hours later or days later when I asked about my hand. Everything is confused when you're ill.

"You can still feel a hand, can't you, even if it's been torn off?"

I realize now how hideous the question must have sounded. But I didn't mean it that way. It was simply that I knew that people who've lost a bit of themselves (let's say it's a hand) report that they still feel it. They don't really, of course, because the hand is miles away, in the swamp. But their brain thinks they feel it. I know because I read this in the *London Loudmouth*.

I'd never seen Father and Eldric so flustered. They rushed to assure me that my hand was still attached to my wrist. They interrupted and spoke over each other, which was not like either of them, but their meaning was clear. My hand was badly injured—injured, yes, it was injured—

They were trying to avoid words like *mangled*. I could tell. No wonder my arm was so heavy. It had been plastered up, like something in a Poe story. Dr. Rannigan set the bones as best he could.

"How many bones did he set?" I cared about it much less than they did. It's my Florence Nightingale calm, I suppose.

There was a pause.

"Twenty-seven," said Father.

There was a question mark in that pause. "How many bones are in a hand?"

Another pause.

"Twenty-seven," said Eldric.

"What on earth were you doing?" Eldric asked, the next time we were alone.

"Doing?"

"You left the knife beside the bog-hole," said Eldric. "After I'd got you home and cleaned up a bit, we saw the cuts."

The cuts? Of course, the knife, and my mushroom skin, and spilling blood for the Boggy Mun. How long ago that had been.

"How did you find me?"

"Don't try to sidetrack me," said Eldric. "What were you doing?"

"But really," I said. "How?"

"I can always find you," said Eldric. "Don't ever think you can hide from me. Now—"

"You have to tell me first," I said. "Because I'm sick."

"Oh Lord," said Eldric, but he laughed. "It was brought forcibly to our attention that you'd left the Parsonage when your father found he had something more to say to you. My manly intuition told me to look in the swamp. You weren't on the Flats, I found the knife in the Quicks—" He turned away, sat on the end of the bed. Up I went.

"You found me in the Slough?"

A pause; Eldric cleared his throat. "And I'd had the good sense to bring a Bible Ball. What were you thinking? Or not thinking?"

"I wasn't not thinking anything," I said. "What did Father want to talk to me about?"

"You'll have to ask him."

"He'll never tell me now," I said. "It was just the energy of the moment when he thought—well, you know."

"You are not a comfortable girl to be with," said Eldric.

"I shall persist in being uncomfortable until you tell me."

"You're going to be sorry," said Eldric.

"I shan't."

I could feel Eldric shrug. "It had to do with the *Well, you know* part of it, with his assumption I'd lured you into the swamp to—well, not to put too fine a point on it—to seduce you. And then it occurred to him to wonder whether you actually knew what a seduction involves. The details, I mean."

I spread my wicked left hand over my face, but surely slices of crimson tide showed between my fingers. "You're right," I said.

"That you're sorry?"

"That I'm sorry."

"What shall I tell your father?" said Eldric.

"Don't tell him anything!"

"You teased it out of me," said Eldric. "You ought to answer. It has your father worried, actually."

"Tell him I read a lot." I could almost hear the curling lion's smile in Eldric's voice.

"Very well. Now will you answer my question? Tell me what you were doing in the Quicks, with that knife."

But I couldn't tell him. "It's unfair, I know, but—"

"You can't tell me, of course." My end of the bed went down. Eldric stood beside me. He pulled my hand from my face.

"I have a request." Eldric rolled back his shirtsleeve, offered me his forearm. "The next time you need to make a blood offering, please ask me for a contribution."

I stared at his forearm, bulging with bad-boy veins.

"It's as red as yours," he said. "I promise."

I nodded.

"I know you won't, though," said Eldric. "Because despite being Fraters—"

"Frateri," I said.

"Frateri, you still keep everything to yourself and don't

ask for help. The blood offering, the pumping station—tell me this, at least: Are the two connected?"

A gulp of silence hung between us.

"I have the advantage," said Eldric, "of being able to wear you down. You have the disadvantage of being wearable and of not being able to leave. I shall keep at it until you tell me."

I nodded.

"Are you telling me they're related?"

I nodded.

Eldric knew more about me than anyone since Stepmother.

"I'm here to make a bet with you," said Eldric.

"What sort of bet?"

"I'm willing to bet that you'll go to Blackberry Night."

"Have you been talking to Cecil?" I said.

"Never, if I can help it."

"He mentioned it too, at your garden party. But the reverend's daughter can't go to Blackberry Night."

"I'm not finished," said Eldric. "I'm betting you'll go to Blackberry Night if we can guarantee you one hundred percent—yes, one hundred percent, ladies and gentlemen—that the Reverend Larkin will never find out."

"That's an odd sort of bet." But it wasn't a bet at all. It was an invitation. He wasn't inviting Leanne; he was inviting me.

"Pearl and I have been plotting. She's making you a frock woven of moonbeams, and you shall wear it to Blackberry Night."

"I really could never do that."

"Why not?"

Why not? Because Father disapproved? Because he delivered his mighty sermon against Blackberry Night?

Do I want Father to guide me in such matters? Do I want Father to place his fingerprints on my thoughts?

I do not.

I woke up to Rose coughing.

She stood over me, coughing and staring so hard a person couldn't help but wake up.

"Eldric prefers that I not awaken you," she said. "He says you need rest. But I prefer to talk to you, so I can make you better. It was quite a difficult decision."

"I shall get better on my own," I said.

"It's not that sort of getting better," said Rose.

"What sort of getting better is it?"

"That's a secret," said Rose.

At least I needn't fret about Rose's illness. The Boggy Mun had frozen the progression of her disease until Halloween, at which time she'd either get better, or die.

"I knew it!" She sat on the bed. She almost sat on the Brownie. "I knew you were all one color. Your face matches your nightdress. But Eldric says not to worry. You'll be pretty again when you recover."

"Eldric said that?"

Rose nodded.

"Perhaps you should bring me a looking glass," I said.

"I prefer not," said Rose. "I have no time to lose."

"Not yet, mistress," said the Brownie. "Don't look yet."

"I prefer so," I said. "I have all the time in the world."

In the end, Rose fetched a looking glass. I studied my face as one might look at a portrait of oneself.

"You're not listening," said Rose. "I made a very difficult decision. I want you to be able to see the secret."

Rose was right about my all-one color, and worse: There were thin vertical lines to either side of my mouth. I knew what a soppy sort of novel might call them: lines of pain. I knew what a non-soppy sort of Briony might call them:

Ugly.

"Where is Eldric?" I said.

"Lessons," said Rose. "I have a very important question to put to you."

"Is he with Mr. Thorpe?"

Of course he was, but Rose is not an *of course* sort of person. "Yes."

"Is he with Leanne?"

"Yes," said Rose. "Now, you really must attend properly: How does midnight look to you?"

"Late."

"I don't mean that," said Rose. "How does it look to your eyes?"

"Dark," I said. "But sometimes there's a moon."

"How does before midnight look to you?"

"How much before midnight?"

Rose paused. "I think that might be a secret."

"You have so many secrets, Rose!" I ticked them off on my fingers. "My birthday. That book of yours you wished had burnt. The different sort of getting better, the one that doesn't have to do with my hand. The secret you want me to see."

"Yes," said Rose. "How does before midnight look to you?"

"If it's five hours before midnight, it might look like twilight, which means the sky's a very deep sapphire blue and the air is like a Persian cat. If it's ten minutes before midnight, it looks just the way midnight does."

"That's no help at all," said Rose. "I shall be obliged to consult Eldric."

My hand hurt more than usual. How horrid it would be if my hand were really missing, and the pain was that long-distance pain I'd learned about in the *London Loudmouth*. My missing hand might never stop hurting because the pain would be all in my mind.

I raised my arm and looked at the monstrosity of bandages. They said my real hand was in there. That's what they said.

Pearl buttoned me up and attended to the other tasks she believed my left hand incapable of performing. There was to be a tea party that afternoon, but I knew no more than that. A surprise was brewing, in addition to the brewing of tea. The past few days had been full of whisperings, followed by sudden silences whenever I drew near.

Rose came dancing in to fetch me. "We've a surprise for you, but I mustn't tell. That's what Father said."

Father needn't have said anything. Rose has a strict sense of honor, or perhaps it's a simple inability to break the rules.

She was rosier than usual, and she smiled her real-girl smile. She was Pinocchio at the story's end.

"Am I to see it now?" I said.

"If you prefer to come." Rose led me down the corridor, which smelled of sawdust and paint and varnish. I hesitated at Father's study because there was nothing else down the corridor save the remains of the library. But Rose passed the study. I dragged myself on.

We were mixed up today, Rose and I. Usually, I was the one who sped along on wolfgirl feet. Rose was the one who dawdled and stumbled and complained. But my legs had gone all snively, and now that we were nearing the library, they went all wet-handkerchief-y, which was probably because I'd been ill, but it could also be because I don't like surprises.

"Hurry up!" said Rose. "You have to go in first."

But still, I hesitated. The house-fixing smells were in there, as well as the voices and laughter, and among the voices was Leanne's. Leanne? Some foolish part of me had hoped she and Eldric were no longer friends. After all, Eldric hadn't gone on the hayride.

Foolish Briony. A regular girl would have known.

"I prefer that you open the door," said Rose.

My right hand was still encased in plaster. I turned the knob with my scarred left hand. The door opened upon the color of honey. Upon honey-colored wainscoting, gleaming with beeswax. Upon a honey-colored floor with an island of crimson carpet.

"Briony preferred to attend the party!" said Rose.

And more. A piano; Father's fiddle; Mother's rocker; window seats tucked beneath diamond mullions; a table, too new to have accumulated the usual rubbish that breeds on horizontal surfaces.

"Are you surprised?" said Rose.

"Very surprised!"

But my memories of the library were stronger than this

214

new reality. The flames; my hand; my screams; the smell of burnt flesh, horribly delicious.

I looked about for something familiar, beyond the acres of honeyed wood and glinting teeth, surrounded by smiles. Eldric stepped forward and with him came Leanne. She'd foamed herself up with pearls and lace.

She looked like a rabid dog.

"I want to give Briony my present first," said Rose.

"That's right, Rose," said Father. "You be first."

"It's not against the rules to give you a present." She handed me a slim packet wrapped in a sheet of the *London Loudmouth*. "That's because you have no birthday."

Beneath the sheet of newspaper lay more sheets of paper, but these were precious papers from Rose's collection. Creamy paper, and linen-y paper, and pebbled and ragged-along-the-edge paper. I looked at them, sheet by sheet.

"Do you like them?" said Rose.

"I like them very much, Rose. They're beautiful."

I found myself extending my forefinger and after a pause, Rose did the same. We touched fingertips. I'd all but forgotten this old ritual. It's a way to hug Rose without actually hugging her. Rose doesn't much like people to touch her. Father suggested it, I think.

"Now you can write your stories again," said Rose. "I like the ones where I'm the hero."

I drifted about the library. It was a crisper, younger version of its old self. There was even a scatter of books on the shelves, *David Copperfield, Jane Eyre*, a collection of Yeats. We used to spend a great deal of time in the library before Stepmother entered our lives.

The tea was already laid out: lovely little sandwiches and blueberry pie—the blueberries were at their peak.

Cecil waved me over from one of the window seats. He'd been lying in wait for me, with two plates of pie. I took the one with more whipped cream, set it on the seat between me and Cecil. How convenient to be unable to hold it. I let my left hand take the fork; no one could expect me to use my right. My hand was like a puppy, delirious at being let out at last.

A train shrilled into the square. The London–Swanton line had been launched while I was ill. How I wished I'd been clever enough to talk the Boggy Mun into curing Rose of the swamp cough, rather than pausing it in its course. Then she and I would be off on one of the trains. Good-bye, Cecil. Good-bye, Leanne. Good-bye, good-bye, good-bye.

But at least I needn't worry about Rose getting worse. The Boggy Mun had promised that Rose would survive Halloween. She would likely die later if the draining didn't stop, but for the moment, there was no need to take special care of her. She wouldn't get better, but she couldn't get worse.

The library was divided into little fiefdoms: Cecil and I on the window seat; Father, Mr. Clayborne, and Mr. Thorpe at the table; Rose at the piano, plunking out random notes; and Leanne and Eldric leaning against the back wall, far from the fire, despite the chill. I remembered Fitz always teasing me, pointing out that Stepmother never liked to stay too long near a fire. He didn't care for Stepmother and loved to provoke me into defending her. I always thought he'd change his mind once he became better acquainted with her, but you can't become better acquainted with a person when you refuse to spend time in her company.

Here came Leanne, marching across our border without so much as showing her papers. Eldric followed, wagging his tail.

"Eldric has a gift for you," said Leanne. Eldric reached past her, a chain of crystals dangling from his fingers. He'd gone pale and ill, just as he'd been at the garden party. That would teach him to take up lessons without me!

"It's beautiful," I said. Eldric had strung the crystal pendants of a broken lamp onto one of Father's fiddle strings. It was as lovely and mysterious as a snowflake.

Only Father and Mr. Clayborne did not quite admire it. Father said nothing, but I suppose he'd envisioned another future for his fiddle string. Mr. Clayborne said it was lovely but when would Eldric ever find a focus in life?

"I beg your pardon, Mr. Clayborne," said Leanne's dusk-lined voice. "I don't mean to be discourteous, but I cannot agree with you."

Didn't she ever get sick of wearing green?

"I believe there are many things about Eldric's playful projects that are useful. It's his gift, don't you see?"

"I have a gift," said Rose.

"So you do," said Eldric, but his eyes never left Leanne's face.

"He creates the most astonishing pieces from absolutely nothing." Leanne smiled at Eldric as though she'd invented him. "Just imagine what he might do if he were to turn that sense of play and humor into a business. Designing children's games, perhaps."

"With firemen!" said Rose.

"And treasure maps," I said, but I had to swallow hard. Why hadn't I been the one to recognize Eldric's gift? I swallowed

217

again. Jealousy lodges in the throat like a hard, green apple.

"And lollipop trees," said Eldric, swiping at his brow. He was sweating. "We mustn't forget the lollipop trees."

Even Mr. Clayborne laughed, and everyone drifted away, except Cecil.

No wonder Eldric sought out Leanne. She defended him to Mr. Clayborne. She recognized his gift.

"Come here, Rose." I patted the cushion beside me. "Tell me just what sort of story you want."

Rose sat between me and Cecil, thank goodness. She made a better shield than the pie plate.

"What heroic act do you want to perform, Rose?"

I almost called her Rosy. Rosy Posy, Briony Vieny.

"I want a story where I save you."

I could do that. I could imagine Rose into saving me. "Which of the papers shall I use first?"

I began writing when everyone had left. I wanted to let my left hand frolic. No need to make the poor thing feign the awkwardness they'd expect.

I read the ending aloud. "And thus it was that clever Rose saved her sister from the monster of the sea."

You could write your way into happiness. It might not be the happiness you'd experience if Eldric pushed Leanne from a cliff, but there's a firefly glimmer in writing something that would please Rose.

"And they all lived happily ever after."

Comin' Thro' the Rye

The moonlight slipped and shifted beneath my feet; my legs dissolved into mud. The swamp has no beginning, it has no end, it's all fringes and wisps and foreverness.

I was porous. I had my own fringes—my ten fingers, my fringe of mucky toes.

It was September 29, it was Blackberry Night, and I dissolved into the swamp. My naked foot merged with iris and orchid and lily. My frock of moonbeams purred against my legs. The earth quivered as I ran, I quivered as I ran, as I ran on spider legs of moonlight, in an ecstasy of fear, in a fear of ecstasy.

My feet were naked, my hands were naked, no more plaster of Paris. My right hand was a shriveled root. But that's all right, here in the swamp.

I avoided Cecil; I avoided Eldric. I chose to come alone, even though Eldric had invited me. But I'd rather be alone than with Eldric, when what he really wanted was to frolic with Leanne.

Feet sloshing and splattering, shouts and screams. I brushed through fringed gentians. I brushed through comb-edged alder leaves. I brushed through netted moonbeams. I brushed—but an arm caught me round the waist.

"Drink up!"

My throat was tilted back. Bees-wine buzzed down my throat. The drink-up voice ran his fingers down the curve of my neck. My elbow jabbed, sank into belly. The belly grunted. On I ran.

My moonbeam skirts were pale moths, fluttering past the skulls of giant mushrooms. I sank into peat moss and autumn leaves, into the musk-stink of dying cabbage and the splosh of decay.

Voices laughed and ran past me in the shadows. I ran through a tangle of moonlight; I ran into a copper sea. *If a body meet a body, comin' thro' the rye.*

I was wild, I was wolfgirl. I was light as a moonbeam, my bones were filled with lace. I ran past chiming voices. "Pretty girl love pretty boy."

A figure came at me.

"Briony!" Cecil, calling, running. "Why didn't you wait for me!

"It's Eldric, isn't it? He's your protection!" Cecil's voice was thick. He'd been drinking.

"I don't need protection."

"No?" Cecil's raw-fish eyes looked into mine. "Let's see if you're right."

I didn't want to talk to him, but Cecil snatched at me,

seized my wrist. "You've kissed him, haven't you?"

"Let me go!"

He pulled me close. I remembered how to make a fist. I punched. But my fist glanced off Cecil's chest. I hadn't known he was so solid.

Cecil's lips were wet. "By God, you'll kiss me too!"

Kiss me too! Fear whispered at the margins of my thoughts. I twisted and tugged, but he held me fast. He had no lacework bones, no latticed chambers, no spaces or echoes or songs.

"You've been drinking!" My hand lumped itself into a fist. That's right, Briony. Squeeze out all the spaces, squeeze yourself to stone.

"You're the one I want." Cecil's voice had lost its edges; his words ran together. His pupils were huge, the iris no more than a pale rim. Splinters of fear ran down my back.

His hands crunched into my wrists. Too hard! His lips pressed into my lips. Too hard! My lips pressed against my teeth. His man's weight pressed against my girl froth; his chest crumpled my girl-lungs.

I bit. I tugged. I ripped.

He reared back, blood ran down his chin. I smashed my stone-fist to his face, but he snatched my other wrist too.

He licked the blood from his lips. His eyes were a lunar eclipse. He pulled me close. I smelled the starch in his shirt. Such a very clean smell. He forced my head back. I smelled lavender. It's shaving cream; Father uses it too. Such a very clean smell.

He held my chin. "No more biting!" He leaned forward. His hard mouth pressed, broke my lips. Blood and spit and sick pooled in my throat. I gagged. His hot fingers crushed, bent my wrist the wrong direction. He parted my lips with his—

But I staggered back. I was free, I was froth. Moonbeams and air touched me. Just moonbeams and air.

Here came a lightning fist, sizzling past my shoulder, crashing into Cecil's middle. Cecil folded in on himself.

Eldric. It was Eldric.

I was froth. I could breathe.

Cecil lumbered to his feet. Eldric slammed him with an elbow. Cecil yelped and fell.

Eldric picked him up and hit him again.

Eldric picked him up and hit him again.

Eldric picked him up. He meant to hit him again, but Cecil flopped about like a rag doll. Eldric picked him up by the belt and hauled him away.

I sat. The rye waved above my head. I should run. A wolf-girl would run, but I was sitting and clutching my skirts. My hands were shaking. Those bird-bone hands, they shook as they clutched a fistful of moonbeams.

Eldric found me in the sweet, damp earth, clutching my skirts. He found me in the rye. He looked at me with his switch-on eyes. "Did he hurt you?"

I shook my head. Why, of all the words in our bounteous language, did those four tip me into ordinary girlness? I couldn't speak. My throat was clotted with words. There was a pressure behind my cheekbones. I wished I could cry like an ordinary girl; I wished I could relieve the pressure. But a witch doesn't deserve to cry.

Eldric wrapped his arm around me.

I looked into Eldric's electric eyes. Cecil has switch-off eyes. Eldric felt along my arm. Up my jaw and cheekbone, over the crown of my head. He was checking to see if I was broken.

I thought of offering him my wrist. It needed to be cradled and rocked and lullabied. I turned, but my cheek got in the way of his lips. He melted his lips into my skin. Not a kiss, a melt. I could allow a melt. That wasn't what Cecil tried to do. I let the melt soak in.

I wanted to look at him. I turned, my lips brushed his.

I leaned into the warm-bread softness of Eldric's lips. They were soft and wet, just a little wet, but I could drown in them.

Drowning. Only that.

Electricity trembled between us. I tasted Eldric's lips. They were butter and silk. We hardly touched, but there was so much electricity.

Now a kiss, deep and soft, and deeper still. Eldric was never hard and crushing; he was only soft and deep. Only that. Time flew by on fringed moth wings. I was blooming, petals unfurling, soft as cream. Those silk-and-butter lips slid down my neck, traced the margin of my neckline.

Only that.

He lowered himself on top, never hard and crushing. He wrapped his forearms under my shoulders, laced his fingers behind my head. He looked down, I looked up. Our lips didn't touch, but all the rest of us was touching. A velvet-and-cream electricity trembled between us.

Only that.

Only that, but Eldric pushed himself up, onto his palms. I looked up at him, he looked down at me, down the length of his arm.

"We can't do this." His mouth made a red hole in his face. "I meant what I told your father. I'll take you home."

I was shaking again. I pulled at my skirts, which were riding up my legs. My wrist hurt. I couldn't make myself decent. That kiss, that electricity, those silk-and-butter lips—those belong to regular girls. It's regular girls who have that I-don't-want-to-stop feeling. It's regular girls who have surprise weddings at Advent. Not Briony Larkin.

Eldric made a queer noise, something between a groan and a sigh, and pushed himself to his feet. He was slower than usual. He didn't leap his usual lion's leap.

He reached for my hand. Eldric, the bad boy, would help me to my feet.

I didn't take his hand. I was wolfgirl; I sprang and ran.

Eldric called after me. "Wait!" But he didn't mean it. He'd come to meet Leanne in the moonlight, in the rye-shadows. He meant to lay her down in this copper sea, in these copper shadows. He meant—

But the wolfgirl ran. She was strong and fast, except for her wrist, which hurt. She ran away from her thoughts. She ran.

Eldric didn't follow.

· 22 ·

How Is Mister E|dric?

Eldric took ill. He took ill on Blackberry Night, and kept to his bed.

How do you suppose this witch reacted? Can you guess what she might have thought?

Such a relief!

That's what she thought.

The very sight of Eldric would curl the witch into a shriveled pea of embarrassment.

A witch does not make a good friend.

Let's remind ourselves how this particular witch works: She is near a person, she is jealous of that person, that person falls from a swing and bashes her head.

The witch meets a person on Blackberry Night. There ensues a shriveled-pea of a situation, and that person falls ill.

How is it that I am always surprised?

I was alone at breakfast the first day, save for the Brownie. I was relieved. I began a new story for Rose.

I declined to answer a letter from Cecil.

I was alone at breakfast the second day, save for the Brownie. I was relieved. I finished the story.

I declined to answer a second letter from Cecil.

I avoided breakfast the third day, because I was sure to see him. I declined to answer a third letter from Cecil.

I was alone at breakfast the fourth day, save for the Brownie.

A strong young man might have a cold for a couple of days, three at the outside. But four days?

"You doesn't got no appetite?" said Pearl, clearing my plate. I shook my head. I was wedged tight inside my rib cage.

I rose. The Brownie rose too. But just now, I'd rather look at the Brownie than at the poached eggs, quivering in their cups. "How is Mister Eldric?"

Poached eggs? What kind of person would invent such a thing?

"He don't be well, miss, an' that Miss Leanne, she be making him worse." Pearl's words poured out, as though they'd been pressing against a dam.

"She don't let Mister Eldric rest. Such a deal o' rubbish she been fetching him, bits o' sea glass an' shells an' driftwood, but to her it don't be rubbish. She setted Mister Eldric to making—I doesn't know what-all, miss."

A regular person wouldn't stand there, looking at Pearl's hands, thinking she might be making Puree of Christ. A regular person would say something. She would sound as though she cared. "How does he look?"

You're an idiot, Briony: There must be something more regular.

"Mister Eldric's face?" said Pearl. "It minded me on your stepmother's face, miss, when she been took ill."

Eldric, as ill as Stepmother? Did he look as—as reduced as Stepmother had? Like bread scraped of butter, milk skimmed of cream, cups drained of ale.

"Mister Eldric, he be working hisself hollow," said Pearl. "If you'll pardon the liberty, miss, Mr. Clayborne, he best fetch Dr. Rannigan, an' that right quick."

"Thank you, Pearl." How calm I was. I was too big for my skin. "I'll see to Dr. Rannigan."

See to Dr. Rannigan. What did that mean? Ought I to consult Father? Mr. Clayborne? My decision-making machinery was jammed. The Brownie followed, lacing his grasshopper fingers in distress. He had a nasty habit of picking up my thoughts.

I looked into the parlor, into the library—empty, empty. I knocked on Father's study door. Silence, empty. Time snarled in on itself.

I spoke aloud. "What should I do?"

"It be early yet, mistress," said the Brownie. "Could be tha'd catch the doctor at breakfast."

"You'll come with me?"

Why on earth did I speak to the Brownie?

"O' course, mistress."

Perhaps he'd worn me down.

And now I was speaking to him, although it was yet another betrayal of Stepmother. I'd already betrayed her in so many ways. Going into the swamp, frolicking about rather than working out how to apprehend her murderer.

Out we went, the Brownie and I, into the snarl of time, twisting and tangling through the village to Dr. Rannigan's house.

His housekeeper said he was attending another patient.

"Do you expect him back soon?" I said.

His housekeeper was sure she didn't know.

"Might he have stopped at the Alehouse?"

His housekeeper said it was not her place to remark upon the doctor's attachment to the demon drink, and that I might perhaps take myself off, as she had work to do.

"How dare he!" I said to the Brownie, which made no sense, but the Brownie, being the Brownie, understood. Dr. Rannigan was our Dr. Rannigan. We needed him now.

I sat on a stile outside the doctor's house and waited. The Brownie waited, crouched at my feet. "I missed you," I said.

"It were a worry, mistress, when tha' setted tha' lips an' didn't say nothing."

I missed you. What had made me say that? But it was true, especially in the last few months of Stepmother's life, when she grew worse and I grew better.

"But I'm afraid," I said. "We could easily hurt someone again."

I saw the world those last few months as though through a magnifying glass. The world shrank to a three-inch circle. It was reduced to bits of lint and flakes of paint and nibblings of fingernails.

"But mistress," said the Brownie. "Us never hurt nobody."

"That's what I thought," I said. "But I know differently now."

"But mistress!"

I slid from the stile. I didn't want to speak of Stepmother and Mucky Face. "Perhaps Dr. Rannigan's finished with his patient."

I knew what kinds of arguments the Brownie would offer; I'd offered them all myself. I hadn't the patience for them now.

The day was taking forever. Where was the loose end of time?

The Brownie and I peered into the Alehouse. No Dr. Rannigan.

He was at none of the usual places. He wasn't playing at draughts with the mayor; or discussing herbs with the apothecary; or in the teashop, reading the *London Loudmouth*. We returned to Dr. Rannigan's house and peered in the garden shed. His guns were still hanging from the wall. So he wasn't out shooting pheasant, although hunting season had just begun and Dr. Rannigan loved to hunt.

Back to the Alehouse, where Dr. Rannigan and Cecil sat sharing a table and a plate of fried fish. Cecil saw me first.

"Milady!" One coiled-spring move, and he stood before me. He was stronger than I'd thought, faster than I'd thought.

"Not now, Cecil. I must speak with Dr. Rannigan."

"But Briony—" Cecil blocked my way.

"Let me pass, Cecil." I was shouting. "Let me pass!"

All at once I was looking into Dr. Rannigan's patient cow eyes, holding his hand, walking with him through the Alehouse door, hearing him tell me to stay in the Alehouse, to sit and rest. Hearing him tell me I looked tired. Watching his rumpled back cross the square—

The world leapt back to its mad pace. The day had passed while I wasn't looking. Shadows leaned against the windows, candles sprang into flame.

"Milady!"

I turned my back on Cecil, rounded the corner of the Alehouse. But that was stupid, because there was only more Alehouse. No part of the Alehouse is safe if one is to avoid Cecil Trumpington.

"Please talk to me!" Cecil's voice came pleading and scratching at my back.

We'd rounded into a sprinkle of outdoor tables, where eel-men were fortifying themselves for nightfall. The eels were running, and eels are best caught in the dark.

"Please! I shall go mad otherwise."

I sat at the nearest table; I couldn't be bothered to care, not about Cecil. But the thought of eels wriggled its way into my mind. Eels, sent to inland cities; eels, smoked or jellied or simply made into soup. Any method will do for those of homicidal disposition. Just add your favorite poison. It will never be detected beneath the taste of eel, which is so, well, eel-ish.

"I'm awfully tired," I said. "Can you be quick about it?"

Poor Cecil, consumed by a *grande passion*, only to be told to compress his love manifesto into a haiku.

"I won't try to excuse my behavior," he said. "It was despicable."

Or a limerick.

> *There once was a rotter named Cecil,*
> *Whose Love Interest wished he could be still.*

Oh well. Unlike some, at least, I've never pretended to be a poet.

Cecil clutched at his hair, although he would undoubtedly prefer that his biographers describe him as having *rent his hair*. The effect was not unattractive. "I can't explain what came over me."

"I can."

> *He rent his dark tresses,*
> *Resulting in messes,*

Thus prompting his L.I. to flee till,
  she reached the end of the world and jumped off.

Perhaps I have untapped potential.

"You do understand! You know how it drives one mad."

"What does?"

"Unrequited love," said Cecil.

"Unrequited lust, you mean."

"It's no such thing!"

"Really?" I said. "I can hardly take that as a compliment."

Cecil's tongue stumbled over itself, trying to explain the fine distinction between passion and lust—

"And drink," I said.

"Briony, please." Cecil reached across the table.

My hand jumped away of itself. "Don't touch me!" My voice went funny, making us both pause and lean back.

Cecil broke the silence. "Are you afraid of me?"

"Would you enjoy it if I were?"

Of course I wasn't afraid. I'd been afraid on Blackberry Night, but only in a primitive, reactive sort of way. The startle-fear of tripping on a stair, or hearing a noise in the dark.

What could Fitz possibly have seen in him? They spent such a quantity of time together.

"Whatever did you and Fitz talk about?"

Cecil blinked, twice, as though that would help him catch up with the conversation. "We were drinking mates. We didn't talk much."

"You can't drink and talk at the same time?"

"Oh, I showed Fitz a few things," said Cecil. "He's older than I, but less experienced in the ways of the world."

231

Fitz, less experienced? Fitz, who's been to Paris and Vienna? "What ways?"

"I don't want to talk about Fitz," said Cecil. "I want to talk about you, about us. First Eldric came, and now you've changed."

"You're the one who's changed." I showed him the pale underside of my wrist, the bruises left by two fingers and a thumb.

If there were such a thing as a vampire-puppy-dog, it would be Cecil. Big pleading eyes, asking for an ear-scratch and a nice warm bowl of blood.

"Why don't you have any bruises?" I said. The vampire-puppy-dog looked all about.

"Eldric hit you hard."

"He hit me where you can't see," said Cecil at last.

Where you can't see? Most satisfactory!

"Forget Eldric," said Cecil. "I was useful to you, admit it."

"Useful?" I said. "How do you mean?"

"Are you back to that game?" His eyes went narrow and chilly. Terrifying, I'm sure. "Pretending you never took me into your confidence about it."

"We'd get on better," I said, "if you could tell me what the *it* is."

"I'd never have thought it of you," he said. "I did it out of love."

Either I was mad, or Cecil was mad. I am not the sort of person to go mad, so the honors go to Cecil.

"Look at you," said Cecil. "That angel face, that lying tongue."

"What can I say to convince you that I'm utterly in the dark?"

"You could start with the truth," said Cecil.

What a fine bit of irony: I tell the truth for once, but

232

am thought to be lying. "Just tell me, Cecil! Then we'll have something concrete to talk about."

Cecil shouted; his head and shoulders came at me across the table. I startle-jumped away, rammed into the back of the chair. It wasn't real fear, just the startle-fear that helps you run fast when there's danger about.

I rose. "I can't talk to you when you act like a spoiled child."

"You mind your tongue!"

"Oh, I do," I said. "I sharpen it every evening on your name."

"I could make things hot for you." Cecil's lips were blood-less. "I could make you squirm."

My hands were shaking. "Are you threatening me?" I clasped them behind my back.

"What if I am?"

What a stupid question. "Then I shan't bother to stay." I walked off, but he shouted after me.

"I'll expose you, I swear I will. You don't believe I will, but just you wait. One of these days, there will come a knock at the door, and what will you think when you open it to see the constable on the other side?" And more of the same, much more.

I was halfway across the square before he stopped shouting.

Dr. Rannigan had come and gone, leaving gloomy news and gloomy fathers. I found it hard to attend to what Mr. Clayborne told me. I felt as though I were listening to him through the wrong end of a telescope. My startle-fear still hung about, which was distracting. *Go away!* I told it. *I don't need you anymore.*

"Pearl told me something," I said. "She says Leanne's visits tire him."

There! I'd achieved one happy result. No visits from Leanne, for the present. Not until he improved. Mr. Clayborne himself said so.

And still the startle-fear hung on. It had outlived its purpose, which was to help a person spring into action, spear the woolly mammoth, stake the vampire-puppy-dog. But it didn't help a person understand how she caused Eldric to fall ill. If I knew how I'd done it, perhaps I could reverse it.

I don't need you any longer, I told the startle-fear.

It didn't care.

You've become a nuisance.

It didn't care.

You are no longer adaptive. Have you never heard of Mr. Darwin?

It hadn't.

Ignore it, Briony. You shall have to adapt instead. Think! Stepmother was ill; Eldric is ill. Eldric looks just as Stepmother did, like an egg without a yolk. Stepmother fell ill because you called Mucky Face, and Mucky Face injured her spine. Eldric fell ill because—because why?

What did I do?

Dr. Rannigan confessed to being astonished. How could Eldric have made a full recovery in only two days? This had been the damndest season for illnesses, he said. The swamp cough comes and goes. The egg-with-no-yolk illness comes and goes. He didn't know what the egg illness was, mind you. He'd seen it only in our family. When Father grew ill, when I grew ill. Eldric's case reminded him particularly of the late Mrs. Larkin's illness, how with her too the disease came and went. Her decline was slower than Eldric's, but she'd surely have died of it if there hadn't been, oh, you know, the unfortunate incident with the arsenic.

Dear Briony,

Do you think you might meet with me for a quarter hour or so? I've something I'd like to discuss with you.

I am completely recovered and ready to go back to being bad. Will you join me?

Yours in Fraternitus,
Eldric

Dear Eldric,

I'm very happy you're quite well again. Certainly I'd like to meet with you, unless it has to do with the events of Blackberry Night, in which case, I would not. I suggest, in fact, that we contrive to forget Blackberry Night entirely. The Larkin family has a grand old tradition of forgetting unpleasant events, and as you know, I learn my lessons well.

All messages exchanged between members of the Fraternitus are, of course, secret. When you have read this letter, eat it!

Yours in Fraternitus,
Briony

P.S. I'm fairly sure I didn't use the poisoned ink.

Dear Briony,

You suggest forgetting Blackberry Night. I, however, have no recollection of any unpleasant occurrence. But in any event, it is not Blackberry Night I wish to discuss. Might we meet at three o'clock, in the library?

I do not believe you used the poisoned ink, unless it is of the slow-acting variety. Please advise. The next step of the Fraternitus must be to devise a secret communication system. I have an idea that involves the tattooing of scalps and growing of hair, but there are several tricky details I haven't managed to work out. Perhaps you'll be able to, as you're so clever.

Yours in Fraternitus,
Eldric

I heard Eldric come down the corridor to the library. It's astonishing that one can recognize a person merely by the way his shoe meets the floor. Now his hand touched the library doorknob, now the door whispered across the carpet. "It's dark in here."

I'd left the lamps dark in case my face betrayed me. I wasn't as sure of my Briony mask as I'd once been. Rain rattled at the windows, coals spat in the hearth. I sat on the carpet, in the shadows. I reserved the spatter of firelight for Eldric.

"You're looking very well," I said. One couldn't say the roses had come back to his cheeks—he wasn't a pinkish person—but he'd gone gold again.

You're looking very well. How stupid you sound, Briony! You speak just as Father might.

"I am entirely well," said Eldric, "which has Dr. Rannigan exploring first one theory, then another, trying to understand. But not being a man of science, I don't care about understanding. I simply want to go outside and break a few windows."

Say something, Briony; say something! The Briony mask always had something tart or amusing to say, but the underneath Briony could think of nothing. The clock tut-tutted in the silence. How slowly it spoke, so slowly that between tick and tock came the sharp silvery plink of rain on glass.

"I'm glad you're better," I said, which was trite but true.

Better, he was better! As soon as I said the word, I felt relief. For once in my life, I felt relief. It came as a melted-butter drizzle down the back of my legs. It pooled in my knees. Perhaps that's why people's knees grow weak.

"I was a little dishonest with you," said Eldric. "In order to tell you what's on my mind, I have to bring up Blackberry Night."

Blackberry Night. On came the crimson tide. I leaned forward to stir the coals; my hair fell over my face.

"It's uncanny," said Eldric, "how you've adapted to using your left hand."

I had to be careful. I'd been giving my left hand too much liberty.

"Forgive me for being a nosy parkerius," said Eldric, "but I wanted to know if you've seen Cecil since Blackberry Night?"

"It's nosy parkerium," I said. "Twelfth declension, you know."

"Never mind that," said Eldric. "I can't stop fretting about Cecil."

Cecil? Of all the things I imagined he might want to talk about, I never imagined Cecil.

"Don't worry about him," I said, although I thought of the day before yesterday, of how strangely Cecil had acted, of his oblique references and veiled threats. "I can wrap him round my little finger."

"I didn't observe the finger-wrap technique on Blackberry Night," said Eldric. "I keep thinking about what might have happened if I hadn't come along."

"And I keep thinking how stupid it all was," I said. "Stupid that you had to come along and rescue me. Stupid that I practiced boxing with you all those times, but I couldn't punch Cecil, not even once."

"Boxing's not that straightforward," said Eldric. "You can practice and practice, but the real experience will always be different. Lots of things are like that, actually. It reminds me of the time I first visited Paris."

"Lucky thing!" I said.

"On the boat over, I practiced French conversations with myself. I'd say to some imaginary Frenchman, 'The restaurant Chez Julien, she is, if I do not mistake myself, down the Boulevard Saint-Michel, to the right?'

"The Frenchman would obligingly say, 'Yes, monsieur. The restaurant, she is down the Boulevard Saint-Michel, to the right.' And sometimes he'd add, 'Might I remark, monsieur, what very good French you speak.'"

Chez Julien. How I longed to visit a city where the very names of the restaurants were spoken in music.

"But the reality was quite different," said Eldric. "To this imaginary Frenchman I'd say, 'The restaurant Chez Julien, she is, if I do not mistake myself, down the Boulevard Saint-Michel, to the right?'

"But he'd reply, 'La plume de ma boulevard, elle est dans la rue de ma tante, monsieur, et vous êtes très ooh-la-la.'"

I laughed.

"I'd thank him politely, then consult my map."

"You're saying that I can't win a real fight without first losing some real fights?"

"I'm saying that a beginner can't expect to perform as well in real life as she might in practice," said Eldric. "Practice is predictable; real life isn't."

"Can you practice with me unpredictably?" I said. "Predictably unpredictably, I mean?"

"I can," said Eldric, "but let's not leave the subject of Cecil just yet."

The door was ajar. The Brownie squeezed through and swung across the carpet on his double-hinged legs. Had Eldric left the door ajar on purpose? To make sure we weren't quite private? Oh, dear.

The Brownie settled at my side, folding his legs every which way.

"Please listen to what I have to say about Cecil," said Eldric. "I see you aren't afraid of him, but I wonder if you should be."

It was raining harder than before. Shards of sky pounded down the chimney. They set the logs to hissing.

Are you afraid of me? That's what Cecil had said, as we sat outside the Alehouse. I'd startle-jumped back. *Are you afraid?*

"He hurt my wrist." But that was not what I meant to say. My voice went high and whiny. What silliness was this? Did I think I could be a baby again? Grow up, Briony.

"Let's take a look."

I produced my wrist with the finger-shaped bruises.

"Bastard!" It was not exactly what one might say to a baby, but it was comforting.

We sat in silence a long time. Eldric stoked the fire. The flames leapt up and admired themselves in the brass grate. "I wonder if you know quite everything about Cecil," said Eldric at last. "He's fond of drink, as you know."

I nodded.

"I don't like to give away his secrets, but it's not only drink that affects him."

Oh! That was interesting. "Opium?"

"Not quite that benign," said Eldric.

"Morphine?"

"Not quite that bad," said Eldric.

"Then tell me!"

"Arsenic," said Eldric.

Arsenic. Cecil took arsenic. Fitz took arsenic. That was doubtless why they spent such a deal of time together.

Pearl came in to light the lamps.

"I should not like to see you alone with him again. He's lost control, at least where you're concerned."

She poured paraffin into one of the lamps.

"Why does a person take arsenic?"

"It depends on the person," said Eldric. "Women used

to take it for their hair and especially for their skin, which it apparently renders very white and clear."

"And if you're a man?"

He paused while Pearl filled the other lamp and bustled out again.

"It has the reputation of boosting a man's—oh, how shall I put it? A man's virility."

I leaned forward again with the poker, my hair shielding my face.

"Never have coals been stirred so well," said Eldric.

"Never has a young lady been put so often to the blush," I said. "It's rather ungentlemanly of you."

I thought he would laugh, but he said, "It's quite a difficult conversation."

I nodded, sorting through my thoughts. Remember what Father had said about Fitz? About not leaving me alone with him? The effect of arsenic on men—that was surely the reason.

I could have gone on to consider I'd done Father an injustice. I'd thought what he'd said all puff and nonsense. But there were other things tugging at my attention. The smell of paraffin. I gave it a good sniff; it ignited memories of the library fire.

It brought it all back: the spark, the whoosh, the flames, the fire, the flames playing over the books, munching at the titles—*The Reed Spirits, The Strangers, Mucky Face.* The fire liked them all. It didn't care that it had only my stories to eat, that the proper books had been ruined in the flood. It brought back the sound of Stepmother's pink satin house shoes click-clacking on the floor.

Did I never wonder how Stepmother managed to rise

from her bed, thinking to save me from the fire? How could she have, with that injury to her spine?

Did I never wonder what I was doing? How I could burn the stories of the Bleeding Hearts and the Strangers and so many others of the Old Ones?

Why would I burn my stories?

Why would I thrust my hand into the fire?

Stop, Briony: You did no such thing!

I tried to banish the memory, but my mind hung on to the image of my left hand diving into the flames.

Stop remembering! But I couldn't stop.

"So do you?" said Eldric.

"Do I what?"

Memory is a queer thing. The smell of paraffin—why would I remember that? I'd called up the fire; I wouldn't have needed paraffin.

"You haven't been listening at all!" said Eldric.

Why would I remember putting my hand into the flames, when what happened is that the fire blazed out of control? It grew faster, burnt hotter than I could manage.

My memories had grown distorted over time. But I had them, at least: I remembered calling up the fire, I remembered turning Mucky Face against Stepmother, I remembered turning the wind against Rose. But I don't remember turning anything against Eldric.

"Please listen!" Eldric leaned forward. "You want to watch out for Cecil."

What had I done to make Eldric so ill?

I didn't care about Cecil. I only wished I could tell Eldric that what he wanted was to watch out for me.

23

Awkwardissimus

The members of the Fraternitus were assembled. The members of the Fraternitus were boxing. Or at least, one of its members was boxing. The other was trying to catch her breath.

"This is a terrible idea," I said. Or rather, I tried to say it but mostly, I panted. "Bad boys should only ever fight predictable fights."

"Unpredictable fights take a lot of practice," said Eldric. "You're doing very well."

"Liar!"

Eldric laughed. I wiped the sweat from my eyes. "And the worst of it is, you're fresh as a daisy."

One daisy petal: *I love him*. Another daisy petal: *I love him not*. Shut up, Briony!

The October evening was chilly, but the longer we fought, the more clothes I shed. An unpredictable fight is terrifically warming. I now wore the fewest garments consistent with modesty, a pair of trousers and a sort of shirt with no sleeves that looked more than anything like an undergarment. Tiddy Rex had lent them to me.

Darling Tiddy Rex!

In an unpredictable fight, a person's always darting about. She punches at a person, but it turns out he's no longer there. She blocks a kick from the right, but she's surprised by an uppercut from the left. She thought she was a wolfgirl who could run forever. But the wolfgirl has never darted and dodged. The wolfgirl is ready to give up after five minutes. But she's proud and carries on, and now she thinks she may need to be carried home.

The person of whom we speak is Briony Larkin. The other person, Eldric Clayborne, merely lounges about and ruminates on the mysteries of life, and every so often, he delivers a little joke of a punch.

"I've never seen you so pink," said Eldric. "Should we knock off for the evening? You've been going at it very hard."

"But you haven't," I said. "I've been punching you hard as I can, but you've been doling out those silly butterfly punches. I'd think you were cheating, except that the members of the Fraternitus Bad-Boyificus are sworn never to cheat."

"No, we never cheat," said Eldric. "Which means I'm honor-bound to admit I should have given myself a handicap. I have two working hands, and you've just the one right now."

This particular member of the Fraternitus had to breach the code of honor. She couldn't admit that her left hand was very spry indeed and that her right hand had never been useful. All at once, I felt the chill sink into my bones. I wrapped my arms about my middle.

"I shouldn't have let you stop moving," said Eldric. "Let's get you warm."

"Let me?" I said. "That's rather bossy."

"A boxing coach is always bossy. That's one of the sad facts of life. Now, wrap up."

I paused. I was wearing Tiddy Rex's peculiar shirt and beneath, a little bit of hardly anything. They were damp with sweat, horrible in the October chill.

The Strangers were lolly-bobbling all about, murmuring about stories and mushrooms and mud. Murmuring about the cemetery and the Unquiet Spirit who tosses in her winding sheet. "The cold worms lie with her and she be shrilling out a name."

I bent over the clothes I'd shed. They too were damp.

"It be tha' name, mistress," said the Strangers. "It be tha' name she be shrilling."

"Your lips are blue," said Eldric. "You do know the rules, don't you? A person who doesn't mind her coach must be expelled from the Fraternitus."

"But these clothes are too wet."

Eldric went all lion, pouncing at his coat and then at me, holding the coat between us as a sort of curtain. "As one member of the Fraternitus to another, it goes without saying that I will protect your privacy against any and all who might seek to invade our fightibus space."

He meant himself, of course, but he couldn't say so. How raw to say, *I promise not to look.*

It was awkward, struggling out of my wet things, feeling entirely exposed, which I was, to the whole half of the world on the east side of the curtain-coat, including the Strangers.

And on the west side, to a boy-man who could peer over at any time, except that members of the Fraternitus never lied or cheated. I scrambled into my blouse, which was the only thing that wasn't wet. It wasn't worse than nothing, but it was not much better.

"Done?" said Eldric.

"How did you know?" I said.

"I have ears."

How could a boy-man hear when a girl was dressed?

"Done," I said.

He turned, wrapped the coat around me. But his fidgety fingers made sure not to touch me, not even through the thickness of the coat. It had been all ruined by Blackberry Night.

"Come along, blue lips," he said, thinking perhaps that a bit of silliness might smooth over the awkwardness.

"If you were to write me a poem," I said, "you could rhyme it with *tulips*."

But silliness was not a smoother-over. Not for the two of us as we made our way back to the village. Not on this particular October evening, when Eldric's long fingers had just taken such care to avoid any bit of Briony Larkin.

We walked in silence past the pumping station, toward the fields of rye. We'd had no time to revisit awkward memories on the outward journey: We'd loped and laughed through the fields to the Scars; it had been too long since our last fighting lesson. But now—well, if only the rye were already harvested and the fields looked like Tiddy Rex after a haircut. It wouldn't be so awkward then. But we had to walk through a field of awkward memories, through the rye, tall and bronze and smelling of kisses.

Gin a body meet a body,
Comin' thro' the rye,
Gin a body kiss a body,
Need a body cry?

I could feel Eldric struggling to contain that hollow whistle of his. How stupid it was, that we couldn't talk about this. I couldn't bear it if we went all silent, as Father and I were. Can a lifetime of silence begin with a kiss?

I couldn't stand it; I had to say something. "Awkwardissimus?"

"Awkwardissimus!" said Eldric.

We laughed, which broke the silence. There was a bit of me, though, that stood outside myself, listening to us: We managed an impressive imitation of the way we'd used to talk, but I thought that any expert would spot the forgery.

The river ran olive brown, like paintbrush water. As we neared the bridge, Mad Tom's voice broke into our counterfeit conversation. "Give 'em back! I needs 'em sore, I does."

Silence now, except for the kingfishers gossiping in the reed beds.

"I does, pretty lady. Mad Tom, he mind on you. He mind on you fine by that black hair what you got."

We crested the rise of the bridge. Mad Tom was hiding behind the black claw of his umbrella, just his shirttail and trouser legs showing beneath. "You got you your own proper wits, pretty lady." He turned.

Leanne! The pretty lady was Leanne. The sight of her gave me a gray, cotton-woolish sort of feeling.

"Oh, my lilied liver! Oh, my turnip toes!" Mad Tom swung the umbrella from his shoulder, stirred the tip into the pebbles at the foot of the bridge. "I knows the pretty lady's got some wits to spare for poor Mad Tom."

Eldric's face went all un-electric. Heavy eyelids at half-mast, lips tight as curling lips can be.

Is that what love looks like? If you're a twenty-two-year-old man in love with a beautiful woman, and you see her and she sees you? But perhaps Eldric wanted to hide the look of love. A boy-man might not like to expose his tender feelings, especially in front of Blackberry-Night Briony Larkin.

She had a floaty sort of walk, Leanne did, and she'd trained her cloak to float along with her. The floatiness went with the color of her cloak and skirts, blues and greens that shifted as she moved.

She slowed as she neared us, setting Mad Tom to dancing about her, blessing his liver and spying his wits with his little eye. She called out to Eldric in her dusk-lined voice, but her gaze lingered on his coat, which hung about me like a sack.

"Lovely to see you again—Briony." The pause before my name was brief, but effective. It said, *So sorry, but I don't have the name of this lovely child quite on the tip of my—ah, here it is.*

Now back to Eldric. "How sweet of your father to write. I cannot tell you how relieved I was to hear of your recovery." Her eyes roved all over him. "Are you completely well?"

"Completely," said Eldric.

He hadn't seen her since he'd recovered! Ten whole days. Wasn't that a long absence for an ardent lover?

"I wonder," she said, "if you could rid me of poor Mad Tom." Her smile showed her sultan's-harem teeth—beautiful, perhaps, but excessive in number. "I confess, he frightens me."

"Them eyes you got, lady." Mad Tom stepped close, too close for politeness. "They been haunting me, them eyes."

Eldric took Mad Tom's arm. "This way," he said. "The pretty lady needs her privacy." But he didn't hurry Mad Tom. He eased Mad Tom down the bridge, letting Mad Tom set the pace. Eldric was a gentleman. I'd never thought of this before.

"I suppose you're not afraid of the poor fellow?" Leanne leaned toward me, as though we were best friends. She whiffed of scent. I could have guessed she'd never choose something fresh and flowery. Instead, she smelled the way she looked, dark and peppery, with an undercurrent of wild animal.

"You're accustomed to him, of course. I hear he's really harmless, but I can't like him drawing so close."

But the dusk and pepper were merely surface smells. Beneath lay the smells of salt and seaweed and damp. They slipped into my mind like minnows, startling me into a scent memory of Stepmother. Not Stepmother as I'd last seen her, but the gay, laughing Stepmother who'd first come into our lives.

When Eldric turned back to join us, Mad Tom shuffle-trotted behind. "Here he comes again," I said, which made Mad Tom address himself to me.

"I thought I seen you afore, but it be t'other girl I seen."

He lunged at Leanne with webbed umbrella fingers. "You be the real girl what stole my wits."

Eldric grabbed the umbrella, pulled it from Mad Tom's hands. "You want to be careful with that. You could hurt someone."

"No," said Mad Tom, quieter now. "I got me a prettier notion. You takes me back an' works me till I falls. I were good feeding for you, weren't I?"

My breath snagged in my throat. Such queer things he was saying. Until now, I'd thought Leanne an idiot to be afraid of Mad Tom. But for the first time ever, I was afraid.

"Lead him away again, will you?" said Leanne. "Perhaps I should accompany you this time. He'll follow me, poor fellow. Perhaps the constable ought to know he's developed an obsession for me. I feel we may call it that, an obsession."

"I've news of the motorcar." Eldric took Leanne's arm. "But I'm promised to Briony for supper, so I'll have to tell you about it some other time."

He was? What a bouncer of an excuse! Did he not want to be with Leanne? How could you explain it otherwise?

He didn't want to be with Leanne!

Leanne leaned in close again, and she frightened me too. "Might you excuse us, Briony?" It wasn't merely that she pressed herself at me and that she was so tall and dark. "Thank you for sparing Eldric. He'll be just a few minutes, I'm sure." It was also that she was somehow bursting out of her skin, and her voice was too big, and she had so many teeth, and I was shrinking away in my skin, and I had no voice at all.

I shrank away from her. I, Florence Nightingale Larkin, actually shrank away, like any regular wilting violet of a girl.

"I swears, lady!" said Mad Tom. "I swears by marble an' blade to work stone for you till I drops. Just don't leave afore my time. Suck at my life, lady, till I be kilt."

"Off we go." Eldric eased Mad Tom down the bridge again, Leanne floating beside.

Eldric turned suddenly, called over his shoulder. "I'll be back directly."

I turned toward the river, set my forearms on the railing. Mad Tom's scoldings and cajolings grew faint, fainter, then faded away. I stared into the paintbrush water. My mask was one great rumple; it would need hours of smoothing.

Shouldn't I be happy? Eldric didn't want to sup with Leanne. Of course I should be happy.

But how can I tell what happiness is? It's not a thought, it's a feeling. If happiness were a description from a soppy novel, it might read, *She felt as though she were walking on air.*

That was right: I felt as though I were walking on air. Clichés became clichés because they contained a nugget of truth.

Eldric did not return directly.

Eldric did not return indirectly.

The walking-on-air feeling evaporated. The paintbrush water was depressing. He did want to be with her after all.

He couldn't expect me to wait on the bridge forever. I headed for the alley that leads into the square, stepped into the dusty-coal dimness. I blinked it away and there stood Eldric. Eldric and Leanne. Eldric, bent over Leanne, his lips on hers. I knew how they felt, those silk-and-butter lips. I knew how it felt when he held you, your body pressed along his, soft and heavy, never hard and crushing, that velvet-and-cream electricity—

I backed out of the alley. I returned to the crest of the bridge. I set my forearms on the railing. I stared into the paintbrush water.

The boy stood on the burning deck. He deserved to die, that boy. Waiting for someone who never came. But I was doing the same, waiting for Eldric, watching the water, the paintbrush water, which now that I was looking, had turned the color of liver.

It eddied, then boiled. I'd seen this before, the wave rising from the river, too tall, too straight, defying gravity. Now a face, taking shape beneath the cap of foam, whirlpool eyes, deep-sea mouth—

Mucky Face, poised to leap and crush.

His whirlpool eyes met mine. "Mistress! Tha' needs must 'mand me to stop!"

His belly was liver-gray. No schoolgirl paintbrush water for Mucky Face.

"Speak lively, mistress! Say, 'As I be tha' mistress . . .'"

I shouted into the roar and sputter. "As I am thy mistress, I command thee to stop. I command thee to return to the river."

Mucky Face hovered. "More, mistress! It be such a mighty voice what calls, what 'mands me to collect my whole particular self nigh unto thee."

"Return to the river, Mucky Face!"

"The voice, it be 'manding me to cast my whole particular self upon thee."

"Dive into the clouds of minnows, Mucky Face! Return to the river—"

"'Manding me to slay thee!"

"Return to the river, push the river up the banks with thy two great hands, push—"

Foam-crested shoulders collapsed. "Tha' be a canny mistress!" Mucky Face sank. Quickly as he'd risen, he poured himself back into his own element. Whitecaps boiled on the river. Mucky Face sank beneath. All at once, the river was as peaceful as a schoolgirl's painting.

There was nothing to see anymore, save the river and my forearms resting on the railing.

Save the river, the railing, and my forearms, and Eldric's forearms too, resting on the railing just beside mine. I stared at them, Eldric's long forearms, shirtsleeves pushed back, despite the chill. My forearms, lost in the tweedy sleeves of his coat.

"My, my," said Eldric. "You are full of surprises."

I had to look at him then, but I didn't see any of the Eldric faces I knew. His face was still. Only his eyes were alive.

"I'm waiting," he said.

24

Wine Is Cheering

The square was set about with torches tossing their pale hair. Light pooled in the scratches and gouges of our table, glanced off Eldric's tell-nothing face. "I'm still waiting."

"You promise you won't tell? Not a single soul?"

It was safe to tell him here, among the riot of merry-makers, spilling from the Alehouse into the square. Safe to tell him in this bedlam of shouts and songs and cries for ale.

"I've already promised," said Eldric. "Five times now."

So he had, on that long, mostly silent walk to the Alehouse.

I slipped my arms from the sleeves of Eldric's coat and wrapped them around my middle. I was inside my arms, which were inside the coat. But still I was cold.

"I'm still waiting."

I'd never have thought he'd be so angry. He'd caught Briony talking to a great wave, and he was angry. His face didn't show it, but it was evident in everything he did, from his uninflected speech to the few feet of distance he kept between us as we walked to the Alehouse.

"Have you heard of the second sight?"

"When a person sees fairies and the like?" said Eldric.

"I can see the Old Ones," I said.

"That wave, an Old One?" I couldn't read Eldric's face. "You were speaking to an Old One?"

How can regular people bear it when their best friend's angry at them? What do they think? What do they do?

If I were a dwelling, I'd be a cave.

If I were a creature, I'd be a cockroach.

I chose my words carefully. "One of the Old Ones, yes. But the wave itself was sent by another Old One. An Old One whose element is water."

"Someone—some Old One—sent you a wave?" said Eldric.

I nodded. "An Old One with a terrific amount of power. Mucky Face couldn't stop until I told him to."

"Who is he then?" said Eldric. "This Old One with such terrific powers?"

"Perhaps it's a *she.*"

"You've blue lips again," said Eldric. "Where's that idiot of a bartender?" He stepped away, overturning his chair, but he didn't pause to put it to rights. He vanished into the noise and crush.

Why would an Old One want to kill me? That was worth thinking about. The Old One had called Mucky Face to do the job, but Mucky Face and I were . . . Can you be friends with a tidal wave? In any event, Mucky Face warned me, saved me from himself.

What Old One would want to kill me? And why?

Eldric returned with wine and bread and soup. I squiggled my arms back into his sleeves, wrapped my hands around the wineglass. It was hot and smelled of cinnamon. "Are you still in a temper?"

"Why shouldn't I be?" said Eldric.

"Why should you?"

"Because you didn't tell me about all this. How can we be friends—"

Best friends?

"How can we be friends if you're so—so hidden from me?"

Wine is said to be cheering. I took a sip. It left a spreading warmth behind my breastbone. Warmth is cheering.

"Betrayed," said Eldric. "That's the word."

"Do you know why I keep my second sight a secret?" I said.

"I really cannot say."

I really cannot say. How horrid he was, all ice and arrogance.

"It's dangerous to have the second sight. Should anyone find out, they'd think me one of the Old Ones."

"And?" said Eldric.

"And," I said, leaning on the *and.* I wager I can make a single word sound as chilly as he can. "If the Swampfolk think I'm one of the Old Ones, what do you think they'd like to do to me?"

Eldric flinched. "Good Lord!" He went pale, which I found extremely pleasant.

"Who else knows?" he said.

"Only you. And Stepmother knew. She fretted about it a great deal and made me promise to keep it a secret."

"Do you know why—?" He ran out of words.

"Why I can see the Old Ones?"

He nodded.

To lie or not to lie, that was the question. I'd never tell him the truth, of course, but I could pretend not to know. But the pretending would be a lie, and the lie would be a betrayal, and Eldric was my best friend.

"I do know, but Stepmother asked me to keep that a secret too. I promised her not to tell, I promised over and over. Would you mind very much if I didn't tell you?"

"I would mind." When people go pale, they usually get rosy again. But not Eldric, not yet. "I do mind."

Too bad for him. "You don't look very well."

"You've given me a shock," he said.

Serves him right. "Perhaps you should put your head down." I knew this was the thing to do, although I've never fainted and I don't intend to.

He managed a smile, shook his head. "I'll just sit for a few minutes."

Now that we sat silent, I noticed the music that came leaking from the Alehouse. "Lord Randal." Lord Randal, whose sweetheart poisons his eel broth for no particular reason, which is not unlike me, if you think about it. I don't need much of a reason to kill.

O I fear ye are poisoned, Lord Randal, my son!
O I fear ye are poisoned, my bonny young man!

How I hate that song with its queer, ancient intervals. But wine is cheering. Drink Briony, drink!

I may be wicked, but I'm not proud of it. And I'm not proud of being a betraying friend and of letting Eldric sit there, all pale and shocked, without doing anything—even though he'd been acting horrid. Yes, horrid!

"I have some questions about betrayal," I said. "Think

about this: A person who calls you his best friend, and says he has dinner plans with you, goes off with a beautiful woman, saying he'll be back directly, then makes you wait half an hour because he's kissing the woman in the alley. Is that betrayal?"

"Oh, Lord." Eldric tossed back his wine.

"You were such a long time," I said. "I came looking for you."

"I'm mortified," said Eldric. "Mortified that you saw us. But—well—I'd fancied myself over her. When she and I are apart, I get to thinking she's not terribly interesting."

"But then she appears," I said.

"Then she appears," said Eldric, "and I no longer care if she's uninteresting."

I get to thinking she's not terribly interesting . . . I no longer care if she's uninteresting. It was peculiar—more than peculiar—the way the presence of Leanne pulled Eldric's emotions about, like taffy. It wouldn't be so peculiar if the memory of Leanne also affected him. But no. *When she and I are apart, I get to thinking she's not terribly interesting.* A lover is expected to moon over the girl of his dreams when they're apart, writing love poems and the like. How else do such things get written? A proper lover wouldn't have time to write and sing when his love appears. He'd be busy doing other things.

"Have you a pencil and paper?"

"My coat," said Eldric. "Breast pocket."

I fished them out. "I know this sounds queer," I said. "But will you tell me about Leanne? And if you don't mind, I'll write it down."

"Whatever for?"

"I don't know." That was not quite true. In the days when I used to write, I was sometimes able to write myself into knowing something. Or, rather, uncovering something I already knew. "But will you indulge me?"

Fine, he said.

He didn't care, he said.

I took scattered notes, at first, as Eldric described meeting her at the courthouse, being struck that she'd ridden all that way from the Sands, what a marvelous horsewoman she was, and more of the same. But when he started describing how she adored his ability to fidget something out of nothing, I wrote everything, best I could.

The following is not at all what I wrote, but it describes what Eldric meant better than anything he said.

> *This is the boy-man called Eldric.*

Let's just skip to the last one, shall we?

> *This is the boy-man called Eldric; who fell in love*
> *with a woman called Leanne; who was terribly*
> *interested in his fidgets, the making of which she*
> *encouraged and facilitated; and once she got Eldric*
> *to making the fidgets day and night, he fell ill; but*
> *when Leanne was barred from his sickroom, he*
> *recovered immediately and, in fact, rather despised*
> *her; but when he saw her again, he could not resist*
> *her spell; and Mad Tom took an unusual interest in*
> *her; and Eldric's friend Briony was there and it may*
> *have been that Leanne felt Briony threatened her*

relationship with Eldric, for why otherwise would
Mucky Face have appeared right then with orders
to kill her, Mucky Face, who, we must remember,
can be controlled by an Old One whose element is
water, and—

"Don't you see!" I heard my own fish-gasp of surprise. "She's a Dark Muse!"

"It was stupid to have fallen for her so," said Eldric. "I freely admit it. But please give me credit for some brains."

"It's not about brains. She cast a spell upon you; you said so yourself."

"I only said I felt as though I'd been under a spell," said Eldric. "I wasn't being literal. You of all people should understand that. You're rarely ever literal. You're too—"

"Abstruse?"

"If you say so," he said. But I didn't say so. That wasn't the right word at all.

"You fell ill once you started fidgeting night and day. She encouraged you. She was drinking down your energy."

"I'll never believe it," said Eldric.

"You recovered the moment your father cut off her visits. She was worried I was distracting you from her; she tried to have me killed."

"Leanne, worried about *you?*" Eldric punched at the *you* as though he were boxing with it.

The punch came like a kick to the breastbone. I shrugged as though to say, *Believe what you like.* But I had no breath to speak.

Wine is cheering. Drink up, Briony!

Slower than slow, Eldric's fingers curled themselves into a fist. Or perhaps it was my mind that went slow. I had plenty of time to see his knuckles go white, plenty of time to say, "Smash the table, why don't you? Kick things about. It's ever so nice to see you embrace the true spirit of the Fraternitus."

Slowly, slowly, Eldric set his fist upon the table. Slowly, slowly, he stretched his fingers. "It's one thing to keep secrets. It's quite another to lie."

"I only lie about important things," I said. "Not about Leanne."

Wine is most certainly cheering.

We fell to eating cold soup and drinking warm wine and eating tepid bread and listening to the music.

"No one had any idea about Mad Tom," I said. "No one imagined he'd be worthy prey for the Dark Muse, not a mere stone carver. Cecil will be ever so put out."

"Blast Cecil!" said Eldric.

"You have my permission," I said.

The canal agent was singing now. He had a fine tenor voice. *There was blood in the kitchen, there was blood in the hall.* When you grow up with these songs, hearing them over and over, you might reach the age of seventeen before you realize how bloody they are.

At some point, Eldric must have fetched more wine. Wine is cheering. Have I said that before?

Thoughts are strange creatures. They lead you from one thing to another. Sometimes you don't know how you got from one to the next. I went from the Dark Muse, to Lord Randal, to Stepmother. I wished I didn't know that she must have suffered when she died. I wished I didn't know about arsenic poisoning, but I'd asked and I'd found out.

I jumped as Eldric tapped my shoulder. "You're far away." He set down a plate of chocolate biscuits.

But I was no farther than Stepmother's grave, just outside the cemetery gates, all in the raggle-taggle grasses-o.

"I want to apologize," said Eldric. "I've been an ass."

Sorry? I would never be sorry! But then I couldn't remember what there was to be sorry about. Leanne, Leanne—it had to do with Leanne.

"Cecil, by the way, is staring at you," said Eldric. "From the shadows."

"He's lurking," I said. "It's so romantic to lurk in the shadows with a broken heart. Is he wearing a long, black cloak?"

Eldric smiled and shook his head.

I'd been thinking about Leanne, hadn't I? Not Cecil. Yes, I had some thoughts about Leanne. "May I ask you something?"

"It depends on what it is." Eldric handed me a biscuit in a delicate, tentative way, as though he were handing me a flower.

I was going to ask him, yes I was. "You remember Blackberry Night?"

The torches were alive with yellow butterfly-flames. "I can't forget it." His eyes were whiter than white.

"You remember the thing we might have done that night, but it turned out to be a thing we didn't do?" It was late and my tongue had gone bleary. "The thing you stopped us from doing?"

"I especially can't forget that."

I was asking about lust, wasn't I? I was fairly certain of

it. But isn't love supposed to come before lust? It does in the dictionary.

"Did you do that with Leanne?"

He flung out a hand. It's silent London language. I believe it's meant to hail a cab. Which also means the cab must stop. "What do you think I am?" His lion's eyes matched the candlelight. "I don't go about preying upon young and virtuous ladies."

"Leanne's not a virtuous lady."

"Let's not get into that again."

"She's not even that young."

"Just wait until you're twenty-two—"

I interrupted him. "She's twenty-three." But when one is cheerful, one doesn't mind interrupting. "Do you remember what she said to Rose? Leanne said she was very old indeed."

"I do remember." Again, I couldn't read his expression.

My tongue thought of a cleverer thing to say. "Never mind Leanne. Have you done it with ladies who lack virtue? They're often rather old, aren't they?"

Eldric laughed quick and loud, as though he'd been startled. "You've had too much wine." His eyes were golder than gold.

But I liked wine. Wine was cheerful.

"You're making me squirm," he said. "Let's hope you don't remember this tomorrow."

"I have an excellent memory."

"I know," said Eldric. "It's quite a problem."

I'd forgotten about the chocolate flower-biscuit. I'd eat it, although one doesn't usually eat a flower. "Just answer me, and we'll pretend I'll have forgotten by tomorrow."

This time Eldric flung up both hands, which I knew wasn't to stop a cab but to surrender. See how quickly I'm learning this silent language?

"How can I put it—without blushing, at least!"

"You're already blushing," I said.

"Not much like a bad boy, am I?" said Eldric. "I could perhaps start by mentioning that I'm a man—"

"A boy-man," I said.

"A boy-man? How am I to take that? Shall I thank you or challenge you to a boxing match?"

"A boxing match," I said. "But no more of those silly butterfly punches!"

Eldric smiled. "Very well. I'm a boy-man, then, and a boy-man who's twenty-two years old—"

I saw where he was going. "What a terrible way to put it!"

"How so?"

"If I were to give you the same answer, it would have no meaning, would it? Isn't it assumed that a young lady of seventeen, or twenty-two, even, has refrained from acting upon, well—"

Here my tongue, until now so merry, failed to find a non-squirmy word.

"Impulses?" said Eldric.

"Impulses." Actually, it would be assumed that the young lady had no such impulses at all, but I'll tell you something: Chocolate melts on my tongue too.

"It's unfair, I suppose," he said. "But it's true. It's simply true that a twenty-two-year-old man has more liberty than a girl."

"If she's a girl of virtue."

"Just so."

"Am I pretty again?" I said.

"You're always pretty!"

"I wasn't when I was ill. You told Rose!"

"Rose told you that! It was just by way of explaining to her—yes, you're pretty again."

"Am I beautiful?" I said.

"Beautiful," said Eldric.

"Leanne is beautiful," I said.

"No more wine for you," said Eldric.

It is possible that at this point I slipped from my chair. Eldric said we must be getting home. "I have a surprise for tomorrow. I want you to feel well enough to enjoy it."

I said I was fond of wine and chocolate biscuits. But Eldric said I mustn't have any more. I kicked him under the table.

"Time to go," said Eldric. "I hope we can keep this from your father."

"I hate my father."

"Do you really?" said Eldric. "That's probably the wine talking."

I said wine couldn't talk, and leaned against him, making him drag me along. Then the tune of "Lord Randal" popped into my head, and it seemed a pity not to sing along, so I did for quite a long while, until Eldric said to hush because we were home and Father would hear me.

"The wine hates Father and I hate Father too." My feet were surprised to find themselves on the garden steps. I turned round to make sure. There was the garden, and there was Eldric, and it was funny that I was almost as tall as he.

"Your lips are blue again."

265

"I'm not the least bit cold," I said.

"That's also the wine talking."

I slopped forward.

"Steady!" Eldric caught my shoulders.

But I wanted to slop forward. "Give us a kiss, then, love!"

I leaned into him; he pushed me away. "Please don't do that," he said. "It's too hard." And there was something so sad about it, I wanted to cry. Except of course that I couldn't.

He kept hushing me as we made our way through the dark to the staircase. "Up you go, quick now. You're on the third floor, remember?"

"I have an excellent memory."

"Right!" said Eldric. "Go straight to bed. I'll see you to-morrow. You might not feel very well, I'm afraid."

"Up I go!" I held tight to the banister.

"I'll watch you go up," said Eldric.

"Watching people isn't polite," I said. "Up I go!"

And finally, up I went. Rose was asleep. "Shh! Mustn't wake Rose!" I believe I nursed some unkind thoughts about the do-not-cross line; and then, like a good girl, I went straight to bed.

I awoke in the dark with a cotton-wool mouth and a hammering in my head. I turned my head; the hammering sloshed to the other side. I grew gradually aware of my surroundings. I lay beside Rose, but on top of the bedclothes. Eldric's coat hung all about me.

Bits of the night came back. Snippets of "Lord Randal." I sang it—yes, I'm sure I did. I staggered through the square, singing, just like any drunken fisherman. How could I show my face in the village again? I should have to stay at home for the rest of my life. It could be done, I knew. I'd heard of an American poetess who never left her house. But I hated poetry.

Eldric had helped me home, hadn't he? Had he held me upright, or might I have dreamt it?

A thought about Eldric sloshed through my head, passed out the other side.

How thirsty I was. I swung my legs over the side of the bed. The hammering sloshed all about; I felt vilely unwell. *You might not feel very well.* That was Eldric's voice in my head. I hadn't dreamt it; he'd been there. Did I make a fool of myself?

The thought sloshed back, daring me to remember. Whatever it was, it was worse than weaving and singing through the square. I didn't want to remember, but I kept picking at the memory—Eldric, Eldric and Leanne. Leanne was dangerous—she was consuming him alive. But Eldric could not—or would not—believe.

I swallowed hard, but the sick still rose, and all at once I was scrambling across the floor. I was wretchedly sick in the ewer.

The smell of sick jumped out at me, the fishy, gritty smell of eel. *Eels boiled in eel broth.* With the smell came the memory of Stepmother. Sick, and eel-smell, and Stepmother. They belonged together.

I didn't want to remember Mucky Face bearing down upon Stepmother. But I couldn't help it, couldn't help remembering that livid belly rounding over her, curling, cresting, crashing. I'll never know if Stepmother screamed. I heard nothing but the smack and smash of water.

Stepmother vanished beneath Mucky Face, but he hadn't

finished. On he surged, into the Parsonage, and only in the Parsonage. He preferred it to any other house. He surged through doors and windows, and nooks and crannies, and holes too small for an ant. And there he stayed for weeks, loitering in the dining room and the parlor and the study and the library, where he turned the books into bloated corpses to fester and rot on the shelves.

I sagged to the floor, leaned against the bed. Images of last night slid behind my eyes in a mad kaleidoscope. Prying into Eldric's past with Leanne. Prying into his past in bars and bedrooms and brothels. Kicking him beneath the table. Standing on the garden steps. The charm of finding myself eye to eye with Eldric, of leaning into his lips. *Give us a kiss, then, love!*

And the horridly urgent question of making Eldric understand the danger he was in.

It was almost a relief to be sick again in the ewer.

25

Jaunting

That afternoon, Tiddy Rex knocked at the garden door. "Miss, oh miss!" He'd gone pale with excitement; his freckles stood out in livery spatters. "Come see, miss!"

"What is it, Tiddy Rex?"

"Sorry, miss. I were supposed to say it with them other words: Mister Eldric would take it very kindly if you might look into the square."

Eldric. My stomach curled up on itself, like a hedgehog. *Give us a kiss, then, love!*

"Honest, miss, you've never seen nothing like it. It be a surprise. An' Mister Eldric requests the presence o' Miss Rose, as well."

"Rose!" I called into the house. "Eldric has a surprise for us in the square."

"I prefer surprises," said Rose.

I had to face Eldric sometime. Staggering and weaving, singing "Lord Randal"—

"Let's hop along, then."

"I don't hop," said Rose.

It was not quite raining, but the air was wet. You could see the wind. The gallows rose tall and lonely, skin and bones against gray clouds. The wind set the noose to swinging. I turned my back on its Cyclops eye.

The surprise stretched and purred before me.

It was a motorcar. ("Motorcar! O Motorcar!" sing the heavenly angels.) Long, but not too long. Red, but not too red. Sleekest of sleeks, shiniest of shines. And sitting at the wheel was Eldric Clayborne, letting a slop of urchins lay sticky hands all over its redness.

Not really red, but cardinal. Yes, cardinal—Cardinal!— with its overtones of High Churchiness. (Hallelujah! Hallelujah!)

"Don't she be a beauty?" said Tiddy Rex.

She?

"All us lads, us be jaunting in her soon. That be the properest word, says Mister Eldric. Jaunting."

She. Of course the motorcar was a lady. Briony Larkin might fall in love with a lady. That would be quite proper. There would be none of the nastiness of men and their cigars.

The motorcar had been acquired with Leanne in mind, of course, but I'd love her anyway. The motorcar, that is.

Mr. Clayborne's men had left off their work to gaze at her. Rose walked round and round, touching the candy-apple skin with one finger. All the while, Eldric was helping dirty little boys and girls into the motorcar and sitting their horrid backsides on the white leather seats. One of the boys sounded her goose-voice of a horn.

270

White leather. I must pause for another color adjustment. Not white, cream. Thick, melting cream, with darling little buttons to fix the decorative pleats and puffs—cream leather buttons, of course. Even the insides of the doors were padded with cream leather.

Each wheel was a spun-candy confection of metalwork. In front, protuberant car eyes peered from protective brass hoods. A brass eagle perched on her nose.

"Do you like her?"

I jumped at Eldric's voice. "I'm in love."

"So am I," said Eldric, "which works out well, as I've saved the first ride for you. Pearl has made us a picnic. I took the liberty of thinking you and Rose might join me."

"I should have thought you'd give Leanne the first ride."

"After what you told me?" he said.

"You didn't believe me, though, did you?"

"No." He smiled; I smiled. *Give us a kiss, then, love!* Ugh. Hedgehog stomach. Ugh.

Rose and I shared the passenger seat. I sank into cream leather.

"Miss!" Tiddy Rex pressed his nose to the window. I found a cunning little crank to open it. "You be taking me next time, miss?"

I always used to be the one who stayed behind, minding Rose, while the others were off eating ice cream or riding sleighs on cold, crisp nights.

I don't care so much about cold, crisp nights, but I have never tasted ice cream.

The motorcar shivered into life and slid forward.

"Miss? Miss!"

"Next time, Tiddy Rex," said Eldric. "You can sound the horn."

Rose talked to Eldric. She actually conducted a conversation. How did the motorcar work? Why did it make such a noise? I could barely hear them, and what I could hear, I didn't understand. It was all springs and drive trains and liters and cylinders and horsepower. Horsepower? Isn't the very point of a motorcar the absence of horse?

It was a peculiar exchange, but peculiar things will happen in this new world of motorcars.

The afternoon was weepy and gray, but the car was cozy. I held my hand out the window. There's a peculiar pleasure in having just a bit of oneself grow cold, while the rest is snug beneath a lap rug.

I sank into the cream leather. "The motorcar makes me feel I am truly a Dresden figurine," I said.

"Dresden?" said Rose.

"Something precious and fragile," said Eldric. "Something that ought to be treated with utmost care."

"Briony's not fragile," said Rose. "She always says how strong she is."

"That's rather embarrassing, Rose!"

"She's right," said Eldric. "That's what you're forever saying."

"Still more embarrassing," I said. "Don't you think it's true?"

We bumped along a rough road, through heather and peat and gorse. The moor rose in lavender folds, dotted with a few arthritic firs.

"In certain ways, perhaps," said Eldric. But then he got quiet and didn't finish his thought.

"In what ways?"

"In Amazon of the Swampsea ways," said Eldric, but I had the feeling I'd just pulled him back from a faraway place and that that was not at all what he'd meant to say.

Now the earth rose around us, cutting off our view of the moor. Banks to either side dripped with rusty mosses and yellow ferns and mushrooms, brown and rugged, like leather. Autumn had taken hold. Just a bit more than a week until Halloween, which was when Eldric would learn I'm a witch.

I watched him adjust the turning wheel. If Michelangelo had lived in this age of motorcars, I knew just how he'd sculpt Eldric's hand. The long, fidgety fingers, the energy that might, at any moment, turn the wheel into a crown.

We splatted through soggy leaves, then hissed onto pebbles to climb a long rise of moor.

I imagined what those fingers would do on Halloween, when I revealed my true self. They'd go very still while he absorbed the information. And then what? Would he want me to give him back the things he'd made?

I touched the gray-pearl wolfgirl that hung against my chest. If he did want things back, it would be too late. I'd have vanished.

But I couldn't bear to have him find out that way. What if I were to tell him?

What if?

We pulled over at an untidy pile of boulders. The almost-rain had given over to almost-sun. Eldric spread a blanket on the sunward side of the boulders, which were flushed and warm.

273

Rose turned away, even though the blanket suggested picnics, and Rose was very fond of picnics. She looked down the spill of moor, at the wind tearing through the scrub, at a bundle of ponies tumbling by.

Eldric produced the picnic basket; we set out our supper. A thermos of tea; cold chicken; buns with raspberry jam and cream; and biscuits.

"Look, Rose," I said. "Buns and biscuits—shop-bought biscuits!"

But Rose did not appear to have heard. She stood smiling, not her anxious-monkey smile, but a real-girl smile. She did have her own thoughts—nice thoughts. Of course she did.

Pearl was a picnic genius. The picnic was the very essence of picnic-ness. She'd given us a quilt, worn and faded to just what a picnic blanket should be. The buns were wrapped in a blue-and-white cloth, and if I were a girl in a story, I'd have exclaimed, *Look, they're still warm!*

Which they were.

"I suppose it's time to get it over with," I said. "While Rose isn't listening."

"About last night?" Eldric didn't pretend not to know what I meant.

"I'm so mortified. Asking you those nosy-parkerium questions, and . . . and singing!"

"But I'm glad you did!" said Eldric. "You have a—a dazzling voice! I should never have heard it otherwise."

I shook my head. "I used to sing well enough, but I grew out of it."

"You haven't," said Eldric. "I'm telling you, you haven't."

"Perhaps I can only sing when I'm tipsy." I smiled to show

I didn't mean it. "And then, on the stairs—oh, I'm so sorry."

"Too bad about that terrific memory," said Eldric. "I'd rather hoped you'd forget."

"I wish I had," I said. "And this horrid thought keeps coming to me. What if I'm no better than Cecil? What if when I get to drinking, I go about kissing people?"

"You're not at all like Cecil," said Eldric.

"What's the difference?"

"Well," said Eldric, but he paused, and again, I had the feeling he'd drifted far away.

"Well?"

"I'd never invite Cecil on a picnic," said Eldric.

"I thought for a moment you were going to be serious," I said.

"Not even for a moment."

"I did feel dreadfully unwell," I said. "Just as you'd predicted."

"I've been under the weather myself," said Eldric, "in just that way. But I think that members of the Fraternitus, young and high spirited as we are, sometimes need to do such things, just to learn not to do them again."

"I've no intention of doing that again."

"Not ever drinking?" said Eldric.

"Not like that, at least."

"A toast at your wedding, perhaps?" said Eldric.

"I shall never get married," I said. "But I do like champagne."

Funny how I'd started off feeling so comfortable with Eldric last spring, but that now prickly little pauses kept growing between us. It's dead opposite to my experience with other people. I usually start out feeling uncomfortable and have to ratchet up the tart-and-amusing side of Briony. But as I begin to despise them, it grows more and more easy, and witticisms fall from my lips like toads.

"Look!" Rose pointed down the bluff. "It's a horse."

It was awkward because of Blackberry Night. Blackberry Night ruined everything.

"Oh," said Eldric, his voice so devoid of inflection that I looked up. He stood beside Rose, looking along her pointing finger, shielding his eyes against the sunset.

"I can tell who it is from that particular shade of green," said Rose. "I have an eye for color."

My mouth turned sour. "The horse is green?"

"I can tell that's a joke," said Rose.

I joined them, knowing what I'd see. A horse and rider, thundering across the moor. The horse wasn't green, but I was—turning green, that is. A taste-memory from last night rose beneath my tongue, all sick and eel and grit. I swallowed hard.

The wind strained through the peacock feather in her hat, tugged at her riding habit of hunter's green.

"She rides rather well," I said.

"Yes," said Eldric.

"She appears to be heading our way."

"Yes," said Eldric.

"Do we have enough chocolate biscuits?" said Rose.

"Let's eat them all up," said Eldric. "Now!"

Leanne was now urging the horse up the bluff, now slowing, now slipping from the saddle, turning toward us, smiling with those overripe teeth.

"What a surprise," said Eldric.

Leanne was pink and glowing and robust, looking indecently healthy. "I thought you might come back here."

Back here. Eldric and Leanne had been here before.

Rose flung herself on the blanket and reached for the packet of biscuits.

"What's the rule, Rose?" I said.

"Sweets are for after." Rose set it down. "But I prefer to ask a question now. A person must always keep a secret, mustn't she?"

Come back here.

"Indeed she must," I said. I'd thought this place so fresh and new, but they'd been here before. It was all worn out.

"Even if she doesn't prefer to?"

"Even then," I said.

"I hope you don't mind my joining you," said Leanne. I minded. After all, she'd tried to kill me. A girl in a novel would say it was hard to believe, but it wasn't.

"I don't agree," said Eldric. "Some secrets are wrong and ought to be told."

"What if a person can tell it without telling it?" said Rose.

"How do you mean?" I said.

"I have a different question," said Eldric. "Why do you want to tell?"

"It's a wicked secret," said Rose. "It's wicked to say you'll hurt a person if they tell a secret, isn't it?"

"Yes," said Eldric. "Most wicked."

We were all sitting now on the blanket. There came a strong smell of musk and salt. Leanne must have drowned herself in scent. For the first time, Eldric looked at her. He adjusted his position ever so slightly, opening the circle, letting her into the conversation.

"It might not always be wicked," I said. "What if in telling the person to keep the secret, you're actually protecting her? What if she'll do herself a harm if she tells?"

Was that what men liked, musk and salt?

"Quite right," said Leanne. "There are always two sides to every story."

"It is never acceptable to hurt somebody, or threaten to hurt him," said Eldric.

"But you punched somebody," I said. "I saw you."

"He was hurting someone else." Eldric ought to have looked at me. I was the person who'd been hurt. But he looked at Leanne. He was falling under her spell, wasn't he? I had to remind him—

I mustn't allow him—

"Was it only yesterday," I said, "that you asked me to give you credit for some brains?"

"I believe so." Eldric's fidgety fingers reached for a bun. "How long ago it seems." He spread the jam very thin, piled the cream very thick.

"He was hurting someone else." I mimicked Eldric. "It's always different when it comes to oneself, isn't it? But just remember: You yourself admitted you'd been stupid."

"Touché!" Eldric handed me a creamy sunset of a bun: mounds of cream, a mere splash of pink.

"Eldric's much too hard on himself," said Leanne.

"Thank you," I said, meaning the bun. "It's just the way I like it."

"I know," said Eldric. "I'll never come to grips with the

thirteenth declension, but I do know what you like."

How lovely to eat a sunset, still warm and spread with clouds.

"Eldric is far from stupid," said Leanne. "He's quite a genius in his way."

But that was my idea! I'd said he was a genius the night of the garden party. Leanne couldn't try to kill me, and steal my idea too!

"He was truly stupid." I hadn't said it aloud, though.

"You are unkind, Miss Larkin." *Miss Larkin,* ha! She couldn't distinguish me from Rose.

"I think not," I said. "We are all stupid, aren't we, from time to time?"

"But I more than most," said Eldric, smiling.

Leanne began to speak, but Rose interrupted.

"You can stop talking now. You are distracting me from a very difficult decision." She paused. "I need first to lay the groundwork."

"Lay away!" Eldric all but sang the words. He'd gone electric. "Shall I fix you a bun, Rose?"

Rose nodded. "Do you remember what Father used to call me?"

"Rosy Posy!" I said, which was the answer, but turned out to be more of an exclamation.

"He used to call you Briony Vieny."

Briony Vieny. "I remember."

But I wished I didn't. How mortifying to remind Leanne of one's childish pet name.

"Do you know how Briony and I match up?" It is sometimes unclear to whom Rose is speaking, because she looks all about, not into one's eyes. This time, though, she made it clear to whom she wasn't speaking: She had turned her back on Leanne.

"Your faces match up quite a bit," said Eldric.

"Faces are only genetic." Rose was really very clever in her own way. "But names aren't genetic."

"May I make a guess on how you match up?" said Eldric.

"You may," said Rose, which was generous, because she's fond of announcing her ideas.

"You match because a rose is a flower and so is a briony?"

"It's a vine," said Rose.

"A poisonous vine," I said.

"I never can guess correctly," said Eldric. "It must be because I'm so stupid."

"Please, Eldric!" said Leanne.

I wanted to laugh, I wanted to fling my arms about Eldric. He was playing with me, he was playing against Leanne.

"Because we're both plants," said Rose. "Our faces match up, and our names match up, but there's something that doesn't match up." And Horrors take me if she didn't produce one of her collages.

"Do you like it?"

I did, actually. It was a riot of blues and purples, with a few splashes of peach and gold to give it life.

"I like it extremely," said Leanne, although she hadn't been asked. "How did you know just what colors to use?"

"I have a gift." Rose sat rather closer to me than usual. "But it's not the sort of gift you give someone. I have it all for myself, Eldric said so."

"I did the cutting and gluing," said Eldric. "Didn't I do an excellent job?"

"Eldric's the Administrative Assistant of Scissors and Glue," said Rose.

As I looked at the collage, the colors resolved themselves into patterns, and the patterns resolved themselves into an image. "Do I see people?"

"Yes!" said Rose, and her voice actually managed an exclamation mark. "Who are the people?"

The people were rather abstract, mostly peach-colored blobs with eyes.

"Are they babies?" said Leanne.

"Yes!" said Rose, still sitting with her back to Leanne, which was wonderfully rude. "Who are the babies?"

I stared into the collage, but the baby-blobs did not give up their names.

"I don't know," I said. "Who are they?"

"I can't tell you," said Rose. "Because of the secret."

"But Rose," I said.

"I like Rosy Posy," said Rose.

"But Rosy Posy," I said.

"I prefer that you see it," said Rose. "Because then you'll get better."

"But I'm no longer ill," I said.

"You're ill in a different sort of way," said Rose.

"What way is that?" said Eldric.

"She's ill in her thoughts," said Rose.

"I am not!"

"You are so," said Rose. "You think certain things about yourself and they don't make you happy."

Eldric glanced at me, but I pretended not to notice. Shut up, Rose! "What makes you think I have unhappy thoughts?"

I don't tell Rose things like that—intimate things.

"Because you talk when you're asleep."

Oh.

"May I hazard a guess?" said Eldric.

"A hazard is dangerous," said Rose.

"Hazard a guess about the babies, I mean. Are they you and Briony?"

"Yes!" Rose actually grew pink from all those exclamation marks.

"You're ever so clever," said Leanne.

"This one's you, Rose." Eldric pointed. "That one's Briony."

"Yes!"

"How on earth can you tell?" I said.

"I've told you dozens of times that you and Rose are nothing alike," said Eldric.

"Eldric has an eye for art of all sorts," said Leanne. "Don't you, darling?"

"If you say so," said Eldric.

Darling! Had they *darlinged* each other when they were here? I imagined them, magnificent on horseback, tossing *darlings* to and fro.

"You are not attending," said Rose.

I leaned closer. The babies were little more than oblongs of paper, yet they were clearly babies. How had she done that?

"It's fantastic, Rose."

"I know," said Rose. "What else do you see?"

I looked, and Eldric looked, but we couldn't make out anything else. "I prefer that you see it," said Rose.

"Perhaps Leanne can see it?" said Eldric.

Leanne gazed but finally shook her head. "I'm sorry."

"You see, Rose," said Eldric, "we haven't your eye for color."

"You may call me Rosy Posy," said Rose. "Leanne, however, may not."

"Rose!" I said. "That was extremely rude."

"We didn't ask her to come," said Rose.

I turned to Leanne to apologize, but Leanne smiled and shook her head. "Don't let it trouble you. I quite understand."

"Don't give up!" said Rose. "Briony must get better!"

I looked deeper into the collage, into an overlay of dark blues with spots of white and yellow.

"The night sky?" I said.

"Yes," said Rose. "Eldric has corroborated my theory that it's all right to say *yes* when you guess correctly."

"I intend only to make correct guesses," I said.

The collage was divided into halves with a vertical line of black. At first glance, the halves were identical. A pale moon in each, and a pale peach baby with a single eye.

The babies were identical (unless you chose to believe Eldric), but the moons were not. The right-hand moon hung in the twelve o'clock position, but the left-hand moon had not yet risen so high.

"Hmm," I said.

"Hmm," said Eldric.

"My dear Rose," said Leanne. "You're quite the artist too."

Good thing she couldn't go after Rose. Good thing the Dark Muse only preyed on men.

"Rosy Posy," said Rose, but not to Leanne. "Briony Vieny."

"Our names match up," I said.

"Quite right," said Rose.

"Our names match up, but the moons don't match up."

"You are exceedingly correct," said Rose.

"Did we have a conversation about this before, Rose? When I was ill?"

"Yes," said Rose.

It had been a conversation about how one might describe midnight. I remember being rather breezy and saying that ten minutes before midnight looked just like midnight. Rose had said that was no good.

"Is the one with the moon straight overhead meant to represent midnight, and the other represent before midnight?"

"It doesn't represent," said Rose. "It is."

"Is it then?"

"You are exceedingly correct."

But there I stuck. Rosy Posy and Briony Vieny? Babies at midnight?

They oughtn't to be up so late.

"Don't stop thinking," said Rose. "Otherwise you won't get well."

"I'm thinking," I said. "But Rose—"

"I prefer Rosy Posy."

"But Rosy Posy." I had to make her understand that I was neither ill nor injured. "How is this going to cure unhappy thoughts?"

"You won't have to think them anymore."

Twilight crept upon us; we tore into the packet of biscuits. Eldric offered a share to Leanne, but she cared only for the homemade kind. We leaned against the warm boulders. Shop-bought biscuits are delicious! Too bad for Leanne.

"Don't stop thinking," said Rose.

"Can you give us a hint, Rosy Posy?"

"It's against the rules."

My attempts to work out Rose's secret felt rather as though I were performing brain surgery by the light of a glowworm. "I believe you're too clever for us, Rosy Posy."

I held out my forefinger.

"Yes," said Rose, touching her finger to mine.

Rose lay back on the perfect picnic quilt. She closed her eyes, but she was still smiling. "This is how I want to live my life."

The rest of us sat in silence while mist and moon and moorland worked themselves into a lather of romance. Leanne was doubtless wishing me and Rose far away. All that lather, but no privacy for a two-person scrub.

"Except I want you to know the secret," said Rose, her eyes still closed.

"I'm trying, Rosy Posy."

"Does everyone have a secret, do you suppose?" said Eldric.

"Mine's a mad husband in the attic," I said.

Leanne laughed. It struck me I'd never heard her laugh before. "This is not a proper secret," she said, "but I don't tell many people, as it sounds hideously conceited. I know I can trust the three of you to understand what I mean to say."

But there were only two of us now, for Rose was asleep. Her dreaming eyes shifted beneath butterfly eyelids. She wanted to be called Rosy Posy. She had an unconscious, of course she did. *This is how I want to live my life.* How could I ever have doubted she was a real girl?

"I'm not an artist myself," said Leanne, "but I believe my

gift is working with artists, bringing their works to life. Teasing out of the artist the very best that he can do."

And gobbling him up! Just look at her—all pearly eyes and come-hither teeth.

"I quite agree," said Eldric. "That's clearly your gift."

How did he mean it? Not, I hoped, in the way Leanne took it. Look at her smile. She thought it a compliment.

"What's your secret, Eldric?" said Leanne.

"The problem I have with telling my secret," said Eldric, "is that it's a secret."

"There's no one you would tell?" said Leanne.

"One person, perhaps," said Eldric. "But as there are three of you here, this cannot be the time to reveal it."

One person, perhaps. Rosy Posy knew how she wanted to live her life. Briony Vieny would like to live hers knowing Eldric's secret.

26

A Proper Punch

I raised my hand to knock at Eldric's door. Go on, Briony; don't be a coward. You have to talk to him again about Leanne.

Go on, knock!

But the door was unsmiling, and Eldric might be too. He'd been gloomy this morning at breakfast, stabbing at his kippers, telling Mr. Thorpe he was too ill for lessons.

I knocked.

The door swung inward, Eldric's head poked round. "Why, it's never Briony Larkin!" His face was a blank.

"It's not *never* her." Why had I come? But here I was, and there he was, swinging the door wider, beckoning me inside.

How dark he kept the little room. He'd only a fire at the hearth, and the afternoon was drawing in.

"Not never, perhaps," said Eldric. "But seldom."

He sounded like Cecil, master of indirection, forever entering by the exit door and slipping backward through the looking glass.

Why did I care if I was talking to Eldric or Cecil? Aren't men fungible? Won't one work as well as another?

"Not very tidy, I'm afraid."

Eldric had transformed the sewing room with a new approach to housekeeping. The bed was unmade, he'd slung his shirt and vest over the back of a chair. He kicked aside a shoe as he ushered me in, sat me by the fire.

"We can't have you sitting on the bed, can we?" He sat on the bed himself. "Not on the bed of a notorious bad boy."

There was one difference between Eldric and Cecil, a difference peculiar to Briony Larkin, and that was lust. I lusted after Eldric; I shuddered away from Cecil.

I didn't sit. On a nearby table lay a half-written letter and a blotter, sopping up a leaky pen. "I'll come back. I've caught you in the middle of something."

Eldric sprang from the bed. "What an idiot!" He snatched at the paper, flung it into the fire. The flames blew bright and hot. Black lips crunched across the paper; the words crumbled into ash.

"What was that?" I said.

"If I wanted anyone to know," said Eldric, "I wouldn't have burnt it, now would I?"

"I thought members of the Fraternitus were not to keep secrets from each other."

But lust is just a matter of chemistry. It's just that Briony molecules and Eldric molecules have a bit that hooks together.

He said nothing; I turned round. "I'll come back."

And it's just that Cecil molecules have no Briony-molecule hooks.

"Don't go!" Eldric grabbed my shoulder. "I'm in a foul temper, I know, but do stay!"

I hated this. It snapped at bits of my insides as though they were elastic. "I'd like to be able to say I'll make it quick—isn't that what characters always say in books? But I've rather a lot to bring up."

"Fire away." Eldric pushed at my shoulder. I sank into the chair.

"I did, actually, want to speak to you about firing away," I said. "Perhaps I'll start with that."

Eldric leaned past me and touched a candle to the fire. Why couldn't he just sit down!

"Do you have a gun?"

He whistled a few hollow notes, then drew the candle toward my face. "No, but I can get one."

I blinked back the light. "Can you shoot?"

"Tolerably well."

"Would you take that candle away? I look just the same as ever."

He'd seen it all before: the corn-silk hair, the Dresden-shepherdess face, the black eyes—iris, pupil, lashes.

He backed away. "What would you want me to do with this hypothetical gun?"

"Bring it to the Feast of the Dead, on Halloween night."

"And then?"

"I'll tell you on Halloween. But the real reason I came is that I have to talk to you about Leanne."

"I've had enough of her for a lifetime," said Eldric.

"You have?"

"Once I leave her sphere, I find I don't much like her. But I told you that. You were right, as always: I was under her spell."

"You rejected her?"

"I will."

"Then there's something else I have to tell you. A Dark Muse can only feed on one man at a time. If she's rejected by him, she can only feed on a blood relative."

"My father?" said Eldric.

"You have to warn him."

"I still don't believe Leanne's a Dark Muse," said Eldric. "And listen here: You say the Dark Muse feeds on artistic energy. But I'm no artist."

"Leanne thought you were," I said. "She liked the way you're always creating something from nothing."

"And once I reject her she can't eat?" said Eldric. "I mean, feed?"

"Unless she gets to your father, she'll dwindle and die."

"Dwindle and die, just as I was doing? Not that I believe any of this, you understand."

I paused. "Not exactly like you. You'd have gone mad first, but when you died your soul would have lived on. But a Dark Muse has no soul. When she dies, she'll turn to dust and blow about for all eternity."

I couldn't stop thinking about Halloween, when I would reveal what I really was. I'd turn witchy in front of everyone, in front of Eldric. I couldn't stop thinking of how his fingers would go stiff, how the light would leave his eyes. How he'd say, *Why didn't you tell me?*

"I've been wanting to tell you something for a long time."

"So have I," said Eldric. "What's yours?"

"You first," I said.

"Guests first, my father always says."

"I'm not a guest."

"Girls first, then," said Eldric.

"Mine is not an easy thing to say."

"Mine's harder," said Eldric. But he smiled for the first time that night.

I'd promised Stepmother never to tell. My tongue curled over on itself, protecting its soft belly. But the alternative was worse: Eldric finding out along with everyone else, and I, never knowing what he thought, going into the future, never knowing.

There came a swallowing-up kind of silence. "I'm a witch."

There, it was done. I'd ruined everything. *Snap!* went my elastic insides.

"You don't look like a witch."

I wished I could see his face better.

"Witches don't look like anything. Witches are. Witches do."

It was so quiet, I heard the candlewick collapse. The flame turned into a blue corpse of itself. I watched it struggle. I watched it drown in its own spit.

The dark blot of Eldric came at me.

"Prove it. Prove you're a witch!"

There we stood, fire snapping at my wicked left hand, the tumble of Eldric's underthings grinning at my virtuous right.

"Prove it!"

"You don't believe me?"

"I need proof," said Eldric. "Why should I believe anything you say?"

My spit turned to powdered glass.

"If you were a game," said Eldric, "you'd be a puzzle. If you were a piece of writing, you'd be a code."

"But I can't prove it." I snapped my fingers. "Not just like that!"

"Can't you? How peculiar!" Eldric laughed, a horrid splat of a laugh. "Show me the most wicked thing you can do."

How dare he be angry!

I'd walked my own anger on a leash all these years, but it was always just a spark away. I'd work myself into a rhapsody of witchiness. I'd spark into fire.

Fire!

I thought about fire. I thought of the library—the burst of flame, my hand, the smell of burning flesh.

There came no fire.

I thought of the piano burning, crashing to its knees, like a camel. I thought of all my stories. How long it had taken me to write them, how quickly they had burnt.

There came no fire.

"You can't prove it." Eldric's eyes were hollows of darkness.

The taste of sulfur clawed at my throat. Let my words strike sparks!

Nothing. I needed the Brownie to explode my powers into sparks. I needed Mucky Face.

There we stood, on the divide of dark and more dark. Eldric pressed his cheek into my silence.

"I'll tell you something that will make you believe," I said. "Have you never wondered how Rose got to be the way she is?"

I'd never told anyone about Rose.

"I did it myself, with witchcraft."

I'd never thought to say those words.

"I don't believe you," said Eldric.

"I meant to hurt her. It's only hatred. A Dark Muse feeds on artistry. A witch feeds on hatred. Hatred is easy."

"But you love Rose!" said Eldric. "I know you do."

Quiet, Briony. Don't say any more. Don't tell him you don't love anyone.

"Then prove you hurt Rose," said Eldric.

I shrugged. "I remember lots of it. I remember Rose falling from the swing and screaming. Stepmother told me the things I can't remember."

"Damn your stepmother! Maybe she's the witch."

"Don't you dare say that!" I shoved him in the chest, hard as I could.

That had no effect, except that he clamped his hands on my shoulders.

"Have you been drinking?" I said.

"No, but that's quite a good idea. Listen, I don't understand why you adore your stepmother so. And since we've been speaking of feeding, I have to say that she seems to have done nothing but feed off of you. I can't stand it when I think of her lying in bed all that time, letting you neglect your education, letting you wait on her."

"I'm the one who injured her spine," I said. "Just in case that changes your mind."

"I don't believe that, either."

"You don't need to believe it for it to be so. I called upon Mucky Face to smash her. She'd have died of it eventually, had the arsenic not come first."

"Mucky Face, the creature we saw from the bridge?"

"The very same."

"You may be mad," said Eldric, "but you're no murderer." He ground at my shoulder bones.

"That hurts."

He let go at once. "Sometimes I want to squeeze something from you." He wrung his hands. "Squeeeeze, like that." He squeezed his knuckles white.

The fire burnt low, muttering and tossing and closing its eyes.

"How stupid I am," he said. "I need to remember that if I squeeze, you'll only break."

But he kept squeezing his own hands, squeezing until one of his bones cried out.

I couldn't speak, but then, I never do speak. Not really. I'm always wearing my mask. The underneath Briony is stuck in her own silence.

Someday, silence will make me explode!

Out went my fist, back went Eldric, onto the bed. He held his face in his two palms. Blood leaked between his fingers.

Pretty girl love! The Bleeding Hearts' voices chimed in my head.

Love pretty boy.

Eldric pinched the bridge of his nose. His shoulders— how they shook!

The Bleeding Hearts had come close to the truth; they couldn't have known I'm incapable of love. *Lust pretty boy!*

I sat on the bed beside Eldric, put my hand on his shoulder. "I have a handkerchief." He peeled his hands from his face.

He was laughing.

Be honest now, Briony. You hit a person and he laughs? That is adorable.

Pretty girl laugh with pretty boy.

"Well done!" Eldric spoke through my handkerchief. "If you'd done that with Cecil, he wouldn't have had a chance." He caught at my fist, wrapped it in his bloody palm. "You used your left hand!"

"It's my wicked hand. My witch hand."

I could almost see him thinking about this, how quickly I'd adapted to using my left hand, how clumsy I'd always been with my right.

"You really do believe you're a witch!" Eldric uncurled my fingers, exposing the scribble of scars.

"Why would I lie about that?"

"To get rid of me?" said Eldric.

My hand was red with Eldric's blood. I drew it to my chest.

"What had you been going to tell me?" I said, but I was already backing away from him, pushing at the swinging door. I mustn't get too near. What if I threw myself at him, just as I had when I was tipsy?

Eldric shook his head. "Another time, perhaps."

I was backing away, and I'd keep on too. After Halloween, I'd back away into the swamp, and if I managed to make it to London without being caught, I'd never see him again.

It's just lust, Briony. There'll be plenty of men in London for you to lust. But don't punch them in the nose, because odds are, they won't laugh.

27

The Face
in the Mirror

The Halloween sky was a splash of pea soup. The sky held its breath, waiting for rain. I stood in the square, voices muttering and crackling all about like dying coals. Everyone was waiting.

"Now!" cried the mayor. The bonfire leapt into life. Torches burst into flame, illuminating stalls with beaded canopies, baskets spilling with brandy snaps and licorice and butterscotch. Figures in beaded masks, passing platters of crystallized ginger, gooseberry tarts, floury buns. And scattered everywhere was toffee: Toffee wrapped in silver paper; heaps and piles and mounds of toffee; silver paper glittering like mountains of ice.

"Ooh!" said the children.

"Ooh!" said the grown folks.

"Ooh!" said Briony.

You couldn't avoid your reflection. Mirrors hung in every twist and turn of the stalls. They caught at their own reflections too, doubling and tripling and reflecting themselves into infinity.

Despite the half-masks, I recognized most of the villagers. Who could mistake the constable's sloppy lips, the Reeve's plucked-chicken skin? Who could mistake a mane of tawny hair and long lion muscles?

The mask turned toward me. The eye-holes glittered; the head tilted into a question mark; the gloved hand beckoned. *Come with me!* The lion muscles pounced into one of the stalls, disappeared into a shadowed recess.

I followed, past the mirrors that showed their faces to the public, toward the hidden mirrors at the back. Some girls wanted their privacy, for it was said that on Halloween night, an image of the man they were to marry would emerge in the looking glass beside their own reflections.

A gloved hand pulled aside a flap of canvas. I pushed into the mirk.

The mirror was a dark hole until Eldric lit a candle. Our reflections stood side by side, masked but unmistakable. I'd never thought about how different we were. Tall and short; gold and pale; broad and narrow; tawny and flaxen.

"I must leave the instant the clock strikes the half hour," I said, like a twentieth-century Cinderella. Both Cinderella and I needed to keep an eye on the time. She had her slipper problems, I had my ghosts.

"I've been thinking," said the Eldric image.

"Ooh, thinking!" I said. "Shall I tell your father?"

"Very funny," said Eldric, but he was laughing. "You may be clever, Miss Larkin, but I've spotted a few holes in last night's story. Yes, even I!

"Take Rose, for example. Would Rose ever climb willingly onto a swing? Rose, who's so cautious she doesn't even toast bread without wearing gloves?"

I hadn't thought of this, but I had an answer. "We don't know what she was like before she struck her head. Perhaps she was quite the opposite."

He slipped off his mask. "Please remind me not to argue with you again." Bruises ran from the bridge of his nose into his eye, which was swollen shut.

"I'm so sorry," I said.

"It's all right. I quite enjoyed telling my story about the great brute with the powerful left hook who surprised me in the night."

"Poor Eldric!" I said. "And where did this great brute overtake you?"

"On my way to call on Leanne."

Oh! My mouth echoed my thoughts: O!

"Take off that mask, will you?"

I shook my head. What if my own Briony mask were not securely in place? Look at my lips, look at how they gave me away: *O!*

"And?" I said.

"I set it to rights, put her out of my life. It was rather horrible, but it's over."

The mirror Briony smiled.

Eldric tugged at the strings of my mask. "Won't you take this off? I have something to say to you, and I'd like to see your face."

What could I do but slip it off? It left me entirely exposed, my face raw as a peeled apple.

"First." Eldric tapped one index finger against the other. *Tick.* "Apologies for being in such a very bad humor when you visited me."

The mirror Briony had no amusing answer. She nodded.

"Two." Eldric ticked his second finger. "Do you remember the paper I burnt?"

Another nod.

"It was a letter, to you. It was that which put me in so foul a humor."

To me? The lips of the mirror Briony mouthed the words.

Eldric nodded. "It was also the secret I mentioned the other night, the secret I'll tell only one person.

"Three." *Tick.* "Remember what you said about marriage, during our picnic?"

Briony nodded.

"That made me upset, which made me angry.

"Four." *Tick.*

The candle sputtered. Eldric cupped his hand round the flame, coaxed it to life. It shone between his fingers, tracing his hand with fire.

"A person might get angry when the girl he loves says she'll never marry."

Girl he loves.

My face was raw. I cradled it in my hands. Give me a mask, any mask! I swung my hair forward.

"I'm almost out of numbers," said Eldric. "As you know, my mathematical skills are limited." He laid his fire-traced hand on the back of my neck. What was I to do? I wished I could love, how I wished!

"That's what I didn't say the other night."

I turned my peeled-apple face to him. I'd make myself look at him. I owed him that. His touch lingered on my neck as though he'd left a handprint of melted light.

His brow was pinchy and he was paler than usual. His scar looked very pink.

The clock struck the half hour. I jumped. "I must go!"

"But the gun!" said Eldric. "What am I to do with the gun?"

"Make sure they don't hang me. I don't want to hang!"

And then I was out, into the square, where nothing had changed. The torches still burnt as before, and the toffee wrappers still glinted, and the children oohed and grabbed and ate, and the sky was still holding its breath.

· 28 ·

Unquiet Spirits

The graveyard yawned with its rotting breath. My skirts fluttered past Mother's grave.

How might I summon the ghost-children? I knew no spells, poor witch that I was. Might I simply talk them out of their graves?

"Harken to me you little ones, taken by the Boggy Mun. Those were woeful days, indeed they were, and there will be many and many a woeful day to come unless you help me. Come with me, to the village, else more little bones will rot beside you."

A scuttle of rats plunged by, their tails like dirty string. I gave a little shriek, just to try it out, to see what it might be like to be a regular girl. What else might scuttle by? I had no Bible Ball, not that it would discourage a rat. It would, however, discourage an Unquiet Spirit. It was for that very reason I had no Bible Ball. I wanted the children to approach, to follow me to the square.

"Indeed, I speak to all of you who lie restless in the earth.

It is All Hallows' Eve, the night you may rise from your graves and show yourselves to the living. Come! Walk with me into the village where you were born. Come! Tell your mothers and fathers and aunts and uncles and grandmothers and grandfathers—tell them it's the Boggy Mun bringing the death sickness."

The sky leaned on my shoulders, it dripped down my spine. It dripped into the graves, which were yawning now, opening their mouths around tiny caskets. The graves were open; they stank of cold.

I'd expected the world to tilt on its axis, as it had done every time I wandered into the spirit world—the skull of Death, the ghost-children. I thought that when the children answered, I'd be standing upside-down on the underside of the world, hair streaming into space. Perhaps the rules were different when it was I who did the calling.

"Hold my hands, come with me. Come and tell the whole of the village that the waters must bide in the Swampsea."

Something touched me. No, not something: someone. Someone set the tip of a small finger against my own finger-tip. The shock of it sizzled through my flesh.

Now another finger, and another and still another, fingers, hands, small hands, wrapping themselves round mine. Hands piled one atop the other, but still I felt them all, each sinking into the others. I could count them. The twenty-nine hands of the twenty-nine children who had heard and risen from their graves.

"Thank you." I spoke but did not look. I passed through the cemetery gate. There were little stumbles in my walking, as though I were crossing a field of thunderbolts.

"Once upon a time," I said, "in the far reaches of the Swampsea, there lived a spirit of the bogs. The Swampfolk called it the Boggy Mun, and it had power, oh, a vast deal of power. It could be kindly, but it could be cruel. When it felt ill-used, it sent the deadly swamp cough to prey upon the people. And as is the way of things, the cough carried away the innocent and the weak: It carried away the children."

"Ah!" The ghost-children sighed like rustling leaves. "Ah!"

On I spoke, telling of the dams and the sluice gates and the pumping station; of the cough and the growing number of little graves; of the grown folks who didn't understand that it was the Boggy Mun sending the sickness.

I spoke of how I, the witch girl, came to ask the ghost-children to climb from their graves and speak the truth of the matter.

"Ah!" sighed the ghost-children. Their hands were not cold. Their hands were not warm. "Ah!"

"The ghost-children came out of the darklings, into the village, holding the witch by the hand. How the Swampfolk cried out! They were scareful and their knee-bones knocked together. The tears poured from their eyes, for whom did they see? They saw their own dear children who had died."

We drew near Hangman's Square and the darkness softened. The gallows was just steps ahead.

"And when the Swampfolk heard them, heard their very own children, they went to work at once. They tore apart the pumping station, and they opened the sluices, and the water flowed back into the swamp.

"The brave ghost-children saved the ailing babies lying

in their cradles, pale as spilt milk. They saved the ailing children coughing out bits of their lungs. They saved the witch girl's ailing sister, and for that, the witch girl promised to tell the story of their bravery over and over as long as she might live."

I stopped. The ghost-children stopped. I'd never thought to climb the gallows, but this was a day for doing things I'd never thought to do. The ghost-children and I must climb the gallows so that everyone might see.

There were no stairs at the gallows' back, but I hoisted myself to waist height, clambered onto the platform. The ghost-children followed, weightless as dandelion puffs.

The Swampfolk saw us now. The barkeep stood frozen, a clutter of boiled sweets in his outstretched palm.

Boys played at hoops, a skip-rope churned. Silver toffee wrappers blew about the children's feet.

The ratcatcher dropped a bar of peanut brittle. The unmarried girls turned away from the looking glasses. They turned away, from bright hopes of future husbands, to dead brothers, and sisters, and cousins, and friends.

"The babies and the children grew well and strong, and so did Rose Larkin, thanks to the heroic ghost-children. And the babies and the children and Rose all lived out the rest of their lives in great peace and contentment."

The skip-rope girls were the last to notice. *Slap-slap* went the rope.

> *The water is high,*
> *The water is low.*
> *In comes the swamp cough:*
> *Out . . . you . . . go!*

Slap . . . The rope stuttered into silence, the handles clattered against the cobblestones.

How the Swampfolk stared! They stood staring in a lump, like cold potatoes. Father's mouth opened. *Briony!* he said, but he made no sound.

But I had the ghost-children. They formed a circle round me. They waited.

· 29 ·

A Crumpled Page

"Maggie!"

"My Jess!"

"Willy!"

The names of dead children filled the night.

"Kevin!"

"Baby Shirley!"

The ghost-hands slipped away; the ghost-children gathered at the gallows' edge, reaching out to flesh and blood. I saw them properly now. There was nothing horrid about them. No dripping flesh, no unspeakable ooze.

"Speak!" I said. "Tell them!"

"'Twere the Boggy Mun!" said a small voice.

Then another. "'Twere the Boggy Mun what kilt us."

"I be scareful o' the darklings!"

I looked into the crowd. Eldric stood at the front, his face bright as flame.

"The Boggy Mun kilt us on account o' the water."

"The water what leaved the swamp."

"The water what goed to the sea."

"I miss you, Mam! My bed, it be so cold!"

Mothers and fathers reached for their children.

"The Boggy Mun kilt us on account o' them engineering men."

Fisherfolk are stolid, usually weeping only when drunk. But now they wept openly, and sobbed, and called for their children.

"Where is she!" howled a woman's voice, all dark caves and echoes. "Where!" The voice struck me between the wings of my shoulders.

The crowd fell back and lost its edges. It oohed and screamed and ran all shimble-shamble.

I spun round, faced the black squall of a mouth.

The bones dripped with flesh. The black squall opened wider. "There she is!" Maggots crawled between her teeth. Maggots oozed through her eyes.

Softer now. "There you are." Her voice was the only thing I recognized. That, and her hair, knots and clumps of sooty hair. *Black is the color of my true love's hair.* Her flesh was real; she was not like the ghost-children, whose flesh did not decay. Blue petals of skin drifted to her feet.

"I've been waiting to talk to you." Stepmother set a finger on the tatters of her lips. I'd forgotten this gesture of hers. "You are a good girl, calling me from my grave." She might have been chatting at a tea party.

The worst thing was that she still had her eyes. Or one of them. The other bulged from its socket, tipped with fish-belly gray.

"Come closer." She reached for me with a tattered arm.

307

Bracelets clinked on her wrist-bones. They sounded much as they used to, just as they might have at a tea party.

The air tasted of thunder. It lay on my tongue like a rusty coin.

"I've been screaming; this whole time I've been screaming." Her bracelets were the color of cinders. "What else can you do, lying in the cold clay, the worms sewing up your shroud?" Her teeth were straight and white, horrific to see in that storm of decay.

"I don't understand." My voice had gone funny and distant. I heard it as though I were listening to myself listen to myself.

"No?" The wind tugged at her flesh, spattering gobbets into the night. "Even though you called me from my grave?"

Or perhaps it was my ears that had gone far away. "You, an Unquiet Spirit?"

"Spirit?" Stepmother paused; fat maggot-tears oozed down her cheeks. "I don't believe that's the word your father would use. But restless, yes. Exceedingly restless. The situation at hand—well, I believe your father would call it ironic."

It was impossible, I know, but my faraway ears heard Father's throat stick together.

"Ironic that after all your attempts to slip away from me, burning your hand when I first turned to you, and then when I turned to Rose—no; let's save that for later."

Stepmother's face was a howling wilderness, but she spoke in her tea-party voice. Could the others hear? They were quiet as death.

"Ironic that after all you did to destroy me, you should call me from my grave. That now I may scream out to the world the name of the person who murdered me, that then at last, I may depart this world."

Murdered. I'd known Stepmother wouldn't kill herself.

"Even we Old Ones—yes, even we are unable to depart this world with our business unfinished."

"Old Ones?" said my faraway voice.

She took a step forward. "Aren't you afraid, Briony? Afraid of what I might say?" Her jaw dropped, and she was once again a black squall, howling into the crowd.

"You are fools, all of you. I didn't take my own life."

Stepmother's cheek slipped from her bones, splatted onto the gallows floor. "My murderer stands before you. Her name, Briony Larkin."

Briony Larkin? My mind could not react to *Briony Larkin.* But my body could. I felt the shock of it, cathedral bells clanging at my neck and wrists.

"Peace at last," said Stepmother, and it happened all at once. Stepmother's skin wilted from her bones. She turned to a pile of petals.

A regular girl would feel something. She'd feel something as the petals crumbled into dust. But a witch merely looks away. Father's face was a crumpled page. The rest of the faces were a blur. The ghost-children had vanished. They'd set themselves free. They too might now leave this world.

The wind whipped across the gallows floor, snatched at the dust that had once been Stepmother.

"Murderess!" shouted someone from the crowd.

Stepmother eddied about my feet.

"Witch!" shouted another.

Stepmother dissolved into the wind. She was gone.

Now a chorus: "Hang the witch!"

The chorus's eyes were slitted windows.

"No!" Cecil blasted through the crowd, but a clot of men grabbed his arm.

"Leave me be!" Cecil struggled, but the men held tight.

"Easy, lad. It be us grown folks as doesn't be fooled by no witch."

Cecil. Cecil, who did a mysterious favor for Briony. Cecil, who's addicted to arsenic.

Stepmother died of arsenic.

I jumped back as a figure leapt the gallows steps. But only one person could make that lion's leap. "Stand back!" The memory of Eldric's hand shone on the back of my neck.

The crowd surged forward, growling and clawing.

"Hang her!"

"I always suspicioned her for a witch."

Eldric raised the pistol. Silence crackled through the crowd. "I'll shoot the first person to move."

"She don't need no trial," said the constable. "Us all seen she be a witch."

"No!" shouted Father.

The constable looked about from under his inside-out eyelids. "Us seen what us seen, hey?"

The crowd growled and pushed closer.

"Look at them eyes she got," said the Reeve. "Black as Hisself they be."

The crowd turned into one great beast with a single mind.

"I always did mislike them eyes."

The crowd tossed its horns and pawed the ground. Its jowls shook.

It ran at the stairs, but Eldric's lightning hand struck. The pistol leapt. The night went white and blank. Reality shattered. I kept picking up bits and putting them together in the wrong order.

The constable reeling back, hand to shoulder.

But that must have happened last.

The constable climbing the gallows steps—

That must have happened first.

The pistol cracking—

That must have happened in the middle.

And over everything, the smell, the tongue-curling tang of gunpowder. That, at least, was as it should be.

"Next I'll shoot the Reeve," said Eldric. His gaze roamed the crowd. "Then I'll have to decide."

"He don't got no more than five shots," said the crowd. It licked its lips. It carried torches that blazed with yellow tulips.

The crowd crashed forward.

Yellow tulips with crimson hearts.

"Go!" Eldric bumped me with his shoulder. I staggered. White nothingness blasted the night.

The tulips paused, their hearts pulsed.

The wind whistled beneath its breath; the first raindrops fell. Eldric shouted, "Run fast as ever you can!"

I ran across the platform. White nothingness blasted a hole in the crowd.

"Run, wolfgirl!" shouted Eldric.

I leapt into the hole. The air shattered. I ran.

· 30 ·

Eels in Eel Broth

The sky wrung itself out like a sponge. Rain fell like daggers; I shielded my eyes. The sky flashed white, silhouetting twisted trees. Lightning played darts on the Flats, with wolfgirl as bull's-eye.

Despite the trees, the Slough provided no shelter. The wind tore at the treetops, tossed about handfuls of oozy leaf-splats. I'd never known such dark. It leaned in all about me. It pressed at my eyes with great, hard thumbs.

Expose my murderer.

Her name is Briony Larkin.

The memory came to me in bits.

I'd never tried to kill an eel. I could not have imagined it would be so hard, that it would wriggle and writhe and slam itself about. I had to skewer it to the table to cut off its head. I skewered it through the middle, but still, it thrashed and writhed. It writhed when you cut off its head; it writhed when you gutted it; it writhed when you skinned it.

What got ye for your supper, Lord Randal, my son?

How can you skin an eel when the skin is tough as leather? When even after it's dead, it thrashes about? Here's how I did it.

What got ye for your supper, my bonny young man?

I fetched Father's pliers. The eel flung itself about, but I grabbed its skin with the pliers, tore it off in strips. The pot was already on the fire. I tossed in the eel. Oh, how it jumped!

I got eels boiled in eel broth; Mother, make my bed soon,
For I'm sick at the heart and I fain would lie doon.

I'd sung "Lord Randal" dozens of times, never once thinking about Lord Randal's sweetheart making that eel broth. I'd sung it before I knew the writhe and grit of eels. Before I knew their stink sinks into your skin, that you scrub and scrub but can't get it out. Before I grew afraid of my own hands, afraid I'd carry the eel-stink forever. Before I discovered the lemon juice that washed it away.

Remember when you asked yourself why you hadn't turned into Mr. Sherlock Holmes? Why you hadn't tracked Stepmother's murderer down?

That's poetical irony for you.

"Mistress!"

I whipped round, into the smell of algae and dead fish, into the foam and roar of Mucky Face. "Mistress, tha' lad be busking the swamp for thee, an' the Dead Hand, it be draggling behind."

"Behind Eldric?"

"Aye, mistress."

"The Dead Hand, following him!"

"Aye, mistress. It draws ever nigh."

I made a sound like peeling paint. The Wykes sparked up, laughing, teasing, trying to lead me astray. The wind screamed and boxed my ears, but it couldn't hide the other scream.

"Briony!"

The Wykes skittered and sneered.

"Briony!" Eldric's voice was a rusty nail. My teeth cringed. Thunder gnashed its teeth.

"Eldric!"

I followed his voice through the rabid underbrush. "Briony!" Only thunder now.

"Eldric!"

Yellow flames skittered ahead of me. "Briony!" Eldric's voice, raw and tattered. The Dead Hand glowed beside his writhing shadow, beside a long darkness of screams. I dove upon the bloated flesh of the Dead Hand, releasing the sweet, rank smell of death.

I pried at its fingers. My nails sank into its flesh. Eldric had brought no Bible Ball—the fool! I wrung out yellow ooze, like curdled cream.

The Wykes watched the witch girl. They saw she couldn't budge the dead fingers. They crackled and cackled.

"Briony!"

I stabbed my fingers into the fleshy web between the Dead Hand's forefinger and thumb. I stabbed at the join between the oozing web and Eldric's warm, living wrist. But they might have been fused together. Not even a shadow could have slipped between.

"Briony!"

I tasted my own sick, I swallowed it down. I let go the hand, tore at my frock. It resisted. I set my teeth upon it. On my feet now, yanking at the placket. Buttons exploded. Off with the frock, tearing at the shoulder seam. Damn you, Pearl, for those strong, tiny stitches. Tearing again, tearing. Curling my finger through a tiny hole, ripping. Tearing and swearing.

I couldn't save the hand, I could only save Eldric.

The Wykes sparked up again, yellow, blue, glinting, laughing. I flung myself to my knees, fell into a slippery wetness. The Wykes, yellow, sparking, glinting, lighting the wetness to crimson. A fountain of Eldric blood. Don't look! You'll be sick if you see his non-hand. You've no time to be sick.

I twisted the sleeve round Eldric's forearm.

The Wykes ebbed and vanished. Dawn sifted through the trees like ashes. The Dead Hand melted away. Did it carry away its prize—don't look!

My petticoat was a crimson stain. Eldric's lips were pale worms. His face raged with bruises. "Help me up," said the worm lips.

He held out his left hand. His eyes were empty rooms.

I took his hand in both my own. I pulled; I pulled again. Finally, I stooped and slipped my shoulder under his left arm.

"One . . . two . . . three!"

He did a great deal of the getting up himself. But he staggered at the end, crashing onto my shoulder. I waited, swallowed the pain, before I said, "We'll get you to Dr. Rannigan."

Eldric stepped, stumbled, clutched. His fingers bit into my bones.

"That's right," I said. "Wrap your arm around my shoulder."

He wrapped, he leaned. "Talk to me," he said.

Talk? There was only one thing to talk about. *Murderess.* The word hung in the air between us.

315

Only one thing to talk about, but nothing to say. If only I had some excuse, something to explain it. Even witchy jealousy would be better than nothing. I remembered the how of it, the eel and the pliers, but I couldn't remember why. It must be in there, someplace, but you can't get at a memory as you might get at a splinter. You can't poke about in your mind with a sterilized needle.

Eldric's forearm, his good forearm, dangled past my shoulder. I held it in a crisscross of my own forearms—as though that would help anything. That wasn't the arm that needed Dr. Rannigan.

But there it was, pressed against my middle, bulging with bad-boy veins. He'd offered his own red blood from those veins, offered it even though I wouldn't tell him anything, not about the Boggy Mun, not about the pumping station. I might tell him that, at least, tell him about Rose and the Boggy Mun.

I meant to start at the beginning with the ghost-children and go straight through to the end. But I ended up jumping into the middle and splashing about in both directions, talking about the swamp cough and the draining and Rose.

My shoulders screamed under Eldric's weight. But if he could keep going, I could keep going.

"Talk some more."

My memory of those days is always of the time after Mucky Face roared through, leaving the Parsonage smelling of paper bloat and cellar scum. Of sitting on the library carpet, in a patch of sunlight, finding myself staring at a scatter of mouse droppings.

Storybook characters are always praised for keeping their

houses neat as pins. But no one writes about characters who are too weary to clean, characters who can't be bothered to care. No one writes about a character who sits on the floor and looks at mouse droppings. Who looks and looks and leaves them be.

"Where are you going?" Eldric's voice was flat and slow, an elastic band, stretched lengthwise.

The character doesn't decide to leave them be. She simply does. She does anything that requires no decision and no action.

"The village."

"You can't go to the village," said the gray, elastic voice. "They'll hang you."

If I were an author, I'd write about people who sit on the floor. About people who look at mouse droppings and don't care. About people who can only feel a black hole inside.

"Turn around," said Eldric. "Run."

"You need to get to Dr. Rannigan."

My memory grabbed at the doctor's face, at his high forehead, his patient cow eyes. If only he were here now, he'd know what to do. My chest slammed shut. My breath went silent; I heard the drumming of my heart.

Dr. Rannigan!

What should I do, Dr. Rannigan?

I couldn't breathe, my heart beat faster. But I couldn't die, not yet. That was for later, on the gallows. I had to get Eldric to Dr. Rannigan.

Breathe, Briony! Breathe so Eldric can keep breathing. I willed my heart to slow, I willed myself to breathe. The door to my chest creaked open. I drew a breath.

"I'll walk myself to the village." Eldric already sounded dead. "You run."

I was used to the idea of dying but not of Eldric dying. The thought hurt my chest. When a person hurts, she cries. But a witch can't cry, she has to go on hurting.

"Run!" said Eldric.

Run? Run and leave Eldric to die? Run into a lifetime of loneliness and guilt? He must be mad.

Memory shards now, falling like rain. I watched my hands dip a ladle into a cauldron of eel broth. I watched them pour the broth into a bowl. My fingers now, tugging at a twist of white powder.

How lucky we twentieth-century witches were. Macbeth's witches had to find poisoned entrails for their cauldron, generally not available at the local apothecary. Briony Larkin had only to measure out four grains of the powder, add a pinch more for good luck, and stir it into the broth.

At first, Stepmother said she was not hungry, but I urged her to eat, saying she'd never otherwise regain her health. If she ate, I said, I'd write her a story.

That's why she ate.

A story, for her and her alone.

She ate it all up.

It started about an hour later, the first symptoms, abdominal pain, nausea, then an urgent need for a chamber pot, the results of which were bloody—all of which I'd expected. I'd written Fitz, asking if he didn't ever worry about overingesting arsenic, and as I'd known he would, he wrote me a treatise on the stages of arsenic poisoning, both chronic and acute.

Stepmother's was acute.

"Talk some more," said Eldric.

I remembered exactly when the skull of Death appeared on her shoulder. Her face had collapsed, her eyes gone red. *Murderess.*

Eldric's knees buckled. I grabbed him round the middle. He slumped against me, toppled me over. We juddered into a log, which slammed into my ribs.

The slump of Eldric pinned me to the log. I hardly felt him breathe. Was he in shock?

"Eldric?"

A person could die from shock.

"Eldric?" I couldn't move him.

I'd never known the true meaning of dead weight. If the mountain wouldn't get off of Muhammad, Muhammad would get out from under the mountain. I squiggled out, bit by bit, scraping myself over moss and bark. My ribs yelped and whined.

Stones and twigs and leaves and blood—blood, leaping from Eldric's wrist. I tightened the tourniquet, watched the spill of blood slow to a weepy drizzle. I watched myself lift his arm with my two hands and lay his hand on his chest. I watched myself examine the raw edges of his wrist. I watched myself worry that I might see severed bones and ligaments. I watched myself being relieved to see nothing but red ooze. I watched myself being ashamed at being relieved. I watched myself work out what to do next.

He'd lost so much blood; his eyes were closed. I should be obliged to drag him. But first, I needed to secure his arm to his body. I mustn't let it bump about.

I could pass another length of frock under his back. I could tie it over his front, which would pin his upper arm to his side, secure his forearm and hand to his chest. But how was I to do that? He was very heavy. I'd have to roll and push and—what if I hurt him again?

But as long as you're thinking about rolling and pushing and hurting, why not think about rolling him onto your cloak? It might work as a sleigh. You could pull him on a cloak-sleigh, jiggety-jig, all the way home.

You may take one—two—three breaths, Briony, and then you have to move!

I worked at a seam in my skirt, tearing through the stitches. Why didn't I have a knife? Florence Nightingale would have had a knife. I laid four lengths of fabric widthwise on the ground, one at shoulder level, one at elbow level, one at hip level, one at ankle level. I laid my cloak over the lengths of fabric.

I could think of only one way to do it. I slipped my arms under Eldric's arms, dragged him backward, over the cloak. The cloak bunched up beneath him.

Hell!

I was wrung out by the time I'd wrapped the cloak around him, looped and tied each length of fabric round the front to hold the cloak in place.

I grasped the collar of the cloak, stepped back, tugged. It could be worse, Briony. It could be your leg that's hurt, not your shoulder and ribs. Don't think about it, keep walking. Think about the snickleway ahead. Think how to get Eldric across without drowning him. Think! Think!

Time ceased to exist. I could not think into the future, I

could not remember the past: There was only now. There was only the present tense.

The Slough is the worst part of the journey. There are so many obstacles—logs, scrub, snickleways. The snickleways are both the hardest and easiest, the water both help and hindrance. It eases the burden of Eldric's weight, but it also wants to drown him. You have to hold his head above water, which means the bit of snickleway you're fording can't be too deep. Which means you plough through it yourself first, to test the depth, and when you do ford the snickleway with Eldric, you have to wrap your arms around his chest. You have to pull him as high as you can, you have to press his neck and shoulders into your middle. When you emerge from the snickleway, you are shaking with the effort. You are tempted to let yourself rest.

But you don't.

You ford another snickleway, you tremble with effort. You tremble with cold. You've given most of your clothes to Eldric. You wear only your petticoat and chemise. *Slough*. It's an appropriate word. Perhaps you'll slough off your skin.

Blood seeps through the cotton that holds Eldric together. You lay him down, settle his head in moss, gently as a lark's egg. Gently now. You untie the tourniquet, but you are slow to tie it again. Your fingers are cold. All of you is cold.

The blood streams, weeps, trickles. Eldric's lips are the color of clay. His eyebrow scar is the color of a rat. He opens his eyes. They do not shine whiter than white.

You could say something. You could say, *I lust you*. You could say, *I love you*.

I love you. The words are not unfamiliar. I believe I heard them more than once when I was little. Perhaps when you hear them over and over, the words stomp out a path in your memory: *I am loveable.* But what if you cease to hear *I love you* and start hearing *Oh, Briony! We musn't ever tell your father.*

Now you have an *I am wicked* path. And surely, the *I am loveable* path begins to fade.

The swamp goes on forever, you go on forever. Your bones mutter curses. The rain turns to spit. Rain spits on Eldric. The edges of the world draw close, and closer. The world is gray and small.

I do not see the bloodhounds until they begin to bay. We are the ferrets, Eldric and I. The constable is almost here. Now I may rest.

I sink to the ground. I settle Eldric's head in my lap. I bend over; I shelter his face from the rain. I do not think of the future, but I remember the past. I remember Stepmother's vomit, streaked with bile and blood.

Stepmother called for water. She was so thirsty, she tasted metal, she said. She must have water, she said. I turned away.

"Briony!"

"Eldric!"

The figures come nearer. Father's mouth makes a black hole in his face.

It took Stepmother fifteen hours to die.

· 31 ·

The Trial

It's the last day of my trial. The spectators have arrived early; the benches are almost full. Why, I don't know. There will be no surprises. I've been a model defendant. I've confessed to everything. Everyone knows what the judgment is to be.

Rose, Father, and Eldric sit in the front row. I don't want to look at them, but my eyes are out of control. There they go, glancing over Eldric's tie; over one tweedy sleeve; over a bulge of gauze, swelling from the cuff like a Christmas pudding.

I will make my eyes obey. I look away, up at the windows. It is snowing. This trial has been a long one. We are drawing near Advent, season of surprise weddings. I do not, however, believe I shall attend any of them.

"All rise!" My bird hands jump at the bailiff's voice. A cold tide of faces surges below.

I grow dizzy when I stand. Dr. Rannigan says I ought to be in sickbed. He says I'm not well. He says I ought to be in a warm bed, not in a damp bunk, not in a cold cell. Judge Trumpington gave permission for me to stay at the Parson-

323

age. He said he could count on the reverend to bring me to my engagements at the courthouse.

But I wouldn't stay at the Parsonage.

It's one thing if a person learns you're a witch. It's quite another if he learns you're a murderer. I almost forget I'm a witch now that I know I'm a murderer—murderess, actually. Murderess sounds so much worse.

Judge Trumpington clears his throat. He is about to begin. I have grown horribly accustomed to the rhythms of his speech. The Brownie sits on the hem of my skirt. I like that. He holds me to the ground. I wish he could stay in my cell with me, but there are too many bars, too much metal.

"As usual, in a case that involves an Old One, we have dispensed with the traditional formalities." He looks at me. "I think I speak for all of us when I say we have been most impressed with the defendant's candor."

When I told Dr. Rannigan I wouldn't stay in the Parsonage, I told him I knew I was going to hang. And if one's going to hang, what's the point of recovering?

"Aye," says the Chime Child in her rough-and-ready way. "She be wondrous candorful. I never seen a defendant as confessed to such a quantity o' wickedness."

I'd never seen Dr. Rannigan so angry. He shouted at me. He shouted that he knew exactly what I was doing. That I was clinging to every bit of strength I had in order to get through the trial. But that I'd really given up. That once the trial was over, I'd let myself die. Which was precisely my point. I'd rather die from illness than be hanged. But other than that, what's the difference? I'll turn to dust. The church bells will take an inventory of Briony Larkin: one chime for each year of life, eighteen chimes in all.

"I knows I been getting old," says the Chime Child. "I maked a grievous misjudgment on poor Nelly Daws. I doesn't got the stomach for judgments no more. But there don't be no one else, an' the judge, he be desirous for my recommendation."

The spectators stir. It's been a long trial, but at last, we're getting to the end, which is bound to be satisfactorily gruesome.

"All you as be here today," says the Chime Child, "you heared the candorous confessions o' yon Briony Larkin. You heared most o' the story an' I heared it all. Briony told me the bits what be particular an' private to her. I knows the whole story, but I doesn't got no answers. I got only questions."

"Go ahead," says the judge.

"This question, it be tricky-like to answer." The Chime Child looks at me. "Supposing it be you, Briony Larkin, you what be judge an' Chime Child today. How does you pronounce on your own self, innocent or guilty?"

I feel the press of spectators' eyes as they wait for my answer.

"You should hang me."

Why such mutter and stir? I'd been wondrous candorful, so what did they expect?

"What be your reasons, Miss Briony?"

"I told you about Stepmother and the arsenic. Isn't that reason enough?"

"But she be an Old One," says the Chime Child. "There be times us allows the killing o' them Old Ones."

"Not unless there's a trial first," says Judge Trumpington. "The system is flawed, we know that, but we can't proceed without a trial. We can't take the law into our own hands, Mrs. Gurnsey."

Mrs. Gurnsey. It's queer to remember the Chime Child has a real name. A real name and a real life. That she's married and has children, that her husband is a fisherman, that she plants poppies in her garden.

"Us be at a trial right now," says the Chime Child.

"Let me make sure I understand you correctly, Mrs. Gurnsey," says Judge Trumpington. "You suggest putting the stepmother on trial?"

"Aye," says the Chime Child.

There follows a long discussion about courtroom rules and how the judicial system doesn't allow you to try a person if she's not present to defend herself. But finally the Chime Child puts an end to it. "It don't matter nohow. The stepmother, she be dead. But Miss Briony here, she be alive. She be the one us doesn't want to kill if there don't be no reason."

Everyone's sorry to have hanged poor Nelly Daws, but don't let that prolong my trial. Please don't. There'll be no last-minute exculpatory evidence, I promise. Just let me lie down.

For I'm sick at the heart and I fain would lie doon.

"Did you never suspect your stepmother was one of the Old Ones?" says Judge Trumpington.

"Never," I say. "She was always very kind to us."

Something has happened. Judge Trumpington and the Chime Child look away from me, into the mass of spectators. Someone has risen. I see him only from the corner of my eye, but I know it is Eldric.

He doesn't offer up his name, or beg pardon, or say a word about pleasing the court. He is already stepping forward as he says, "I believe I can help." Judge Trumpington nods and says, "Please."

Soon I shall be obliged to look at his face and I can't bear it. *Murderess.* He knows me to be a murderess. I can't bear it.

I look away. The spectators' faces are splats of snow. My head is filled with white.

I don't understand Eldric's idea. He wants to make me a story. I will say the words, he will write them.

I say nothing. Judge Trumpington says nothing. The Chime Child approves.

Eldric lowers his voice. He speaks for me, alone. "When you wrote me into an understanding of Leanne, you'd a notion there was something about her we had yet to learn, had you not? I've the same sort of notion about the late Mrs. Larkin. Perhaps I can do the same for you."

There's nothing to understand. She was an Old One. I procured arsenic from Cecil, I poisoned her.

Eldric stands at the defendant's box. He lays a sheet of paper on the ledge. Rose has given it to him. I recognize it as twin to one she gave me in the library. She wanted me to make it into a story. I associate it with the smells of sawdust and paint and polish. The smells of hope and life.

I face the Chime Child. Eldric faces me. The sooner I start, the sooner I end, the sooner I lie doon.

Eldric taps the pencil point onto the paper. He asks me to speak of the time I was ill. Not the Dead Hand illness, the earlier one, the long one, before Stepmother died. He isn't accustomed to writing with his left hand. He grips the pencil so hard his fingertips go red.

What can I say about it? That I was ill, that Stepmother

nursed me? Eldric taps at the paper. He taps it into a Tiddy Rex of freckles.

"She was very kind," I begin.

"Let's start with specifics," says Eldric. "What sort of illness was it?"

That's easy enough. It wasn't an illness as much as an exhaustion. I awakened every morning wearier than before. One morning I was able to rise, the next I was not.

I pause frequently; I wait for Eldric to catch up. He writes like a child, dragging his left wrist across the paper. His fingertips have now gone white. He turns letters into spiders, sentences into valleys.

No one offers to help.

"What did she do to amuse you while you were ill? To help you pass the time?"

I say that Stepmother brought me paper and ink. That she thought it might be healing for me to write. *Healing,* that was her word. So although I was often too tired, although the writing often wore me down, it was difficult to refuse. She was so delighted to help. Delighted with everything I wrote.

"You're saying, then, that the writing was not healing?" says Eldric.

I suppose that's what I was saying, although it feels like a betrayal to admit it. "It ground me down, rather. I felt as though I were a music box in want of winding." Yes, as though I were a music box and the tune were my life, playing more and more slowly with every passing day. Finally, not even I could recognize it. The notes were stretched too far apart. They were no longer notes, they were *plinks.* I wound down to a *plink.*

"You were unwinding," says Eldric. "What then?"

My gaze betrays me. It moves to Eldric's face. He looks much as usual, in obvious, surface ways. A month must be enough time for a strong young man to recover from the loss of his hand. But he looks different in underneath ways. Gone is the pounce and bounce. His eyes are dark, and although he smiles, he doesn't mean it.

He hates me.

"Then I got better."

He hates me because I murdered Stepmother. He hates me because the Dead Hand took my clumsy right hand and left me with my useful left. He hates me because the Dead Hand took his useful right hand and left him with his clumsy left. What's a strong, fidgety boy to do without his dominant hand? What happens when there's a Cecil Trumpington to knock about?

"Tell me about the fire."

I know even less about the fire. "I can't say why I started it."

"Not the why," says Eldric. "Just the details. How did you start it?"

I have two sets of memories about the fire. Both start with me dragging myself into the library. I hurry, best I can. I must do what I need to do before I am entirely unwound. My nightdress drags on the floor as though I've shrunk.

I pause in my telling. Here, the memories diverge.

"This is where you have to forget you're Briony Larkin," says Eldric. "Forget that you're clever, that you always have the right answer. The only right memory is the one that first comes to you."

This, I cannot believe.

But Eldric doesn't care whether I believe. He just wants

me to be as honest as I can, with the court, of course, but also with myself. This seems a peculiar thing to say, but I proceed.

"I brought paraffin and matches with me into the library. I doused the books with paraffin, the piano too. I struck a match."

I pause, look into Eldric's switch-off eyes. "The problem," I say, "is that that's not the true memory. I didn't set the fire. I called the fire up; I know it."

"Are you sure?" says Eldric. "I remember a situation in which you were unable to call up fire."

Yes, just before I punched your nose. If I weren't so weak, I'd do it again. But if you want the wrong story, you'll get it. What do I care? Hanging is hanging.

"There was a great whoosh of fire," I say. "I stood there watching for a bit."

I do not say aloud that I watched the exercise books whoosh into flame. There went the story of the Reed Spirits. There, the Brownie's story. There, Rose's favorite, in which she gets to be the hero. I do not say aloud that this cannot be the true memory. Why would I have destroyed the stories I'd labored over so long? I'm wicked, not mad.

"I heard my stepmother in the corridor. I suppose she smelled the smoke. She was almost at the door when I shoved my hand into the flames."

I haven't expected there'd come a great gasp, that dark caves would open in those snow-splat faces. Father hid his eyes behind his forearm.

It's a waste of emotion, although regular people seem to have an overabundance of the stuff. I'm playing Eldric's game, telling my false memories. But the truth is that I called the fire, which raged out of control and bit me.

"I don't know how Stepmother managed to make it to the library. I've already told you how I injured her spine."

"Perhaps you didn't," says Eldric.

"But I saw Mucky Face strike her," I said. This conversation is just between the two of us, too low for the others to hear. "If I didn't call him, who did?" I shall wither him with sarcasm. "Stepmother?"

"Perhaps." Eldric writes for a long while. What exactly is he writing? My every word? When he looks up, his eyes shine with wet.

"Stepmother assured me she wouldn't tell anyone. She was terrifically loyal. She never told anyone the other wicked things I did."

"What other wicked things?"

But I don't care to discuss Rose in front of the entire village. For that matter, I don't care to discuss Rose in front of Rose. There she'd be, under the magnifying glass, the butterfly with the torn wing, the whole village looking on.

"Those wicked things are private. I told the Chime Child; they're not for everybody's ears." Eldric knew, though. I told him the night of the bloody nose.

"I'll tell then," says Eldric.

"I told you that in confidence!"

"I took an oath, on the Bible," says Eldric. "I swore to tell the whole truth."

"But you have no right hand," I say.

Eldric's eyebrows jump. He makes a line of his curling lips. I have wounded him.

"In Italian," I say, "the word for *left* is *sinistra*. 'Sinister.' It would be wrong to lay your sinister hand on the Bible."

Eldric does not respond. He is going to tell.

I squeeze all the lace from my hand-bones. I turn my fist to cement. "Don't you dare tell!" I whisper, so he has to draw close. I can easily reach that beautiful face of his. I jab, but I am weak and slow, and his left hand is quick—quick enough, at least, to catch mine.

Eldric speaks very low. "Don't throw your punch from your elbow."

"Stupidibus," I say.

He almost smiles.

I refuse to listen. I put my fingers in my ears. But my imagination keeps following the story. What's he saying now?

When will Father know what I did to Rose?

Does he know now?

Now?

What about Rose?

Does she know now?

Eldric taps my hand. He is done.

No, I amend that: He is done for.

I am going to kill him.

Father has risen. He doesn't know where to put his arms. You wouldn't take him for a clergyman, accustomed to speaking in public.

"I'm trying to sort through what happened here," he says. "But one thing I do know: Rose was born who she is and she's remained who she is. I know she sustained no injury that—"

He searches for the *mot juste*.

"—that compromised her."

Father is lying to save me. Stepmother was wrong. Father's

not so righteous that he'd have turned me over to the constable. I wish I could feel happy about this. Eldric, of course, thinks Father's telling the truth.

"I know it's hard to believe," says Eldric, in his just-between-you-and-me voice. "Do you remember how at first I couldn't believe Leanne was a Dark Muse? It was too great a shock. I couldn't accept that my feelings had clouded my judgment, and that my feelings themselves were the result of a spell."

I could hit him so easily. "Are you suggesting Stepmother was a Dark Muse?" More sarcastic withering.

Father speaks into Eldric's silence. "We were married a year before I understood she was a Dark Muse, feeding on my music. I absented myself as much as possible, so she'd have nothing to feed on."

My mouth tastes sharp and bright.

"We have misunderstood the powers of the Dark Muse," says Judge Trumpington. "She's able to feed on girls."

I have bitten my tongue.

"Happen," says the Chime Child, "us never knowed the powers o' yon lasses. The art they does, it be strong enough to feed the Dark Muse."

"Perhaps Briony misunderstood her own powers," says Eldric. "Perhaps she's not a witch at all."

Eldric's voice again, now for me, alone. "You've gone whiter than I'd have thought possible. You ought to put your head down."

"I told you once to put your head down," I say. I don't recognize my own voice. "But you didn't." He'd gone all distant and wavy, as though I were looking at him through old glass.

My own strange voice rises, speaks loud as Rose. "Don't

tell me I'm not a witch!" My voice is all blisters and scars. "How do you explain that I have the second sight?"

And then my voice, which I recognize this time, except that it belongs to Rose.

"I didn't prefer to tell the secret," says Rose, "but Robert assured me I ought to."

I let myself look at her. She wears a white coat, not terribly practical, but she does look lovely in it.

Rose understands, doesn't she? I think she has known for a long while. Is it because I talk in my sleep? You tell them, Rose. Tell them I'm a witch.

My throat is full of liquid, but my eyes are deserts of sand.

"Stepmother," says Rose, "was a bad person. Once I told her that Briony had no birthday, and she asked why. I showed her the register in which the midwife had written our names."

"What register?" says Judge Trumpington. "What midwife?"

It was the midwife, Rose says, who attended Mother when we were born. The midwife had brought a book with her that said *Register* on the front. Inside were written the dates and times of all the babies she'd delivered.

How does Rose know it belonged to the midwife?

Rose assures us it's simple. Over and over, the midwife had written, *Ruth Parks, midwife to*, and the name of the baby. Or babies, in the case of twins.

Not even Judge Trumpington can quarrel with Rose's conclusion.

My heart squeezes in on itself.

"I found it when I was very little," says Rose. "But I was a terrifically early reader."

The register. It's not surprising the midwife forgot it in the turmoil of twin babies and a dead mother.

"At first Stepmother was nice," says Rose. "I showed her the register, and she told me never to tell anyone. I promised. She said she'd hurt Briony if I told, which was exceedingly unnecessary because I prefer to keep secrets. I'm breaking my promise now because Robert says I must."

"What was the secret?" says Judge Trumpington.

"Robert says I may tell a secret if it's a bad secret," says Rose. "I know it's bad because it keeps Briony thinking bad thoughts."

It stands to reason the midwife might have chosen not to return to the Parsonage. That she may have decided it was better to forgo the register than to collect it from the reverend, whose wife had died under her care.

"That's right," says the judge. "You mustn't keep a bad secret."

"Midwife Parks wrote it like this." Rose scribbles the air with her forefinger.

> Rose Larkin, born November 1, 11:48 pm.
> Briony Larkin, born neither November 1 nor yet
>   November 2, but at the sixth and seventh chimes
>   of midnight.

My heart wrings itself out. I am drowning in heart juice.

"Why might your stepmother want to keep it a secret?"

Rose opens her eyes very wide. Hasn't the judge realized by now? "So Stepmother can make Briony think she's a witch, not a Chime Child."

My heart juice is pressing at me, building up pressure, just as secrets do. I think of Rose's insistence that I cover my ears

335

before the first chimes of midnight. She was trying to keep the secret. I think of Rose's collage, of her desperation that she be able to portray the difference between ten minutes to midnight, and midnight itself. Rose was trying to keep the secret yet reveal the truth. I think of Rose's desperation that I see that the Rose baby blob belongs to ten minutes to midnight, that the Briony baby blob belongs to midnight.

Where is my heart juice to go? I squeeze my eyes, but I cannot keep it from leaking out.

Rose couldn't bear that I not know. Rose knew I thought I was a witch.

Judge Trumpington asks Rose to show him the register, but adds that there's no hurry. The trial will end now, register or no.

"I used to prefer that the register had burnt," says Rose. "But now I prefer that it not have burnt, which it didn't."

There is a hubbub of time where great smiling faces press themselves at me and shake my hand and say they always knew I couldn't have done it, but I did do it, and I don't understand: I killed Stepmother.

I begin to rise, but the Brownie lies on my skirt. I don't want to stay here, crying with everyone gathered round, leaking as ordinary girls do, wet inside and out.

Now the Brownie's beside me, clicking at my side as I leave the defendant's box. Great smiling faces back away as I navigate the aisle between the benches. The Brownie and I leave the courthouse, alone.

But someone waits on the steps. I don't want to see her. I can't help but see her. A green coat, a peacock feather. Leanne, returned to her old habit of visiting the courthouse. I don't allow myself to look, but I do anyway. Her skin is plastered to her bones. She draws the gray shrivel of her lips to her gums.

"Briony!" She reaches for me. Her sleeve drips from her arm. "Help me! Help me get at Mr. Clayborne and I'll help you escape. I've worked out a way . . ."

I walk on. Leanne's too wound down to realize I'm already free, that I must be, as I've neither constable nor manacle to keep me from going wherever I like.

"Briony, listen!" says Leanne.

She'll lose those teeth soon. She's winding down to her final *plink*.

"Briony, stop!" says Leanne. "Briony!"

I round the corner, where months ago, I was sick on the smell of eels. The Brownie swings on beside me. Leanne is a Dark Muse. I don't know what I am.

Snow falls on my hair. The world is small and white.

Stepmother was a Dark Muse. She fed on me, she fed on Rose.

"Briony!"

I come upon a tangle of alleys. Weave yourself into them, Briony. Go round one more corner, Briony. Perhaps they won't find you.

I sit beside a rubbish bin.

Snow falls. The world outside is small and white. The world inside is vast and dark.

A figure emerges from the gray and snow.

"Briony?"

My tears go on forever. Snowflakes fall like shredded clouds. My tears go on forever. The figure comes nearer. Eldric's lips are so red they hurt.

Word Magic

I am stomping out new memory paths.

It is difficult. There are too many *I am wicked* paths crossing and crisscrossing my memory. I don't believe the nice things I say to myself.

I like you! I tell myself.

I answer myself: *What a stupidibus!*

Stop saying that, Briony. If you don't have anything nice to say, don't say anything at all.

I like you!

Briony pinches her lips. She says nothing.

I like you!

I don't believe it now. I shall have to reverse the false memories that Stepmother stomped into my brain. *You're a witch!* She trod out paths to memories that never existed. *You hurt Rose.* She trod them out over and over, so they appeared to be real, even though they led to nothing at all.

I like you!

It would be easier to believe myself if Eldric said something. *I love you.* He said it once. But he hasn't said it since. It would be so easy: He sits a mere table's width away. But he stomps out no paths. He is indifferent.

"Wrap that bit around the end, will you?" he says.

"The squiggly bit?"

"That's the one."

It's only March, but today comes with a whiff of spring. From the front porch, Eldric and I have a terrific view of the square. Father and Eldric rebuilt the porch after the trial, while I was ill. I've seen Dr. Rannigan any number of times, but he never says *I told you so!* I was ill for months. You'd think a person who's lost his hand would need a great deal of time to recover, but it seems that a person who wanders the swamp in her petticoat, then bides in jail for five weeks, needs even more.

A river of steel flows into the village. On it stands the *five thirty-nine,* snorting and pawing the ground. She's ready for her run to London. But for now at least, the plans to extend the railway into the swamp have been suspended. There's been no draining of the swamp since Halloween. But Mr. Clayborne's contemplating the possibility of sinking great posts into the swamp and floating the railroad on top of them. Then the queen will be happy and the Boggy Mun will be happy.

"This fidget needs a bit of a twiggle," says Eldric, and I twiggle. We have a terrific working vocabulary. But Eldric needs my help less than he pretends. He's worked out a way to tie a knot with just the one hand. I've seen him.

"Tell me the story again," says Eldric. He says his memories of the Dead Hand and the swamp are like a dream. He remembers, but he doesn't remember.

"Which version do you want?" I say. "The one in which I am terrifically heroic? Or the one in which I am extraordinarily heroic?"

"The latter," says Eldric, but then he looks at me sideways, and I know what he's going to say.

"For goodness' sake!" I say. "I am not too tired. Would you and Father please stop treating me as though I'm going to break?"

"But you did break," says Eldric. "That's hard for us to forget."

"You broke too," I say. "But you don't see me worrying about you."

"But you do worry, I think. You worry in a different way."

Eldric's right, although I'll never admit it. I do worry about him. I worry that he has horrid feelings about having lost his hand, his dominant hand. He was a boy-man who boxed and fidgeted and climbed roofs, and now— What does he say to himself when he's alone?

I hate myself? Is that what he says?

I can only guess at his feelings. I know what Dr. Freud would guess, but he'd be wrong.

"You could at least complain," I say. "I adore complaining. It calms the nerves."

I wish I'd lost my hand instead. I have no particular need for it, except for writing. But even so, I need only the one.

"Ha!" he says. "You didn't see me all the while you were ill. Just ask my father if I didn't complain. Or Pearl. Pearl knows."

It's true. I've lost time, all sorts of time. I've lost memory time with Stepmother; I've lost real time with Eldric. I feel as though he and I are just now meeting all over again. I try to identify what's shifted between us. Perhaps the best word for it is *guarded*. Eldric has grown guarded.

I tell a highly colored version of our journey through the swamp on Halloween night. But there's enough truth that I let Eldric shake his head and say, "How did you do it, though? All those miles, and me, such a weight!"

"Robust," I say primly. "You're robust."

"You're very kind." Here comes his curling lion's smile. "I rather think my father would call me hulking."

"Only when you ask for thirds at supper. You tell him I say you're robust, and that I'm the one to know."

The *five thirty-nine* whistles. Eldric and I jump, then laugh. The skip-rope girls scatter. The *five thirty-nine* tosses her luminous hair and chuffs away from the station.

Someday I will gallop away with the *five thirty-nine* to London. And someday, I will take one of her sisters from London to Dover, then sail to France, and I know just what I'll say. "Pardon, monsieur." I will be very polite. "Le restaurant Chez Julien, il est sur le Boulevard Saint-Michel, à droite, si je ne me trompe pas?"

I mention this to Eldric, but he shakes his head. "Let me remind you of the correct phrasing, and please note my perfect accent: The restaurant Chez Julien, she is, if I do not mistake myself, down the Boulevard Saint-Michel, to the right?"

I speak again in my French voice. "I must note one error, monsieur, one oh-so-small error. A restaurant, he is a boy, not a girl."

"Really!" says Eldric. "The French have certainly got that wrong!"

"You can correct them on your next visit."

"I shall be sure to." Eldric sweeps his newest fidget into his palm, admires it from all sides. "We are ready for paint. Or, as they'd say in Paris, *Voilà!* French is an admirably economical language."

"I'll fetch Rose." I peel off my lap rug, but Eldric springs up first.

"I'll do it."

"I am not going to break!"

"Not if you keep quiet," says Eldric. Dr. Rannigan has told Eldric and Father he was astonished I managed to hang on through the end of the trial. But he also says he's seen it before. That sometimes people stave off the symptoms of illness to finish something else. Then, though, the illness comes crashing down upon the person like an avalanche. It makes Father and Eldric feel guilty, which is nice, but tiresome.

Eldric speeds through the front door, but I call after him. "I won't stay in this chair. You'll come back sometime to find I've disappeared."

Hmm. When might *sometime* be? It might be this evening.

It might, and it will. I mean to walk to the fields to check on the green mist. That's what the Swampfolk used to do every spring when I was small. We'd rise before dawn. We'd wait and watch. For days and days, we'd watch the sun rise over fields of plain brown earth, and we'd turn about and go home. But one morning, the sun would rise on fields of green mist, and we'd stay to welcome the earth. We'd tell her how glad we were she'd awakened once again. We'd sprinkle salt and bread on the ground and say strange old words that no one understands anymore.

Tonight wouldn't be like those not-so-very-old days. I'd be watching in the evening, and I'd be watching alone. But I wouldn't let another day pass without watching for the earth to awaken.

"You may as well have let me fetch her," I say as Eldric emerges with Rose. "While you were gone, I ran around the square. Twice."

"Don't even think about doing that," says Eldric.

"Or?" I say. I listen to myself. I sound, perhaps, a touch childish.

"Or I'll pound you into a pulp," says Eldric with the utmost good humor.

"I know that's a joke," says Rose.

"Quite right, Rosy Posy." I hand Rose the box of paints. "I have a color request for this fidget."

Rose opens the box.

"Let's paint it the exact color of the motorcar."

"I'm the one who has an eye for color," says Rose.

"I'm the one who's ill," I say.

"You've been ill too much," says Rose.

"Hear! Hear!" says Eldric.

I feel the prickle of tears behind my cheekbones. I lie back and close my eyes. They're joking, I tell myself. Or at least Eldric is. Rose doesn't know how to joke. But sometimes I cry at the stupidest things.

Rose sets out the paints; she mumbles over them. Eldric whispers. Mumble, whisper, mumble. Finally, Rose says, "What color is the motorcar, Briony Vieny?"

Eldric has coached her, of course.

"Cardinal." (Hallelujah! Hallelujah!)

The two of them rattle about in the paints.

"Is this one cardinal?" says Eldric.

"No, it's this one," says Rose.

"You've got an eye for color, right enough," says Eldric.

I get what I want, but I still feel like crying. What a stupid baby!

Stop, Briony! Don't you remember about treading out the paths? You don't want to deepen the path to *stupid baby*. You want to tread out a path to kindness. What might Father have said? *Poor girl, you've been so ill, and no one's looked after you for such a long time.*

That's actually no longer true, although truth is entirely irrelevant to the treading out of brain paths.

Eldric sends Rose to the kitchen. We need a bite to eat, he says. "Ask Pearl for some of those sunset buns your sister likes so well."

I smile. I know Eldric sees it. He may be indifferent, but at least he forbids me to say I'm not a hero. There! Another brain path in want of scuffing.

I'm a hero. Briony Larkin is a hero.

I am drifting into sleep. I'm thinking mad, mixed-up thoughts, or perhaps I'm dreaming, but my dream thoughts are true, true in the real world. I wish that Eldric had cared for me while I was ill, as he did when I was recovering from my encounter with the Dead Hand. But, instead, it was Father who cared for me. He sang, and bathed my forehead, and took to singing again at night. It's awfully silly with daughters who are eighteen, but I don't have to pretend not to like it. Rose likes it, which means that even if I didn't like it, I wouldn't say so because one doesn't say one doesn't like things if

Rose likes them, unless one doesn't value one's hearing.

After a few pints of ale, Father even manages a few *I love yous*. He was devastated that he'd left us alone with a Dark Muse—even now he can hardly bear to say the words. I tell him he couldn't possibly have realized she'd turn to us for her next snack.

I tell him it was reasonable to think he'd dealt her a death blow when he stopped singing and locked away his fiddle. She should have unwound and died.

But Stepmother was too clever, of course. The very day Father locked away his fiddle was the day she told me— "reminded" me—that I hurt Rose and that I was a witch. And that meant I couldn't leave the Parsonage. Stepmother had made me believe it was too dangerous to enter the swamp, and anyway, I couldn't leave her alone to care for Rose. Stepmother made sure I'd stay close by. Stepmother wasted no time in beginning to feed off me.

I tell Father no one imagined a Dark Muse could feed on girls.

Father tells me it's awful to realize how long ago she started planning; taking her first steps when I was seven; making me believe I was wicked; keeping me tethered to her larder should Father discover what she was.

I wish he'd told me from the beginning, when he realized the truth about Stepmother. But it wasn't possible for him, the Reverend Larkin, to tell his daughter he married a Dark Muse. It was too shameful. He had to hide the fact. He left her to die for want of feeding, or so he thought. He never thought she'd feed upon his girls.

I hear Eldric pause, hear him pad over to me, lion soft.

He pulls the coverlet up to my chin. He often performs these small kindnesses for me when he thinks I'm asleep. And when I am asleep too, I suppose.

But I wish he would do the same when I'm awake. I wish he'd help lay down new brain paths for me and scuff out the old. I wish he'd tell me how perfect I am, just as Father did when I was small. That he'd exclaim over my darling apricot ears and perfect fingernails. That he'd scuff out the paths Stepmother stomped into existence, paths of wickedness and guilt.

I fall into mad dream thoughts of fingernails and babies. I put a baby on the wrong train, and no one can find it, and I'm running about, looking for the baby, but the air is thick as glue. What a relief to wake up and realize I've been asleep. Rose has gone, leaving behind half a plate of sunset buns and a litter of crumbs. Eldric holds the paintbrush in the tips of his fingers.

"Damn!" he says.

"I can give it a go," I say.

The paintbrush pauses. "Sorry, did I wake you?"

"I don't think so." I try to shake off my dream.

He reaches for the plate of buns. "Give it a whirl, will you, while I get things warmed up." He glances at the bowl of soggy cream. "And get things colded up."

I give it a whirl. Painting a tiny fidget is not as easy as it sounds. Every little mistake looks huge. A dribble of paint has run into a corner and dried.

"Damn," I say. I was never as wicked as I'd thought, so I have some extra goodness to balance out a bad word or two.

The truth will set you free. That's both true and not true.

346

It was certainly liberating to learn I'm not a witch. To learn I hadn't hurt Rose, or even Stepmother, at least not with Mucky Face as my weapon. To learn that Stepmother was never really ill, except for a brief period after the fire, before she turned to Rose, and of course, the last day of her life. It was not so liberating to remember I poisoned Stepmother, but for that, I am forgiven. It seems that if someone (Stepmother) is killing someone else (Rose), the law permits you to kill the someone in order to protect the someone else.

I like myself.

I like myself.

Or, for example, the law permits Eldric to wing the constable in order to protect Briony Larkin.

Eldric returns with a sunset-lathered bun. We speak of a certain person who has an eye for color but can't manage to finish painting a certain fidget. We speculate that she has gone to visit Robert: Rose has become awfully independent these days. We are relieved of our conversation when Tiddy Rex comes running by.

Eldric looks at me. "Shall we?"

"Is it dry?"

Eldric nods.

I call Tiddy Rex onto the porch. "You are just the boy we want to see. We hope you will agree to join our secret society."

"The Fearsome Four," says Eldric.

"The mission of the Fearsome Four is to fight for justice," I say.

"To go on quests," says Eldric.

"I never been on no quest," says Tiddy Rex. His eyes are wide and exactly match the color of his freckles.

"In the olden days," I say, "people set off on quests by horseback. But in these modern days, heroes go by motorcar."

"Motorcar!" Tiddy Rex's voice is just a squeak.

"The existence of the Fearsome Four is a solemn secret," says Eldric. "Will you join us and dedicate yourself to our mission?"

Tiddy Rex flushes. "Aye, aye!"

"Kneel, then, Tiddy Rex, that you may be sworn into the secret society of the Fearsome Four."

Tiddy Rex kneels. I glance up as though this is a holy moment. The sky is all stretchy clouds, like elastic lace. "Do you solemnly swear to face all perils in order to rescue those in need? Do you swear to be relentless in the eternal quest for justice?"

"Aye, aye!"

"Do you solemnly swear to motor from one end of the world to the other, rooting out evil wheresoever you may find it?"

"Aye, aye!"

Eldric rises. He sets a leather cord around Tiddy Rex's neck. "I now pronounce you a member of the Fearsome Four. Welcome, Tiddy Rex! Rise and walk among us."

Tiddy Rex's face is a starry map. He touches the fidget hanging on the cord.

"Mister Eldric!" he says, for the fidget is a brilliant copy of the motorcar, right down to the tiny brass eagle. The eagle's not made of brass, of course, but it's painted gold, and you can see its beak and its every talon.

I look at Eldric and he looks at me. That was fun! For a moment, we actually had fun.

I'm expected to rest after supper, to prepare myself for the next grand adventure in life, which is sleep. Father and Eldric think they've bullied me into this with the suggestion that I shan't be well enough to study with my new tutor. Yes, Father has engaged a tutor for me, just as brilliant as Fitz. James Bellingham. I haven't yet told him his pet name. I wonder if he'll like it?

But neither Father nor Eldric is particularly skilled at bullying. I sit on the upstairs landing until I hear Pearl bid Father good night. I think about Jim Bellingham. What would have been better? To have allowed Father to send me away to school, or to have remained in the Swampsea, to have met Eldric?

But I had no choice, had I? Stepmother saw to that, making me believe I called Mucky Face and injured her. She knew I couldn't leave her then, not for school, not for anything.

I slip downstairs. I have an excuse ready, should anyone see me, but I don't need it. I slip out the kitchen door, over the bridge.

I step in the hoof prints of the Shire horses, as Eldric and I used to do. But I'm lonely, and I'm already tired. I shuffle along, I ignore the hoof prints. All I want is to see the green mist. Tears come to my eyes.

Honestly, Briony, enough of the self-pity. What a baby you are!

Stop, Briony: Amend that thought!

What a darling baby, and such delightful apricot ears!

I clamber up the riverbank and cut across the Flats. But it's harder to walk on the sloppy ground. Where's wolfgirl? She never minded a bit of slop.

I'll have to reinvent wolfgirl too. But she won't be so hard

349

to reinvent. I'll have to stomp out muscle paths for her, not brain paths. Muscle paths are easy; the brain is a tricky thing.

I think of the moment I discovered that Stepmother was a Dark Muse. I remember my hand moving across paper, my pen leaving a trail of ink. I remember myself, sitting in a sea of crumpled bedsheets, beside the do-not-cross line. I remember that I was ill, that the pen was heavy.

I wrote that Stepmother brought me writing materials. I wrote that the more I wrote, the sicker I got. I wrote about Father's illness and of his immediate recovery once he abandoned the fiddle and left the Parsonage. I wrote myself into understanding. I wrote myself into realizing I had to make sure I could write nothing anymore. I knew I hadn't enough power to refuse to write. I couldn't resist Stepmother's spell.

I wrote myself into understanding I had to burn my hand.

But the brain is tricky. I couldn't allow myself to remember what Stepmother really was. I made myself forget. I scuffed out my own real memories while Stepmother trod in false memories.

"Such a vasty time to bide away, mistress!"

I have come upon the Reed Spirits. I've not been to the swamp since All Hallows' Day.

"I've been ill," I say. "I'll come back and talk to you properly when I'm recovered."

"An' tha'll fetch our sweet story along with thee?" How sweet their voices are, and how mournful. Careful, Briony, or you'll cry.

I understand better, now, the appetite of the Old Ones for their story. The Chime Child has told me. She may have made a mistake with Nelly Daws, but she is terrifically clever and knows ever so much about the Old Ones. It's only the mortals, she says, who can write down a story, so that it doesn't vanish with memory. And of course, it's only we, the Chime Child and I, who can hear the Old Ones and set their story down.

"When I am better," I say, "I shall come to set down your stories."

How they sigh and sing. "Mistress!

"Mistress!

"Our thanks to thee, mistress!"

And when I'm better, I shall apprentice to the Chime Child. Sometimes the Chime Child says she's made so many mistakes of late, she should apprentice to me. But I don't know. It's a difficult job. There is much she has to teach me.

I walk on slowly. I am tired, but I am also thinking. I think about the Old Ones, that they have a past but no history. I think about the inevitability of death, and whether it's not that very inevitability that inspires us to take photographs and make scrapbooks and tell stories. That that's how we humans find our way to immortality. This is not a new thought; I've had such thoughts before. But I have a new thought now.

That that's how we find our way toward meaning.

Meaning. If you're going to die, you want to find meaning in life.

You want to connect the dots.

The Old Ones are born immortal. They've lived hundreds upon hundreds of years. But they're going to die. Someday soon—in five days, or five months, or five years—we humans will come up with a cure for the swamp cough. Then Mr. Clayborne will light the illuminating gas and set the machines going and drain the water from the swamp.

I look about the Flats, I try to imagine it. Men will dig up the ancient trees. They'll shrivel the Flats into a toothless granny. They'll drain the swamp into a scab. The Old Ones will have nowhere to live. And if that doesn't kill them, industry will. The factories and hospitals and shipyards that are sure to come. The Old Ones can't survive a world filled with metal. They can't survive the clatter and growl of machinery.

I leave the Flats. The fields are not too far now. Just down the road. But the road looks long and I feel the prickle of tears again. It's because I've been ill, I know. That's all it is.

And when the bog-holes are puckered shut, where will the Boggy Mun go? Will he go to the sea? And if he does, what then?

Is the sea too big to drain? Probably not. Look what mankind can create. Now you can photograph a person moving, and when you look at the photograph, you'll actually see him moving, which is why it's called a moving picture. This is hard to believe, I know, but still, we humans are inventing such astonishing things. I shouldn't be surprised if, in time, we'll be able to drain the sea.

And what of the Old Ones?

Only the stories will remain.

Another quarter mile to the fields of rye. You can manage it, Briony. Don't cry.

I don't cry. I walk and walk and I arrive.

There are fields, but there are no fields of rye. Not yet. There is no green mist.

I sit down. I am too tired. I am a baby with apricot ears who needs to cry. But I don't. I sit at the edge of the fields and stare at the brown earth.

Everything is still, save for a puff of dust in the distance. It is accompanied by a sound. The puff and the sound come closer. It turns into a beautiful shade of red—one might call it cardinal.

The motorcar stops a few yards short of where I sit. Eldric emerges. I look up when his shadow falls over me.

"Well, if it isn't Miss Briony Larkin," he says.

"Let's say it isn't. You might like me better."

Eldric sits beside me. "How do you mean?"

"I wanted to check on the green mist," I say.

"Like you better?" he says.

I shrug, which I should remember not to do. My shoulder still hurts. "It's just one of those things people say."

"No it isn't."

What does he know about it? We are silent for a bit. What does he know about anything? Then I surprise myself and say, "I don't feel I know you anymore."

"You know everything about me," he says. "Including a few things you oughtn't."

Girls, he means. I know things about Eldric and girls that I oughtn't. I was tipsy at the time, but I know from Cecil that that's no excuse.

"You never talk about your hand," I say.

"This hand?" He holds out his right arm. His sleeves are rolled up. He never bothers to disguise the stump.

"That hand."

"What about it?" he says.

"Remember what I said about complaining? You never complain."

"You want to know if I miss it?"

"Yes."

"The answer to that depends on other answers," says Eldric. "But I don't have them yet. Here's an example: Do you miss my hand?"

"Only if you do," I say. "I want to know what it's like for you. Is it horrible when you want to make something and you have to ask for help? Or is it horrible in a boxing sort of way?"

"Do you mean that I can no longer take on a Cecil Trumpington?"

Cecil Trumpington, magnanimous Cecil, distributing arsenic to his friends, including Fitz. Including me. I've apologized to Cecil dozens of times, but I know he still doesn't quite believe I could have forgotten about him, about the arsenic, about the murder.

"I suppose so," I say.

I've tried to remember the day I realized Stepmother had started to feed upon Rose. I remembered it as vividly as I could. I remembered that I watched the two of them together, under the parlor table. I remembered that I watched Stepmother snip-snip-snipping at Rose's endless bits of paper. I remembered looking at my hand, thinking I burnt it for nothing: Stepmother could no longer snack on Briony's writing, but there was another Larkin sister who might be just as tasty.

Eldric turns his stump this way and that, examining it. "What makes you think I can't take Cecil on?"

"I don't know. I just assumed—"

"Please don't assume anything." His voice goes tight. "You do realize I haven't been emasculated?"

Emasculated. That's the word Dr. Freud would want to use.

"Who said anything about being emasculated?"

354

"You did. You do. Every time you look at me, you do. I hate the way you slide your eyes away from me."

"I do not!"

"You do! You think, Poor fellow. What he wants is a dose of arsenic. Liven things up."

He leans in close, too close, and now I'm shrinking back. "I can still kiss a girl, you know. I can still unbutton her frock."

I try to push him away, but he pushes me, instead. Two fingers is all it takes, two fingers pushing at my breastbone, and I'm tumbled to the earth.

"There are, of course, certain disadvantages to missing a hand," he says. "If the girl's inclined to run away, you have to sit on her—so!" He doesn't quite sit, but he kneels to either side of me. He traps my middle with his knees.

"Get away!" I pound his middle, his chest, whatever I can reach. But he catches the two of my hands with the one of his. The sun is behind him. His eyes are all in shadow.

"I can still unlace a girl's chemise."

All the Cecil awfulness comes back to me: crumpled girl froth; and hard lips; and lunar eyes; and blood, and spit, and sick, and choking and choking; and the memory of the choking makes me choke again. I turn my head to the side so I don't drown.

Eldric lets go of my hands. *I can still unlace a girl's chemise.* But he doesn't touch me. He lays his hand on his face.

He is weeping.

I feel very unwell. "Will you let me up, please?"

Eldric stands. I stand. I walk into the field. I walk between the rows of grain. Everything has changed. I am breathing and walking, breathing and walking.

I won't say I hate myself.

I won't say I hate myself.

It's difficult, though. There was a certain comfort in hating myself. Then, at least, I knew what I was. But now that I know I'm not a witch, I've lost my way to myself.

I will not hate myself.

I stand in the middle of the field. It is a Chime Child time of day, an in-between time. The sky pushes her blue shoulder through bits of the moon.

"Briony!"

I walk faster.

"Briony!"

"Go away!"

He's coming close. I whirl around. "Don't touch me!"

He stops. He raises a hand of surrender. He's a messy crier. He has great red splotches on his cheeks. "Please let me show you the real reason I came to find you."

"You didn't come to rape and pillage?"

He flinches. "May I show you?"

"You didn't answer my question."

"Let me show you. Then you'll know."

"Show me, then leave me alone."

He opens his fingers. On his palm lies the tiniest fidget. "I have to confess I didn't make it all by myself."

The fidget is a dazzle of gold and pearl, except that pearl doesn't glitter and this does.

"I don't expect you to take it. But I wanted to show you that I didn't come to—" He bites at the insides of his lips, but tears come to his eyes.

"On Halloween night," he says, "I told you I loved you.

You didn't say anything then, you haven't said anything since. I meant to tell you again, tonight, but the very first words out of your mouth were about my liking you better if you weren't yourself."

Why did I say that? If I weren't so angry, I might be ashamed.

"But I can't possibly like you any better than I do. And when you said that—well, I've taken a lot of blows in my life, boxing and whatnot, but I've never felt one like that. Like a mule kick it was, to the chest."

Why did I say that?

"A person gets to wondering, he gets nervous, he loses his confidence along with his hand. The girl laughed with him when he had both hands. The girl kissed him when he had both hands. But now she hardly looks at him. He blames his hand."

"That," I say, "is the stupidest thing I ever heard. You don't laugh with your hand. You don't kiss with your hand.

"Do you Blackberry-Night with your hand? I wouldn't know, of course, because I had no young man on Blackberry Night. He ran away."

"I didn't run away!" says Eldric, but his lion's lips begin to curl.

"I find myself wondering what a proper Blackberry Night might be like," I say. "The sort of Blackberry Night where the young man doesn't remember words like *virtue* or *Advent wedding*. The sort of Blackberry Night where the young man stays in the rye."

Eldric is smiling.

"You can get by without a hand."

357

"You don't love a person for his hand."

"What do you love a person for?" he says. "I mean, what do *you* love a person for?"

Here it comes at last. I have to admit I don't love anyone.

"I love a person for knowing I need to be touched. I love a person for cleaning blood off my forehead. I love a person for knowing I need to be a baby again and singing lullabies. I love a person for knowing I'm not a Dresden figurine. I love a person for fidgeting me up a wolfgirl."

What am I saying? I'm brave when it comes to punching Petey or fighting the Dead Hand, but I'm a coward with words. What am I saying? My scalp crawls with centipedes of fear. But how can I know something if I don't say it?

"I love a person for communion, communion with wine and coats and help and trust—even if that person feels he's doing all the trust and gets grumpy. I love a person for knowing I'm the Amazon of the Swampsea, and for helping me be even more Amazonian, although he oughtn't to deal out those little butterfly punches, because that's cheating.

"I love him for making me laugh, and I love it that I make him laugh—"

There are no end to the things I might say. I feel my heart unfolding. I've felt that unfolding before, but I haven't let it be real. Pay attention, Briony; pay attention!

"I love a person for knowing I should run about on Blackberry Night, even if I didn't know myself, and even if certain unforeseen and complicated things ensued, and I love him for playing with the children, and for making the children adore him, and for trusting that I can be Robin Hood—"

Really, I could say anything, and it would be true. Except—

"Except when a person acts like Cecil, and worries about his own manliness, and thinks it a good thing to show a girl he's manly, because girls love strong men, of course they do, they love it when someone holds their wrists too hard, and makes their lips bleed, and crushes out all their lace and froth and gleam."

Eldric draws a forearm across his eyes. He's crying again. "How stupid I am."

"Yes," I say.

He laughs and he cries. "You're right, and I can't bear it. I never thought that I could ever act like Cecil."

I lay my hand on my heart. Our parents teach us the very first things we learn. They teach us about hearts. What if I could be treated as though I were small again? What if I were mothered all over again? Might I get my heart back?

My heart is unfolding.

But isn't that what Eldric did? He mothered me and fathered me and gave me back my heart. I have to tell him.

I tell him my theory about the treading in and scuffing out of brain paths. I explain about going back to being a baby.

Eldric cries and he laughs.

"Every so often," I say, "I might like to hear about my adorable apricot ears."

He laughs, he cries, he holds out his arms.

I step toward him, I let him fold his arms around me. It's not embarrassing when Eldric cries.

"I'd like to look at your fidget," I say, "but I feel I must warn you about all the paths I have to scuff and tread. It hardly seems fair. Perhaps you should return when I'm grown."

I'm joking, of course, except that I'm not. By the time

I'm grown, Eldric will have moved on to a girl who's really grown-up.

"This is the grown-up girl I like," says Eldric. He takes my hand. He slips his fidget on my finger. "The watchmaker was very kind," he says. "He let me use his shop, and he loaned me his two hands."

Moonstones. Those are the non-pearls that glitter. I don't recognize the yellow sparkling stones. I ask and he tells me. The ring is set with moonstones and yellow diamonds.

"I think of us as sun and moon," he says.

My heart is a smushy mess. If hearts truly had strings, I'd say he was plucking mine.

He whispers to the baby Briony. He adores her darling apricot ears and tiny fingernails. He whispers to the grown-up Briony. "I don't want another girl. We can tread out the paths, I know we can."

"But I don't know if I'll ever sing again." And now, at last, I'm crying. One can stomp out brain paths, but one can't stomp out a voice path.

"But you trod out the path of the memory of your darling apricot ears," says Eldric. "Did you think you ever would?"

I did not.

"Then we can tread out other paths," says Eldric. "We'll stomp them out, just like that. Some will be hard, some will be easy. We'll do it together."

Perhaps he was right. I look at the ring. "How did you know it would fit?"

"I don't know the twelfth declension," he says, "but I know how you like your cream and jam. I know every one of your fingers."

"I love it," I say. "Did you know I would? Did you know that too?"

"Yes," he says.

We walk to the motorcar. I step on the running board, but he catches at me.

"I love you."

Word magic. If you say a word, it leaps out and becomes the truth. *I love you.* I believe it. I believe I am loveable. How can something as fragile as a word build a whole world?

· Acknowledgments ·

Love and thanks to the HTGs and the Foos, who inspire, celebrate, console, and encourage. I can't imagine a writing life without each and every one of you. Thanks in particular to Dian Curtis Regan for the crucial feedback she gave in her eleventh-hour role as "innocent" reader, and to my brilliant editor, Kathy Dawson, who throughout the many tricky revisions, never lost sight of the soul of the story. Thank you!

chime

Author Q and A with
New York Times bestseller Libba Bray

You are a spectacular world-builder with a singular voice like a Tim Burton, Jonathan Carroll, or Kelly Link, so that, when reading a Franny Billingsley novel, I immediately feel as if my own world has fallen away and I am somewhere strange and wonderful and somewhat menacing. In *Chime*, Swampsea is an early twentieth-century English town that feels slightly Victorian, slightly modern, slightly not-of-this-earth, and wholly original. How do you go about constructing your worlds? Is there some magical Franny wisdom you can impart to us mortals?

Libba, it's interesting that my answers to many of your questions are tangled up in and with other questions you asked. This question about world-building, for example, is connected to the question about the genesis of *Chime* (below):

You and I were at Cynthia and Greg Leitich-Smith's wonderful WriteFest workshop in Austin, Texas, in 2005, where I had a first draft of *Going Bovine* and you had a first draft of *Chime*. It's astounding to me how much *Chime* changed in those six years. What was the initial inspiration/seed/spark for the novel, and can you tell us about the changes and the process of revision you went through?

I do have to talk about that initial spark to explain how I ended up in the Swampsea. The kindling for the spark was handed to me by my daughter, Miranda. When she was about five, I read her "A Fair Exchange," a changeling story from the collection *The Maid of the North*, and when I had finished, she said she wished I'd make a novel of that story. I wanted to, as well. It's a wonderfully gripping story, about a mother willing to do anything to retrieve her baby from Fairyland. But I was then still finishing *The Folk Keeper*, and so I tucked the idea away in the back of my mind.

Like the woman in the story, I had a baby, too. Miranda's baby brother was then about six months old.

A year passed, two years, three. . . . The baby brother was pretty darn perfect, except for one niggling worry: he had not yet started to speak. I started taking him to see doctors of various kinds, doctors who saw only his weaknesses but not his strengths, which were prodigious. It was those doctors—damn them—who put a match to the kindling Miranda had handed me three years earlier. My idea was this: there's a girl, like Miranda; maybe she's about twelve. She has a little brother; maybe he's about six. The brother doesn't speak, but he's prodigiously talented in other ways: he's very musical, for example, and this talent shows up in all kinds of ways when he fools around on the piano.

Enter the fairies: they don't care about talking; they care about music. They steal the brother away to Fairyland and leave in his place a changeling: a fairy child magicked into a perfect resemblance of the brother. The parents (dumb old parents) are delighted that their son seems to have turned the developmental corner overnight. But the sister, who knows the brother best, knows he's not the real brother. There are many clues, but the biggest clue is that the fairy child has no music inside of him: he can't fool around on the piano. It's up to the sister to find her way into Fairyland and rescue her true brother.

It's a great plot—I thought so then and I still think so today. But I couldn't write it. I couldn't write it because I couldn't figure out the physical nature of Fairyland. I knew it wasn't a place with enchanted forests and white stags and jeweled fruits. I knew it was a sinister sort of place, but that's all I knew. I tried to superimpose various landscapes upon it: a volcanic landscape, bright with flowing lava; a labyrinth of twisted stone spires. But however intriguing each landscape might be, I knew I was simply imposing it upon my book. The geography of Fairyland needed to spring organically from the needs of the book itself—the characters, the plot—and I never could find that organic connection. That's the book, Libba, you read in Austin.

Being nothing if not stubborn, I held onto the changeling/Fairyland idea for just a little longer—just a few years, just a few long years of my life. Meanwhile, my son grew, learned to talk, and in third grade was reading the *Lord of the Rings.* He was okay, more than okay, and the initial situation that had fueled the story drizzled away.

Finally, I sat myself down for a serious talk: I was never going to succeed in finding a Fairyland organic to the story, and even if I did, I'd lost interest in the story itself. "Franny," I said, "what about finding another setting for the story? Perhaps other story elements will emerge because plot and setting are, of course, inextricably intertwined."

"They are?" I said.

"Just kidding," I said. "I knew that."

How did I come to choose the swamps? I have no memory of how I got there, but it was the right decision. The sinister creatures arose organically from the swamp setting rather than my planting the fairies in a setting not their own. And although the details changed, the plot was essentially the same: the sister (Briony) had a sibling (a twin sister this time) who was threatened by the creatures of the swamp. Briony's job was to save her.

Same plot, different geography. And now I circle back round to your question, Libba—now many paragraphs ago. How did I come up with this world?

It was handed to me by history and folklore. The British wetlands had been drained again and again, so often that folk stories had grown up around it. They were, often as not, stories about the chief spirit of the swamp who objected to the draining of his water, which meant he had a nasty tendency to kill the people who came to drain the swamp: engineers and other workers. I used these stories and I used the history: the people who dwelt in the wetlands (the real people) were stuck in the past; they resisted the pull and romance of technology, of the future. But the future came upon them of itself: the swamp was drained, and the folks of the wetlands had to find another way to live. There was no more fishing, no more weaving of reed baskets. They were forced to race after the future in order to survive. And so it became clear to me that *Chime* would be set just then, at the fulcrum of history, when the balance shifted, when the folks of the wetlands were forced to embrace the future. And had the swamp creatures really existed, what would have happened to them—what? They would most likely have died. It's not that I made any of this up. It's all in the folklore and history of the wetlands.

Maybe there's a shorter answer to this question:

I steal from history and folklore. It doesn't seem to me as though I'm building a world. I take what already exists and stir my characters into the brew. That's why, in the swamp setting, there was never any question about the setting and plot being organic to each other. The history and folklore that predated my novel made them so.

I take; I steal.

I recommend it.

Language always plays a huge part in your novels. There are turns of phrase and word choices that are so unusual and unbelievably beautiful that I have to read them again just for the sheer enjoyment (and jealousy!) of your craftsmanship. Has language always been important to you? Is it a way for you to discover the voice/feel of the novel? How did you come to be such a wordsmith?

The answer to this question is woven into the answer to the question below:

I know you've talked about the importance of ballads and fairy

tales in your life. Can you tell us a little more about that and about how they came to shape *Chime*?

It's not so much about how ballads and fairy tales came to shape *Chime* as about how they came to shape my voice as a writer. It was the ballads more than the fairy tales, and it was the nursery rhymes and, later, the poems my father read me. My father sang to us (us kids), sang lots of songs, American folk songs as well as British ballads, and he read to us aloud, starting with *Mother Goose*. He started when I was young—young enough to have a sponge-brain that could soak up the poetry and the melody, soak up the rhythm and the rhyme—young enough so that later I could speak this language without an accent.

I won't say that the language comes to me easily—I write as many shitty first (and second and third) drafts as the next writer. More, probably, because I happen to be slow. That's just wiring, I think, nothing existential. It doesn't come to me easily but it comes to me naturally. It has its limits, though. I think I would have an accent were I to try to write a Western, say, or try to assume the voice and manners of the American South.

Which leads me to this question:

There is a great deal in *Chime* about the importance of storytelling. The Old Ones beg Briony to write their stories again. And, without getting spoilery, the telling of stories, of getting down to the bones of truth, plays a crucial role in the plot. What sort of power do you think storytelling has for us now? Like the Old World magic versus industrialism in *Chime*, is storytelling changing for us in the wake of e-books and social networking and what-not?

I think we'll always need stories and tell stories—the vehicles may change but the essence will not. I don't worry about that. The one thing that perhaps I do worry about is whether people read nursery rhymes and poetry to very young kids. Whether they sing to very young kids. My bookstore experience leads me to believe that they (mostly) do not. Certainly, kids get exposed to rhythm and rhyme and melody when they're older, but are they too old? Are their brains still sponges? The cut-off age for learning a foreign language perfectly—to be able to speak it as a native would—is terrifyingly young, and I feel that the same is true about learning the poetry of our language. But generally, I'm not in despair about the state of civilization: I don't believe that the snow was deeper and colder when I was a child than it is today. (Well, okay, maybe it was cleaner.)

Briony is a fascinating character. Haunted by guilt and self-loathing, she is by turns hard, witty, arch, vulnerable, and unflinchingly honest. She is not trying to win friends and influence people. She is not concerned with being "likable." What drew you to tell her story? Were you concerned that you would catch shit for writing such a take-no-prisoners sort of girl? And do you think that we are, in subtle ways, encouraged to make our female characters more "likable"? (There is no Holden-Marie Caulfield. I'm just sayin'.)

It never occurred to me I'd catch shit for writing a Briony type of girl. But then, a lot of stuff never occurs to me.

I do think we're encouraged to make female characters more "likable," whatever that means. Beauty is certainly part of what it means. I know I haven't yet broken the beauty barrier. If my protagonist isn't beautiful (which Briony is), then she's sort of exotic and interesting looking, which is much the same. I really admire Philip Reeve in the Mortal Engines books for creating Hester with her knife-scarred face. Do we love Hester despite the scars, or because of them? Or do we love her simply because she's Hester? I think the last is true, but I haven't been brave enough to test it out.

There is, of course, a romance in *Chime* between the witty, affable Eldric and Briony. I really enjoyed the ways in which they complemented and challenged each other. And Briony thinks quite a bit on both lust and love. In your estimation, what makes for a satisfying romance? Are there romances you particularly like?

One of my favorite books is *Jane Eyre*, and I love you saying that Briony and Eldric complement and challenge each other, because that is exactly how I perceive Jane and Mr. Rochester. He's longing for someone to be honest with him; he's longing to shake off his jaundiced view of the world, and that's exactly what honest, straight-talking Jane does. Eldric does the same for Briony in *Chime*. He's playful, irreverent, nonjudgmental; and once he comes into Briony's life (Briony, who does nothing but judge herself), she can't help but view herself differently, take life less seriously. Briony, who thought herself incapable of either lust or love, mixes them up but gets a healthy dose of each. Although I love a little lust and steam in a romance, the romances I go back to again and again are mostly the complementing and challenging sort. I love Robin McKinley's *Beauty* (which is really *Jane Eyre* in disguise), and *I Capture the Castle,* and *The Perilous Gard.* And although not a true romance, I love *David Copperfield.* I love it that David—although he initially makes a mistake in love—finally realizes that Agnes (whom he's known for years) is the complementing and challenging life partner he's been yearning for. I guess I can sacrifice steam for that.

Of course I have to ask: what's next from the fabulous Franny Billingsley?

As I was finishing *Chime,* I had a sort of epiphany: the two most interesting story ideas that had come to me as I was writing *Chime* actually belong to the world of *Chime.* They're companion books, not sequels; they're related thematically. The first is tentatively called *Shadow,* the second (again tentative) *Cloud.* I'm hoping and assuming that because I know the world, I can write these rather more quickly than I did *Chime.* Perhaps I need no longer worry that I'll die of old age before I can publish another few books.

Discussion Questions

- Briony keeps several secrets to herself. What are they and what impact do they have on her happiness, her sense of self-worth, and her sense of responsibility?

- Briony describes herself: "I'd lived in a hollow all the past year. A Fitz hollow, a Brownie hollow, a Stepmother hollow. When you live in a hollow, your life is small" (p. 160). What does this passage say about Briony's self-perception?

- Why does Briony hate herself? Why does Eldric make her want to cry?

- Billingsley references a number of children's fairy tales. Identify at least one and explain how its use contributes to the story.

- What role does superstition play in the story? Religion? Cite examples or influences of each in the story.

- Throughout the story, Briony references her inability to feel emotions. She says she understands the "idea" of emotions, but she does not feel them. For instance, when eating with Eldric in the Alehouse, she tells the reader, " . . . the idea of happiness returned to me. Not the feeling, the idea" (p. 81). Do you agree or disagree with her statement? Explain.

- What does the story say about manipulation and our responsibility as human beings to care for others? What does it say about betrayal and deception?

- In what way is *Chime* a story of guilt? A story of mercy?

- Might this story be classified as a "Cinderella" story? Explain.

- Mystery writers often use red herrings to throw the reader off the trail of the mystery and/or to keep the reader guessing until the end. What red herrings can you find in the story? What clues point to the resolution?

- At the beginning of the story, Briony is filled with self-contempt; however, by the end of the story she is learning to love herself. What accounts for this change and why will this change take time? How has Briony been wounded?

- The truth about Briony's stepmother is revealed at story's end. What clues does Billingsley plant throughout the story that speak to her true character?